BE WITH ME

A DARK MAFIA ROMANCE

HOUSE OF FERRARO

GABRIELLE SANDS

BE WITH ME

GABRIELLE SANDS

PLAYLIST

"Okay" – Chase Atlantic
"Bury Me" – Friday Pilots Club
"PERFuMITO NUEVO" – Bad Bunny, RaiNao
"touchin' me" – Chandler Leighton
"Espresso" – Sabrina Carpenter
"Call Me By Your Name" – Sophie Castillo
"Kiss Me Slow" – Vanés
"Goodbye" – Sophie Castillo
"Revolving door" – Tate McRae
"Cherry Red" – Vanés
"test drive" – Artemas
"Scream My Name" – Thomas LaRosa
"Hardcore Romance" – Beach Weather, Ari Abdul
"how could u love somebody like me?" – Artemas
"DEVOTION" – KiNG MALA

CONTENT WARNING

Please be aware this book contains graphic scenes meant for a mature audience.

Trigger Warnings: explicit sexual content, violence, on page SA (flashback, not to the heroine)

CHAPTER 1

Mia

My best friend's engagement party was today, and I wasn't invited.

I only found out because of a baffling text that landed on my phone about five minutes ago. I'd managed to read it three times before it vanished—deleted by sender.

Clearly, Fabi hadn't meant to send it to me.

If I hadn't been glued to my screen, trying to reschedule a fitting with one of my personal styling clients, I would've missed it. Instead, the words were imprinted in my memory, as if written in permanent ink.

"How close are you? Cosimo just got here for our pre-engagement party photoshoot, and I already want to shoot myself. Emotional support required. BTW, when you type the address into the app, it might take you to the wrong place. Here's the pin with the exact location."

I'm sorry, what? An engagement party?

Fabi hadn't even told me she *was* engaged.

"You ready?" Jenny asked, her voice barely cutting through the crowd chanting *Morales for mayor! Morales for mayor!*

"Uh-huh." My palm was clammy around the phone as I zoomed in on the pin.

It was in Scarsdale. Wasn't that where Fabi's brother lived? The drive from here to there would take a half hour. I was scheduled to stay until the end of Dad's rally, but there was no way. As soon as I wrapped up my speech, I was out of here. Fabi and I needed to talk. Face-to-face.

"You look a bit flushed," Jenny said.

"I'm fine," I lied, pretending my mind wasn't whirring at an alarming speed as I tried to process that text and what it implied. Fabi and I were best friends. Why would she hide the fact that she got engaged from *me*?

Engaged to Cosimo. Her mysterious long-distance boyfriend. Just weeks after first mentioning him, Fabi had dropped a bomb. She was quitting her dream job at the UN in Geneva and moving back to New York to be closer to him. A man she'd only just met. A man she'd barely told me a word about.

Like any good friend, I'd asked questions. Lots of them. I'd wanted to make sure she'd really thought this huge decision through.

Nice one, Mia. You probably came off as unsupportive. Maybe you'd offended her.

I rolled my lips together. Did I? Was that it?

It had been three weeks since she returned to New York, and we still hadn't seen each other even though we'd always dreamed of living in the same city again.

There'd been plenty of excuses—we were both insanely busy. Her with settling back in, and me with the never-ending demands of the campaign.

But what if she was just avoiding me?

Crap.

Heat crept up the back of my neck. This was a nightmare. I hated upsetting people. Especially those closest to me.

"If you elect me as the mayor of this great city, I promise to dismantle the organized crime families that have plagued our community for far too long." My dad's voice boomed over the speakers, so loud I could feel it vibrating inside my chest.

I glanced up at the stage and exhaled. It was almost my turn. I didn't want to get up there right now—I rarely did—but skipping my speech wasn't an option. Jenny was already going to scold me when I asked to leave early. She was one of my dad's assistants. As my de facto boss, she controlled my calendar.

Dad slammed his hands against the podium. "The lawless mobsters and their cronies will be put behind bars."

"Get them off our streets!" someone shouted from amongst the crowd.

"We will make New York a safer place for our children. That is my promise to you, and I am a man of my word."

My dad was a powerful orator. He knew how to hold his audience captive, how to win them over with his rhetoric and his charisma.

Me? Not so much. I preferred to stay in the background. To let other people shine.

Getting shoved into the spotlight this year hadn't been fun. But there was no one else who could take my place. My stepmom would love to be here—in theory. But since her stroke, she was too self-conscious to go out in public like this.

"Thank you, thank you." Dad beamed at the audience. "Now, I have a special guest I'd like to bring on stage. My beautiful, talented daughter, Mia. Can you please help me welcome her?"

The crowd erupted in cheers, and Jenny nudged my

back. "Just read the teleprompter," she whispered, as if I needed the reminder.

That teleprompter was quite literally my lifeline. Without it, I'd be spewing nonsense in front of everyone, especially right now when I was anything but present or focused.

I took a deep breath and jumped right into it. My father was born in New York to a French mother and a Mexican father. When he was twelve, he lost his older brother—my uncle—in a shootout, caught in the crossfire of two warring factions of the Ferraro family.

An innocent bystander. Wrong place, wrong time.

After my granddad died, my dad took over the family business. But he always dreamed of making this city a place where no one else would suffer the way our family had. So at fifty-five, he sold the business and decided to run for mayor—to honor his brother's memory by fighting for justice, safety, and hope.

I recited the words but my heart wasn't in it. I couldn't stop thinking about Fabi and the apology I was starting to think I owed her.

Dad returned to the stage when I finished and tugged me into a hug. "You did great, *cariño*."

I squeezed him back. "I love you, Dad."

He pulled back and smiled at me before returning to the podium to welcome his next guest.

He didn't say it back.

He's just distracted.

I pushed aside that brittle, needy feeling inside of me and walked off stage to where Jenny stood. The situation with Fabi was making me way too sensitive.

"Well done," Jenny said, patting me on the arm.

"I've got to go," I said to her.

Her brow furrowed as I handed her my ID badge. "Go? Where? You're booked until seven."

"I know. But I have something important. And you don't need me here anymore, not really."

"What's so important?"

"It's my friend's engagement party." I grabbed my purse and slung it over my shoulder.

She frowned. "That's not on your calendar."

Believe me, I'm aware. "I'm sorry. I don't know what happened, but I totally forgot to add it."

"Which friend?"

"Fabi Castellano."

Jenny sighed, looking irked. "Fine. Just don't let this happen again, all right? You know we run a tight ship. Give me a heads-up next time."

"I will."

I rushed out of the venue and flagged down a taxi. A warm, late-August breeze pulled on the strands of my hair as I tugged open the door and climbed into the back seat.

The cab inched its way through Manhattan, the driver honking impatiently at the cars cutting him off, while suicidal bikers swerved around us.

I closed my eyes and massaged my temples.

It was a bit nuts to just show up at this thing when I was apparently not wanted there, but if Fabi was mad at me, why hadn't she just talked to me about it? Keeping her engagement a secret in response to something I'd said seemed like a huge overreaction. It just didn't make sense.

And what about Nina and Zo? Fabi had to have told them about this. So why haven't they said anything to me?

The four of us didn't have secrets from each other.

At least, that's what I'd thought.

Twenty minutes later we were pulling into a neighborhood. This was a wealthy area, full of sprawling estates and huge homes—exactly the kind of place I'd expect Fabi's family to live.

I didn't know much about them, but Valais Academy, the Swiss boarding school where Fabi, Nina, Zo, and I met, had cost a hundred grand a year. Unless you were a genius like Zo, who got a full-ride scholarship, your family had to be rich to afford that kind of education.

We turned onto the driveway that ended in front of a grand Colonial-style mansion with imposing white columns flanking the double front doors.

The gate was open, the security booth empty. The taxi driver paused for a moment as if giving someone a chance to stop us, but when no one appeared, he drove through the gate.

I pulled my phone out of my purse and shot off a text.

> Hey, we need to talk.

Fabi's response was immediate.

> 100%. Next Monday?

> Actually, I'm outside.

> What????

> Where??

I sent her a photo of the facade. Thanking the taxi driver, I slipped out of the car and started toward the front door. Music and laughter drifted from the backyard—it sounded like the party was in full-swing.

I braced myself.

This was going to awkward, but it needed to happen. I wasn't trying to ruin her party. I just couldn't let our friendship fall apart over some misunderstanding.

Fabi and I weren't teenagers anymore. We didn't text

every hour or get together for weekly sleepovers in our dorm like we'd used to back at school. But for two twenty-five-year-olds who up until three weeks ago had spent years living on different continents, we were still close. Really close.

You sure about that? Maybe you mean a lot less to her than you think.

My chest squeezed. No, I wasn't going to go there. If I dipped my toe into the vast pool of my insecurities, it would only make the situation worse.

All I planned to do was apologize for being skeptical about her boyfriend—I mean, *fiancé*—and explain that I was only trying to watch out for her. If they were head over heels and wanted to move fast—fine. As long as she was happy.

If after hearing me out she still didn't want me here, I'd leave.

I was halfway up the walkway when—

"Mia! What the HELL!?" Fabi sprinted along a path to the side of the house, her heels clicking against the pavement, her thick curls bouncing wildly, her cocktail dress hitched in her fists.

Hurt sliced through me. Was she really this upset that I'd shown up? I opened my mouth to explain—

"Miss Messero," a voice called out. "Everything okay?"

Fabi froze a few feet from me, her face losing its color. She gulped and glanced over her shoulder at a man in a suit with a walkie-talkie clipped to his belt. He stood at the end of the path where Fabi had just come down.

"Yes! Just greeting an old friend! I'll be right back."

Miss...Messero?

That wasn't Fabi's last name.

Unease took root, spreading like ice through my veins. All of the sudden, it felt like I was missing something. Something important.

"All right," the man said, turning back.

She faced me again and pressed her index finger to her lips, signaling for me to stay quiet until the security guard left.

My pulse pounded against the side of my neck. "Fabi, what's going on?"

"You're not supposed to be here. How did you get this address?"

"I saw the text you sent."

She shut her eyes, looking pained. "Shit. I hoped you wouldn't."

The weird thing was that she didn't sound angry.

She sounded...kinda scared.

Alarm bells rang inside my head. "Why did that man call you by the wrong name?"

Her throat bobbed, but her eyes stayed closed. "He didn't. My last name isn't Castellano. It's Messero."

I frowned. *Wait, but that's—*

"My brother is Rafaele Messero," she said, her voice breaking as she finally looked at me, "and my fiancé is Cosimo Ferraro."

My heart dropped all the way to my toes.

"Messero and Ferraro," I echoed as my brain scrambled to make sense of what she was saying.

Fabi nodded.

I swallowed. Hard. "Your family is involved with the mob."

"No, Mia. My family *is* the mob."

CHAPTER 2

Mia

This had to be a prank.

Highly upsetting. Terribly unfunny. If I had to guess—Zo's idea. She never meant badly, but sometimes she took things too far.

The alternative was almost impossible for me to comprehend: Fabi lying to me for over a decade about her name.

Her identity.

Her *fiancé's* identity.

She was *not* getting married to Cosimo Ferraro. No way. That man was the heir to the Ferraro family empire. The family who were responsible for my uncle's death. The family who were at the top of my father's tough-on-crime crusade.

It was too crazy. "This is a joke, right?" I scanned her face, looking for a tell.

"I wish."

The light crack in her voice. The shiny, green eyes. The way she gnawed on her bottom lip.

Shit. She wasn't *that* good at pretending.

I pressed my hand against the side of a polished white

column. "You're seriously telling me you're a mafia princess?" Rafaele Messero—the man Fabi claimed was her *brother*—was the don of another major mob family in the state.

Fabi's eyes jumped to my hand. "Oh God, Mia. Are you feeling faint? Sit down." She pulled me toward the bench by the front door. "I should have asked you to sit before I told you. I'm not thinking straight."

I scanned my body for any signs of an impending episode.

No nausea.

No flash of heat.

No dark spots in my vision.

A small relief. Vasovagal syncope was an annoying condition to live with, and the last thing I needed right now was to spontaneously lose consciousness.

I had so many questions. "Wait, so—"

"Shit," Fabi cut me off, her gaze flicking to something above me. "Don't look up. There's a camera right there. We can't let them see you." She slid off the shawl she had wrapped around her shoulders and tossed it at me. "Here, take this. Wrap it around your head."

"What? Why?"

"Because every single person your dad wants to put behind bars is out there, right this second, in my brother's backyard," she whispered urgently. "The name Morales isn't exactly popular around here. How do you think they'll react if they know his daughter is on the premises?"

My stomach bottomed out. I was on enemy territory.

Oh boy. My lack of an invitation to this party was starting to make a lot more sense.

I fumbled with the shawl, hands shaking. I'd gotten this whole thing wrong. But how could I have gotten it right?

Fabi's family had always been a mystery. I only knew her

twin sister, Elena, who went to the same boarding school, but she had her own friend group and never really hung out with us. No one had ever visited the twins at Valais Academy and there were only vague mentions of a brother. I remembered Fabi's father died a few years ago. She'd confided that he'd been abusive to her mom, but nothing more.

Even if I'd suspected her and Elena were hiding something about their family, I would never have suspected *this*.

"Give me." She snatched the shawl back, wrapped it over my hair, and reached into her clutch. A pair of oversized sunglasses appeared, which she promptly slid onto my face. "We need to get you inside. Now. Some people are running late, and they might arrive any second. We can't risk anyone recognizing you. Are you okay to stand?"

"Yes." This was exactly the kind of situation that usually triggered an episode, but it seemed like my body had decided to have mercy on me.

"Head down, don't look at anyone, and for the love of God, do not look at the cameras. There's the one above you and one in the lobby. Let's go."

Fabi corralled me through the front door, her hand pressed firmly against my back. We power walked through the house. It smelled like roses and a hint of masculine cologne. I kept my gaze on the floor, watching it change from pristine marble, to hardwood, then to a plush blue rug as we entered a room and stopped.

A door clicked shut behind me.

"You can take it off now," Fabi said.

I slipped off the shawl and the glasses and tossed them onto a four-poster bed. We were in a guest bedroom with a small window that faced the backyard.

Fabi rushed over to it and pulled the curtains closed. "I'm so sorry. I wish you didn't have to find out like this." When she turned around, her eyes were glistening. "The last few months were impossible, Mia. I didn't know how to tell you. I didn't know what you'd think."

"Start from the beginning," I said, trying to stay calm.

"Hold on." She took a buzzing phone out of her clutch and pressed it to her ear. "Yes, she's really here. Go inside from the back, take a right, and walk until the third door. We'll be waiting."

As soon as she hung up, she flung herself at me. "God, I missed you. I missed you so much, you have no idea."

I gave her back a few tentative pats. Warring emotions were battling it out inside my chest. I was hurt, confused, and a little scared. I wasn't ready for a heartfelt reunion. I just wanted the truth.

"Can you please explain what's been going on?"

She pulled back, her expression all guilt. "I will. Trust me, I will, if you just—"

The door cracked open, and Nina stepped in.

The hurt surged forward, flooding my entire body. Nina knew, and she didn't say a word.

Nina's gaze connected with mine. She was wearing the red off-the-shoulder dress I picked out for her weeks ago. She'd said she needed it for a charity gala she was attending this month.

"You lied to me," I accused, looking between her and Fabi. "Both of you."

Fabi's lips wobbled. "I'm so sorry. I never meant for this to go on for so long."

"I know you're pissed," Nina said, raising her palms. "But we can't do this here. We need to get you out."

My chest tightened with indignation. "I spent the last hour since I received that text freaking out. Imagine finding out your friend's having an engagement party when you didn't even know she was engaged. I thought I did something to upset Fabi!"

"Oh, Mia," Fabi sobbed. "It's not you. It's me. I've made a horrible mistake."

Nina sighed, grabbed a box of tissues from the nightstand, and shoved it into Fabi's hands. "Don't cry. You'll ruin your makeup." Then she turned to me. "We owe you an explanation—I'm not saying we don't. But you know who's out there, right?" She pointed at the window. "Someone's going to start wondering where the bride-to-be has gone off to, and they won't wait long before coming to find her."

God. If they found her, they'd find me. I was easily recognizable thanks to the news coverage of the campaign.

Cold fear wrapped around me. The few safety trainings I'd received from my dad's security team definitely hadn't covered what to do if you accidentally crashed a mob party.

I was out of my depth.

And even though I didn't like what Nina was saying, I couldn't argue with her logic.

"Fine," I said. "We'll talk later."

"Go, Fabi," Nina commanded. "I'll handle this."

Fabi grabbed her things off the bed, gave me a final, anguished look, and slipped out of the room.

Nina's expression was grim. "I'm calling you a cab."

I sat down on the edge of the bed. "An Uber might be faster."

"We don't need a digital record of you being here," she countered, already dialing.

She had a point. I gnawed on a fingernail as she spoke to the dispatcher. Questions clawed at me, and I was so desperate for answers, but I wasn't going to get any right now.

Nina hung up. "Fifteen minutes." She moved to the door. "Once the cab arrives, I'll come and grab you."

"Where are you going?" I asked, alarmed.

"I'm going to scope things out. Make sure the path is clear and that no one's hanging around the entrance."

I didn't like this—not one bit—but I nodded anyway. What other choice did I have?

"Just stay put until I get back," Nina said before slipping out.

Nerves prickled beneath my skin as I moved around the room, familiarizing myself with my surroundings. I peeled back the curtain just enough to get a glimpse of the party outside. The backyard was packed with men in crisp suits and women in glittering cocktail dresses, their laughter and conversation drifting through the night air.

From here, they looked so...ordinary.

But it was a facade, at least according to my dad. The mob families had tried for years to clean up their reputation, and they'd succeeded to some degree. Many of them owned legitimate businesses, some of which even traded on the stock exchange. But my dad said that beneath that polished veneer, they were still ruthless. Still dangerous. The same people flooding the streets with drugs and orchestrating crimes that made them far richer than any legal business ever could.

I swallowed and let the curtain fall back into place.

While I waited for Nina, I slipped into the en suite to use the bathroom. At the sink, I washed my hands and dried them on a towel monogrammed with the letter *M*. That must have—

CRASH.

My heart slammed into my ribs. I froze, fingers gripping the edge of the sink, breath caught in my throat.

Someone had just barged into the room.

And neither of the voices coming from out there belonged to Nina.

CHAPTER 3

Mia

"Calm down." A man's deep voice drifted through the crack in the bathroom door. "What's gotten into you?"

"I'm tired of this," a woman said, her speech slightly slurred. "I can't stand him. The way he talks to me. The way he looks at me. Just listening to him chew makes me want to break a plate over his head. I'm *done*."

Crap.

Why didn't I close the bathroom door all the way?

There was a five-inch gap through which they could spot me if they moved to the other side of the room.

I backed away from the sink until my shoulder blades touched the cold tile wall. I was slightly more hidden here.

"You're drunk. Go home, Harper. We can talk in the morning once you sleep this off."

"No! I FUCKING LOVE YOU, ROMOLO!"

My breath caught.

Romolo?

As in, *Romolo Ferraro*?

The youngest of the three Ferraro brothers, or as my dad called them, Gino Ferraro's spawns.

Like their father, they were criminals. I didn't know

which crimes they were guilty of, just that there were many. My dad didn't share his research with me, and I'd never been tempted to ask. It was his passion. His purpose.

I had my own. And it had nothing to do with taking down criminals.

"Lower your voice." Romolo's tone was filled with warning.

Cold sweat sprang from my pores. He sounded scary. Dangerous. A little mean.

"Kiss me. Just kiss me."

"Jesus fucking Christ. Get off me," he snapped.

Okay. He sounded *a lot* mean.

"The cab just messaged," he said. "He's outside. Let's go."

"Romolo. Oh, Romolo. Didn't you hear me? I *love* you."

She moaned his name like a porn star.

I winced.

Yikes. I felt bad for her. But also... had she completely lost the plot? The guy radiated jerk energy.

He let out a loud sigh. I'd never heard someone sound more done. "Harper, we're over. What we had has run its course."

"No! You can't do this! I can't live without you. Don't you see? I don't *want* to live if we're not together. I'd rather throw myself under a train and just end my misery."

My mouth fell open. Who needed reality TV when this was your life? Were all mob relationships this dramatic?

"Harper," Romolo barked. "Smarten the fuck up. All we did was screw for a few weeks. It wasn't that fucking deep."

Ouch.

She started to cry.

I pressed my palm over my mouth, mortified on her behalf. He was so cold. So goddamn rude. I couldn't even imagine talking like that to someone.

Where the hell was Nina? And what was she going to do when she walked in on *this*?

Footsteps padded closer. A shadow passed the crack in the door.

I flattened myself tighter against the wall.

Please don't see me. Please don't see me. Please don't—

The shadow moved back the other way.

"Here." A dull sound reached my ears, like something landing on the bed. "Clean yourself up. Let's go."

Harper's cries slowly died down. She blew her nose. "Will you walk me out?"

"You can find your own way out."

She sniffed. "I'll call you."

"Don't."

A few seconds later, the door slammed.

Finally. Thank—

A sigh.

Crap! He was still here. Why hadn't he left?

The clicking sound of him scrolling through his phone poured through the air.

I bit on a nail. Was he doomscrolling? How long was he going to stay here for?

A minute of silence passed. "Fuck. Gotta get back out there," he muttered to himself. He must have been just by the door, because I couldn't see him at all from this angle.

I heard the door open and then shut.

Gone. He was gone.

I waited a few seconds just to make sure he didn't come back. When no sound came, I exhaled, peeled myself off the wall, and took a few tentative steps.

Still silent.

Slowly, I peeked my head out.

Big mistake.

A man stood by the door, his powerful frame filling the space, arms crossed over his broad chest, studying me.

My stomach dipped.

This was him. Romolo Ferraro.

Dressed in a suit, he was every bit as huge and imposing as I'd imagined. But what I hadn't expected was that face.

Strikingly, breath-catchingly handsome. The kind of handsome that made you do a double take.

"Did you enjoy the show?" he asked, his voice a low rumble that rolled over my skin like distant thunder. He didn't sound even a little friendly. He sounded *pissed*.

Fear knotted my stomach. I was so screwed.

"Uhm—no. I'm just...uhh..." Words. I used to have those. I used to know how to form coherent sentences. But all that knowledge seemed to have been vacuumed out of my brain, leaving it completely blank.

Romolo arched a brow, clearly unimpressed with my eloquence or lack thereof. "Not exactly a glowing review."

"I didn't hear anything," I tried.

His lips curved into something that wasn't quite a smile. "We both know that's not true. Do you know what we do to eavesdroppers around here?"

Nope. And I had zero interest in finding out.

My adrenaline surged. My gut screamed at me to move. *Right. Now.*

I lurched toward the heavy lamp sitting on the nightstand at the same time as he moved toward me.

My hands curled around the base. I raised the lamp above my head, and whirled around to face him. "Stay back!"

He took another step.

"I said, stay back!" I lifted the lamp higher.

Another step. "Don't you fucking dare."

I hurled the damn thing at him.

God, what *was* that aim? He barely had to duck to avoid it. The lamp hit the wall behind him, bursting into shards.

Stupid. If it weren't for the music thundering outside, the crash would've drawn every set of ears out in the garden.

He ignored the crunch of ceramic beneath his dress shoes as he prowled toward me, anger flashing in his eyes.

Panic rose up my throat. In retrospect, I should have thought this through. I was boxed in by the bed with nowhere to go.

A large hand clamped down on my shoulder.

I shrieked. He tensed, jaw clenching as he grabbed me and pulled me hard against him. My back hit his chest. His arm slid across my collarbone, the other clamping a hand over my mouth.

"Stop," he hissed into my ear.

I didn't listen. Of course, I didn't. My animal instincts had taken over, and I was fighting for my life.

I bucked against him, doing everything I could with my five-foot-five frame to fight him off. My heels dug into the tops of his shoes. I kicked backward at his shins and landed a hit.

He grunted, lost his balance, and fell, taking me with him.

My body hit the bed, and he landed on top of me. He was *heavy*. The impact pushed all the air out of my lungs.

I bit the hand he still had pressed over my mouth. What else was I supposed to do?

"Goddamn it," he growled, yanking it away.

He rolled off me and flipped me over. I tried to sit up, but he shoved me back down and stood up. He bracketed my legs with his, squeezing them together, and bent over me, trapping my wrists at my sides.

I couldn't move at all now. My hair was in my mouth, and I coughed around it. The more I coughed the more hair fell in. I felt like I would choke on it until Romolo let go of one wrist just long enough to swipe the strands away from my face.

And then he stared.

Panting, I tried to catch my breath.

His eyes made a slow descent over my body, stilling on my chest.

I glanced down and felt my cheeks heat. My dress had gotten twisted during our scuffle, and my white lace bra was showing.

His jaw tightened. He yanked the fabric back into place with more force than necessary, but the anger in his expression had been replaced with mild curiosity.

I could handle that. What I couldn't handle was him recognizing me.

If he knew I was Mia Morales... My lungs shriveled at the thought of what he might do to me.

I started squirming, trying to get away again. "Let me go!"

"Enough," he said gruffly. He moved my arms and pinned my wrists above my head, clamping down on them with one hand.

"No! N—"

He shut me up by pressing his forearm straight across my mouth. I tried to bite him again, but the fabric of his suit prevented me from doing any damage.

"I'm not a chew toy," he said through gritted teeth. "Fucking behave."

I shook my head. I wasn't going to go down without a fight. I just needed to get him off me. Then I could run. I'd walk back to Manhattan if I had to.

"No?" He raised a dark brow.

Another shake.

"All right then." He crawled *onto* the bed and sat down

across my upper thighs, his heavy bulk pressing me into the mattress. "I'll have to call backup. If you think I'm bad, wait until you meet my brothers."

That froze me. The prospect of two more Ferraros storming in short-circuited my brain.

Satisfied with my reaction, he lifted his forearm from my mouth a few inches, as if he was ready to slam it back down if I made another peep.

It dawned on me that screaming was probably not the smartest idea. Would Nina hear me—where *was* she?—or would another guest?

Romolo's gaze drilled into me. "Why were you in there spying on me?"

"I wasn't spying on you." My voice came out hoarse and much weaker than I wanted it to.

"Then what were you doing?" He sat up and let go of my wrists, but his body stayed exactly where it was—on top of me.

I pushed at his thighs, desperate to put some space between us, but it was like trying to push a brick wall. He didn't budge. Not even an inch.

All I could do was huff in frustration. "I was using the bathroom when you and your girlfriend barged in. I didn't know how to interrupt your fight."

"She's not my girlfriend." His eyes swept over my face, lingering, assessing.

It made me feel exposed.

"If you weren't spying on me, why the fuck did you throw that goddamn lamp?"

"I-I don't know," I stammered. "I just acted on instinct. You were threatening me."

He raked his fingers through his thick, raven-black hair. "You know who I am?"

I hesitated and then nodded.

"Then you should have thought twice about doing something like that." His gaze dragged over me again, like he was pondering my punishment.

My teeth sank into my bottom lip. My body practically vibrated with fear. He looked like he was close to my age, but he was twice my size, and I felt like a little kid being picked on by the big bad bully in the sandpit.

"Instead of terrorizing me, maybe you should go check to see if your friend actually made it to her cab," I said with far more bravado than I felt.

I didn't think of myself as a particularly courageous person. But if Romolo was a bully, weakness would only egg him on.

He cocked a brow. "Who's terrorizing who? You're the one who just destroyed what was probably some Messero family heirloom."

Whatever blood was left in my face drained. "Shoot."

His lips made the tiniest quirk. "I'll take the blame if you tell me your name."

Did he really think that would convince me? I'd apologize to Fabi about the lamp if indeed it *was* a family heirloom, but there was no way in hell I was giving him my name.

"No."

Romolo's mouth twisted into a smirk, and he leaned down, anchoring his palms on either side of my head, and bringing our faces closer. Thick, dark lashes framed his gray eyes. "See, when you say things like that, it makes it hard for me to believe your story. I didn't see you down there at the party. What are you doing here?"

The irritation in his voice had been replaced with something smoother. More coaxing. Like he'd decided to use a different tool in his arsenal other than pure intimidation.

Whatever it was, I didn't like how it made a flutter appear low inside my belly.

"I'm Fabi's friend." My hands pushed against his flat stomach, trying to force him away. It didn't work. He had abs made of steel.

"Okay, *Fabi's friend*," he mocked. "Why are you hiding in a guest room during her engagement party instead of celebrating with her?"

"I wasn't feeling well when I arrived, so Fabi took me here." It wasn't a total lie.

His eyes dropped to my mouth. "Is that right?"

"It was something I ate. I'm better now." I pushed my nails into his abs, hoping it would hurt enough for him to ease up a bit.

But it seemed to have the opposite effect. He made a low grunt that sounded more appreciative than pained. "Yeah, you look just fine to me."

The air between us thickened. My pulse thrummed against my neck. "How long do you plan to hold me hostage?"

"Not sure yet," he murmured. He still hadn't recognized me, but I had a feeling he thought I looked familiar. It would explain why he was staring so intently at me.

"Well, I'm done talking to you," I whispered.

He huffed in dry amusement and sat up, moving his entire weight back onto my thighs. "I'm Romolo." He offered me his hand.

Was he joking? Did he really think I was going to shake his hand while he was cutting off all circulation to my legs?

A spark of anger flared inside my belly. "Trust me, I got it. If I get dementia and forget everything, your name will still haunt me. Your not-girlfriend's moans are burned into my brain. Rooooh-moooh-lo. Rooooh-moooh-lo."

His eyes widened slightly beneath the dark slashes of his brows, like he hadn't expected that from me.

I hadn't expected that from me either.

But I was spent, scared, and it was starting to feel like he was playing with me.

A rough chuckle. "Not bad."

"Can I go now?"

"I think I'm going to need you to moan my name a couple more times just to make sure you've got it right."

My mouth formed an O. He *was* playing with me. "You know, most men have to earn a woman moaning their name, and you *definitely* haven't done that."

I shouldn't have said that, because he suddenly seemed very intrigued. "Are you asking me to earn it?"

Oh God. I was *provoking* him.

I was losing my damn mind.

My fists rained against his thighs. "I can't feel my legs. Get. Off. Me!"

He smirked and flipped us over in one effortless move, settling me onto *his* lap. "Better?"

I sucked in a breath and scrambled off him like he was on fire. Halfway to the door, he caught up to me and yanked me against his front.

Heat rolled off him. I was sweating. "You never answered my question," he said, looking down at me, while my chest rose and fell against his.

"The answer is no."

"If you change your mind, let me know." He shot me a very male grin.

"I'd rather die."

He laughed and lowered his face to mine, his dark gaze burning at the edges. "A little death? That can be arranged."

My eyes widened at the innuendo. Then narrowed at how amusing he seemed to be finding all this.

The one hour of self-defense training I did a few months ago rushed back to me. I braced myself and drove my knee into his groin.

He made a pained groan and doubled over, letting go.

I didn't waste a second. I grabbed my purse from where I'd dropped it on the floor and got the hell out of there.

As I sprinted through the house, my heartbeat was louder than the music thudding from the garden. I barely remembered the path Fabi and I had taken, but I had to find my way out before Romolo goddamn Ferraro caught up to me.

Where was Nina? She'd said she'd come back, but it had been at least fifteen minutes—though it felt like a lot longer. Apparently, time slowed when a six-foot-something monster of a man had you pinned to a bed, demanding your name.

I skidded into the foyer and tore at the front door. Beyond it was a waiting cab—*thank God*. The driver was leaning against the car, casually smoking a cigarette.

"Hi! I'm here! Let's go!" I shouted, practically diving into the back seat.

The cabbie raised a brow and flicked his cigarette to the ground before sauntering to the driver's side. He slid into his seat, giving me a glance in the rearview mirror that teetered between concern and suspicion.

"Miss, you okay?"

"Fine. Just drive. Please. I'm really late for something." I must have sounded like I'd just robbed the place blind. But with only my small purse clutched to my chest, I supposed I didn't scream *thief*.

The car rumbled to life. Relief swept over me, so palpable it was like angels singing from above. Then I caught my reflection in the rearview mirror and almost screamed.

My hair was a disaster—tangled and sticking out at

angles that defied physics. My makeup was a mess—eyeliner smudged into dark streaks that made me look unhinged. But it was my eyes that scared me most. There was a wild, ravenous gleam in them, like I'd just been unleashed from a cage after being starved for days.

I fell back against the seat, choking down an anguished groan.

If my luck hadn't run out, I would have gotten out of there undetected.

I really, really wish it hadn't run out, because I had a feeling those assessing gray eyes were going to haunt me for a very long time.

Romolo Ferraro was terrifying.

But it hadn't been just fear coursing through me in that bedroom.

Or now.

My whole body buzzed like a live wire. I felt hot and *alive*.

Not the good kind of alive—like the rush after a long run or the icy clarity of a cold plunge. The dangerous kind. The kind that pointed out just how little you've been living up until now.

I couldn't remember ever reacting to a man this way.

And I wanted nothing to do with it.

I stared out the window as the streetlights blurred past, forcing myself to breathe, forcing myself to calm down. I was safe now. He hadn't recognized me. He didn't know who I was.

And as long as I stayed far, far away from Romolo Ferraro, he never would.

CHAPTER 4

Rom

I hobbled to the bed, one hand wrapped around my aching balls, and sat down on the edge with a groan.

Jesus fucking Christ.

Tonight wasn't going the way I'd planned. I was supposed to be sipping my future brother-in-law's most expensive whiskey and gloating about the fact that my nightclub had been voted the number one spot in the city, beating out his.

Instead, Harper had shown up wasted and uninvited. That ridiculous love confession was bad enough, made worse when I realized someone was eavesdropping on our conversation.

Annoyance pulsed at my temples.

That girl. Something about her was awfully familiar. I hadn't seen her earlier at the party—no, somewhere else. Somewhere I couldn't place.

Thick dark hair, peachy skin, and lips the color of raspberries. Pretty. Very pretty. A tiny thing.

I was starting to enjoy our tussle until she kneed me in the damn balls and fled the scene.

She'd been gone a few minutes now, but her scent

lingered. Floral. Sweet. Delicate. Something about it tugged at me. Like her face, it teased at the edges of my consciousness, a memory just out of reach.

I glanced down at the wrinkled duvet where I could still see the imprint of her small body.

Should I? Ah, fuck it.

I bent down and pressed my face into the fabric.

One deep inhale and...

My chest panged.

Lily of the valley.

The same flowers our old housekeeper used to leave in a blue vase in my room when she cleaned my parents' penthouse on Wednesdays. That scent yanked me straight back to a different time—before I got made, before I became the man I was now.

She kept leaving the flowers even after I told her to stop. Even after I shouted at her that I didn't need her fucking pity. She was the only one besides my mother who knew what had happened that summer.

My jaw clenched. Damn that girl for sending me down memory lane. It was an ugly place I had no interest in revisiting.

Shaking off the tension in my shoulders, I got to my feet.

The thrum of music filtered into the house through the open windows along the hall. I was about to turn the corner when another sound caught my attention—a movie playing in the background.

Taking a detour through Messeros' living room, I smirked when I saw who it was. "Lasted all of two hours, huh?"

Alessio was sprawled on the sofa, a remote dangling loosely from his tattooed hand, the last few minutes of *Good Will Hunting* playing on the TV. "I needed a break."

My brother hated socializing. He usually skipped out on these things, but Mother had insisted he show up today.

"Shove over," I said, sitting down beside him. I fucking loved this film. "Did you figure out why Mother was so adamant about having you here?"

"Yeah. Something with Aunt Lisa. Mom told her I'm getting into plants."

"Weed?"

"No, regular plants."

I glanced away from Chuckie on the screen who'd just realized Will left. "Are you?"

He gave me a look like, *what the fuck do you think?* "Nero's wife gave me a cactus for the palace. When Mom stopped by the other day, she saw it. Now she's making out like I've got a green thumb or something. Told Aunt Lisa she should come by to drop off some trimmings and give me tips."

I huffed a laugh, imagining Aunt Lisa—best known for her baked ziti and her love for gardening—showing up at Alessio's "palace," a twenty-thousand-square-foot warehouse decked out with every torture device imaginable.

Alessio was the family's enforcer, responsible for the darkest parts of our business. The parts most of the family liked to pretend didn't exist—especially now that we'd gotten so big, so legitimate on the surface. My uncle was a CEO, my cousin a COO, and so on and so forth.

Some of them could almost pretend they weren't criminals.

Almost.

But no matter how buttoned-up we got, our empire was built on crime, and we'd never hesitate to commit more of it to achieve our goals.

"And what's Mother's aim with all this?" I asked as Sean —Robin Williams's character—pulled out Will's letter from the mailbox.

"You know her and Aunt Lisa never got along. Mom isn't happy with how her and Uncle Mario have been running the packaging business. She probably figured if Lisa got an up-close-and-personal reminder of how I handle those who get on her bad side, they'd hustle a lot harder."

That would probably work. That was the thing about my mother's plans—most of the time, they worked. And in this business, the ends justified the means. No matter how ugly those means were.

We sat there and watched the last minute of the movie. When the credits started to roll by, Alessio tossed me the remote. "See if you can find anything good."

I flicked through the channels.

"Look who it is," he said when I hit the news. "Another day, another fucking rally."

It was the mayor-to-be.

The camera zoomed in on Morales as he droned on about how my father deserved to be behind bars.

I swore under my breath.

"Still nothing?" Alessio asked.

"No."

If you elect me as the mayor of this great city, I promise to dismantle the organized crime networks that have plagued our community for far too long.

"He's a fucking broken record," I muttered.

In our family, I was the one who got information. Seduction, blackmail, threats—whatever got the job done. I was an expert at figuring out leverage, uncovering weaknesses, and then using it all to my advantage.

And I was damn good at what I did.

Which made the current situation really fucking frustrating.

I hadn't been able to find shit on Morales's campaign.

Mother viewed him as an existential threat to us. My

orders were to figure out who was funding him—because no way was it all grassroots donations. The man was too well-connected, too well-supported for that. None of us bought his sappy story about his dead brother being the real reason he was doing all this. Someone was using him to get to us.

The question was who.

Alessio rubbed his jaw. "He's sticking to his message. If he gets elected, it'll be bad for business."

I wanted to believe otherwise. Just because Morales wanted to take us down didn't mean he could.

We'd been exceedingly careful.

But all he needed was one weak link.

"If he is being funded with dirty money, they covered up their tracks well," I said.

Harper's husband was a banker at Credit First—the bank Morales's campaign used. He liked to monologue Harper about his clients during dinner, spilling confidential details to a wife who hated his guts.

She told me everything she knew, but none of it was what I needed.

Which meant I had no use for her anymore.

With Harper officially out of the picture, I needed a new target—someone with insight into Morales's finances.

"Now, I have a special guest I'd like to bring on stage. My beautiful, talented daughter, Mia. Can you please help me welcome her?"

The camera panned over the cheering audience.

"The daughter?" I asked. "Is this the first time he's bringing her out?"

Alessio bumped me with his knee. "Have you been living under a rock? She's always with him at these things."

I hadn't been watching the rallies. Why would I when Mother gave me what felt like daily updates on the future mayor's statements? The last thing I wanted to do when I got home was hear more from him.

The camera panned back to the stage, showing someone walking on.

And the moment it did, the world around me fell away.

Alessio's voice faded. The room disappeared.

It was just me, that TV, and *her*.

What. The. *Fuck*.

The girl I'd pinned beneath me five minutes ago.

Slowly, I opened my palm. The traces of her bite were still there. It was real. I hadn't hallucinated having Mia Morales, *the future mayor's fucking daughter*, biting me in Messero's guest room.

"Dude, what's your problem?" Alessio sputtered as I shot off the sofa. "Where are you going?"

I didn't answer. I just ran.

Ten seconds later, I was tearing the front door open.

But she was already gone.

CHAPTER 5

Rom

"We are not delaying the wedding, Cosimo," Mother said in a clipped voice.

Gone was the serene, warm woman the rest of the world knew, and in her place was the dictator who'd raised us.

When it came to the family, Vita Ferraro sorted people into two categories: useful or useless. You'd better fucking pray you were the former.

Cosimo was stiff in an armchair, his jaw tight. They'd been going at it since we sat down for our Friday morning meeting. I had news, but I couldn't get a word in edgewise.

I was still pissed at myself for not recognizing Mia. No wonder she'd seemed familiar. I had a whole fucking file on her. But she hadn't looked like the prim and proper woman Morales dragged up on stage with him. Not with her hair mussed, her eyes wide, and that raspberry lipstick smudged on her lips as she stared up at me all scared while looking freshly fucked.

Heat pooled in my veins. Somehow, the fact that she was who she was didn't stop my cock from twitching when I thought of that image.

"Why don't you make Romolo marry her?" Cosimo snapped, pulling me back.

"Me? Married?" I drawled. "Hilarious, Cos."

I didn't do relationships. I definitely didn't do marriage. Any woman who would even consider tying herself to me for more than a few weeks had to seriously hate herself. Case in point—Harper. My reputation generally prevented anyone from getting those kinds of ideas about me.

Mother pressed her fingers to her temples. "This is getting tiresome."

"We've already delayed the wedding twice. At your request, Cosimo," Dad said calmly as he trimmed a bonsai tree at his desk. Six more sat on the windowsill. "Your work is never going to get less busy."

Cosimo's fists tightened over his knees. "It might. We can delay it again."

Mother shook her head. "Enough. This alliance is happening. We'll need Rafaele Messero's support if Morales wins and pursues his agenda against us."

I had a hunch about why Cosimo was so resistant to marrying Fabiana and it had nothing to do with work. But he hadn't come to me for advice and I wasn't going to get involved in his business unless asked. I had my own shit to deal with.

Plus, he was the eldest. Next in line after Dad. There was no question he'd get married to who he was told to. He just needed to get the fuck over it.

"Let's move on," Dad said. "Speaking of the election... What's the latest?"

Cosimo's jaw ticked. "Wilson's numbers are continuing their sad descent in the polls. Morales's people still won't return our calls."

I cracked my neck. Rupert Wilson had been our guy, but no amount of money seemed to be doing the trick this time around. He was deeply unpopular, and Morales was winning.

"We know whoever is backing Morales has a vendetta against us," Alessio said. "Have we gone one by one through that—probably very long—list of people?"

My father's expression gave nothing away. "We did. It didn't yield anything."

Mother shot him a look—one of *those* looks that were laden with unspoken meaning.

Secrets. So many fucking secrets between them.

They had a partnership that was legendary in our circles. She was the yin to his yang. He loved her. Was obsessed with her.

And her? I wasn't convinced that woman was capable of love, but if she was, our dad would be the only one on the receiving end of that emotion.

She moved closer, placing a hand on his shoulder while he snipped at his bonsai tree. "We should go over the list again, Gino. See if we missed anyone."

Dad's gaze lifted to her, an indulgent smile on his lips. "As you wish."

She bent down and kissed the top of his head.

I looked out the window so that I didn't have to watch them. I hated seeing her affectionate with him—the way she'd never been with me or my brothers. She pretended in public—she was a great actress—but it was all an act.

Vita Ferraro wasn't who people thought she was. Not even close.

I dragged my tongue over my teeth and turned back to them. The sooner I told them what I'd discovered, the sooner I could get the fuck out of here and prep for the meeting I had planned this afternoon. "I have an update. Harper was a bust, but I've found a better target."

"We're all ears, Romolo," Mother said, her fingers drumming against the desk. Her voice was smooth but threaded with impatience. Because of my failures to get us something we could use against Morales over the last six months, I was teetering dangerously close to the useless category she despised so much.

"Mia. His daughter. She was at Cosimo's party last night."

The drumming stopped.

I savored the stunned look on my mother's face. It was like I'd detonated a bomb in my father's office. Catching her off guard was rare. Satisfying.

Rising from my seat, I buttoned my jacket. "She's friends with Fabiana, apparently. But from the look on her face, I don't think she had any idea what she was walking into. I found her hiding in one of the bedrooms."

Cosimo let out a dry laugh. "Unbelievable."

I brushed a bit of lint from my sleeve. "If she's that naïve about her friend's family, she might be a weak spot. And given how tight she seems with her dad, she could have insight into who's backing him."

As they absorbed that, I headed for the door, eager to be gone.

"Where are you going?" my mother called after me.

"To introduce myself properly," I said over my shoulder, stepping into the hall.

The door clicked shut behind me, and I exhaled, tension easing from my spine. It always felt like I could breathe better once I was out of Mother's line of sight.

Now onto the fun part.

I rolled my shoulders, letting the anticipation take over —the memory of wide, frightened eyes and trembling lips humming in my blood. A slow smirk curved my mouth.

Let's see what Mia Morales is really made of.

CHAPTER 6

Mia

It turned out that shortly after Nina had left me in the bedroom yesterday, she ran into Fabi's sister-in-law. Cleo Messero cornered Nina for a full twenty minutes, grilling her about Fabi's likes and dislikes for the bachelorette party she was planning. It was long enough for Nina to miss the entire fiasco with Romolo.

When Nina finally called me, panicked after finding the room empty with a broken lamp on the ground, I told her I was fine and already in a cab. What I didn't tell her was how shaken I was—how I'd clawed at the front door of that house like my life depended on it.

And I definitely didn't tell her a word about Romolo. That story would have to wait until tonight, when I met up with her, Fabi, and Zo. They were finally going to explain to me, in person, why they'd kept me in the dark.

Right now, I had more immediate problems to deal with. Another client was ghosting me. She was more than an hour late for our meeting and hadn't responded to my texts.

I leaned back in my office chair. I'd rented this studio in SoHo three years ago. It was small, but I'd made it work.

The space had high ceilings and exposed brick that was

softened by a vintage Persian rug and warm pendant lighting. A floor-to-ceiling mirror leaned against the far wall, framed in antique gold. Closer to where I sat was a sleek rack where I kept my latest styling pulls—handpicked outfits curated for clients based on their personalities, their lifestyles, and the images they wanted to project.

A few blocks over, the high-end boutiques buzzed with life, but Broderick Lane was quieter. Most of the storefronts here were short-term rentals for pop-ups. Some weeks, the street pulsed with energy, and lines of people snaked around the block for the latest "it" brand. Other weeks? Ghost town.

This space wasn't cheap, but I'd told myself I'd be able to cover the rent in no time. Back then, I'd been so full of hope, so sure of myself.

For a while, everything had gone according to plan. I'd built a solid roster of clients, carving out a name for myself in a city where the competition was ruthless.

Then my father announced his run for mayor.

His campaign advisors decided his messaging needed to lean into his family values and his unwavering commitment to fighting organized crime. Since my stepmom was too sick to be by his side, I took her place—attending campaign rallies, shaking hands, smiling for cameras.

No one asked me if I'd do it. It was simply decided.

Even if someone had asked, I would've said yes. How could I not? I wanted to support my dad. But I hadn't considered what that support would cost me.

It wasn't the hard work—I could handle long hours and late nights. What gutted me was losing control over my time. I was a piece on someone else's chessboard, moved at will. Client appointments didn't matter. Shopping for my business didn't matter. If I was needed at a lunch, a rally, an interview, I had to drop everything at a moment's notice, without question.

I'd lost ten clients in the past year. Ten. And every time, it felt like a part of me withered and died.

This wasn't just a business. It was my passion and my last, fragile link to my mom.

To me, she was the most beautiful woman in the world —always smiling, always expressive, always draped in color. Fashion wasn't just something she wore. It was how she lived. And it had rubbed off on me.

We used to play dress-up with the treasures in her closet. Later, she taught me to sew, to alter clothes, to make them my own.

She died when I was nine. An aneurysm. No warning. No goodbye.

For months afterward, I wanted nothing. Nothing but her. My room felt cold and empty, so I slept in her closet. My dad let me. He didn't know what else to do. I curled into my sleeping bag on the carpeted floor, one of her dresses clutched in my arms, and cried into the fabric that still smelled like her.

It was during one of those nights—wrapped in the scent of her and cocooned in her world—that I decided what I wanted to do with my life.

I wanted to dress people the way Mom had dressed me. I wanted them to feel what she'd made me feel—confident, seen, beautiful. And every time they smiled, it would be a smile for her too.

Swallowing past the tightness in my throat, I retied the shoulder straps of my dress, adjusting the bows until they sat just right.

Not everything was lost.

I just had to make it to November 8th.

If my father won? Great. If he lost? I would be devastated

for him, but at least the campaign would be over. I'd be off the hook. Jenny had promised.

I could start putting my business back together.

If there was still a business left to save.

The door swung open. I didn't get a ton of walk-ins, but when it happened, it was always a nice surprise. Especially now.

"Hi! Come on i—"

My greeting got strangled on its way past my lips. It wasn't a prospective client standing on my doorstep.

It was *him*.

Romolo Ferraro tilted his head, his gaze drifting over my body.

I blinked once, twice, praying he was an apparition. He wasn't. He was still there, staring at me like I was something he couldn't wait to sink his teeth into.

How had he found me? He didn't even know who I was. Or at least... I'd thought he didn't. Clearly, I'd been wrong.

His intense stare unsettled me, but worse was the slow, dangerous smirk that curved his lips as he slightly turned. Flashing me the snake and dagger tattoo on the side of his throat, he reached behind him, and...

Locked the door.

My heart rate soared. If one of my fainting spells hit right now, it would be the worst possible time.

I waited for that telltale flash of heat to appear, but it didn't. Not yet.

"I have an appointment coming any second now," I warned him, rising from my seat while I gripped the side of the desk, just in case I started feeling woozy.

His eyes glittered. "Doubt it."

He couldn't possibly know that. But the momentary flicker in my expression must have given me away. I was ninety-nine percent sure my client wasn't going to show, and I wasn't a good liar.

He began walking toward me.

Fear and panic tangled with something much worse—something dark and electric that spread through my chest, buzzing through every nerve. His presence turned the dial up on reality, every detail sharper, more intense.

It thrilled and terrified me all at once.

Was he here to punish me for my parting gift? I was sure a man like him didn't love getting physically bested by a girl.

Do something, Mia.

Keeping my gaze locked on him, I shoved my hand into my desk drawer, fingers fumbling until they closed around the cold metal of my nail file. I yanked it out and held it up like a dagger. "Stay back."

He stopped, amusement dancing across his features as he took in my makeshift weapon.

"What exactly are you hoping to accomplish with that?"

"Don't patronize me," I hissed, tightening my grip.

He gestured lazily toward the nail file. "You're a lot more likely to hurt yourself than you are to hurt me with that thing."

I groaned internally because he was right. This man was a six-foot-something wall of muscle, and I knew that because I'd felt it. Felt *him*. On top of me. Against me.

And now here he was again, standing in my studio in a navy suit made from what looked like high-quality Italian wool, tailored to emphasize the shape of his lethal body.

Let's get real. Yesterday had been a fluke. I wouldn't stand a chance against him if he wanted to hurt me. Even if I lunged, he'd swat me away like a fly.

I tossed the useless nail file back into the drawer with a clatter. "What are you doing here?"

He rolled his shoulders and glanced around the studio.

"Is this how you greet all of your prospective clients? By threatening them with personal grooming objects?"

"You're not a prospective client. How did you find me?"

"Fabi told me."

Lie. "She'd never."

A mocking smirk tugged on his lips. "Just checking to see how loyal you think your friends are."

"Loyal enough that if I called her right now, she'd get here fast and demand to know why you're intimidating me."

"Intimidating?" He took another step forward, gaze pinned to mine. "We're just having a conversation, *Mia*."

The way he said my name—low, deliberate—sent an unwanted shiver down my spine.

"I saw you on TV. You're all over the news."

I winced. *Damn it.*

"It's a shame I didn't place you right away." His voice dropped lower, became silkier. "If I'd known you were the enemy, I would have enjoyed having you beneath me even more."

My thoughts scrambled, tripping over themselves. What was I supposed to say to that? I hated the way my skin warmed, hated the way my gaze suddenly couldn't leave his. Why did he have to be so impossibly beautiful? The kind of beauty that made you forget—momentarily—how dangerous he was.

Romolo pulled out the chair in front of my desk and lowered himself into it, looking as comfortable as if he owned the place. He gestured for me to sit, like I was the guest in *his* studio.

After a second, I sat down. I hated giving him the impression he could boss me around, but I just wanted this over with. Maybe playing along would get him the hell out of here faster.

That condescending smirk was still playing on his lips.

"I kept trying to figure out why you showed up at the party only to hide inside. Now that I know who you are, I'm back to thinking I was right about you being a spy." Elbow propped on the armrest, he dragged his index finger over his bottom lip and then slowly leaned back in the chair, letting his jacket fall open to reveal...

A gun holstered at his side.

He brought a *freaking gun* into my studio.

I barely contained my panicked squeak. "I'm not a spy! I already told you. I was in the bedroom because I wasn't feeling well."

"We both know you shouldn't have been there in the first place. Your last name is more than enough to keep you off the guest list."

"Why don't you ask Fabi?" It didn't feel great, throwing her under the bus, but she was his future sister-in-law. Maybe he'd be more civil with her.

"To ask Fabi, I'd have to loop in her brother. You really want me to get Rafaele Messero involved in this too?"

I grimaced. No. No, I absolutely did not. One mobster was more than enough.

Why *had* I shown up last night? I could've waited. Reached out to Fabi after the party.

But that would've meant sitting with the possibility that I'd hurt someone—and I was *terrible* at that.

As a result, I was in this mess.

Maybe it was better to just tell Romolo the truth.

"All right." I exhaled. "If I tell you, will you promise to leave?"

He chuckled, as if he was amused at my attempt to negotiate with him. "Deal."

I didn't trust him. He didn't strike me as a man of his word. Not at all. But what choice did I have?

"Fabi and I went to boarding school together. She used a

different last name. I didn't know she was a Messero until last night. She didn't invite me to the party, I just showed up, and then... Well, then I found out why I wasn't invited."

KNOCK KNOCK.

I shot to my feet, nearly tripping over my chair.

Romolo twisted, looking over his shoulder. "Your appointment?"

Panic clawed its way up my chest. I doubted my no-show client would appear this late, which meant it could be anyone. The glass on the door was frosted, but the window beside it wasn't. Whoever was out there would look through the clear glass in seconds if I didn't open up. That's what everyone did.

What if it was Jenny? Or someone else from my dad's staff?

They couldn't see Romolo here.

Our eyes locked.

I grabbed the curtain that separated the changing area from the front of the studio and yanked it aside. "Go. To the back."

It wasn't an order. It was basically a plea.

To my relief, he rose out of his seat. He brushed past me, his arm grazing mine for the briefest moment before he ducked under the curtain.

I let it fall back into place and hurried to the door, praying—*praying*—that I could quickly get rid of whoever it was.

CHAPTER 7
Mia

The face that appeared in the window belonged to Kassandra Proctor.

I'd never been so relieved to see her.

Which was saying a lot, considering Kassandra was the self-appointed Grim Reaper of my career. But at least she had no connection to my dad and no interest in politics.

I tried to look calm as I unlocked the door.

Over the past year, Kassandra had gone out of her way to poach my clients. She'd flooded their inboxes with offers and sent weekly emails to make sure they knew she'd always be more available than I was.

I didn't blame my clients for leaving me when I wasn't able to meet their expectations, but Kassandra seemed to take sick pleasure in taking me down.

What did she want now?

"Kassandra. Can I help you?"

She stood there in her usual monochrome ensemble, a silk wrap covering her red hair. She was the queen of sad neutrals.

"Hello, Mia, sweetheart," she cooed. "Just stopping by to let you know Angie has decided to join my client list."

The client who'd gone radio silent. The last sliver of hope I'd had for her melted into nothing. I'd known it in my gut.

Kassandra adjusted her glasses. "I thought it was only professional to tell you in person. Since, you know, we've had so many clients migrate from your list to mine." She sighed dramatically. "I think that makes it eleven now. Honestly, I feel like I should be paying you a referral fee."

The polite smile on my face was frozen. I was barely holding on to the fraying edges of my composure. My day had gone from bad to worse to apocalyptic.

With another client gone, I was going to have to dip into my savings just to cover the studio's rent next month.

My throat itched.

Don't. Cry.

I would not. Not in front of Kassandra, who'd probably feign pity and only make me feel worse, and definitely not in front of Romolo, who could hear every word of our conversation from behind the curtain.

"Thank you for the heads-up." Despite my best efforts, my voice cracked.

Kassandra's smile sharpened. "Of course, sweetheart. I know you've had a lot on your plate lately, but in our industry, clients expect excellence. If you can't deliver... Well, you can't blame them for going elsewhere."

It stung because it was true.

I'd disappointed my clients by being flaky and unreliable. I was trying so, so hard, but it wasn't enough. Whenever I tried to push back against Jenny dropping something on my calendar at the last minute, she'd lay on the guilt trip so thick it felt like I was suffocating.

I dug my nails into the palm of my hand, hoping the pain would distract me from the tears blurring my vision.

It didn't.

"Oh, and—" Kassandra added with a triumphant glint in her eye "—if you're ever looking for work after your father's campaign, I'd be happy to bring you on as an assistant."

Don't. Cry.

"This fits well, Mia." A deep voice cut through the air. "But I think we'll need something more dramatic for The Golden Circle party."

I whirled around to see Romolo stepping out from behind the curtain.

What is he doing?

He slid his palms over the front of his suit, as if he'd just put it on and was straightening the folds.

"Did he just say The Golden Circle?" Kassandra asked, her voice hushed.

I thought so, but I must have been hearing things. The Golden Circle was the most exclusive social club in New York City, with a membership fee of a hundred grand a year, and a waitlist longer than Fifth Avenue. Their parties were legendary, filled with only the cream of the crop of this city's high society.

Romolo was a member? I guess he had the connections and the money to find his way in, criminal reputation notwithstanding.

He strode toward me. "We still have two weeks to get it right. I gave you an unlimited budget for a reason. Get creative. Make me stand out."

Kassandra swallowed. I watched the gears turn in her head while mine did the same.

He was helping me save face. Dressing someone for a Golden Circle event was something few stylists in the city got to do.

I didn't have time to react before his gaze slid to Kassandra.

"The door was locked for a reason. We're busy. Get out." His voice was so cold that Kassandra visibly recoiled.

She sputtered. "I-I didn't realize—"

He stepped forward, crowding her. "A word of advice? Look somewhere else for your assistant. Given the astronomical rate I'm paying Mia, I doubt you can afford her."

She backed up. Fast.

I just stood there, stunned, as he forced her out of the studio.

He shut the door, locked it, and closed the blinds.

Then, he turned to me.

Something dangerous swarmed inside his eyes, something that sent a series of shivers racing down my spine.

He walked toward me with measured steps. I forced myself to stand my ground, even though my animal instincts screamed at me to run.

"Has she always been such a cunt, or is this a new thing?" His voice was a low rumble inside his chest.

He stood so close that my next inhale caught his scent. Rich, spicy, unmistakable, and *so* familiar.

Was that...?

Angel's Share. My favorite cologne.

Why? Just why?

It was like someone had conspired to make this dangerous predator as physically attractive as possible.

"I'm pretty sure she was born that way," I whispered.

In this light, his eyes were a pale, piercing gray—the color of dense morning fog. "And here I had the impression you were the kind of person who never had a bad word to say about anyone."

I *was* that kind of person. But something about Romolo made me a little sharper around the edges. I didn't think I could survive around him if I stayed all soft.

"Guess you don't know me."

"I'd like to change that." He lifted his hand and took hold of one of the ends of the bow hanging over my shoulder. There was something sensual about the way he rubbed the gauzy fabric between his forefinger and thumb.

My stomach did a flip I refused to analyze too closely.

Fear. That's all it was. The same fluttering, disorienting sensation I'd felt yesterday when he'd pinned me to the bed, his body overwhelming mine.

I tugged the fabric free from his grasp and took a step back, heat prickling my cheeks. "I'd like you to leave."

"I'm not going anywhere. Not when you just became my new stylist."

A hysterical laugh bubbled up. "Look, I appreciate you saving me from further embarrassment just now, but we both know I'm not dressing you for anything."

He crossed his arms over his chest. "You left your agenda open on a stool in the dressing area. Five cancelled appointments in the last week. Ten out of nineteen clients crossed out. I guess it's eleven once you account for the one you just lost. Your business is crumbling."

I clenched my hands at my sides. Shame clawed at me. I brushed past him and retreated behind the safety of my desk. It wasn't much of a barrier, but it was something. "My business is none of your business."

He settled back into his chair, all relaxed confidence, while I busied myself with opening my laptop. The fact that he'd seen me in that moment of vulnerability—and knew just how screwed I was—was a bitter pill to swallow. I hadn't even told my friends the full extent of my business problems. It was too embarrassing. Too raw.

"Dress me for this dinner, and I'll get your name out there."

"No."

"The theme is Moon Signs and Merengues."

My pulse skipped.

If there was one thing New York loved, it was a ridiculous theme. I'd styled at least ten absurdly themed parties every year for the past three years.

And I loved it. Okay? I *loved* it. It allowed me to get creative. It allowed me to take risks.

"Normally, I don't bother dressing up for these things. But this year, I feel like giving it a try."

Slowly, my gaze slid back to him. He'd look good in midnight-blue with his lightly tanned complexion. Maybe if—

Stop. Just stop.

I slammed my laptop closed. It was out of the question. A disaster waiting to happen. "My answer is still no."

Romolo's brow arched. "Do you know what a feature in The Golden Circle monthly newsletter could do for you?"

A lot.

The Golden Circle's members were some of the most fashionable people in the city—socialites, artists, cultural icons... They graced the pages of glossy magazines, got photographed every time they stepped outside, and were watched by everyone else who wished to be like them.

A roster full of them would be a dream.

"Are you the owner of The Golden Circle?" I asked.

His brow furrowed. "No."

"Then why should I believe you have the kind of sway needed to get someone of your choosing into their heavily curated newsletter?" I clipped out, annoyed at myself for even engaging with this delusion.

"Heavily curated by my cousin, Caterina Ferraro. A glowing recommendation from me would be all it takes."

Anger was starting to bubble up inside of me. He was dangling a shiny, golden ticket in front of me—the answer to my problems.

But it didn't matter.

I couldn't do it.

As he said, I was the enemy. He was my enemy too.

"What would you get out of this, Romolo?" I demanded.

He didn't answer. He just smiled. Of course, he wasn't going to tell me his real motives, but I knew they wouldn't spell anything good for me.

I tucked a strand of hair behind my ear. "There are plenty of other stylists in this city who could do exactly what you're asking for."

"I don't want them. I want *you*."

The way he said it—low, firm—made the air in my lungs feel thin.

I shook my head. "It's not going to happen." Yes, I wanted to save my business. But not like this.

If anyone saw us together, it'd be a headline. If anyone found out I was working for him, it'd be a full-blown scandal. Knowing the damage that could do to my dad's campaign, I wouldn't risk it.

No, I would fix my business problems on my own. I didn't need Romolo Ferraro's help.

I tipped my chin up. "We're done here."

He didn't seem disappointed. He simply reached into his jacket pocket and handed me a card. "Call me if you change your mind."

There was no name, only a number. I flipped it over to see the initials R.F.

"I won't change my mind." When I glanced up, he was already halfway out the door, and if he heard me, he didn't reply.

He stepped outside, his tall frame moving past my window before he disappeared out of sight.

I had no intention of calling him.

But something told me he wasn't done with me yet.

CHAPTER 8

Mia

That evening, I stepped through the doors of the speakeasy, ready to demand answers.

Potions and Co was an old pharmacy turned apothecary-themed drinking haunt. A wall of shelves lined with antique pill bottles and glass apothecary jars doubled as a hidden entrance. I rang the bell and waited until an attendant appeared and invited me inside.

The space beneath the shop felt more like an alchemist's lab than a bar. A narrow staircase led down to a dimly lit room where candlelight flickered against stone walls. Behind the counter, flasks of green liquid bubbled over burners, while jars filled with dried herbs, mouse tails, and pickled eyeballs sat among the usual liquor bottles. I made a point not to look too closely at those. They made me queasy.

Sitting in the corner booth—the one Nina and I always got whenever we came here—were my friends.

"You made it," Fabi said, sounding relieved, like she'd been worried I wouldn't show.

"Of course I made it." I slid in beside Zo, who'd dyed her hair purple since the last time I'd seen her, and handed

Nina my tote so she could put it on the shelf behind her. "But the three of you better start talking."

Zo reached for the cocktail menu. "Let's get a round first—"

I snatched it out of her hands. "No. Answers first. Alcohol later."

She raised her palms. "Okay, okay. For the record, I told Fabi she needed to fess up to you a while back."

"Oh yeah? Why'd you go along with it then?" I was coming in hotter than usual, but I didn't care. I couldn't remember the last time I was this angry with them.

Fabi reached across the table, fingers curling around my hand. "Mia, it's not Zo's fault. It wasn't her secret to tell. I feel awful about how I've treated you these last few weeks."

I pulled my hand away and crossed my arms over my chest.

"I didn't know how to tell you," Fabi pleaded. "Your dad was on TV talking about how he was going to take down the Ferraros and put them behind bars, and in the meantime, I was picking out the flower arrangements for my wedding to Cosimo. I was scared, Mia. Scared you wouldn't want to have anything to do with me after you found out."

"So instead, you made it seem like you didn't want anything to do with *me*?" My voice rose, incredulous. "Make it make sense, Fabi."

She shook her head. "It doesn't. I know. I was paralyzed, and I kept kicking the can down the road. I kept thinking, 'I'll talk to her next week. No, next week. No, next week.' And then—"

"I showed up and forced the conversation."

Fabi nodded, her eyes glassy. "I'm glad you did. It killed me keeping this from you. I'm so sorry, Mia."

I shook my head. She sounded genuinely remorseful, but I wasn't ready to let it go just yet. "I don't understand why you never told me who you were. We've known each other for over a decade. Far longer than my dad's campaign."

She grimaced. "It was supposed to be a secret. My brother gave Elena and I a different last name so that no one could trace us back to him. It was about safety, especially while we were living abroad."

I picked at a cuticle. Okay, that kind of tracked, but it still hurt. Fabi should have known she could trust me.

I gestured at Nina and Zo. "You told them."

Fabi shook her head. "I didn't."

"Then how did they find out?"

Zo shrugged. "You know me, I like to poke around."

"Poke around where exactly?"

"The FBI database," Zo said so casually you'd think she was talking about checking the weather. "I hacked into it about two years ago."

"Zo! Jesus Christ. That's the kind of thing that gets people arrested," I said.

She waved a hand. "I was careful."

I wasn't comforted by that.

"Naturally," she continued, "the first thing I did was look up all my friends. Imagine my surprise when I found out Fabi Castellano wasn't a real person. I got curious. And you know how I get when I get curious."

"You dig," Nina said.

Zo flipped over a coaster. "I sure do. Found her and her sis's birth certificates eventually."

Unbelievable. "Wow. Easy."

She cocked a brow. "Oh, it *wasn't* easy. Took forever to hack into the FBI in the first place. Don't downplay my brilliance."

"God forbid," I muttered. "So you knew all this time and told Nina, but not me?"

"It was *her* secret," Zo said, nodding toward Fabi. "And Nina figured it out before me."

"How?" I turned to Nina. She didn't have Zo's hacking skills. She must have pieced it together another way.

Nina fiddled with the small pendant she always wore around her neck. "I'm related to Cosimo Ferraro."

My jaw hit the floor. "*What?* But your last name's Liu. Your dad's Chinese."

"Yes, but my mom's Italian-Albanian. And her sister is Vita Ferraro."

The Ferraro matriarch was Nina's *aunt*? According to my father, Vita was an important player in the criminal organization.

I couldn't believe what I was hearing. Nina was even more by the book than me. She was the last person I'd ever imagine having extended family involved in organized crime.

I sank back into my seat, trying to wrap my head around all of this. "So Cosimo is your—"

"He's my cousin."

And so was Romolo.

Oh God.

"You must've known all along, then," I said. She was part of the same world as Fabi.

"No." Nina shook her head. "I put it together during the winter break just before we graduated Valais Academy. My parents have nothing to do with the Ferraro business, but we still get together now and then. The subject of the Messeros came up at a big family dinner, and when someone said Rafaele Messero's sisters went to a private school in Switzerland, I had a feeling. When I got back to school, I asked Fabi straight up, and—"

"She turned red," I guessed.

"So red. Like, horrifically red."

My head fell back against the booth. "Okay. I'm ready for a drink."

Zo flagged a server down. As soon as he'd taken our orders and left, Fabi reached for my hand again. This time, I didn't pull away.

"Will you forgive me?"

I wanted to. But I was still hurt. "You hid a big part of your life from me. For a long time."

"It wasn't really my life until the engagement," she insisted. "My brother doesn't talk to me about his business. I'm not involved in his companies. I was happy to live in Geneva, doing my own thing. Same with Elena."

"Is she back in New York now too?" I asked.

Fabi shook her head. "She's on a mission in Botswana. It'll be over just in time for the wedding."

"So what happened exactly? You fell for Cosimo and decided he's worth leaving Switzerland for?"

Fabi's hand clenched around mine, and her expression fell. "I..." Her voice wavered. "I didn't fall for him. It's an arranged marriage."

My heart stopped. I felt the blood drain out of my face. "Come again?"

Fabi smiled, but it looked forced. "It's okay. I always knew it would be this way. My brother picked Cosimo for me. It's for the good of the family."

That text she'd sent yesterday. I hadn't thought much of her saying she needed emotional support—who didn't at an event with your entire family present?—but now I suspected there was more to it.

"Fabi, do you like him?" I asked.

"Uh-huh. Sure."

That was the least convincing answer I'd ever heard. All the secrecy about him—God, it was all starting to click.

I squinted at her. "Do you even *know* him?"

She nibbled on the corner of her mouth. "A bit. Yeah."

The server returned with our drinks, but I barely registered him rattling off our order. My ears rang.

This wasn't right. Fabi deserved better than having to marry some guy she hardly knew.

Correction—not just some guy. A dangerous, ruthless criminal like Cosimo Ferraro. How could her brother do this to her?

The anger I'd felt at her earlier was gone. Now I was just worried.

"Do you want to marry him?" I asked as soon as the server walked away.

She let out a breath. "I don't have a choice. But honestly, it's fine. That was the deal my brother made with Elena and I. We could live our lives in Switzerland, far from all of this, as long as when the time came, we'd return home and do our duty."

Fine. It wasn't fine.

If anything, it seemed cruel. Letting them taste freedom just to rip it away.

My gaze flicked to Nina and Zo. "This isn't okay. Right?"

Nina didn't look fazed. She sipped her drink, taking her time before answering. "I know it must seem strange, but this is how that world works."

I stared at her. "Seriously? So you're okay with Fabi being forced to marry a killer?" My voice sharpened. "Because he's your cousin?"

Nina frowned. "Cosimo's not going to hurt her, Mia. He's not like that."

"And how can you be so sure? Zo, back me up here."

Zo tilted her martini glass between her fingers. "There are plenty of arranged marriages in the world. Not all of them are bad. My own parents' marriage was set up by their families back in Serbia."

The two of them were so casual about this. Probably because, unlike me, they'd had time to accept it. To rationalize it.

But had they forgotten about Fabi's mom?

Her mother had been abused by Fabi's dad. That alone was horrific. But knowing now that he was a mafia don made it worse. Going to the police? That probably wasn't even an option for her.

And it wouldn't be for Fabi, either.

If history repeated itself, she'd be trapped.

"Look, Cosimo wouldn't dare lay a hand on me. My brother would kill him if he did."

She sounded sure. I wasn't. It seemed to me these men treated women like cattle, no better than property.

I met her gaze. Her expression was resigned.

But I was worried for her. So, so worried.

She'd been carrying a heavy weight these last few months. She hadn't chosen this. Any of this. And knowing she thought she might lose me over something she had no control over? That had to have been unbearable.

I sighed. "Fabs, I forgive you. And I'm not going to ditch you as a friend. Come on. You really think I'm capable of that?"

Her eyes shimmered, and her grip on my hand tightened. "I'm sorry for being such a coward."

"You're not. But no more secrets, okay?"

She nodded. "No more."

Zo lifted her martini. "Let's toast and put this behind us. To us all being in the same city again."

Yes, at least we had that. If Fabi needed anything, we'd be close to her. We could help her.

Nina set her glass down. "Your turn, Mia. What happened yesterday? With the broken lamp?"

The question wrenched me back into my own problems.

Romolo's card was somewhere at the bottom of my purse. I should have tossed it into the bin, but something made me keep it.

"The lamp wasn't like a...family heirloom, was it?"

Fabi waved a hand. "Not at all."

"Good." I sighed. "Here's what happened."

I told them everything.

Every ridiculous, mortifying detail. Romolo Ferraro and that woman barging into the bedroom. Me throwing the lamp at him. My business problems. Him showing up at my studio today.

And his offer.

His damned offer.

"I told him there was no way I'd ever dress him," I said. "I mean, I can't believe he thought I might agree to something like that."

"He's out of his mind," Nina said without hesitation.

Zo, meanwhile, pulled out her phone. "I'm sorry, I'm still stuck on the fact that you two basically cuddled last night." She started typing. "I need to see what this guy looks like."

"We did not cuddle," I muttered, remembering his hard body pressing down on mine. I could still remember the feel of his six-pack against my palms.

My fists curled. *Ugh. Stop.*

Fabi looked concerned. "I hate that you're on his radar. Who knows what he's really after?"

"I think it's pretty obvious what he wants," Nina said. "He's trying to get something from Mia to use against her father."

A knot formed in my stomach. "Yeah. Probably."

"*This* is who we're talking about?" Zo slid her phone in the center of the table so we could all see the screen.

It was a photo of Romolo at some high-society event. A stunning woman was draped on his arm. He had a drink in his hand, and that signature smirk curved his lips. The kind that didn't hold an ounce of humor and was impossible to look away from.

"That's him," I said weakly.

"He's *hot*," Zo declared. "Now I'm even more upset I didn't come back from my business trip a day early. No one told me there'd be eye candy at the party last night." She grinned. "I think it's a brilliant idea for you to dress him."

"How's that?" Nina arched a brow.

"C'mon." Zo slid her phone back in her bag. "Mia's business is struggling, and he's offering her a solution. All she has to do is dress him for one party, and he'll get her in front of the crème de la crème of New York society. This could be huge for her!"

"I'd never do anything to put my dad's campaign at risk," I said.

"What's the risk?" Zo flicked her hand. "He looks too pretty to be clever. You can win against him at his own game."

I sighed. "I wish I had your confidence."

"Don't we all," Nina muttered. "Zo, I can promise you Romolo Ferraro isn't some idiot. He *is* clever. And ruthless. When it comes to women, he ensnares, conquers, and discards. Romolo isn't someone I'd want any friend of mine spending time with. He'll do whatever it takes to get what he wants, and he doesn't care who he hurts in the process."

A chill slid down my spine.

That was a damning description of Romolo, but what about Cosimo?

They were brothers, raised under the same roof by the same parents.

If Romolo was this dangerous, how much better could his brother be?

Even though I was finally in on the secret, I still felt like an outsider at this table. How could they all be so okay with what was happening to Fabi? It was like they were in denial —telling themselves everything would be fine because they saw no way out.

But what if it wasn't all fine?

What if Cosimo was actually horrible? What if he was an abuser? Nina said they weren't close. Just because she was family didn't mean she knew how he treated women.

But there was one person who would.

His brother.

And if I agreed to dress Romolo, maybe I could find out.

I traced my finger around the rim of my glass.

Could I?

Despite Nina's and Zo's drastically different outlooks— one the voice of reason, the other a devil on your shoulder —they were both logical and unflinching. Meanwhile, Fabi and I led with our hearts. Calculated masterminds, we were not.

But if this was my one opportunity to figure out what would await Fabi after she'd walked down the aisle...wasn't it worth the risk?

"How many times would you even need to meet him in person to do the job?" Zo asked, flipping through the cocktail menu again.

I thought about it. "Two or three times? The party's in two weeks, so there's not much time for back-and-forth. We'd have one meeting to agree on the look, and then a fitting or two."

"Three meetings. Three measly meetings where you just have to stay sharp," Zo said before her gaze darted to Nina. "You think she can't handle that? Have some faith. This could change everything for her."

Nina frowned. "Romolo might not even hold up his end

of the bargain. Especially if he manages to get what he wants from Mia. You can't trust him."

I flattened my palms against the table. "Does he really think I'm stupid enough to hand him information about my dad?"

And what information would that even be? My dad wasn't hiding skeletons in his closet. He was an honest man trying to fix this city.

The Ferraros must be nervous about being in his crosshairs.

What was their plan?

I rolled my lips, thoughts tangling. Maybe that was another thing I could try to figure out.

"The men in our world always underestimate women," Fabi said. "Just forget about him, Mia. If he comes to see you again, tell me, and I'll talk to Cosimo. Romolo has no right to bother you."

"You think your fiancé would do something about it?"

Fabi's cheeks reddened. "I-I don't know."

And that was the problem.

She had no idea who she was marrying.

Dressing Romolo for this event could give me a chance to find out.

But according to Nina, he was dangerous and smart.

Could I really hold my own against him?

Could I afford not to?

CHAPTER 9

Rom

Mia Morales was almost too perfect.

The interviews, the speeches at her father's rallies—they painted a picture of a dutiful daughter, the kind who'd sacrifice anything for her family. Her stepmom was sick, so Mia stepped in as the radiant proxy, always at her father's side.

The media adored her. She had the face of a saint, all soft smiles and big brown eyes, and was forever being caught in the act of doing something noble. Volunteering at soup kitchens. Shaking hands with elderly veterans. Laughing with wide-eyed kids at youth centers.

She smiled like there was nowhere else she'd rather be.

But it was a lie.

Her posture was too stiff, her shoulders too tight. Her smile was beautiful, but it didn't reach her eyes.

Despite being all over the news, it was clear she hated the spotlight. And yet, she endured it. For her father.

I was sprawled out in bed, laptop balanced on my stomach, whiskey glass in hand as I scrolled through her Instagram for the dozenth time. Her Facebook was a fossil from her teenage years, abandoned long before the Morales political machine got its claws in her. The Internet was all curated interviews where she stuck to the party line. But Instagram? That's where the real Mia lived.

Her account was private, but she wasn't careful about who she let in. I made a burner profile for a fake clothing brand, posted a single vague teaser about an upcoming launch, and sent her a follow request. She accepted within an hour.

Little Mia probably prided herself on supporting small businesses.

Her grid was full of food shots, artsy cropped photos of New York, and outfit pics. Lots and lots of them. She dressed her clients in all kinds of wild shit, but her own style was more subdued. Especially in the last year. She was dressing for the campaign now. For her father's voters.

If I had to guess, she was counting down the days until it was over.

That girl wanted to be in her studio. It wasn't just a workspace for her. It was her temple, her sanctuary. I'd felt it the second I stepped inside. She'd spend all her time there if she could.

Her business meant a lot to her. But her father meant more.

That's why I wasn't sure if she'd take my offer.

It had been a few days, and she hadn't contacted me.

Fine. I just had to work harder to uncover more of the secrets she hid beneath that polished do-gooder facade. Eventually, I'd find another way in.

Whoever handled security for the Morales campaign should be fired. Mia's location was tagged in almost every photo. If I wanted to piece together her schedule, I could do it with ease. She was practically begging to be stalked.

Didn't her father realize how reckless that was? He wasn't stupid. He knew we were dangerous.

So what made him so confident she was safe? Pure arrogance, perhaps?

Outside, thunder cracked.

My gaze snapped to the window. The rain hadn't started yet, but it would soon. I hated the sight of it. The way the droplets would slither down my floor-to-ceiling windows like slow-moving tears.

I got up and yanked the blinds shut.

Returning to my nightstand, I downed the rest of my drink. Another few minutes of scrolling brought me to the bottom of Mia's feed.

Her first post. She was fifteen, maybe sixteen. Four girls posed in front of the backdrop of Valais Academy, that snobby Swiss prep school.

Mia. Fabi. Nina. And a fourth I didn't recognize.

I had first discovered Mia and my cousin were also friends when I looked into her after Cosimo's engagement party. But I still hadn't called Nina to fish for intel.

Maybe it was time.

She picked up on the third ring. "Rom. I was wondering when I'd hear from you."

My lips quirked. Nina and I barely saw each other these days. Long gone were the summers we spent together as children, playing board games in her parents' basement. It used to drive her insane when I cheated. Which I did. Constantly.

She was bossy, sharp, and no-nonsense, traits that hadn't faded with time.

If she suspected I was up to something, she'd warn Mia to stay the hell away from me.

"Let me guess," I said, leaning back against the headboard. "Mia already told you I stopped by her studio."

"Yes. And I won't tell you a damn thing about her if that's why you're calling. The women who land in your crosshairs typically end up depressed, fleeing the country to 'find themselves,' or filing for divorce. I'm not signing Mia up for any of that."

My brow arched. "Who's filed for divorce?"

"That footballer player's wife you had on your arm at Black Silk the one time I was there."

I wasn't aware. I didn't keep tabs on old flings. "You know her?"

"We have some friends in common. Rumor is things at home went downhill the moment you entered the picture."

Sounded about right. I excelled at many things, but there was one thing I discovered a long time ago I was particularly good at—destroying people's lives.

Sometimes, I barely even had to try.

I chuckled dismissively. "You know better than to believe in rumors."

"Whatever you're planning, it won't work. Mia's not desperate. She knows better than to get involved with you."

"So protective," I mused.

"She's a good person, Rom."

I bet she was. Which meant she'd be easy to manipulate.

"Like you?" I asked.

"Is that an attempt at flattery? Give me a break."

"Fine. But at least tell me what you told her about me."

"Only the truth, and nothing but the truth."

"Ouch." I clutched my chest mockingly, even though she couldn't see it. "We're family. Family's supposed to stick together."

"Mia's my family too. Maybe not by blood, but in every other way that matters. Don't forget that."

The *or else* hung in the air.

"Good catching up, cuz," I drawled. I wasn't going to get anything out of her.

"Good night," she said dryly and hung up.

I set my phone on the nightstand. It was safe to assume Mia had been thoroughly warned about me.

Forcing Nina to give me something wouldn't be difficult —I could mess with her business in some way—but I didn't need to do that. Not yet. I could research—

My phone buzzed with a text.

> "I'll dress you for The Golden Circle party. Can you come to the studio on Tuesday at 8 a.m.?"

A spark of excitement zapped up my spine.

Well, well, well.

Guess Mia wasn't so selfless after all.

She was open to crossing some lines to save her precious business. And that was even after hearing the warnings I presumed Nina had given, which had likely been as long as the tax code.

I raked my fingers through my hair.

Mia thought she could handle me, then. It looked like arrogance ran in her family.

I let out a low chuckle, shaking my head. She had no idea who she'd just invited into her life.

But she'd learn.

Oh, she'd learn.

CHAPTER 10

Rom

On Tuesday, I parked in front of Mia's studio and let a delivery biker pass before opening the car door.

It was eight a.m. The day was going to be a scorcher. Even now, it was already oppressively humid and hot.

A few streets over, cars blared their horns, and an ambulance wailed, threatening to cleave my skull in two. I was running on fumes. Last night, I'd barely slept.

I'd gotten in bed by one, determined to be sharp for today, but just as I'd started drifting off, the general manager at Black Silk called.

Four armed Albanians had tried to get into my club. On a fucking Monday night, when it was basically dead. My men got them and dragged them into my office, not knowing if they should let them go or not. By the time I arrived, they were still high on something, babbling excuses about how they'd gone to the wrong club. Maybe they were telling the truth. Maybe they weren't. Didn't matter.

They left with something to remember me by.

Flexing my bruised knuckles, I crossed the sidewalk and walked up to Mia's studio.

She opened the door before I even knocked. Clearly, she'd been waiting for me.

My gaze trailed a path down her body. She was dressed for the weather—light-blue skirt stopping mid-thigh on smooth, toned legs. A white silk blouse fitted just right. It skimmed over her curves, making me want to see what it would look like untucked, unbuttoned.

The sight of her made this shitty heat suddenly seem a lot less shitty.

"Morning," I drawled, masking the gut-punch of arousal. I couldn't remember the last time I'd found a woman this attractive.

It pissed me off.

I wasn't worried it would interfere with my plans, but it was a distraction. An annoying one.

She gave me a once-over, eyes lingering on my belt for a second too long. "No gun this time?"

I smirked. "I can get it, if that's what gets you going."

She huffed but didn't take the bait. "Come in."

The studio was as I remembered it. Small. Tidy. Feminine.

A clothing rack stood beside her desk with a few garments already prepped. Looked like they might be my size.

We sat across from each other at her desk. She laced her fingers neatly over a leather sketchbook, her back straight. She seemed nervous and trying so damn hard to hide it.

This was going to be fun.

"I sketched a proposal for your outfit," she said, diving straight in. "The plan is for you to review the design and try on some of the pieces I picked out. We'll have one more meeting for a fitting, and we'll be done."

Two meetings.

She was trying to get me in and out of her life as quickly

as possible. Maybe she wasn't as arrogant as I thought. Maybe she sensed it was dangerous to be around me for too long.

I smirked. "You never asked for my moon sign."

She reached for a thick stack of papers and pushed it my way. "I got it from Nina," she said. "Did you know she's into astrology?"

I glanced down. The cover page said it was a birth chart reading, and it had my full name, along with my birth date, time of birth, and location.

The fuck?

I flipped the page and stared at some graph I had no idea how to read. The next page was a wall of text. It was in-depth. More detailed than any of the bullshit horoscopes I'd seen in magazines.

She was prepared.

"You're Gemini sun, Venus square Saturn, and an Aries moon. Your moon sign is fire, ruled by Mars, which signifies action and energy."

"Astrology's not really my thing," I said, brushing it off. Fucking Nina. She sold me out. Not that I put much weight into this stuff, but—

"You're confident, bold, assertive. You crave excitement and independence and hate when people try to control you. Boredom is your enemy. You need constant mental stimula-tion, or you start to feel like you're crawling out of your skin."

I froze mid page flip, a prickling sensation creeping up the back of my neck. That was...uncomfortably accurate. Especially the last part. My days were packed, sure—but every night, the silence hit me like a wall. I had this ritual: put on a film the second I got home. Just so I wouldn't have to sit in it.

"She must have been thrilled to help, considering she

told you to stay the hell away from me," I muttered, slapping the pages down and pushing the stack away from me.

"She thinks I shouldn't do this," Mia admitted. "But at the end of the day, it's my choice."

Interesting. Just when I'd thought she was nothing more than a helpless little lamb, she showed a bit of backbone.

She was a lot more interesting than I'd initially pegged her to be.

She opened her sketchbook and turned it toward me. The way she leaned forward gave me a tantalizing glimpse down her blouse.

Suddenly, I was wide awake, every cell in my body hyperaware of her.

Fuck.

I've seen enough tits for two lifetimes. At this point, a good rack was like a well-made whiskey cocktail at the club—appreciated, sure, but nothing that stopped me in my tracks.

Except hers, apparently.

Heat rushed straight down to my cock, and my mind went to places it shouldn't. Like imagining her sprawled on my bed, nothing but moonlight licking at her skin.

"In Roman mythology, Mars is the god of war, so I thought we could play with that." She tapped the paper. "Tell me what you think."

I dragged my gaze to the drawing, forcing myself to focus.

The sketch was clean and precise. A tailored military-style suit, the jacket with a double-breasted cut and a high collar. Ornate silver clasps ran down the chest, and a thick leather belt wrapped around the middle. A deep red cape was pinned to the suit with a brooch, and draped over one shoulder, giving it a dramatic flair. The pants were slimmer than my usual, tucked inside a pair of leather boots.

It looked like the uniform of a celestial warlord.

The god of war.

Yeah, I could see it.

I looked at her. "Sold."

She tucked a strand of hair behind her ear. "Yeah? You can tell me if you don't like it."

I liked it, all right. She had talent. And although that fucking birth chart was an intrusion, the vain part of me was pleased that she'd put so much thought into this instead of just phoning it in.

Most of my suits were made by our family's tailor—Giuseppe. He was a cranky old man who lectured me about menswear while holding me hostage in his office.

I had a feeling I'd enjoy her fussing over me a hell of a lot more.

"You did well," I said, picking up a small tube that lay on her desk.

It was her lip gloss.

Berry.

The same one that made her mouth that deep, fuckable shade of red.

She snatched it from my fingers. "Will your brother be at the party?"

My brother? "Which one?"

"Cosimo."

Why was she asking about him?

Hold on.

I sat back, tipping my head slightly as I took her in.

Mia Morales wasn't selfish. Everything I'd learned about her said the opposite. So what was more likely—that she'd taken this job to save her business?

Or to save someone else?

"Why do you want to know about my brother?"

She shifted in her seat. "He's marrying my best friend. Is it so surprising that I'd be curious about him?"

There it was. She was concerned about Fabiana.

Cos had been a shitty fiancé so far, and I was sure Mia had heard all about it from Fabi this past week. After she'd finally learned the truth about her friend. After she'd crashed a party she had no business being at.

And now she was swooping in, trying to protect her.

Fuck me. This girl had a savior complex.

I dragged my palm over my lips. I could use this.

"All right," I said easily. "I'll tell you about him. But it's a question for a question. One from you, one from me."

Her brows furrowed. "Fine."

I smiled. She was so eager for information, so desperate to know if her best friend was walking into a nightmare. She wasn't even trying to hide it.

Her throat worked around her next words. "Is he going to hurt her?"

I held her gaze. "Cos doesn't hurt women." I paused. "Not physically, at least."

She stared at me, waiting, expecting me to say more. I didn't. I never said more than I needed to.

It was my turn now.

"What's the real reason your father is so fucking obsessed with my family?"

Her lips—those soft, *berry*-coated lips—pressed into a thin line. "Haven't you watched any of his rallies? Your family is the reason my uncle is dead."

"Yeah, I know. Caught in a shootout a fucking century ago."

"More like thirty years," she corrected.

"Before either of us were born. Your dad really knows how to hold a grudge, huh?"

"He only wants justice."

"He was happy enough living without it for more than half of his life. You know there has to be something else."

She seemed confused. "Something else? I don't know what you mean."

Was that a lie? I searched her expression, waiting for a tell—the flick of her gaze, the twitch of her fingers.

Nothing.

"You really—"

"I answered your question," she said, cutting me off.

"Fine. Your turn."

"No. That's enough." Pushing back from the desk, she looked flushed. "I don't want to play this game anymore."

She was rattled. Why? Because she was hiding something? Or because she hated toeing the line?

This girl wanted to help Fabi and also wanted to protect her dad.

She was so goddamn busy trying to be everything to everyone that she was allowing her business to crumble in the meantime.

If this wasn't fully self-inflicted and if I possessed a heart, I might have felt sorry for her.

Instead, I cocked a brow. "What now?"

She grabbed a few hangers off the metal rack. "I need you to try these on so I can check the fit. Then I'll take your measurements for any alterations."

I began unbuttoning my shirt.

Her eyes sprang wide. "What are you doing?"

"Changing."

She practically threw the clothes at me, her hands flying up as if to block her view. "Not here! Go to the back." She gestured to the curtained-off area at the back where I'd hidden last time.

"What if I need some help?" I asked, getting up.

Her nostrils flared. "You're capable of putting on pants without assistance, I assume?"

I shrugged, stepping closer. "If I must. But we both know it'd be more fun if you helped."

"That's not happening," she muttered and brushed past me, her shoulder grazing mine.

I chuckled. It was far too easy to get a rise out of her.

The dark slacks slid on without a problem.

The shirt was another matter. I got my arms halfway through the sleeves. The fabric wrapped around me like shrink wrap, and I took it off.

"Shirt's too small," I called, stepping out of the changing room with it hanging off my index finger. "Got another?"

She was leaning against her desk, typing something on her phone. Her gaze lifted, widened, and darted away just as quickly.

"Let me check." She rushed over to the rack of clothes.

I ran a hand over the tattoo on the side of my neck, enjoying how fucking flustered she looked. She walked over to me with another shirt, clearly trying to avoid looking at my bare chest. Was she afraid I'd mesmerize her with my six-pack?

I mean, fair. It's happened before.

"Here," she said, giving me the shirt.

I took it. "Thanks."

Her eyes locked onto my bruised hand.

"What happened?" she asked, her brows knitting.

I slid my arms through the sleeves. "Nothing."

Mia didn't move, just stood there watching as I started on the buttons. "Looks like it hurts."

"Just a bit stiff." I flexed my hand against the ache as I fumbled with a button.

She frowned. "Here, let me." She stepped closer and

made quick work of the buttons, her fingertips brushing against my skin through the fabric now and then.

Those featherlight touches sent sparks all the way down to my cock.

It was *ridiculous*. What the fuck was going on with me?

On paper, Mia wasn't my type. I didn't chase good girls or get off on the idea of luring them into my world. Women were either part of the job or one-night stands to take the edge off.

Mia was just another job.

And yet, my reaction to her was throwing me for a fucking loop.

"I've got it," I said, my voice rough as I tried to push her hands away.

She ignored me, her stubborn fingers continuing their work.

Jesus. She just couldn't help herself. She was even trying to save *me*.

"What happens when you stop rescuing the people around you?" I asked, watching the way her frown deepened, tugging at the corners of her lips.

She hesitated. "I don't know what you mean."

"You care too much. Have you ever been selfish, or is that word foreign to you?" I tilted my head, studying her. "You're such a fucking good girl—practically a caricature."

Her eyes snapped to mine, flashing with indignation. "You're a jerk."

She tried to step away, but I caught her wrists with my bruised hands, ignoring the sharp stab of pain. I moved forward, forcing her back. She stumbled, shoulder blades meeting the wall with a soft thud.

"I should've known you'd never agree to work for me if the only person who stood to benefit from this arrangement was you."

Her eyes widened. Was she surprised I could read her so easily? She was an open fucking book.

"Romolo," she said, voice tight. "Let go of me."

I leaned in, lowering my voice. "I'll let you in on a secret." My grip tightened slightly—not enough to hurt, just enough to make sure she was listening. "Not everyone deserves to be taken care of."

Her breath hitched. "That's a sad way to look at life."

"Is it?" I murmured.

"Do you think it's a burden? Taking care of people?" She tried again to pull away. "Because it's not. I like doing it."

"Oh yeah?" I inched forward, closing the distance between us. "Tell me...who takes care of you?"

Her lips parted, but nothing came out.

I could see the way my words were sinking in, making her think. Making her wonder.

How long would it take for her to come to a conclusion she wouldn't like? I mean, shit. Her father hadn't even bothered telling her to stop broadcasting her location.

"Let go of me, Romolo," she whispered. Her gaze flicked —just for a moment—to my mouth.

"Is that really what you want?"

Her pupils dilated, and a shallow breath escaped her lips.

Those lips. Those goddamn lips. I wanted to bite into them. To find out what they tasted like.

Why the fuck not?

Outside, the city churned—car horns, footsteps, the distant hum of voices—but here, in this studio, we were in a bubble. A charged, electric bubble neither of us appeared willing to break.

I leaned down, shrinking the distance between us until my nose nearly brushed against hers.

Was I fully in control? Not really. But I was here to find

leverage, and this felt like moving roughly in the right direction. I'd find some way to use this. Eventually.

Just as I was about to satiate my curiosity, she jerked her hands out of my loosened grip and said, "Yes. That *is* what I want."

The moment snapped.

Clearing her throat, she sidestepped me, grabbed a suit jacket off the rack, and held it out. "Put this on." There was a slight tremble in her voice.

I dragged my tongue over my teeth. Annoyed. Frustrated. Turned on. "Sure."

She busied herself with straightening out some clothes, pretending she wasn't affected by what just happened. But she wasn't fooling me.

Jacket on, I strode toward the full-length mirror.

"It's too tight in the shoulders." She appeared behind me with a piece of measuring tape. Her hands smoothed over my upper back, dragging down my arms as she assessed the fit. "And the sleeves are too short."

Her touch was light, barely there. But it might as well have been a brand.

I grunted like I agreed and clenched my fists against the heat tunneling through my body. Why couldn't I shake it off?

"I was hoping to use this suit as the base of the look," she said. "I'll have to sew some of the embellishments on." She moved around to my front, tugging on the front of the jacket, brushing her fingers along the collar. Her brow furrowed in concentration, oblivious—or maybe pretending to be— while my body went tight as a wire.

"This works." Her fingers grazed just beneath my ear as she adjusted the neckline. "I want you to keep it buttoned all the way up."

And I wanted her on her knees in front of me, those pretty doe eyes looking up as her lips wrapped around my—

I clenched my jaw and dragged my gaze away from her, cursing under my breath as I willed my stiffening dick back under control.

When was the last time a woman touched you like this? a voice in the back of my mind whispered.

It wasn't sexual, just...intimate. So why the fuck was this such a turn-on?

"Okay, I think I have what I need." She dragged her hand down my back one more time. "You can go change now."

The dressing room was a relief—a much-needed fucking chance to breathe.

I yanked off the jacket and forced my mind elsewhere. Torture. Nails scraping on a chalkboard. The smell of week-old garbage—anything to get my dick down.

"When are we meeting next?" I asked once I stepped back out.

Mia took the clothes from me. "Once I have the alterations done. Let's plan for Tuesday next week. That will give us a few days before the dinner on Saturday to fine-tune anything." She glanced away, moving to put everything back on the rack.

While she wasn't looking, I swiped her lip gloss off her desk and shoved it into my pocket.

Why? Fuck if I knew. Probably because I was losing my goddamn mind.

I walked out of there frustrated, feeling like I'd lost the round.

Next time I came back, I was going to make sure I got some sleep. Because this game between us was only getting started.

CHAPTER 11

Mia

Today was one of my stepmom's bad days. She greeted me with her cane in hand—the one she hated using. She only reached for it when the muscle stiffness was particularly rough.

Normally, the three of us had breakfast together on Saturday mornings, but today, my dad had a meeting, which meant it was just Aris and me.

They lived in a beautiful prewar building on the Upper East Side, right across from the Met. Stepping into the lobby always felt like stepping back in time—black-and-white checkered floors, gold-plated elevator doors, the kind of place where the doormen knew every tenant's name. Their apartment had three bedrooms, two baths, a small office, an even smaller kitchen, and an extravagantly large living room where my stepmom spent most of her days. She'd curl up on the sofa with a book or spend hours on the phone with one of her sisters in California.

For four years after boarding school, I reclaimed my childhood bedroom. But three years ago, I moved out.

I told them it was to be closer to my studio, because the

real reason made me feel like a terrible daughter: I needed space from the oppressive weight of this place.

I made us breakfast, and we ate in silence at the dining table.

"Are you sure you don't want some more eggs?" I nudged the dish toward Aris. "They're good, aren't they?"

She sat across from me, wrapped in the robe I bought her for Christmas last year—one of the few gifts from me she actually seemed to like.

"I'm full."

"You barely ate anything."

"I don't need you to micromanage my meals for me, Mia. I said I'm done." She pushed her plate away. "Get my iPad from the bedroom. I want to check my email."

I bit on the inside of my cheek. I still didn't know how to handle her bad moods. They made me feel like a little girl again. A little girl who secretly wondered if her dad and stepmom had sent her away to boarding school because she'd done something wrong.

When she got like this, it felt like I was drowning in guilt.

What happened to her wasn't my fault. I knew that. But it never stopped me from feeling like I owed her something.

She and my dad got married two years after my mom died. They immediately started trying to have a baby, but nothing happened. After a year, they turned to IVF.

It was around the same time my dad sat me down and told me I was being sent abroad.

He never said it outright, but I know part of the reason was due to my stepmom. My dad worked late most nights, so she was the one who took care of school pickups and drop-offs. The one who shuttled me to my after-school activities. The one who filled the space my mom left behind.

But we never bonded. She wasn't cruel, but I always had the sense that she tolerated my presence more than she enjoyed it.

Being sent off to Switzerland only strengthened that feeling.

The IVF journey ended years later when she had a stroke—triggered, apparently, by the years of hormone treatments. I was finishing high school when it happened. My dad missed my graduation. I didn't blame him.

Afterward, he asked me to come back to New York for college instead of going to Milan, where I'd been accepted into Istituto Marangoni. He said he could use my help taking care of her.

I agreed without hesitation. I'd also gotten into FIT's fashion styling program in New York, so I could still pursue my career goals while being closer to them.

A part of me had hoped it would allow us to bond. That it would make the three of us feel like a real family.

"Mia?" Her sharp voice cut through my thoughts. "Did you hear me?"

I met her dark-brown eyes. "Sorry. I'll go get it, Aris."

In the bedroom, her iPad sat on the nightstand next to a framed photo of her and my father. It was taken before the stroke, when she was still optimistic that she and my dad would have the big family they wanted.

But it never happened.

I was their only daughter. And there were no pictures of me in their room.

Oh, come on. Don't you think you're reading too much into it?

I rolled my lips and grabbed the iPad.

In the dining room, Aris was still in the same position, fingers tapping absentmindedly against the table. I handed her the tablet.

"Do you know what time your father will be home?" she asked.

I checked my watch. "Should be any minute now."

I hoped he wouldn't be late. I had plans.

Fabi, Nina, and Zo were already on their way to pick me up. It was Labor Day weekend, and we were going to spend it at the Hamptons. Fabi's mom had a gorgeous house out there, and since she was in Italy for the summer, the place was empty. Fabi had suggested we take advantage of it—a girls' weekend before fall really set in.

I hadn't had a getaway all year. I needed this.

More than that, I needed to talk to Fabi some more about her engagement.

Romolo's assessment of Cosimo was only mildly comforting. I didn't know if I could trust him to tell me the truth about his brother.

I was starting to think I was in way over my head.

Even before he showed up at my studio three days ago, I'd been having second thoughts.

What was I thinking?

I wasn't a match for Romolo Ferraro, and I knew it. That was why I'd ended our round of questioning before it had even really begun. I was afraid I'd slip. Afraid I'd say something I shouldn't.

Especially when his presence alone made me feel so damn on edge.

"Didn't you say you had plans this weekend?" my stepmom asked.

"Yeah, I'm just waiting for Dad to get in before I go."

"You don't need to wait. I don't need you supervising me."

"Aris..." I hesitated, unsure what to say.

She pressed her lips together and tapped her fingers against her iPad with barely restrained frustration.

I knew it wasn't personal. She was just trying to hold on to whatever sliver of control she had left.

At least, that's what I told myself.

Exhaling quietly, I stood up and began clearing the table. The sound of the front door unlocking came right as I finished.

My dad smiled at me when I appeared in the hallway, my weekend bag slung over my shoulder.

"Mia, there you are." He pressed a kiss to my cheek. "How was breakfast?"

"Good. We missed you."

"I'm sorry I couldn't be here." His gaze dropped to my bag. "Listen, something came up. Jenny was just about to call you."

I stilled. A call from Jenny was rarely good news, especially when I'd booked the weekend off.

"What's up?"

"Looks like my schedule's changed." He scrolled through his phone. "I have to meet a donor at her house at the Finger Lakes."

I frowned. "That's a long drive."

"It means I won't get back here tonight. Probably not until late tomorrow afternoon." His gaze softened as it landed on me. "That's a long time for Aris to be here alone."

My stomach sank. "Dad, I've made plans."

"I know, *cariño*. I'm sorry."

"Who's the donor?"

"An old acquaintance from college. No one you know."

That struck me as odd. I knew all of my father's major donors. I'd sat through countless dinners and events, schmoozing right alongside him. "What's so important it can't be a phone call?"

My father smiled. Did it seem a bit strained?

I felt a flicker of guilt. As crazy as my schedule was, my dad's was even worse.

"She's well-connected in the city," he said. "I'd like her to take on an unofficial role with the transition team. I wish I could skip the trip, *cariño*, but it's not possible. This is the only time she can meet in person for the next few weeks."

The unspoken request hung in the air between us.

His trip was mandatory. Mine wasn't. But I wanted to go. Badly.

Dad placed a hand on my shoulder. "Your friends will understand, I'm sure."

Before I could answer, my stepmom's voice cut across the hallway.

"Carlos, let her go. I'll be fine."

I turned to see her leaning against the doorframe, watching us with that familiar, tight-lipped expression she always wore when she was annoyed.

Dad stepped toward her. "*Mi amor*, the nurse is on vacation this week. There won't be anyone nearby if you need something."

"The fridge is full of food. All my medicine's refilled. What's there to worry about?"

"You know I don't like you being alone for so long."

"Reality TV will keep me better company than Mia sulking about missing her trip."

Our eyes met. Was she trying to help me, or did she just not want me around? I couldn't tell. I never could.

"I won't sulk," I said, forcing a lightness I didn't feel.

She waved a dismissive hand. "If anything serious happens, I can call Jenny, can't I?"

Dad exhaled through his nose, clearly reluctant. But then he sighed and pressed a kiss to her temple. "You get your way, *mi amor*. Just like always."

I felt a guilty type of relief. My stepmom shot me

another unreadable glance before turning and disappearing into the living room.

"I'll walk you out," Dad said, grabbing my bag.

I followed him to the elevator, my chest still tight.

"You've seemed distracted this week. Is it work?" he asked while we waited.

Distracted was putting it mildly.

For the past few days, I'd been debating whether or not to tell him about Romolo.

Would it help him to know that the Ferraros were questioning his motives?

I didn't see how it could. Their suspicions were baseless. I would know if my dad had some other reason for going after them beyond getting justice and making this city a safer place.

If I told him Romolo was a client—even temporarily— he'd tell me to stop working with him right away. No doubt. The man brought a gun to my studio, and then showed up with bruised knuckles he must have gotten as a result of a fight. He was a bad idea wrapped in a tailored suit.

But what if I still *could* get something more from him?

We had one more meeting left. I could handle it. Couldn't I? Yes, he almost kissed me last time. But that was because I'd let myself get caught off guard. Now, I knew better. Now, I'd be ready.

"I didn't sleep well," I said.

It wasn't a lie. The last two nights, that mafioso hadn't just occupied most of my waking thoughts. He'd also appeared in my dreams. Shirtless. Inked. Wearing that smirk.

In the dream, I couldn't speak. Couldn't tell him to let me go.

So he didn't. His lips were hard against mine, and when I woke, my heart was still pounding.

I swallowed. "And work's been a lot. There never seems to be enough time for everything."

"We're almost at the end," Dad said as the elevator arrived. "Just a few more months. The polls are looking stronger with each week, and the transition planning is going better than expected. The attorney general is fully on board with prosecuting the crime families to the full extent of the law."

My blood ran cold. "Wow. Is there a case?"

"It'll come together," Dad said, no uncertainty in his tone. "They're looking at the Ferraros and their known associates. It's a tangled web."

Known associates. The Messeros had to fall into that category.

Could Fabi get swept up in this? She'd been gone from New York for many years, but now she was back and about to marry Cosimo. Even if she had no part to play in their business, was she really safe?

"You look worried."

My gaze jumped to my dad. "I am, I guess." About him. About Fabi. And maybe—God help me—even about Romolo, which made no sense.

Not everyone deserves to be taken care of.

That's what he thought about himself. How did someone get to that conclusion?

I was curious about him. About why he reacted so strongly to me offering him just a bit of help. Beneath all that cocky armor, there was something vulnerable. Something he tried hard to hide.

Dad squeezed my shoulder. "We'll get them, *cariño*. We just have to win first."

The elevator dinged and opened to the first floor.

He handed me my bag when we stepped outside. "Enjoy your trip."

"Thanks, I will."

As I waited for Fabi to pick me up, the words *we'll get them* echoed in my mind.

If my dad got his way, Romolo Ferraro wouldn't just be a dangerous enigma.

He'd be behind bars, along with his family.

CHAPTER 12

Mia

It was a humid day in the Hamptons. The air was thick with the scent of sunscreen and apricots. The surround-sound speakers hidden throughout the property blasted Sabrina Carpenter's latest hit.

We were scattered around the pool, each doing our own thing. Fabi floated on an inflatable swan, a glass of rosé in hand. Zo sat on a lounger, painting her toenails a deep purple. Nina and I were hunched over a canvas I'd impulsively bought online. The piece depicting a mask was now getting an excessive amount of rhinestones glued on. I was going through a phase. I had about three of these already completed back at my apartment. Somehow, I'd convinced myself bedazzling was a valid form of therapy.

"I think we should go to a party," Zo announced as she finished off her pinky toe.

I carefully glued on another black rhinestone. "We already agreed we'd stay in."

We'd cracked open the alcohol as soon as we'd arrived three hours ago, and while I appreciated the buzz, day drinking in the sun wasn't the kind of thing that made me want to go anywhere afterward. I was looking forward to making dinner with the girls, passing out in bed by ten, and then doing it all over again tomorrow before heading home on Monday.

Zo took a long slurp of her Aperol Spritz before plunking the glass onto the coffee table. "I know. But that was before I got this text."

She grabbed her phone and held it out to us. Nina and I leaned in to read.

> Hey cutie, saw on your Instagram you're in the Hamptons this weekend. Throwing a big Labor Day bash before we close down the house for the season. You and your girls wanna stop by?

"Who is this?" Nina asked.

"A billionaire whose company hired us for a project a year ago. We've kept in touch."

"You're telling me this is a fully grown man?" Nina sounded unimpressed. "Because he texts like he's a frat bro with a trust fund."

Zo laughed. "He's a fully grown bro. I know, the worst. But he's got a nice dick, and this party is gonna be out of this world."

My brows rose. "You slept with a client?"

"After the project was over," Zo said. "Bumped into him at a bar in Austin, and it seemed like a good idea. The three shots of tequila might have had something to do with it."

I sighed. "I can't even remember the last time I had sex." It was probably with my ex, Sergio. Which was over two years ago. We dated for about nine months before it became glaringly obvious he was secretly in love with his best friend.

And our sex life? Nothing memorable.

Why did I even date him? I pressed my wineglass to my

cheek, trying to recall. I guess he was nice. Maybe that was all I needed at the time.

"Same," Nina muttered.

Zo shook her head. "What a sad life you two live. You know what your problem is? You overthink it."

"I'd rather overthink it than underthink it," Nina said, dabbing some glue on the canvas. "I have high standards. And I'm not about to lower them just for an orgasm. My own fingers do a perfectly fine job."

Zo smirked. "Your own fingers don't have a sexy male body attached to them. Don't you miss big, strong hands? The scent of a man? The little sounds they make when you're gobbling down their—"

"I *didn't* until you put it like that," Nina interjected, slicing her a glare.

Zo laughed. "I can keep going. Just picture tracing those thick veins on their arms, squeezing those rounded biceps—"

I threw a rhinestone at her, somehow landing it straight into her drink. "Okay, enough."

She fished it out, still grinning. "All I'm saying is, we should go to this party. It'll be packed. I'm sure you'll both find someone to end your dry spell."

I shook my head. "I don't feel like going to some insane rager."

"You never feel like going to an insane rager," Zo said. "But that's exactly why you need one. You never have fun. You're always working."

"There's nothing wrong with always working," Nina said.

"Thank you." I clinked my glass against hers.

"You're both workaholics." Zo tugged on her bikini top, fixing it into place. "It's time for an intervention."

"We're not the ones working for a company that sends you on week-long business trips with no weekends off,"

Nina pointed out. Zo worked for a white-hat hacking firm that was hired by companies to test their cybersecurity by trying to break through their firewalls. At least, I thought that's what she did. Whenever she got too technical, I struggled to follow.

Zo looked up at the sky, shielding her eyes with her hand. "Yeah, but then I get to take entire weeks off where I do nothing but play video games, go on dates, and spend all my hard-earned money. It's a good trade-off."

"She's got a point," Fabi called out, apparently listening to the conversation from her float.

Nina just shook her head. We both worked like crazy because we ran our own businesses. The only difference was that Nina's chocolate company was thriving, while mine... Well, as already established, my business was in not a great place.

Although, if Romolo actually followed through on his word about getting me into The Golden Circle newsletter...

He wouldn't. Also, that wasn't why I'd agreed to work for him.

He'd been right when he said I'd never agree to dress him only for my own benefit. I wasn't worth the risk. But my dad and Fabi were.

"Hey, Fabi," I called out to her, watching as she lazily drifted across the pool. "How are you doing?"

She lifted her glass of rosé in a half-hearted salute, her curls piled on top of her head in a messy bun. "I don't know. Fine? But I'm with Zo. I think we should go."

I sat up straighter. "Really?"

Nina groaned. "What happened to our plan?"

"Yeah, but..." Fabi hesitated, pushing her heart-shaped sunglasses up her nose. "I don't know. I just feel like this might be the last time we get to do this kind of thing, you know?"

Something twisted inside my chest. I put the rhinestone picker down. "What do you mean?"

"I don't know what life will be like when I'm married. Or what rules I'll have to follow."

Rules? I rose and walked over to the edge of the pool. "Are you saying Cosimo might not allow you to see your friends?"

I'd been waiting for the right moment to bring him up. Fabi was in a good mood when they picked me up, and I didn't want to ruin it.

But clearly, her engagement was also on her mind.

She blew out a breath. "Honestly, who the hell knows."

Zo and I exchanged a worried look. That didn't sound good.

Nina just sat there with a grave expression, like she wasn't at all surprised by this.

"Has he said something about these rules to you?" I asked.

Fabi took a big sip of her wine. "Nope. Not yet. He's refusing to talk to me. And after what happened earlier this week, I just—"

"What happened?" Nina called out.

Fabi kicked at the water to float closer to us. "I messaged him to ask if we could meet up for dinner and actually talk about, you know...our upcoming marriage."

"Okay," I said cautiously.

"And he texted back with one word: 'Busy.'"

My nostrils flared. What a jerk. This woman was about to become his wife, and he was too busy for her?

I was offended on Fabi's behalf.

"Asshole," Zo muttered.

Nina pursed her lips. "That's not right. You should talk to Rafaele about it."

Fabi stared into her wineglass. "What's the point?"

"He can get Cosimo in line," Nina said.

Frustration pulsed at my temples. "Or maybe if he knew your fiancé was actively ignoring you, he'd change his mind about this whole damn wedding."

What they were doing to Fabi was awful, and I didn't care if "that's just how things were done" in their world. This whole situation was barbaric. She was being handed off to a criminal and expected to smile through it.

Given that their own mother's marriage had been a nightmare, I couldn't understand how her brother could do this to her.

"That's not gonna happen," Fabi said, defeated. "I always knew I'd have to get married to someone I didn't choose for myself, so I'm not expecting fireworks, you know? Honestly, I was prepared for apathy. But it seems like he hates me. Or maybe he's just disgusted by me."

"There's no way," Nina said. "He doesn't know you yet, which is why he doesn't understand you're a damn catch."

"Well, he doesn't seem to have any interest in getting to know me," Fabi said. "Maybe the best I can hope for is that he'll just ignore me once we're married. I mean, one day, he'll expect kids, but it's not like that day has to be anytime soon."

I clenched my jaw. "And what if that's not what happens?"

Fabi stared out toward the ocean. "I'll just have to figure it out." I watched her float to the edge of the pool and set her empty wineglass on the patio. "Guys, let's just go. I want to have a good time tonight. I want to dance. I want to drink." She hauled herself out of the pool, looking a little buzzed already. "I just want to forget he exists for one night."

I bit my lip.

Maybe if Fabi spent tonight like a normal person, she'd

realize what she was giving up. Maybe she'd put up more of a fight.

But then again, I understood family loyalty. I understood duty. God, better than anyone.

Still, what I was doing for my dad's campaign was temporary. It would end.

For Fabi, this was the rest of her life.

Zo twisted the cap back onto her nail polish and tossed it onto the coffee table. "It's settled. We're going out.

I dragged my palms down my thighs. "I didn't even bring anything to wear."

Zo smirked. "Come on. I've got plenty of things you can borrow."

CHAPTER 13

Mia

It was just after eleven when we arrived at the party.

A security guard greeted us at the door and handed each of us a small black sticker. "Put this over your camera. No pictures allowed. If anyone catches you breaking the rule, you're out."

I didn't know how the other girls felt about that, but I was relieved. The last thing I needed was photographic evidence of me looking like *this* on someone's phone.

I tugged my black cardigan tighter around me as we made our way inside. The party was already in full swing. Music pounded through the space so hard that the glassware in the cabinets behind the massive bar rattled with every beat.

"Isn't this great?" Zo shouted over the noise.

I was a little tipsy, but not tipsy enough to feel comfortable in the outfit I was wearing.

Zo had an affinity for going out in barely there clothing, which was how I'd ended up in a slinky, metallic-pink slip dress with slits up both sides and a cowl neck that barely clung to my chest. I wasn't used to wearing so little, and my instinct was to keep the cardigan wrapped tightly around me like armor.

Zo wasn't having it.

She grabbed my hands and pulled me toward her. "Okay, Mia, it's showtime. Take it off."

I shook my head. "I really don't know about this."

"Come on." She gave my arm a dramatic shake. "No one's gonna recognize you anyway. Not under all that glitter."

She was probably right.

Zo had doused me in so much glitter, I could blind someone if I walked into direct sunlight. My cheekbones, shoulders, and even my collarbones shimmered under the lights. My hair was pulled into two space buns, and my eyes were winged with metallic-blue eyeliner.

I didn't look anything like the polished, put-together politician's daughter the public saw on TV.

And with no cameras allowed...

All right. Screw it.

I shrugged off the cardigan.

Zo snatched it from my hands and clapped like I'd just done something groundbreaking. "There we go. You look amazing."

Fabi and Nina, who had disappeared a minute ago to grab drinks, appeared with cocktails in hand. The moment they saw me, they whooped their approval.

"Let's get this party started," Fabi declared, shoving a margarita into my hand.

The dance floor was in the center of the massive living room and already packed.

We wove through the crowd until we found an open spot. The bass was so loud it vibrated through my chest.

I had to admit, this party wasn't as sloppy as I'd expected. The crowd was our age or older, which explained why it didn't have the chaotic, beer-soaked energy of a frat house rager.

Fabi caught my eye and smiled, shaking her hips to the beat. She looked lighter than she had all weekend.

Much better than by the pool earlier.

I wanted to talk to her some more about Cosimo. But I also knew *she* didn't want to talk about Cosimo. Not tonight.

I understood that.

Nina had grilled me about Romolo on the drive here, digging for details on how our first meeting had gone. I gave her the highlight reel, carefully skimming over the part where he'd almost kissed me.

Because that?

I wasn't ready to admit that had happened.

The memory made me feel played—like I'd walked into a trap I should have seen coming. It was exactly the kind of move someone like Romolo Ferraro would pull.

He hadn't meant anything by it. I knew that. He was trying to mess with me. Get under my skin.

So why had I considered—just for a moment—letting him do it?

I really was an idiot. Drawn to him like a moth to a flame, fluttering my wings dangerously close to the heat.

But I didn't need to give him any real estate in my mind tonight. Fabi wasn't thinking about Cosimo, so I wasn't going to think about Romolo.

I just needed to stop overanalyzing everything and—

Zo grabbed my wrist and spun me to the music. I laughed, letting myself relax.

"To the Valais Vixens!" Zo declared, lifting her glass into the middle of our circle.

Nina groaned as we clinked glasses. "When are we going to retire that name?"

"Never!" Zo shouted. "And stop trying to change the group chat name. You know I'll just change it back."

I grinned. "It's part of our lore."

Nina rolled her eyes good-naturedly. "We came up with that name when we were thirteen. Haven't we earned something a little more grown-up by now?"

"Growing up is overrated," Zo declared, throwing back half her cocktail.

"Amen to that," Fabi said, doing the same.

A crack of thunder echoed through the house, sending a few girls shrieking before they dissolved into laughter.

Nina glanced toward the window. "Sky's looking rough."

Dark clouds loomed beyond the glass, thick and heavy, promising a downpour. I vaguely remembered seeing something about a storm in the forecast.

Good thing we were close to Fabi's mom's house—a fifteen-minute drive, tops.

"Oh shit." Zo froze mid-step, the excitement in her expression shifting into something sharper.

"What?" I asked.

"You're not going to believe who's here."

A prickle of unease crawled up my spine.

I turned.

Across the room, a familiar pair of gray eyes locked onto mine.

CHAPTER 14

Rom

I hadn't been sure she'd show up tonight. When I saw her friend's Instagram story earlier about them going to the Hamptons, I knew it was a long shot. But when it came to the work I did, finding the right opportunity to corner a target unexpectedly could be make or break.

Mia had probably thought the last time she'd see me would be at our meeting next week.

She was wrong.

I wasn't ready to be done with her—not even close. She was still my best shot at getting something useful about Morales. Even if she seemed far too innocent to be involved in whatever plan he might be scheming, she was close to him. Close enough to pick up on things she might not even realize were valuable.

I wasn't giving up that easily.

So I cancelled my plans for the day and moved fast.

It took me five minutes to find a mutual connection with Zo in the list of people she followed. Another ten to hear back from him. After I'd laid the bait, I sped down here in my car despite the fact that the weather forecast said it might rain. And I waited.

Hours of waiting.

The last thing Zo had posted was a shot of them lounging by the pool, cocktails in hand, the sun glinting off their sunglasses. That was this afternoon. Since then— nothing. No updates. No way to know if they'd actually show up at this party.

By the time I spotted them walking through the doors, my patience was running thin.

I watched and planned my next move as they made their way through the crowd. And then Mia took off that sweater, and I nearly choked on my drink.

What the fuck was she wearing?

A pulse of something sharp and territorial ran through me.

That tiny slip of a dress was practically falling off her body. Those slits sliced high up her thighs. And all that soft, brown skin was on display.

A muscle in my jaw twitched. I forced myself to take a slow, even breath.

Why did I even care? Mia Morales wasn't mine. She was just a target.

But that knowledge didn't stop me from seeing red.

"You want in on some of this?" Johnny, the host, asked from where he sat, pulling my gaze to the line of coke he was casually cutting on the glass table.

It was our product. Best in the state, courtesy of our Colombian suppliers. They knew it too, which was why they were playing hardball in this year's contract renegotiations. I was more than happy to let Cosimo deal with that headache.

"I'm good," I said. The last time I'd touched the stuff, I was eighteen and stupid, desperate for an escape. I grew out of it fast when I saw what happened to the men who didn't.

Johnny snorted the line and tipped his head back with a blissed-out sigh.

I turned back toward the dance floor. *Fuck.* He'd distracted me, and now Mia was gone. Her friends were still there, but she'd run off somewhere.

Hiding from me?

Good luck. The house was big, but not big enough.

Nina's sharp glare was fixed on me. She shook her head in warning.

I just smirked.

She didn't like Mia getting entangled with me? Too fucking bad. I still needed to have a word with my cousin about that fucking horoscope she put together, but that could wait.

Pushing off the wall, I went in search of my little stylist.

I knew my way around here. Johnny was a regular at Black Silk, and I always got invites to his Labor Day parties, along with the others he threw during summers. By day, he designed software. By night, he liked to pretend he had an edge.

He was the kind of guy who had missed out on partying in his twenties and was now desperately making up for lost time at thirty-five.

But he wasn't stupid.

If photos of him getting sloppy surfaced online, there'd be hell to pay. His PR team had probably begged him to enforce that no-camera rule. Everyone generally obeyed.

Everyone except me. I didn't play by the fucking rules.

Something Mia was about to find out.

I checked behind a few of the doors—empty bedrooms. Halfway down the hall, I stopped.

A familiar scent lingered in the air. Lily of the valley.

My gaze flicked to the door on my right. A bathroom. She was in there.

I leaned against the wall, crossing my arms. I could wait. What was another minute or two when she'd made me wait hours?

The lock turned. The door slid open.

And there she was.

In that fucking dress.

The little metallic thing clung to her curves like a second skin. Did she have any idea? Was she aware that every man in this house probably salivated when she walked past?

Her wide brown eyes locked onto mine.

"We need to talk," I ground out.

"No thanks." She tried to brush past me, like she actually thought I'd let her go. She even had the nerve to look surprised when my arm shot out and blocked her path.

I leaned down, bringing my lips close to her ear. Her whole body stiffened. "It's about The Golden Circle party."

She swallowed. "What about it?"

"Too loud here. Can't hear a word you're saying."

I grabbed her hand and pulled her into one of the empty bedrooms I'd just checked.

Once we were shut inside, I took my time looking at her.

From the bottom of her high heels to the top of her head. She was covered in glitter, and her hair was fixed in two buns on her head. I didn't know what to call that fucking hairstyle, but it was sexy—just like the rest of her—and it made my dick twitch. "Nice outfit."

Her cheeks flushed pink. Her arms folded protectively around her waist, like she wasn't quite comfortable in the dress.

Her friends must have talked her into wearing it. Figures.

"Did you really want to talk about the project?"

"Sure." Of course the fuck not. But I'd been right about this being an opportunity, and it was about to pay off.

I pulled out my phone and snapped a photo of her.

Her eyes widened. "Hey! What are you doing? You're not supposed to take pictures in here. That's the rule!"

"Fuck the rules."

She dropped the tiny purse that was slung over her shoulder onto the ground and lunged for my phone.

I dodged her easily, holding it over my head, far out of her reach.

A frustrated sound escaped her throat. "Romolo, delete it!"

"Like hell." I'd decided when I saw her just now that I was done playing nice. Why waste time trying to coax the information out of her when she made blackmail so damn easy? The quicker I got what I wanted, the quicker I could be done with her. I didn't feel like myself in her vicinity, and I didn't fucking like it.

She tried again, hopping on her heels, her fingers wrapping around nothing but air.

I backed away from her grasping hands until my calves hit something hard.

A sofa.

I dropped onto it, still holding the phone high above my head, pressing it against the wall behind me. Mia—so desperate to get it—didn't think twice before crawling onto my lap.

Her soft, bare thighs straddled me. They were warm against my legs, and my pulse fucking jumped.

"Romolo," she huffed, stretching for the phone, her body flush with mine. "Just give it to me."

"No." My jaw clenched as her breasts pressed against my cheek. I had to bite back a groan.

"Romolo, please," she begged.

Did she realize what she was doing?

Or was she doing it on purpose to distract me?

I had to admit—it was working. She was everywhere. That soft, floral lily of the valley scent clung to her skin, filling my lungs with every inhale. I clenched the back of her barely there dress with my fist and thought hard about whether I wanted to pull her away from me or tug her even closer.

Her hand slid up my arm, the other one pushing against my shoulder as she braced herself. Then, using the leverage of her knees against my thighs, she stretched just enough to snatch the phone from my hand.

She sank back onto my lap, victorious and so fucking absorbed with the phone she didn't seem to realize I was as hard as a damn rock.

The phone was locked.

She turned it toward me, trying to activate Face ID.

"It's not enabled," I said, my voice tight. "You'll need my passcode."

"What is it?" she demanded, eyes snapping back to mine.

She shifted, and I could tell the exact moment she felt my erection.

Her eyes widened. Pupils dilated. Throat bobbed.

"What do you think the news outlets will say when they see how the next mayor's daughter dresses when she's off duty?" I squeezed my fist into her dress, pulling the fabric taut around her waist. She had the kind of body that turned heads. My muscles strained from the effort it took not to grind against her. "Kind of goes against all those wholesome family values your dad loves to preach about, doesn't it?"

Whatever hint of arousal might have been there in her expression moments earlier disappeared in a flash. "You're an asshole." Betrayal ran through her eyes, and it fascinated me.

Because it implied some part of her had trusted me.

Even if just a little.

Jesus Christ.

How the fuck was she still alive and walking around with that kind of naïveté?

My gaze licked over her collarbones, then down to the low neckline of her dress. That fucking glitter. It made her look like some kind of mythical creature—a being not meant for a place like this.

Not meant for a man like me.

At some point, my other hand had settled on her waist.

I didn't even remember doing it.

Her fingers tightened around my phone.

"What do you want?" Her voice shook.

I glanced back up. She was trying not to cry.

The words I needed to say bounced around my head. *I want you to tell me everything you know about who's giving money to your father.*

I didn't know if the photo would be enough leverage, but there was a good chance it was.

I should have been pleased. Should have been thrilled that I had her right where I wanted her.

Instead, something twisted in my chest.

All I could think about was how she'd look at me when she heard the words. Whatever fragile illusions she still had about me would shatter.

It was ridiculous.

I'd trapped my prey, had her exactly where I needed her. And yet, something held me back from delivering the final blow.

Maybe it was because there was something else I wanted from her. Something I wanted more.

My teeth ground together. *Which is it going to be?*

She was watching me, her breath shallow, her fingers gripping my phone.

"Romolo, please," she whispered, clutching the phone to her chest.

I should've said it.

I should've told her I'd delete the picture in exchange for her father's secrets.

But instead, my mouth—completely disconnected from my better judgment—said, "I want you to kiss me. And not just some fucking peck. I want you to kiss me and mean it."

A beat passed. Her big, brown eyes flickered with something I couldn't name. I wished I could read her thoughts.

"Why?"

"I want to know something." I dragged my thumb over her bottom lip. "Do these taste like berries?"

The way she looked at me told me she thought I was insane.

If I was, it was her fault.

Her lip gloss sat inside my pocket. Had she noticed it had gone missing? I wondered if she'd realized I'd taken it, and what she thought it meant.

Maybe she could enlighten me, because fuck if I knew.

Her tongue darted out to swipe over her bottom lip. "If I kiss you, you'll give me the code?"

"It's a deal." I was so fucking angry with myself for giving into this irrational urge I wanted to punch a wall.

She thought about it for another few moments.

"Hurry up," I snapped. "The offer won't be there forever."

Her gaze narrowed. "There's something wrong with you."

"Now you're getting it."

"Fine." Her palm curled around the back of my neck. "One kiss."

"Make it count."

She leaned in. "Stop talking."

I groaned when she slid an inch forward, pressing down onto my cock.

A shiver ran through her. She was close enough that I could see each individual speck of glitter dusted across her cheekbones.

Her lips parted—

REEEE! REEE! REEE!

I jolted. "What the fuck is that?"

Mia let out a startled breath and practically leapt off me. "It's my stepmom calling." She scrambled for her purse.

I dragged my palm over my face. One more minute was all I'd needed.

She picked up. "Hello?" Her voice was tight. "Is everything okay?"

I sat up, adjusting myself. She was finally far enough from me for my mind to clear. I hadn't been thinking with my head—not the right one, at least.

"What do you mean? How bad is it?"

My brows furrowed. Something was wrong.

Mia chewed on her fingernail, nodding along to whatever was being said. "Jenny's not picking up?" A breath of frustration. "Crap. Okay. I'll head back."

Head back?

At this fucking hour?

I got to my feet. The moment between us was gone, disintegrated like it had never happened.

"I'm at least two hours away. Please call 911 if it gets worse. No—Aris." She paced. "Don't be stubborn. It's better to be safe than sorry. Okay, I'm on my way."

Her fingers shook as she ended the call. Before I could say anything, she was already moving for the door.

"Mia—"

She didn't look at me. Didn't even hesitate.

And then she was gone.

Fuck.

Whatever was going on with her stepmom was clearly more important than the photo I still had on my phone.

I followed after her. I wasn't worried. Of course not. This was about unfinished business. Now that my brain was working again, I'd make her a different deal—the one I should have made in the first place.

She weaved through the crowd toward her friends, unaware that I was right behind her.

The girls all looked surprised when they saw me, but they quickly focused on Mia, who was explaining the situation.

"My stepmom's not well. She's having chest pains, and there's no one else around. I've got to go home."

Nina shook her head. "We've all been drinking. Fabi's car is back at her mom's house."

"I'm calling a rideshare," Mia said, already scrolling through the app.

My jaw clenched. She was actually going to call an Uber and sit in the back of some random guy's car for two hours in the middle of the night?

"She can't ask a friend to come over?" I asked.

Mia ignored me.

"We'll go with you," Fabi said.

"There's no point ruining your weekend." Her phone screen blinked *No drivers available.*

"Shit." She tried again. Same result.

"Probably because of the storm," Nina pointed out. "Forecast says it's starting tonight. I doubt there are many drivers wanting to go that far right now."

I glanced out the window. It was too dark to see anything, but the glass wasn't wet. Yet.

I hated driving in the rain. Especially in this fucking place. I rolled my shoulders, the tension already setting in.

But two hours in the car with her when she was agitated and still a bit buzzed... It was the perfect chance to get what I wanted.

Screw it. I could handle it. It was worth the risk.

"I'll drive you," I said.

The girls all turned my way.

"No way," Nina said. "You've been drinking too."

"One drink. I'm fine."

Mia barely looked up from her phone. She was still searching. Still finding nothing.

"I was going to head back tonight anyway," I lied. "You can either get in my car now, or you can still be standing here twenty minutes from now, with no driver, wishing you'd come with me."

That got her attention. Her head jerked up.

I could see the war happening inside her. Her eyes told me she wanted nothing to do with me right now, but she didn't have a better choice. And she knew it.

Her throat worked around a swallow. Apprehension flickered across her face.

Finally, she nodded. "Okay. Let's go."

CHAPTER 15

Mia

A loud crack of thunder split the sky as I climbed into Romolo's Mercedes.

I clipped in and yanked the cardigan I'd gotten back from Zo tighter around me. My stepmom had sounded bad on the phone—short of breath, temper frayed, her every word clipped.

She was probably pissed she'd let me leave in the first place.

I should've stayed home. I shouldn't have even entertained the idea of a weekend away without someone else around to keep an eye on her.

A wave of worry curled hot in my stomach. I needed to get a handle on my anxiety before it spiraled into something worse. Vasovagal syncope wasn't predictable, but over the years, I'd noticed a pattern of it happening when I'm anxious or surprised. The only physical warning I'd get was that telltale flash of heat all over my body. By then, it was usually too late to do anything about it. I'd pass out whether I wanted to or not.

At least I was already seated. But I didn't want to be even more vulnerable in front of the devil sitting beside me.

Romolo's expression was hard as he steered us onto the road. It was almost impossible to reconcile that a few minutes ago, I'd been on his lap about to kiss him in exchange for his passcode.

He'd seemed so angry when he asked for that kiss.

If anyone should have been angry, it was me.

He tricked me. Tried to blackmail me. Made me feel lightheaded with his touch. I hated that my heart beat faster whenever he was around, even when he was being an ass.

But what I hated even more was that photo still sitting on his phone.

I had to do something about it.

My fingers tightened around my cardigan. "Romolo, you need to delete the picture."

He didn't even blink. "What's wrong with your stepmother?"

I stared at him. "Did you hear what I just said?"

"If you want me to delete that picture, you're going to have to answer my questions."

My God. Of course he'd find a way to twist this in his favor. I'd naïvely thought there might be more to him than met the eye, but it was time to admit I was wrong.

"Is empathy a completely foreign concept to you?" I asked.

The car slowed.

"What are you doing?" I demanded.

"Showing you what happens when you refuse to do what I tell you. You want me to drive quickly? You better start talking."

Yep. He was showing me exactly who he was. It was time I believed him. This man had a black hole where most people had a heart. How could someone so beautiful be so heartless?

"Fine," I spat. "She had a stroke a few years ago. Lots of

complications followed. She doesn't like to leave the house because she's self-conscious about her appearance, suffers from depression, and has a slew of other health-related anxieties. She's at higher risk for another stroke, and we try to keep a close eye on her."

He pressed on the gas, speeding up. "Where's her nurse? Surely Morales has enough money to hire one."

"She's out of town. Same with my dad. My stepmom won't call 911 unless she's literally on the verge of death." I scrolled through my phone, debating my options. She wouldn't like it if I called anyone outside her approved circle, which was me, my dad, the nurse, and Jenny. But if it came down to it, I'd make a call to one of our neighbors. Better she be furious with me than jeopardize her health.

Romolo's hands flexed around the wheel. The roads were empty, most drivers probably deterred by the impending storm. Plus, it was late—past twelve a.m.

"Your father's farther away than us?"

"Yes. He has a meeting up by the Finger Lakes. He won't be back until tomorrow."

His jaw ticked. "Meeting with who?"

My phone buzzed. Jenny was calling. I picked up.

"Mia?" She sounded groggy. "I just woke up to use the bathroom and saw the missed calls from your mom. I don't know how my phone ended up on silent. I'm on my way now."

I shut my eyes. "Oh, thank God. How far are you?"

"Ten minutes, tops."

"I'm on my way back from the Hamptons."

"I've got it covered. You shouldn't drive back tonight. I heard they're forecasting a big storm. Come back tomorrow. I'll stay with her as long as I need to."

"It's not raining yet—"

Right on cue, the sky opened up.

Fat raindrops slammed against the windshield, blurring the road.

"Never mind," I muttered.

"I can hear the thunder. Stay safe, okay? I'll text you as soon as I get to your place."

"Thank you." For all the ways Jenny could be a pain, she was someone my dad and I could rely on.

"You got it."

I hung up and let my head fall back against the seat. "Crisis averted."

"That was the assistant?" Romolo's voice was low. Tense.

"Yeah. I don't need to go back anymore, which means I don't need to put up with your interrogation."

"You will if you want that photo to disappear." He slowed the car and made a sharp U-turn.

"Where are you taking me?"

"Back to where you're staying. I assume it's with Fabi. If you don't give me what I need before we get there, that photo will be plastered all over the Internet tomorrow. Who is your father's meeting with?"

Anger surged through me like a flame racing along a trail of gasoline. "I'm not—"

Buzzzz. I glanced down at my phone. A text this time—from my stepmom.

> Jenny is on her way. I'll see you tomorrow.

"Mia."

I ignored him. I was so furious with him that I didn't trust myself to speak. Instead, I typed out a quick response.

> She called me. I'll drive back first thing in the morning. Love you.

I stared at the screen. Two checkmarks appeared.

Then nothing.

She left me on read.

"Mia."

I gritted my teeth. *Don't answer. Don't give him the satisfaction.*

"*Mia*," he growled, his tone dark and expectant, like he was owed my attention.

That was it. I snapped.

"Enough!" I whipped my head toward him. "I'm not going to tell you anything about my dad. I don't know what you want, what you're digging for, but you're not going to get anything from me."

"Listen to me—"

"No, *you* listen to me, you jerk. I realize I made a mistake. I should have never sent you that text. I should have never agreed to work with you. But I'm not going to put up with this blackmail. You want to send that picture to the press? Go ahead, Romolo. I'll deal with the fallout. I'll work until I'm exhausted to fix the situation if that's what I have to do to make sure you never have any power over me."

Silence. Broken only by the rain hammering against the windshield.

Romolo's gaze stayed fixed on the road, his knuckles white as bone. For once, he didn't have a quick comeback.

I was so worked up that I was sweating. I'd never stood up for myself like that before. Never dared to.

It was a revelation. It felt *so damn good.*

And I wasn't done yet. "How do you sleep at night?"

"I don't." His voice was low, strained. He didn't sound like his usual self.

Had I gotten through to him? I hoped he felt ashamed.

The rain was coming down in sheets. The wipers struggled to keep up.

The veins on the backs of Romolo's hands bulged as he

strangled the wheel. He was pale, almost ashen. A bead of sweat rolled down his temple.

Hold on... Something was wrong.

I frowned, shifting slightly to get a better look at him. "Romolo?"

His chest jerked as he inhaled, sharp and ragged.

And then the car swerved.

"Romolo!" My hands flew out, bracing against the dash as the Mercedes jerked across the slick pavement. He was gasping, his chest heaving as he clawed at his collar with one hand like he couldn't breathe.

"Pull over!" I screamed, reaching for the wheel and placing my hand on top of his. His skin was ice cold.

He veered off the road, slamming the brakes just as we skidded to a stop near the edge of a wooded area.

"Stay here." He threw the door open and stumbled out into the rain.

I watched him run in front of the car and disappear in the shadows. My pulse was still hammering, my body still stuck in that moment of panic.

What the hell had just happened?

There was no way I was going stay sitting here while he was having...whatever he was having. A medical emergency? A panic attack?

I couldn't lose track of him.

My heels landed in a puddle as I got out of the car. The rain was so heavy it took only seconds for my cardigan to get completely soaked.

"Romolo!"

I spotted him ahead, his silhouette barely visible through the storm. He stood near a tree, both palms pressed against the trunk like he needed it to stay upright.

I slammed the door shut and ran toward him. The moment my feet hit the muddy grass, my heels sank. I toed them off and left them behind as I sprinted toward him barefoot.

He was trembling. His body shook as he gasped for air.

It was strange and terrifying to see someone so powerful looking so...fragile.

I pressed my palm to the center of his back. "I'm here."

His muscles tensed beneath my touch. The next second, he jerked away from me violently.

"Damn it, Mia. I told you to stay in the car." His voice was a rasp—low and strained but laced with anger.

Normally, that kind of tone would've made me recoil, but he looked like he was barely holding himself together. I wasn't about to leave him like this.

"Do you need me to drive you to the hospital?"

"No." He pushed off the tree and took one slow step forward like he was going to walk back to the car.

But he only made it two steps. His knees buckled. He caught himself before he fully collapsed, his hands slamming into the mud, his breath coming in harsh, uneven gasps.

My heart broke. Something about seeing him like this made me want to weep.

I crouched down beside him, ignoring the way the wet earth soaked my bare legs, and placed a hand on his shoulder. "It's okay."

His fingers curled into the dirt. "Leave me alone." His voice was so low I could barely hear it over the storm.

Lightning cracked above us, illuminating his face.

He looked lost.

What happened to you, Romolo?

CHAPTER 16

Rom

She hadn't listened. Why hadn't she listened?

Mia's hand rested on my shoulder. Small. Warm. Steady.

She was trying to comfort me, but it was having the opposite effect. My lungs tightened even more.

I shrugged her off and tried to get back to my feet, stumbling as the world tilted around me. The memories clawed their way to the surface, unrelenting. The flashbacks were vivid. A horror movie projected straight into my head.

Nails digging into my thigh. Water rushing in with a roar. Her choked apologies, the names of the children—

My chest felt like it was splintering apart, my head splitting open.

Control. I needed to get back in control.

"Romolo, look at me." Mia's voice broke through.

I blinked. I was back on my knees, soaked to the bone, heart hammering like it was trying to break free of my ribs. I couldn't get enough air.

"I said leave me." My voice was raw. She wasn't supposed to see me like this. No one was. And no one had, not since that night.

I'd shut the emotional valve off inside my head back then, and it hadn't opened. Not until now.

"I'm not going to do that."

My eyes squeezed shut. Arms wrapped around me, pulling me close. Her wet cheek pressed against my own. She was as drenched as I was, but still warm somehow. Still trying to comfort me.

That night, I'd almost begged for this. I'd just wanted someone to hold me, to tell me it would be okay. But no one did. No one ever did.

I felt like I was choking on something. I didn't know how to receive comfort anymore. Maybe it was like a muscle. It atrophied if it didn't get used.

"Tell me what's going on," she whispered, her lips brushing against my cheek.

I shook my head. I'd never tell. Not her. Not anyone.

She pulled back slightly, her brown eyes searching mine. "You're trembling."

The words echoed in my head: *"You. Can't. Be. Weak."*

I jerked back, knocking Mia's arms away. "Get away from me."

"No. I'm not going anywhere. I don't care if you don't like it. I'm right here."

After a moment, her hands found my arms and rubbed up and down in slow, soothing strokes.

Something cracked inside my chest. I couldn't look at her. I looked down at my muddy hands instead and fought against my instinct to push her away from me again.

I didn't know how to handle her touch, but it dawned on me I would like it even less when it was gone.

On each inhale, I braced myself. On each exhale, I relaxed.

She kept rubbing my arms, reminding me I wasn't alone.

The cord around my throat began to loosen. Something welled inside me.

Rain poured down on us, unrelenting, but I didn't care. It was better than being in the car, because being in the car felt like I was in a coffin.

Her hands stilled on my shoulders. "That's it. Slow, deep breaths."

I stared at her bare knees plunked into the muddy grass. I'd been an utter asshole to her in the car. And she was still doing what she always did—taking care of people.

I tried to summon some disgust at that. I couldn't. The truth was...nothing about her disgusted me. She just stirred up a whirlwind of strange, fucked-up emotions when she proved to me, again and again, that her goodness wasn't fake.

Not even a little bit.

She held a mirror up to me and in its reflection, I saw all the ways we were different.

She helped people.

I destroyed them.

I kept my eyes on her knees until my pulse slowed. She didn't rush me. She just sat there, her presence a quiet comfort, waiting for me to find my way back to myself.

Shame crept up my spine as I realized what a coward I was being. Hiding from her, from the understanding in her eyes.

Finally, I forced myself to meet her gaze.

And fuck, she was beautiful.

Even now, with the buns on her head falling apart, her mascara smeared, and her black cardigan covered in dirt.

Without thinking, I brushed away the dark-gray streaks on her cheek with my thumb—only to remember too late that my hands were covered in mud.

"Shit," I muttered, my eyes tracing over the streak I'd left on her cheek. "I got you dirty."

She smiled, and it was pure light. The first break of sunrise over the horizon. "Don't think it makes much of a difference at this point."

I huffed. We were both filthy.

Her eyes searched mine. "What happened to you?" she asked again.

I couldn't tell her. Couldn't let her inside that part of me. The ugliest, darkest part. But the walls I'd spent years building around it were weak now. Punctured.

And the way she looked at me—with no pity, no judgment, just quiet concern—made the words slip out.

"A while back, I ran my car into a lake. Almost drowned. Driving in the rain made me—" I swallowed hard, shaking my head. I sounded like a fucking idiot.

"The rain made it feel like we were underwater," she said gently, squeezing my shoulders. "I get it."

I focused on the sensation of her touch. It didn't bother me anymore. It anchored me to this moment instead of letting me drown in the past.

We stayed like that until my body felt like it was back to normal.

But I feared nothing would ever be normal again.

CHAPTER 17

Mia

The road stretched ahead, slick and gleaming under the headlights as I drove us back toward Fabi's.

Romolo was fiddling with the heat.

"It's one night," I said.

"It's not happening. I'm going home."

"You can leave first thing tomorrow morning."

"I'm not staying at Fabi's," he snapped. "It's not even your place to invite me to."

He was right. It wasn't my house. But Fabi wouldn't hold it against me. The storm was an easy excuse for bringing Romolo along. And considering she was about to become part of his family, it wasn't as if he'd be unwelcome.

"I'm not inviting you. I'm telling you that's what you're doing."

"When did you get the impression that you can tell me what to do?" His voice was low and edged with frustration. He hadn't shaken off what had happened back there. For a man like him, that must have been a cataclysmic event. A moment of raw vulnerability in front of someone playing for the other team.

He hated every second of this.

"We all have our weak spots, Romolo." A beat passed. "You don't have to be so angry that I saw yours. The more you try to repress something painful, the more it tends to rupture to the surface when you least expect it."

His jaw ticked. "What painful feelings have you been repressing?"

I sighed. He was trying to deflect the conversation to me so he wouldn't have to talk about himself.

Fine. I'd humor him.

"In high school, I had anxiety. It got pretty bad for a while." I stopped at a light. "Had to see a therapist."

"Anxiety over what?"

I hesitated. "A lot of things. My classes. My grades. My family."

Why my dad sent me away and never visited unless I begged.

It wasn't that abnormal at Valais Academy. Fabi and Elena's family never visited either. Most kids there had parents who were busy running multibillion-dollar corporations or managing their generational wealth.

If my mom had been still alive, I knew she would have been there as often as she could. She would have loved the campus. Especially the view of the mountain range from my dorm window. I'd have taken her to my favorite restaurant in the village and made her try the fondue.

I would have felt wanted and loved, instead of discarded.

"What did you do about it?" Romolo's voice pulled me back to the present.

I cleared my throat. "For a long time, I didn't do anything. I showed up to class and pretended I was fine. But I wasn't. Then, one day, I had an anxiety attack during a final exam. Had to be escorted out and taken to the school medic's office." I winced at the memory. "It was humiliating. But after that, I realized I needed to deal with my problems instead of pretending they weren't there. So I found a therapist."

"Did it help?"

"It did." Of course, I knew that just because it hadn't happened again, didn't mean it never would.

"I'm not going to a shrink, Mia," Romolo muttered. "And I fucking hate the Hamptons. I'll feel a hell of a lot better when I'm back in Manhattan."

"It can start to rain again at any moment. You really want to have a repeat of what happened? Alone in the car this time?"

"I would've preferred to be alone."

"You're more concerned about your pride than staying alive. The male ego is truly something," I said, trying to lighten the heavy mood that had descended inside the car.

He flicked a clump of grass off his jeans "What pride is left? I look like some mud creature. These clothes are ruined."

I glanced at him, regretting it immediately. Heat prickled at my cheeks as I took in the soaked fabric clinging to his chest and outlining the powerful lines of his shoulders and arms.

I found his current state of disarray to be charming. His usual polished exterior was gone. He was unfiltered. Sulking. Grumpy.

But real.

I liked real.

"It'll be fine after a wash," I said, forcing myself to focus on the road. "And there's no judgment here," I said. "I look just as bad."

He shot me a sidelong glance, his gaze dipping to my bare legs just long enough to send goosebumps racing up my skin.

"You're cold." His voice had lost its earlier edge. It seemed I'd won the argument.

He reached behind his seat, grabbed his leather jacket, and tossed it across my lap.

I adjusted it to cover myself.

"Mia?"

"Yeah?"

A beat passed.

"Can you keep a secret?"

He didn't want anyone to know about what had happened back there. That he'd cracked open, even for a moment. "Yeah."

His gaze lingered on my face, warming my cheek. "Thanks."

The jacket carried his scent, and for the rest of the drive, my blood hummed, too aware of it.

Too aware of him.

Fabi, Nina, and Zo weren't back yet when we arrived at the house. I punched in the code to the front door that Fabi had given to all of us and wiped my muddy feet on the welcome mat before stepping inside Fabi's mom's pristine home. Romolo followed me.

The house was dark and eerily quiet. I reached for the light switch and blinked against the harsh glare as the overhead lights flickered on.

We caught our reflections in the entryway mirror at the same time.

Oh God.

We were a mess. Mud-streaked. Soaked. Completely wrecked.

Romolo exhaled through his nose. "Straight to the shower."

It wasn't meant suggestively, but an image of us under steaming water together flashed through my mind before I could stop it. Heat bloomed across my face. When I caught his pensive gaze in the mirror, I wondered if his mind had gone in a similar direction.

We were alone in an empty house. Light rain still bounced against the windows, and just beyond the glass in the living room, waves crashed over the shore. The sound of them filled the air.

It was intimate.

Dangerously intimate.

I felt myself drawn to him in a way I shouldn't be.

Don't forget what you thought of him before the car swerved.

Right.

He'd been awful. He wanted information on my dad, and he'd been ruthless in trying to get it.

No matter what happened tonight, I couldn't risk further associating myself with him. I needed to get him out of my life.

And that picture... God. Was it worth trying to get him to delete it now that I had something on him, too?

The idea felt icky, but I had to use the little leverage I had to protect myself and the campaign.

I'd let him clean up first. Then I'd bring it up.

I nodded toward the stairs. "There's a bathroom upstairs. Third door on the right."

He rummaged through the gym bag he'd fished out of the trunk. "I only have a spare pair of sweatpants in here. Think you can find a T-shirt my size?"

"I can check."

We climbed the stairs, careful not to touch the walls or

railing with our filthy clothes. At the bathroom door, I stopped. "Go ahead. I'll find you something to wear."

His gray eyes lingered on me for a moment before he nodded and disappeared inside.

I bit down on the inside of my cheek. The near drowning must have been horrific to traumatize him. How had he survived? Did someone pull him out, or did he fight his way to the surface?

He wouldn't tell me. But I wanted to know. He'd been a black box before, and now the lid had been lifted just enough for me to glimpse inside. There were layers to him. Dimensions.

He wasn't just the manipulative asshole he pretended to be.

The shower started.

A shirt. Right.

One by one, I checked the bedrooms the girls and I had taken. Besides our stuff, there were only a few bathrobes in the closets.

Finally, I found two neatly folded T-shirts in the master suite's walk-in closet. They were roughly his size.

I grabbed the one that didn't say The Hamptons, Long Island—since he said he hated this place—and knocked on the bathroom door. "Found you something."

The water had stopped. "Come in," his deep voice rumbled.

Steam spilled into the hallway as I opened the door and stepped inside. Romolo stood by the vanity raking his fingers through his damp hair, a towel slung low around his hips.

My mouth went dry.

Broad shoulders. Defined abs. Water still glistening over his skin. Tattoos wrapped around his torso and across his back—intricate images and patterns that must have taken hours upon hours to create.

It wasn't fair.

Our eyes met in the mirror. His brows lifted slightly like he was amused. "What did you find?"

His voice coasted over my skin like a warm summer wind. I flushed, thrusting the shirt toward him. "Just a black T-shirt."

He took it, his fingers grazing mine for the briefest moment. The room felt too small, the air charged and heavy.

"Why do I have a feeling this is Messero's?" he mused, holding up the shirt.

The disdain in his voice made it clear how he felt about Fabi's brother.

"No love lost between you and your future brother-in-law, huh?" I said, forcing my focus on anything other than the smooth planes of his chest.

"For the love of God, don't remind me he'll be family soon."

"Well, just pretend it's someone else's. Maybe Fabi's mom has a boyfriend."

He shook his head, his expression unreadable. A few beats passed before his gaze slid back to me. "You're staring, Mia. See something you like?"

I *was* staring.

I *did* like what I saw.

Too much.

Heat crept up my neck. *Leave. Why are you still here?*

He turned, giving me his back.

The towel dropped.

I made a strangled sound and spun toward the wall, my eyes snapping shut. "What are you doing?!"

"Getting dressed." The fabric rustled as he pulled on the clothes.

I didn't know why I was *still* standing there, but I couldn't move. My feet were glued in place. My brain was short-circuiting.

He chuckled, low and knowingly.

I stared hard at the towel rack like it held all the answers to the universe.

And then I felt him.

Felt his warmth at my back. His shirt brushing against my dirty, damp cardigan. The barest graze of his lips near my ear.

"I'll take that as a yes," he murmured.

A violent shiver ran through me. I wanted to lean back. Wanted to see if he'd—

He brushed past me and walked out of the bathroom.

CHAPTER 18

Mia

I walked down the stairs in my pajamas, a bathrobe thrown on top, still shivering from the ice-cold shower I'd taken.

Painful? Yes.

Worth it? Also yes.

My head was officially screwed on straight again after seeing Romolo naked. And it was a good thing, because I could hear voices drifting up from the main floor.

My friends were back.

Romolo sat sprawled on the living room sofa, a book in hand, looking completely at ease, while Fabi, Nina, and Zo stood across from him, their expressions ranging from confusion to shock, and in Nina's case—outright hostility.

Romolo's eyes flicked to me the second I appeared. "There she is. Alive and well. Mia, mind catching them up? I've already been subjected to a slew of accusations."

Fabi stumbled toward me, unsteady and eyes glassy. She was drunk. So was Zo, who was grinning at me like a fool, her eyes twitching—was she trying to wink?

I glanced away from her, trying not to laugh, and caught Nina's eye. The scowl on her face told me she was the most sober one of the three.

"Mia, are you okay?" Fabi slurred. I steadied her, already knowing exactly what this looked like.

Freshly showered and in a robe.

Romolo, equally showered, lounging like a king who'd just been thoroughly satisfied.

God. Kill me.

I hesitated just a second too long—long enough for Nina to narrow her eyes and stab an accusatory finger at Romolo. "What did you do to her?"

Romolo barely lifted his gaze from the book. "Nothing she didn't want me to."

I glared at him. The bastard was enjoying this.

Fabi and Zo let out simultaneous gasps, their faces a mix of scandalized and intrigued.

I raised my hands. "It's not what it looks like." Then, quickly, before Nina combusted, "And, yes, I'm fine."

She wasn't buying it. "What is *he* doing here?"

Zo's brows knitted together. "Is your stepmom okay? I thought you were driving back to her in Manhattan."

"I was. But one of my dad's assistants was able to go there instead to keep an eye on her. So Romolo and I turned back. It was raining really bad. I invited him to crash here." I looked at Fabi, hoping she wouldn't mind.

Fabi slung an arm around me, nodding dramatically. "Ye-yep. No problem."

Romolo tsked. "She's wasted. Nina, I hope you made sure she behaved appropriately since she's my brother's future wife."

Fabi perked up, looking offended. "Excuse me?"

Nina scoffed. "Please. Who are you to lecture anyone on behavior?" She crossed her arms. "I'm still trying to figure out how you ended up at the same party as us. Big coincidence, isn't it?"

I bit the inside of my cheek. Good question. How *did* he end up there?

Romolo shrugged, all lazy amusement. "What exactly are you accusing me of, cousin?"

"I don't know, Rom," Nina said. "Seems to me like you're stalking Mia."

Fabi gasped again, but late, like she'd just processed the conversation. "Ohhh. That IS suspicious."

Romolo let out a slow, smug laugh. "I don't remember you being this paranoid, Nina." He checked the time on his phone. "It's two a.m. What do you want to do? Kick me out into the storm?"

"No," I cut in. "Nina, it's fine. Just leave him be."

Displeasure radiated off her as she whipped around to glare at me.

Zo wobbled forward. "Mia, we need to talk. Privately."

Oh boy.

We ducked into a small reading room down the hall. The second we were out of Romolo's earshot, Nina and Zo crowded around me while Fabi collapsed onto a sofa with a deep, groggy groan.

"I don't trust him," Nina hissed. "I'm pretty sure he was the one who got us invited to that party."

"I don't trust him either," I admitted. "But I didn't want him to get into an accident on the road."

"That's what airbags are for," Zo said unhelpfully. She looped an arm around my shoulder. "I have to ask... What's with the robe?"

"We were all muddy when we got here," I explained.

"And you took a shower together?" Zo asked.

"NO." I nearly choked.

"What happened?" Nina asked.

"He—" Shit. I couldn't tell them the truth, and I hadn't come up with a convincing explanation. My conversation with Romolo in the car came back to me. There was one thing I could say…

"I kind of freaked out about my stepmom. I felt like I was having a panic attack, so I got Romolo to pull over so I could get out of the car. It was muddy on the side of the road, and I got drenched."

Nina's face softened. "Your anxiety. Shit, Mia. I'm sorry."

They believed me so easily. I hated lying to them, but I'd made a promise to Romolo. And I was still planning on trading my silence for that picture. Zo sighed and squeezed my shoulder. "We should've gone with you."

"It's all good now. I'm just really tired. Is it okay if I go to bed?" I glanced at Fabi. She was already out, snoring softly, one arm dangling off the couch.

Zo nodded. "We should all go to bed."

Nina crossed her arms, still on edge. "And Romolo?"

"There's a guest room downstairs," I said.

"Can we trust him to keep himself out of trouble in there?" Nina asked.

Zo yawned. "Maybe we should be a little grateful he got Mia back here safely, regardless of our opinions."

"Only because he knows if he didn't, I'd kill him," Nina muttered. "He never does anything unless it serves him somehow."

I should have agreed. But to my surprise, I felt the smallest, strangest urge to defend him.

Nina sighed. "I told you it was a bad idea to do this project with him. He's trying to sink his claws into you. Working for him is not the only way to save your business."

My stomach twisted. I hadn't told them the real reason I'd taken the job. I knew they'd try to talk me out of it. Fabi would say she didn't need my help, and they'd all say I was already doing too much for my dad.

But I'd wanted to try. Even if it was starting to feel like I had made a very, very bad deal with the devil.

CHAPTER 19

Mia

The glowing red numbers on the alarm clock said it was just after three.

I yanked the pillow from under my head, threw it over my face, and groaned.

I was dead tired. But I couldn't fall asleep.

My mind kept spinning, replaying a highlight reel of moments from today.

Romolo cornering me at the party.

Romolo on his knees in the rain.

Romolo in the steaming bathroom, towel slung low, voice dripping with amusement—*See something you like?*

Worst of all was the awareness that he was still here, just one floor below me. The image of him lying in bed, black boxer briefs hugging two sculpted thighs, one arm tucked behind his head... It sent heat pooling low in my belly.

He was the last person I should be thirsting after given everything that had happened.

The absolute. Dead. Last.

I kicked the sheet off and sat up, covering my face with my hands. I wished he'd never had the panic attack. It would have been easier to hate him for everything shitty that he'd done. It would have kept things simple.

Nothing felt simple anymore.

Seeing him so vulnerable had softened my anger toward him. And that attraction, the one that had been there from the very beginning, still burned just as brightly.

I climbed out of bed. My throat was dry and scratchy. I'd grab a glass of water from the kitchen and then get serious about sleeping—counting sheep, meditating, maybe even popping the Ambien I'd found in one of the bathroom drawers.

My palm slid over the wooden banister as I crept downstairs, careful not to make a sound. Nothing less than a bomb would wake Fabi and Zo, but Nina was another matter. I already felt bad for making her worry. I didn't want to worry her more.

The kitchen was silent except for the ticking clock above the gas stove. I filled a glass at the sink and was halfway through drinking it when I saw him.

Romolo.

He was outside on the back deck, hands braced against the railing as he stared out at the ocean. The black shirt I'd found for him was stretched taut across his shoulders.

I folded my lips over my teeth. Since we were both up, maybe this was the best time to bring up the photo on his phone.

Just get it over with and move on.

Unease danced inside my throat as I crossed the living room and slid the glass door open.

The sound pulled his attention. He turned, just enough for his gaze to land on me. It slid from my face to the messy ponytail atop my head, then down to where the hem of my pajama shorts kissed my thighs.

The night air was cooler than I'd expected, and my skin

pebbled with goosebumps. Regret whispered in the back of my head. I should have brought a sweater.

"Mia."

He sounded tired. And frustrated. His black hair was tousled, like he'd been running his hand through it over and over again. A tumbler with liquor—whiskey, probably—sat half empty on the railing.

My bare feet stepped across the still-wet deck until I stood at his side. "You raided Fabi's mom's stash?"

"I doubt she'll mind." He pushed the tumbler a few inches toward me. "Want some?"

I shook my head and took a sip of my water. The waves crashed in the distance. It was too dark to see them—the moon was hidden behind the thick clouds—but their song filled the air.

Romolo tapped his fingers against the railing, slowly and rhythmically, the only other sound apart from the ocean. "You told them."

It was a statement, not a question. Tension marred his jaw as he stared—no, *glared* at the water.

That's when it dawned on me.

He had never actually thought I'd keep his secret. He probably didn't trust people. Not unless they'd been bribed, forced, or otherwise coerced into doing what he wanted.

And here I was, about to confirm his sad, depressing worldview.

An ache pulsed inside my chest.

If I used this against him, if I turned this into a negotiation to get that photo deleted, I'd be giving him one more reason to believe the world worked exactly the way he thought it did.

I...couldn't do that to him.

Maybe if I was colder. More ruthless. More driven by logic.

But I wasn't. My heart was placed firmly on my sleeve, which meant it got hurt. Often.

But I could live with my own pain. It was the pain of others I didn't know how to handle.

I bit on the inside of my cheek. One day, I'd might regret this. But today wasn't that day.

"I didn't," I said softly. "And I won't."

Silence stretched between us. His gaze skimmed my face, suspicion dancing at the edges. "How did you explain what happened? Why we showered as soon as we got home?"

"I said I had a panic attack and forced you to let me out of the car. They know my history. They believed it."

He frowned. "You lied on my behalf?"

"I don't feel great about it. I don't like lying to my friends."

"And yet you did."

"I made you a promise."

Something flickered across his face—doubt, disbelief. Like promises didn't mean anything to him anymore. Like every promise ever made to him had been broken.

The ache inside me spread until it took up my entire ribcage.

Men weren't born hardened. They were made that way by someone's heavy hand until nothing soft remained.

Who was Romolo's maker?

I placed my hand over his. It was warm. Solid. "I won't break it."

Another few seconds passed before his shoulders lowered. His breath escaped his lungs in a slow exhale, and then his whole face changed in a million tiny ways.

For the first time since I'd met him, I could read him. I could see exactly what he was thinking.

He was grateful.

Profoundly so. In ways I suspected he didn't even fully understand, and the knowledge that I'd given this moment to him made my heart churn.

His fingers twitched beneath my hand as he held my gaze. "You're not...like who I thought you'd be."

"Really?" I asked softly. He wasn't either, but out of the two of us, he was the one who hid behind a mask.

The wind picked up, sinking its cold teeth into my skin. I began to shiver. Maybe it was time to go in—

Romolo moved. A second later, large hands appeared on the railing, bracketing mine.

A bump against my shoulder blades.

Then warmth. So much warmth. His heat blanketed my back, seeping through my clothes, caressing my flesh.

"Better?" The word came from somewhere very close to my ear.

My eyes were wide. "Uh— Yeah. Better." His huge, muscled body was practically wrapped around me.

This was us crossing another line. I knew it. He knew it.

But something kept me standing still instead of running away like I told myself I would if he ever got too close again.

Each second ticked by in slow motion as I basked in his warmth and his clean, male scent.

Thwomp... Shhhh... Thwomp.... Shhhh...

The whispers of the waves followed a hypnotic rhythm, lulling me into a relaxed state, despite my best intentions to stay on my guard.

"I thought behind that good girl act you were just like the rest of them." His voice was rough, but the way his lips brushed the shell of my ear softened the edge. "But you're the real thing, aren't you? Good all the way through. You went from hating me to helping me in seconds. Didn't even hesitate."

I didn't hate him.

"That's what anyone would've done," I whispered.

"No." His warm breath grazed the side of my neck, making my toes curl. "It's not."

I didn't know what this was. What we were doing. Another game?

His hands fell from the railing to my hips.

We stood still, unmoving, but I felt every single place we touched. Each point of contact burned—hotter than the flashes that warned me I was about to lose consciousness. Hotter than anything I'd ever felt.

Don't let this go any further, a voice whispered, threaded with desperation.

But my body had other plans.

I leaned back, letting my head fall against his shoulder.

He made a sound of satisfaction, low and deep, the kind a person makes when a puzzle piece fits. Then he pulled my hips back against his.

He was hard.

"Your fucking scent." The words rumbled in his chest. "It drives me crazy."

Every nerve ending lit up. He was like a drug. Toxic, addictive, bad for me, but at the same time, oh so good.

His thumb slipped under the hem of my shirt, grazing the bare skin above my hip. He stroked it, back and forth— each pass sending shivers through me that had nothing to do with the cold.

I pushed my butt against his erection.

That low groan. God, it made my thighs clench.

His hand moved, over my belly, then down into my shorts.

I didn't stop him.

I welcomed it.

Until it hit me—if he found out how wet I was...

My eyes flew open. "Wait—"

"Jesus, Mia."

Too late. His fingers were already dragging over the soaked fabric of my panties, and judging by the way his cock twitched against me, he was pleased.

Shit. He knew. I was so hot for him, and now he *knew*.

"What's got you like this?" His tone was pure tease. "Was it when I called you a good girl?" His palm cupped me with firm pressure. "I bet this pussy loves to be praised."

My cheeks burned. Did it?

"I bet it craves being told how wet and warm and fucking perfect it is."

Judging by the way I clenched around nothing—yeah, it did.

A whimper clawed up my throat as he dipped inside my panties, sliding lower, teasing my opening before gliding back up to my clit.

I gasped, hands gripping the railing as sparks raced through my body.

He was too good, too skilled. Every stroke was just right. It was like he'd mapped my body before tonight and knew exactly how to break me apart.

A moan slipped past my lips.

"Shhh." His breath coasted over my ear. "You wouldn't want your friends to know how good I am at making you come."

I bit on my tongue, my eyes watering. I was so far gone, not even the risk of being caught could pull me back.

His fingers moved in circles now. Every few of them punctuated with a gentle pinch. I bucked my hips, silently begging for more.

"That's it." His voice was pure gravel.

"Oh. Oh God." I was already unraveling, breaths coming in sharp, needy gasps.

Cool wind tickled against my bare hip as he slid his

other hand under my shirt, lifting it a few inches on his way to cup my breast.

He pinched my nipple, rolling it between rough fingers, and the sensation shot straight down to my clit. I writhed against him, pressure coiling tighter and tighter inside me.

"Take it, Mia," he growled, thrusting two fingers inside. The heel of his palm replaced the rhythm on my clit. "Come all over my hand."

Thwomp... Shhhh...

He clamped a hand over my mouth just in time.

The orgasm crashed into me like a wave, stealing my breath, tearing me apart. I moaned against his palm and clenched around his fingers. He kept moving, stroking me from the inside out, wet and slick and relentless.

Oh. My. God.

I was still coming down, mind in shards, when he pulled his hand from my shorts.

I looked down and—*Christ.*

My wetness practically dripped off his fingers.

I whirled around, pressing my back against the railing, face on fire. He needed something to clean them with. I'd grab a napkin, a towel, anything.

"I'll get—"

He cut me off with a look. Dark. Hooded. Turned on. And then he brought those fingers to his mouth and licked them clean.

With a groan.

Like I was the best thing he'd ever tasted.

I slumped against the railing. My legs feel like jelly. My core felt like it'd been liquefied. And still, a gnawing hunger pulsed low inside my belly.

More. More. More.

The voice in my head shouting *ABORT ABORT* turned frantic.

If there was ever a time to listen to it, it was now.

Instead, I couldn't tear my gaze away from his lips. If I kissed him now, I'd probably taste myself on his tongue.

The thought drove me wild.

"This is a terrible idea," I muttered, more to myself than to him.

He took a step forward, crowding me against the railing.

"We should stop," I all but whispered.

His hand cupped my cheek, thumb grazing my skin. "You telling me to stop?"

"Rom…" His name broke on my lips. Indecision choked the rest of the sentence. My heart hammered, torn between reason and want.

His lips hovered over mine. So close. Every breath he exhaled mingled with mine in the space between us.

Thwomp… Shhhh…

The waves crashed in the distance. I barely heard them over the rush of my own pulse.

The heat in his gaze bled into me, soaking through my veins and settling in the pit of my belly.

Just a peck.

That was all I needed. I'd simmer down once I satisfied this aching need to feel his lips against mine.

I licked my lips. "No."

And then I rose onto my tiptoes and kissed him.

He responded with a low groan, curling his palm around my waist while his other hand tilted my head back.

Just a peck, just a peck, just a—

Somehow, my fingers were in his hair. Somehow, my tongue was inside his mouth. Somehow, we were biting on each other's lips like we were both starved.

With a whine, I tugged him closer, deepening the kiss that was *definitely not a peck*.

I felt possessed. I wasn't sure anything less than an exorcism would help me.

The kiss was rough. Messy. Unrestrained.

When we finally broke apart, we were both panting. Romolo's chest heaved, and his entire body was vibrating with tension, like he was barely holding himself together.

"Fuck," he muttered, dropping his forehead against mine.

We stood there for a moment, suspended in the aftershock.

Then came his sigh. Heavy. Final. "Four. One. Nine. Nine. Seven. Three."

I pulled away and blinked, confused. "What?"

There was a sudden shift in his expression. It sent a flicker of unease through me.

He reached into his pocket, pulled out his phone, and held it out.

I stared at the device. It took me an embarrassingly long time to piece it all together.

The numbers were his passcode.

"A deal's a deal," he said flatly. His voice had gone cold. Distant. Like a door slamming shut inside him.

My heart stilled.

I hadn't kissed him because of the deal. I hadn't even thought about it. But I guess for him, this *was* all another game.

My prize was six muttered numbers, but I still felt like I'd lost.

Refusing to look at him—I didn't want him to see the hurt in my expression—I took the phone and unlocked it.

The last photo in his camera roll was of me. I deleted it.

The next one slid into view before I could look away. It was a photo of him and a beautiful woman glued to his side in what appeared to be a nightclub.

My stomach sank.

I didn't know when it was taken. I didn't care. All I cared about was getting away from him as quickly as I could.

Expression blank, I shoved the phone back into his hand and walked inside the house without another word.

The next morning, he was gone before I woke up.

CHAPTER 20

Rom

"Mom wants to see you." Cosimo stood in my doorway, a bruise darkening his left cheek.

I'd barely been home an hour. Just long enough to shower, put on a mindless action flick, and collapse onto the sofa, where I'd been mulling over my next steps. I would have stayed there longer if Cos hadn't showed up.

I stepped aside, letting him in. "What does she want?" My mother was the last thing I needed on my plate today.

"An update. She said you haven't responded to her messages for the last few days. Where have you been?"

"Busy. Working." Having my fingers inside the most forbidden pussy in the city.

I could still feel it. Warm, wet, inviting. It was as fucking perfect as the rest of her—including her lips that did in fact taste like fucking berries—and it made me irate knowing those five stunning minutes were all I'd ever get.

The second she said she'd lied to her friends for me, it was game over. Shock hit first—she'd kept her word when I'd done *nothing* to deserve it. And then came something else.

A weird warmth inside my chest. A tightening in my

throat. And a heavy sense of certainty sinking into the pit of my belly.

I'd known exactly what I had to do.

It was something I'd never done before. Something I'd never even considered doing.

I'd given away the only leverage I had.

Mia Morales had infected my black heart with a virus that compelled me to do right by her.

Fuck knows if I'd ever recover.

"I stopped by your club last night," Cosimo said. "You weren't there."

"Since when do I have to report my movements to you?" I moved toward the living room, the hardwood shifting to carpet beneath my feet. "Have a seat. Want coffee?"

"Already had three cups," Cosimo said, following after me.

"Who'd you go to the club with?"

"It was Nate's birthday."

I sank onto the sofa and nodded at his bruise. "That looks fresh. What happened?"

He sat across from me. "Nothing."

I just looked at him.

He swiped a hand over his jaw. "I said it was nothing."

"Since when do you get into fights at my fucking club?"

He frowned. "You know?"

I cocked my head. "You didn't think Alexis would message me the second my own fucking brother decked some finance bro on the dance floor?" I leaned forward. "What's going on with you, Cos? Have you forgotten you're the eldest? The don-in-waiting? You've spent a decade building a reputation as someone reasonable. Steady. Someone the family could count on. And now you're losing your mind over a piece of ass?"

His nostrils flared. "Watch how you speak about my future wife."

I laughed. He really thought I was clueless. Had he forgotten who I was? What I did for this family?

"You son of a bitch, I'm not talking about that poor girl. I saw Fabi last night. She was in the Hamptons with her friends, medicating the depression you're inducing in her by getting sloshed." I sank back into the sofa. "I'm talking about Rosa."

Irritation flashed across his face. "How about you stay out of my business?"

"Trust me, I've been staying out of it, but this has gone on for too long. She's got you wrapped around her little finger. It's fucking ridiculous, Cos."

His voice dropped. "You don't know what you're talking about."

"I know she likes power and money. You happen to have both. If you think there's another reason why she's sleeping with you, you're deluding yourself."

He flicked his eyes to the window. "You have no idea what she wants or what she's like."

Oh, but I fucking did. Like recognizes like, and Rosa? She was just like me. A natural at destruction.

There weren't many people I gave a damn about, but my brothers were on that short list. If Cos didn't cut Rosa loose before the wedding, it would be doomed from the start. She wasn't the kind of mistress who'd be happy staying in the shadows.

But Cos was stubborn. He had to come to that conclusion himself.

"What did the finance bro do?" I asked, rubbing my hand over my jaw.

"Overstepped." His vague response probably meant the

guy had asked Rosa for a dance in front of Cosimo, not knowing any better.

His jaw tightened. "Fabiana was at the Hamptons? Messero is supposed to keep me updated of her movements."

"Don't you follow her on Instagram?"

His frown deepened. "She's on Instagram?"

"Yeah. Along with everyone else under fifty. You'd know if you weren't such a fucking Luddite."

"That shit rots your brain," he muttered, even as he pulled out his phone and started tapping.

I refilled my coffee in the kitchen. By the time I returned, he'd downloaded the app and was scrolling through Fabi's profile.

I huffed a laugh. "Isn't it interesting you thought I was talking about her? Fabi been on your mind a lot lately?"

Immediately, he locked his screen and slid the phone into his pocket. "I don't have time for this. Are you coming or not? Mom's not in a patient mood."

Yeah, I figured. She'd expected me to get something useful from Mia, but all I had to show for my efforts was a stolen tube of lip gloss and a newly rediscovered conscience.

I couldn't fucking stomach the thought of hurting that girl anymore.

She'd done something to me. I didn't like these feelings. I didn't like *feeling*. Period.

What I wanted was to get back to normal, to having no moral qualms about doing my fucking job. I wanted to rid myself of this disturbing urge to protect someone whose last name wasn't Ferraro.

If I told Mother any of this, she'd crucify me. Tell me I lost my damn mind.

And she'd be right.

But I was done. After my next meeting with Mia, I wasn't planning on seeing her again.

She'd won.

I set my half-finished mug on the coffee table. "Let's go."

My parents' penthouse was only a few blocks from mine. But when Cos and I stepped out onto the street, he turned in the opposite direction.

"You're not coming?" I called after him.

"You can handle it," he said, tossing the words over his shoulder. "Good luck."

I scoffed. He was annoyed with me. He'd get over it.

Five minutes later, I stepped out of the elevator into my parents' foyer.

Voices floated in from the living room. Mother was entertaining. If she'd summoned me in the middle of it, she must've really had it.

I walked through the archway, flashing a grin at the five women seated around the dining table. My aunts and cousins greeted me with high-pitched exclamations and air-kisses as I made my way around the room.

Aunt Lisa was nowhere in sight. Guess she was still on Mother's bad side.

At the head of the table, Mother smiled serenely. Not a trace of the irritation I knew was brewing beneath her mask showed.

"Romolo, darling. How are you?" she asked.

"Just fine. Almost recovered from last night."

Aunt Marina clucked her tongue. "You look pale, Romolino. You're not getting enough sunshine cooped up in that club all the time."

I raked my fingers through my hair. "You know how it is, *Zia*. Someone's got to keep the order in that place."

Aunt Paolina beamed. "Look at you. So grown-up. Vita, you've raised three good boys."

Good boys. I swiped my hand over my lips to smother a chuckle. Only in a mob family would my brothers and I qualify for that title.

Mother rose from her seat. "I need to talk to Romolo for a moment." She signaled to one of the household staff. "More tea for everyone, please."

As soon as we entered Father's office, her demeanor changed. I was used to it, but it still amazed me how she could go from warm and pleasant to dictator mode in the blink of an eye.

She moved behind my father's desk and took his chair. "Where were you last night?"

"The Hamptons." I dropped onto the sofa instead of sitting across from her like a schoolboy in the principal's office.

She laced her fingers together on the desk. "What happened with Morales's daughter? You haven't given me an update."

I slid a hand into my trouser pocket and wrapped my fingers around the stolen lip gloss tube.

I should've thrown it away earlier. Tried to. Couldn't do it.

"I don't think she knows anything."

Her gaze sharpened. "That's not what I want to hear, Romolo."

She let the words hang, as if she was waiting for me to correct myself. When I didn't, she pressed on. "Did Cosimo give you an update on what's happening with the Colombians?"

I popped my ankle over my knee. "He forgot to mention it. Enlighten me."

She folded her arms in front of her on the desk. "They're threatening to pull out of the deal because they're afraid Morales will have the police force cracking down on our distribution network as soon as he's elected. Your father flew out first thing this morning to meet with them in person."

I shrugged. "They're bluffing. If they want the New York market, they have to work with us. There's no other option."

"It seems that there is."

"Who?"

Her lips pursed. "We don't know for certain. One theory is that they're negotiating with a biker gang—the Crimson Defenders—who've been trying to expand into the state."

"We'd crush them." We had the manpower to fight off just about any threat.

"We can't risk a fight in the city if Morales is elected. It would only give him more ammunition in his fight against us. We don't want to be sitting here with our hands tied while the gang sets up shop."

Fuck. She had a point.

I rubbed my chin. If the Colombians walked, we'd have a lot more problems on our hands. It would signal weakness. Spook our other partners.

Mother leaned forward. "I want a full report on Morales's daughter. What have you learned? No detail is too small."

Dread pressed down on my shoulders. She was about to grill me, and if I didn't give her something, she'd get suspicious. I had to play this carefully.

"She knows who I am. She's cautious. I've applied some pressure, but I can't risk applying more yet. I have to wait to see how she'll react."

Mother frowned. "You're telling me you're just sitting around, waiting?"

"It's a delicate situation."

Her gaze narrowed.

I made sure my face gave nothing away.

If Morales had a secret backer, Mia had no idea about

any of it. I was sure of it. She was too principled. Her father would know better than to involve her.

To get information, I would need to compel her to spy on Morales. And I'd already decided I wasn't going to do that.

Not after last night.

"We don't have time to wait around," Mother said, her tone leaving no room for argument. "When are you seeing her next?"

"Two days from now for a fitting. I've convinced her to dress me for an event next week at The Golden Circle."

She picked up a pen. "How?"

"Her business is in trouble. Told her I'd get her more clients."

Mother looked thoughtful as she tapped the pen against her lips. "How much damage would an intimate photo of you two cause?"

My blood ran cold. She was dipping into her favorite bag of tricks. "Could be significant. She wouldn't want something like that getting out. But would it be enough to get her to betray her father? I doubt it."

"Unless you have better ideas, I think we should give it a try."

"She's been standoffish. Aloof."

"I'm not going to tell you how to seduce her, Romolo. Surely, you can figure that out?"

A foul sensation knotted inside my gut. "Rhetorical question, right?" I said, my voice low.

Her lips thinned as she stared at me. The pen clicked closed. "Tell me when you think you'll be able to stage it. I can help arrange the tech."

Help. I didn't need her fucking help. What I needed was for her to forget that Mia existed.

But how? She was like dog with a bone. After I said

goodbye to Mia tomorrow, I'd have to keep the ruse going for a while longer. Pretend like I was still pursuing her so that Mother wouldn't suspect I'd given up.

How long could I keep it up until Mother decided to intervene?

Only time would tell.

My hand clenched around the tube in my pocket. "I've got it."

She got to her feet and anchored her palms against the desk. "A week ago you waltzed in here and promised to solve our most important problem. I want results. Have I made myself clear?"

I rolled my lips over my teeth and stood up. "Crystal."

"Good. You're dismissed."

CHAPTER 21

Mia

There were some things I could get away with in life. Boarding with zone three when my plane ticket said zone four. Telling my nutritionist I only had a bite of cake, instead of a full slice. Skipping the occasional campaign event by pretending I had food poisoning.

Hooking up with a mob boss's son wasn't one of them.

The steamer wand huffed angrily as I dragged it over Romolo's finished suit. He was due to arrive for his fitting any minute.

Two days had passed since the night in the Hamptons. Plenty of time to reflect, overanalyze, and go in and out of mental tailspins.

He hadn't texted me since that night. Why would he? His last words to me had been that a deal was a deal. He'd reduced our kiss to a bargaining chip. I had no idea what he was thinking, or if he'd thought about me at all.

On the other hand, I'd thought about him plenty, pondering all his complexities and contradictions.

Lust, I could handle. What I couldn't handle was the rest.

The curiosity. The butterflies. The gnawing *need*. And

most of all, the way I sometimes secretly enjoyed the morally questionable things he did.

Like pinning me to a bed. Cornering me in my office. Coercing me to climb onto his lap and then bribing me for a kiss. He had power, and he wasn't afraid to use it.

Something about that appealed to me, which was seriously messed up. Continuing down this path would lead me to dangerous places.

My only comfort was reminding myself that nothing terrible had happened—yet. No one had caught us doing anything we were definitely not supposed to be doing together. But I'd always believed that breaking rules had consequences, and eventually, they caught up with you.

I wasn't going to gamble with fate. Not when my entire plan—if I could even call it that—was held together by wishful thinking and duct tape.

Fabi was set on this wedding. My dad's poll numbers were climbing, despite whatever the Ferraros were doing on their end. Neither of them needed my help. It was time to admit I was more likely to cause harm than do any good by continuing this. And not just to them, but to myself.

Which was why today had to be our last meeting.

With a sigh, I placed the steamer wand back in its holder. I was rifling through my desk drawer—where *was* my lip gloss?—when the door creaked open.

My head snapped up.

Romolo stepped inside. He was wearing a worn leather jacket over a black T-shirt and dark-wash jeans.

Ugh. The look worked well on him, although I was convinced *everything* worked well on him.

Our eyes clashed.

"Mia." The low rumble of his voice slid through the air and coasted down my spine.

"Rom."

A charged silence settled between us.

We were trying to read each other. At least, I was.

Is he thinking about it, too?

The deck. The rain. His hands on me. His mouth against mine.

Nope. Not going there. It was time to move forward.

"About what happened—"

"That night was—"

We both stopped.

"Go ahead," I said.

"Ladies first."

Now he wants to be a gentleman? Of course. The one time I didn't want courtesy, he handed it to me like a loaded gun.

I exhaled. "It can't happen again."

His expression didn't change. "Right. It was a mistake. We weren't thinking straight."

I blinked. "Exactly. A lot happened that night."

He nodded. "Glad we're on the same page."

"Somehow." Guess he was as eager to move on as I was. "I'm glad you didn't get the wrong idea."

"Which would be?"

I felt my face heat. "Never mind."

He cocked his head. "I'm a grown man, Mia. You think I get attached every time I get to third base with a woman? I'd have a harem of wives by now if I did."

I almost reared back at that statement. I'd expected his usual arrogance, but I hadn't expected him to be so callous.

A humorless smirk appeared on his lips. "We'll wrap everything up today, and then we can say goodbye. For good."

"Sounds great to me," I said, my voice flat. Hurt pulsed inside my chest. "Ready to try on your look?"

His gaze flicked to the garment rack. He stepped

forward, lifted the suit off the hanger, and held it out in front of him.

I folded my teeth over my lips, trying to read his reaction. Not that I should care what he thought about it at this point. He wasn't a real client, and I wasn't holding my breath for that recommendation.

But I *did* care. Maybe it was my professional pride that demanded I do a great job. Or maybe…I just wanted him to like my work.

Ugh. Why? It was so stupid.

"Are you going to try it on, or just stare at it? I have a busy schedule, Romolo."

He arched a brow but said nothing. Then, with a shake of his head, he carried the suit into the changing area.

I crossed my arms, forcing myself to stay composed as I paced the studio, struggling—and failing—to keep my thoughts from straying to the last time we were alone.

I hated how vividly I could still remember the feel of his mouth on mine, his hands gripping my hips, his voice rough against my ear.

The curtain slid open and Romolo emerged. "It fits well."

I froze mid-step.

He looked…incredible. Exactly how I'd envisioned when I imagined the look. The suit molded to his body, emphasizing his muscular build, and the red cape added an element of drama. He was already dangerous. Powerful. Untouchable. But now? Every detail I'd painstakingly added to his clothes amplified those qualities.

Dressed like this, he wasn't just a man. He was Mars, the god of war.

I walked around him, inspecting the fit from every angle, searching for flaws. I found none.

"What do you think?" I asked, coming to stand in front of him.

His gaze flickered to mine in the mirror. "It'll do," he said, his tone dismissive.

My lungs deflated. *That's it?* Quickly, I looked away. "Well, that's great. I'm happy you like it."

"Anything else? Or are we good here?"

It was a dismissal.

I swallowed the lump in my throat. "I guess that's it."

"I'll go change."

I watched him disappear back into the changing area and wrapped my arms around myself.

He hadn't said anything about the design. Not a single compliment. Not one comment on the details, the fit, the time I'd put into it.

It shouldn't bother me. It *shouldn't*. Why was I such a goddamn softie? It didn't matter, damn it.

A few minutes later, he emerged dressed in his T-shirt and leather jacket again, the suit slung over his arm. "We never discussed payment," he said. "You can email me the invoice."

I shook my head. "I'm not taking your money." The last thing I needed was a financial link between us.

His gaze narrowed. "Not good enough for you?"

"That recommendation will be more than enough compensation. If you're still planning on making it."

"Of course I'm still planning on it. That was our agreement." His eyes swept over me one last time, from my hair to the tips of my shoes. Then he turned toward the door.

His steps were slow. Measured. Not entirely natural.

Like maybe he felt more than he was letting on.

Like maybe he was holding something back.

My teeth sank into my bottom lip. I knew that if I didn't

ask at least one question that weighed on me, I'd look back on this and regret it.

"Romolo."

He paused with his hand on the doorknob.

"Why did you ask me to work with you? I'm not talking about the suit. The real reason."

He stood frozen, his back toward me. A heavy silence hung between the walls.

I shifted my weight between my feet. "Did you get what you wanted from me?"

"No," was his quiet response. "And I don't want it anymore."

Pain bloomed in my chest, spreading like wildfire. I couldn't even pinpoint why.

He opened the door and paused for another brief second. "Take care of yourself, Mia."

I swallowed hard. "You too."

And that was that.

He was gone.

He'd walked out of my life as abruptly as he'd entered it.

I sniffed, sat down behind my desk, and opened my laptop. The calendar blurred for a second, before I blinked the wetness in my eyes away.

I'd be fine. It was back to business as usual. Just some emails to respond to before I was supposed to meet my dad and a reporter for lunch. Then my calendar was booked solid until late evening.

Great. No time to think about Romolo. I *would* forget about him eventually if he wasn't constantly waltzing in and out of my life.

My phone rang. Jenny.

"Hey, your dad got a last-minute invite to an event this week, but he can't make it. I was hoping you'd go in his place."

"When is it?"

"Friday, seven p.m. Some fancy private club called The Golden Circle."

I sat up straight. No. No way.

"Seriously?"

"Yeah. Is there a problem?"

I pressed my palm against my forehead. "Can I skip it?"

"It's kind of a big deal to be invited. There will be people there you should network with. We want you to go, Mia."

I sucked in a breath and then exhaled. "All right. I'll be there."

"I'll send you the details shortly. Talk soon." She hung up.

I groaned and banged my forehead against my desk.

So much for never seeing him again.

CHAPTER 22

Rom

It was just yesterday that I first heard about the update to the guest list. The president of the club, in his infinite wisdom, had decided to invite the two frontrunners for the mayoral race to this damn dinner.

Of course, Mayor Wilson couldn't make it—useless bastard. He was down with pneumonia. As if Morales needed any more luck with his campaign. Then the president found out Morales was also unavailable, but naturally, his daughter was coming in his place.

She hadn't even arrived, and I was already on edge.

Well, we were all adults. We could survive an evening together in the same room.

Cosimo signaled for another whiskey, his eyes flicking over the attendees in their ridiculous outfits. "I don't know how you do it," he muttered.

I propped my elbows behind me on the bar. Above us, blown-glass planets and stars were suspended from the high ceiling. On each of the high-top tables scattered around the room were towers of merengues. "Do what?"

"Pretend like you're one of them."

I huffed, swirling the amber liquid in my own glass. "I

don't have to pretend to be one of them. In fact, the reason they can't resist me is because I'm not. I'm like a rare fucking peacock parading around, luring them in."

Cosimo scoffed. "A peacock with poisonous claws." He took a slow sip of his drink, and then his posture shifted. "Look. It's her."

I took my time before turning toward the entrance. I already knew exactly who he meant.

Cosimo, along with the rest of the family, thought I was still working Mia. I hadn't let him in on the truth, and I wasn't planning to. I had no idea how to explain what had occurred between us.

How could I explain something I didn't understand?

My gaze finally landed on its target, and my fists clenched.

She was in a sleek, shimmering dress. The fabric caught the light like stardust. It was pink and silver—probably some cosmic connection to Venus or whatever the hell her horoscope said. I still didn't fully understand what the fuck a moon sign was.

She paused at the threshold, scanning the room.

She was alone.

I waited until her eyes found me.

When they did, I felt an electric jolt. Her shoulder lifted slightly, and then she looked away. It was like I was nothing. Like I was a stranger.

Like I was a ghost.

My jaw tightened.

The president of the club approached her with his hand outstretched. She met him with a radiant smile—one I wished was directed at me—and shook his hand.

Then his palm landed on the small of her back.

A little too fucking low.

I glowered as he guided her toward a passing waiter with

a tray of champagne flutes. She took one, her head tilting back as she laughed at something the old man said. She was animated, engaged.

What the hell did they have in common?

That guy was a million years old and looked like he needed a nap halfway through his own sentence.

And yet she gave him her attention.

Her smiles.

"Wow," Cosimo drawled, swirling the whiskey in his glass as he watched Mia. "You really are her dirty little secret, aren't you? She barely spared you a glance."

I dragged my teeth over my bottom lip, tamping down the flicker of irritation curling through my chest. "I should've known better than to bring you as my plus-one."

"Come on." He chuckled. "You've given me enough shit about Fabiana. Now it's my turn to give you shit about *her*."

I glanced at him. He was still staring at Mia, his gaze cold and assessing.

"Stop staring at her fucking ass," I muttered.

"Wasn't. But now I am."

My grip on my glass tightened. He was just trying to rile me up, and I hated that it was working.

"So are you getting any or what? Mom made it sound like you were still trying to convince her you're worth the time of day."

I exhaled through my nose. "Jesus. Is that what you and Mother talk about? My sex life?"

Across the room, my attention snagged on Andrei fucking Baranov. The son of a bitch had slithered up to Mia and the president. He was wearing the same smug, entitled expression he always did, like the entire world was an amusement park built for his entertainment. The son of a Belarusian construction magnate, he'd been raised on wealth, power, and the belief that everything was his for the taking.

And right now, he was looking at Mia.

Like she was free for his taking, too.

"Not really. I mostly talk with her about business," Cos said, pulling me back. "But she tells me when she's annoyed with you. Probably because she thinks if I apply pressure, you'll work harder."

"And do you?" I asked, barely listening. Andrei was shaking Mia's hand now, his filthy paw lingering too long. She smiled at him—sweet, innocent, oblivious—and it made my blood boil.

"I let her think I do. We both know that's not true. But if nodding and pretending I'll handle it gets her to ease up on you, I'm happy to play along."

"Didn't know you had my back like that with her," I muttered. Baranov laughed at something Mia said, his hand brushing her arm. If he kept that up, I was going to break his wrist.

Cosimo sniffed. "Yeah, well. Making up for the times I didn't."

That got me to glance at him. "The fuck are you talking about?"

"The year after Les and I moved out." He rolled his glass between his palms, suddenly looking thoughtful. "You changed that year."

A muscle ticked in my jaw. "Of course I did. That was the year I got fucking made."

"It was before that too."

I went still.

This was a conversation I wasn't about to have. Not here. Not now. Not fucking ever, if I could help it.

Baranov pulled out his phone and stepped away from Mia to take a call.

I slammed my tumbler onto the bar. "Go make some friends, Cos. I'm bored of this conversation."

I stalked after Baranov into the hallway. He was pacing away from the party, muttering something into his cell.

He didn't see me until he hung up and turned, his brows lifting in surprise. "Rom. How are you?"

"Fucking fantastic. You?"

His gaze flicked over my suit. "You look great. Hell of a suit. Where'd you get it?"

"Someone with taste styled me. Someone good."

"Oh yeah? Can I get their card?"

"I don't think so. Then we'd have something in common, and I'd rather eat shit and die."

Baranov's eyes narrowed. "What's your problem?"

"Montenegro is a nice spot."

"What?"

"Does Gracie know about your little secret family parked in that villa by the sea?"

His face turned ashen. Gracie was his fiancée, and his weak spot.

"How do you—"

"I just do." I knew every piece of dirt on everyone here. "Should I tell her?"

His nostrils flared. "What do you want?"

"Leave."

"The party?"

"And the club. Cancel your membership. Unsubscribe from the damn newsletter. I don't ever want to see your face around here again."

He bristled, fists clenching like he'd take a swing, but he wasn't that stupid. His daddy had power in Belarus, but here, he was defenseless from someone like me.

"Oh, and Andrei?" I took a step, forcing him to take one back. "Don't ever talk to the Morales girl again."

Confusion bled into his expression. "Why?"

"I don't owe you an explanation."

He hesitated and then smoothed his tie, forcing calm. "Fine."

I watched him slink to the elevator, waited until the doors swallowed him whole, and then I strode back into the room.

Mia was gone, but Cosimo was still by the bar. He smirked at me and tipped his head in the direction of the dining room.

I found her in there by the salad bar, alone. The moment she noticed me, she stiffened.

"What are you doing?" she said out of the corner of her mouth.

"Rumor is, he had a nasty bout of chlamydia last year. Thought you'd appreciate the heads-up."

"Who?"

"The guy you were speaking to earlier."

She let out a sharp breath and glared at me. "Forgive me for thinking you're full of shit."

I grinned. I liked her sweetness, but I liked her fire even more.

"You're swearing. Is that a new thing?"

"I've had to expand my vocabulary when it comes to you." She grabbed a plate at the salad bar and started piling on romaine.

I also grabbed a plate and opened my hand for her to pass me the tongs.

"Romolo, we're in public. Please leave me alone."

"Can't I also get some food? You want me to starve just because you're here?"

Her lips pressed together. "Fine."

I started filling my plate. "How have things been the last few days?"

"Busy." She didn't look at me.

"You're not going to ask how my day has been?"

"No. You do realize I had no choice but to show up at this dinner, right?"

"Are you implying I could have bowed out?" I asked. "And miss the opportunity to wear this masterpiece you made for me?"

"A masterpiece? The only thing you said after I gave it to you was, 'It'll do.'" A bitter note slipped into her voice.

Ah. That explained the hostility.

Yeah. I'd fucked that up.

"Mia, it's brilliant. But you know that. You don't need my validation."

Her hand stilled over the tomatoes, the serving spoon hovering midair. A flicker of surprise crossed her face before she buried it beneath that cool, composed exterior. "You're right. I don't. Just like I don't need you issuing me warnings about anyone."

Oh, but she did. She was too trusting. Too naïve. And I didn't know why I cared.

I'd already done the heroic—*blerg*—deed of protecting her from my family. Now I wanted to protect her from others?

Maybe I was having a quarter-life crisis?

"Damn it," I muttered.

She drizzled some dressing onto her salad. "What now?"

"Nothing. By the way, I'm talking to my cousin Caterina this week. You'll be compensated generously for your work."

"Uh-huh," she said, sounding skeptical. She didn't believe me. But I'd prove her wrong. Even sooner than she expected it.

She picked up the next pair of tongs and reached for a bread roll. Some genius decided to stack them in a precarious tower that wobbled when Mia picked one up.

Her mouth popped open. "Oh no. Oh *shoot.*"

Oh shoot. Why was it so fucking cute when she said that?

She frantically tried to stabilize the rolls with her tongs, but they tilted even more, so I grabbed another pair and helped her.

She blew out a breath. "Thanks." Then she glanced at me, her gaze dipping to my mouth. "Why are you smiling?"

I sighed. "It happens when I look at you. Can't explain it. Maybe you have a theory?" I didn't mention the weird warmth in my chest that she also brought on since the night of the storm.

Actually, I did have a theory. That night, she'd taken care of me, held me, helped me. No woman had ever done that for me before. She'd rewired something fundamental inside me, some critical connection in my brain.

The long-term effects were still unclear.

Her throat moved as she swallowed. She stared at her plate, brows pulling together, teeth grazing her lip like she suddenly had a lot on her mind. Then, after a beat, she straightened.

"We said goodbye to each other on Tuesday," she said quietly. There was no anger left in her tone, just resignation. "We both agreed that we shouldn't be in contact. Nothing has changed, except for this unfortunate coincidence with the invite. Let's just get through tonight and move on."

My mood sobered. She was right. Nothing had changed.

She was still Morales's daughter. I was still a Ferraro. If I wasn't going to use her for information, then I had no business left with her.

I cleared my throat, feigning indifference. "Fine by me."

She grabbed a small glass of chilled soup, struggling to balance it in her hands along with her plate and her purse.

I thought about the object in my pocket, the one I'd

planned to give to her today. "I'll help you. Give me your purse."

"No, Rom—"

"I'll walk you to your table, and then I'll leave you alone for the rest of the night."

"All right," she muttered. "Thank you."

I took her purse and followed behind her. As we passed my table, I dropped off my plate, freeing one hand.

Discreetly, I reached into my pocket and slipped the damned thing into the small side pocket of her bag.

A moment later, we reached her table. She placed her plate down by the name tag spelling out Mia Morales in elegant cursive, then turned back, hand outstretched for her purse.

Our fingers brushed as I passed it back.

"Thank you again," she said, meeting my gaze.

I nodded. "My pleasure."

The other people at her table were watching us curiously. They all knew who I was. Who she was.

They were probably wondering what the hell we'd been talking about.

Mia, the picture of composure, gave me a polite smile. "Enjoy your evening."

I returned the expression. "You too." Then I walked back to my seat and sat down.

We didn't speak for the rest of the evening.

But I spent the entire goddamn night watching her.

CHAPTER 23

Mia

The air in my apartment was stuffy and warm when I got home.

I kicked off the heels that had been pinching my toes all evening, walked over to the living room window, and opened it as far as it would go. A barely there breeze skated over my face.

Closing my eyes, I took a deep breath.

The seating arrangement had done me no favors. Romolo had been able to see me. I couldn't see him.

But I'd felt him.

His gaze had warmed the back of my head throughout the appetizers, the entrée, and the dessert. I'd tried to stay present, to feign interest in the people at my table, but I'd only been able to focus on bits and pieces of the conversation. I'd already forgotten most of their names. My awareness had been constantly drawn to the man I was supposed to forget.

His comment about how I made him smile had thrown me off-balance. I didn't know what to make of it. I wished he'd kept the comment to himself.

In short, the evening had been a disaster. It had brought to the surface all of my confusing, frustrating emotions.

The only way it could have been worse was if Romolo had kissed me in front of everyone. And yet I'd spent a good chunk of time at that table imagining exactly that. The way someone might imagine stepping off a train platform just to see how it would feel.

The thought should have terrified me.

It had terrified me.

But it had also made me *burn*.

I rolled my neck and decided it was time to shower, go to bed, and pray that the acute sense of loss that had blanketed me right when I left the venue would be gone when I woke up.

The chances of another coincidence putting us in a room together were slim. I wasn't going to be welcomed at any of Fabi's wedding festivities—a fact she had apologized for profusely last weekend, even after I'd assured her I knew it wasn't her decision to make.

Tonight had been goodbye for real.

Grabbing my purse off the kitchen counter, I carried it into my bedroom and dumped its contents onto the bed.

I had a large handbag collection, each one neatly stored in its dust bag when not in use. That was what I was about to do with the Bottega clutch when I felt something in the side pocket.

Huh. I didn't remember putting anything there.

Frowning, I tugged on the zipper and fished out the small item with my index finger. The clutch slipped from my grasp.

A diamond necklace.

A thin ribbon of paper was spooled around one end.

Heart pounding, I unwrapped it and saw the jagged handwriting.

Something to remember me by.

I held it by one end, slowly lowering it into the center of my open palm.

A string of diamonds. From a New York City mobster I wasn't supposed to see again. He must have slipped it into my bag when he carried it for me.

You'll be compensated generously for your work.

Was this part of that compensation? I'd made it clear I didn't want his money. Did he think this was any better?

My God. It was heavy. I didn't even want to think about how much it was worth.

What did this mean?

Was it his way of telling me my opinions didn't matter? That if he wanted to pay me, he would?

Or was this just another mind game?

I was leaning toward that option.

He wanted me to remember him. Which was the exact opposite of what I was trying to do.

For a fleeting moment, I considered texting him, demanding he take it back. But I dismissed the idea just as quickly. If Romolo Ferraro wanted to waste his money on me, that was his choice.

He could afford it.

But I'd never wear the damn thing. The necklace would spend its life tucked away. Just like my memory of him.

I opened the drawer of my vanity, lowered the necklace inside, and slammed it shut—like that would somehow lock away the tangled mess of feelings the man who'd given it to me had stirred.

CHAPTER 24

Rom

I drummed my fingers against the wheel. "This the right place?"

"That's the one," Alessio said.

"It better be worth the twenty-minute drive."

"You sure you don't want anything? The reviews are saying they've got the best pour-overs."

I huffed. "I'm good."

My brother had a habit of hyper-fixating on things. Video games. Conspiracy theories. Now—coffee.

There was a Starbucks five minutes from the palace. I'd suggested we go *there*, which had earned me the kind of look you'd give someone eating sushi with a fork. Apparently, Starbucks coffee was a notch above espresso-flavored piss. His words, not mine.

"You've lived in Brooklyn too long," I said dryly. "You're turning into a fucking hipster."

Alessio smirked but didn't argue. He patted his pockets. "Shit. I left my wallet behind. You got any cash?"

"Check the glove compartment."

He rummaged through it and then stopped. "Since when do you wear makeup?"

I frowned. "The fuck are you talking about?"

He held up a tube of lip gloss between two fingers, inspecting it like it was evidence in a crime scene.

A sharp pulse went through me.

"I don't," I said. "Some girl must've left it."

"Want me to toss it?"

"No." The word came out too fast.

Alessio's brows lifted slightly. "Oooh-kay."

I exhaled through my nose, my temper fraying. "Just go get your fucking coffee so we can get back to work."

He shrugged, put the lip gloss back, and grabbed a ten-dollar bill from the compartment. "You're always in a bad mood lately," he tossed over his shoulder before stepping out of the car.

The moment he was out of sight, I popped open the glove compartment and pulled out the tube.

It was small and sleek, and the label was starting to wear off from being carried around. I turned it over between my fingers. The familiar shape. The shade she always wore. *Berry*.

I still didn't know why I'd kept it. At least, I told myself I didn't.

A while back, I'd stashed it in the car, out of sight. Otherwise, my habit of constantly rolling it between my fingers was bound to turn into a nervous tick.

I wished I could say my life had gone back to normal after Mia and I said goodbye. That walking away had reset everything.

It hadn't.

Everything felt like it was going to shit.

My father had returned from Colombia a few days after The Golden Circle dinner. It hadn't been a good trip. The

Colombians wanted guarantees we couldn't give and refused to say who else they were negotiating with.

We were now facing two existential threats: Morales's election and the potential collapse of our long-standing deal with the Colombians.

But in a twisted way, it was working in my favor. Both of my parents were too focused on the negotiation to keep me in their crosshairs. My mother, who had been relentless in asking about Mia, had mostly dropped the subject in recent weeks. Now, she spent her time trying to pinpoint where the Colombians were thinking about taking their business.

I was worried about the family—reasonably so—but this wasn't the first time we'd been backed into a corner. We always survived.

We would survive this, too.

With Mia out of my life and out of my family's scrutiny, I should feel relieved.

I didn't.

The longer I spent away from her, the worse everything became.

Nights were the worst.

I slept even less than before. The insomnia had never been this bad—not even after the accident. I'd lie in bed, eyes closed, a movie of her playing on repeat inside my head. No off button. No escape. Sometimes I swore I could smell lily of the valley in my penthouse, a place she'd never even fucking been to.

In the midst of all this family turmoil, I should be staying productive, should be using my skill set to gather intel, find new targets...

But I couldn't bring myself to do it.

I didn't want to talk to people. Didn't want to put on an act.

I didn't even want to fuck anyone.

The thought of it—of touching someone who wasn't her—made my stomach turn.

If they didn't look like her, smell like her, moan like her...I didn't fucking want them.

I needed a distraction.

Alessio slid into the passenger seat and exhaled, lifting the giant cup he held in his hand. "It's fucking excellent. You wanna try?"

My brother didn't sleep much either. He'd go days before finally crashing when his body gave out. The work he did demanded it. When someone was close to breaking, you didn't stop just because it was dinner time.

You pushed until there was nothing left to squeeze out.

I took a sip and handed it back to him. "Not bad."

"It's a Gesha from a micro-lot in Panama, lightly roasted to preserve its jasmine and bergamot notes."

"Tastes like coffee."

He sighed. "You're a lost cause. Let's get back. I want to get a few more names from him before we wrap up for the night."

Two weeks ago, I'd called Alessio and asked if he needed an extra pair of hands at the palace.

He'd seemed surprised but told me to come by whenever I wanted.

I'd been showing up every day since.

I started the car. "It's not even four. You've got some-where else to be later?"

"I'm having dinner at Nero's with him and his wife."

I arched a brow. "Well, aren't you two fucking cozy?"

Nero De Luca was Rafael Messero's consigliere. At one point, he had a brief stint working for Alessio. The position had been meant as punishment, but somehow, the two of them had become friends.

"You bringing a date, Les?" I asked.

"Nah."

"Why not? Not seeing anyone?"

"Mind your own fucking business."

I laughed and began to drive. He was always cagey about his personal life, which made me think he didn't have much of one. In our world, the women were terrified of him because of what he did for the family. But he had to get laid once in a while, right? He was twenty-seven, good-looking, and covered in tattoos that stretched all the way down to his fingertips. Although, maybe spelling out the words "MORE PAIN" across his knuckles wasn't the best way to attract the opposite sex.

"There's gotta be someone out there for you," I said, passing through a green light. "Someone who'll even like the hair." His long, dark strands were tied in a low knot, and I liked to give him shit about it. "You just have to go looking for them, Les."

"I'm used to being alone. I don't mind it."

Lucky him. For me, solitude was the perfect breeding ground for thoughts of her.

Twenty minutes later, I parked outside the palace. Alessio and I got out and moved through the massive warehouse, past stacked shipping containers, toward the reinforced room at the center of the building—Alessio's interrogation chamber.

The guy we'd been working on was slumped over in his chair. He was a low-level recruit who'd been brought into the fold about six months ago on a recommendation from one of our made guys.

He'd turned out to be an undercover agent. It didn't seem like he'd managed to get any information we needed to worry about, but we wanted to be sure.

I narrowed my eyes. He was too still.

"Shit," Alessio swore, shoving his half-finished coffee

into my hand before rushing over. He pressed two fingers to the guy's neck, waited a beat, then muttered another curse under his breath.

"This is your fault, Rom." He glared at me. "I told you we were going too hard."

My jaw clenched. "Thought he could take it."

"That's my call to make, not yours." His sharp eyes scanned me, sizing me up. "Why the fuck have you been so goddamn angry these past few weeks? I don't need that shit in here."

Alessio was steady. Always. He had to be, given the kind of work he did. An emotional interrogator wasn't one who was good at his job. And Les was really fucking good at his job.

I exhaled through my nose. "Look, my bad. It was an accident, all right? It won't happen again."

He folded his arms, unconvinced.

"Why don't we get started on the other guy?" I offered, nodding toward the next room.

"No." He shook his head. "We're done for today." He ran a hand down his face. "You take out whatever the hell you're dealing with on a few punching bags before you come help me again."

"Fine."

"Get out of here."

I walked out, got back into my car, and sat there for a second gripping the wheel. My pulse thumped in my temple.

I didn't want to sit still.

So I drove.

The congestion was lighter than usual, but traffic in Manhattan never truly let up. Taxis honked. Pedestrians weaved through moving cars. Steam billowed from manholes, looking ghostly in the late September air. The heat had finally broken, and the city was slipping into fall. The leaves had started to change—red and orange against a backdrop of glass, steel, and brick.

I'd noticed it on my walks around the city. Walks that always, somehow, took me past Broderick Lane.

I'd seen Mia through the window a couple of times. Just glimpses. Nothing more.

On the days I saw her, I felt a little better. Lighter.

But it never lasted. A few more days would pass, and the gray would seep back in, heavier and darker than before.

Thirty minutes later, I was in the elevator, heading up to my penthouse. Inside, I kicked off my shoes, fell onto the living room sofa, and flicked on the TV.

Jurassic Park. A rerun of *The Office*. And then—*her*.

I set the remote down and leaned back against the cushions.

She was on TV a lot. Interviews. Rallies. Some ribbon-cutting ceremony or another.

For everyone else watching, Mia was a side character given a few minutes to say her piece before the cameras zoomed back in on her father.

But for me? She was the star of the fucking show.

Today, it was a rally at Washington Square Park.

The crowd was massive. Mia stood onstage behind her father, hands linked in front of her, poised and polished as always.

It took me a few seconds to notice something was off.

I braced my elbows on my knees and leaned toward the TV, narrowing my eyes.

Her skin looked ashy. Her smile wasn't quite right. Strained. Like she had to work extra hard to keep it there.

She lifted a hand and pressed her fingers to her temple.

A bad, bad feeling crawled up my spine.

She swayed.

I shot to my feet, watching as one of her father's aides stepped up to her. He caught her elbow to steady her. My relief at him being close enough to help clashed with the violent urge to snap his fingers just for touching her.

He leaned in and whispered something into her ear as he led her off the stage. She didn't say anything. She just gave the smallest of nods and leaned on him for support.

The crowd barely reacted. They were too focused on her father, hanging on whatever empty words he was feeding them.

I stared at the TV, waiting to see if the camera would pan to where she'd walked off to.

It didn't.

My heart pounded against my ribcage. "What the *fuck* are they doing to her?"

She looked exhausted. Maybe sick. Was she getting any rest? Was *anyone* taking care of her?

"Ugh!" I grabbed the remote and hurled it across the room. It slammed against the wall and clattered to the floor.

This wasn't working.

I could stay away if I knew she was fine, but keeping my distance when her piece-of-shit father and his incompetent team were running her into the ground?

No.

Fuck. No.

She deserved better than that.

I thought I'd satisfied my urge to protect her when I let her go. But it hadn't gone away. It had embedded itself in my bones, a need that wouldn't fucking quit. And with it, something else had been simmering. Something I'd tried so fucking hard to deny.

I couldn't deny it anymore.

I. Wanted. Her.

I was done sustaining myself on glimpses through

windows and memories that wouldn't let me sleep. I wanted the real thing. I wanted us in the same room, breathing the same air, having a fucking conversation.

And then I wanted more. So much more. I wanted everything she'd give me.

Even if it wouldn't be her all.

We weren't possible. Her dad was trying to put me and my entire fucking family behind bars. But I wouldn't be asking for a fairy tale.

I'd be asking to be her dirty little secret for a while.

Fucking Cosimo was right.

I tilted my head to the ceiling and dragged my palms down my face.

How the fuck was I going to pull this off when she was constantly surrounded by her father's people? I had no idea.

The only thing I was sure of was that I was done staying away.

CHAPTER 25

Mia

"What do you think about this one?" Fabi asked, turning the laptop to show me another choice for her after-party dress.

I tapped my phone against my lips. "That could work."

"But?"

"But...it's a little safe."

"Safe? Mia, it has a slit up to *here*." She traced a line up her thigh. "You remember my entire extended family and then some will be at this thing, right?"

We were hanging out at my place, our half-eaten lunch sitting in takeout containers on the coffee table. After I'd nearly collapsed from exhaustion on stage last week, Jenny had finally deemed me worthy of a few days off. She wasn't happy about it. The updated schedule she'd sent me came with clear instructions to let her know if I felt recovered sooner. She'd be glad to put me right back to work.

I opened a new tab on my computer and navigated to a website. "I don't mean safe as in not revealing. It's just stylistically boring. You're the bride. You can bring a little drama, you know? How about this brand?"

Fabi hummed as I scrolled through their latest collection of cocktail dresses.

I'd ordered one of them for a client just last night. I'd spent all day yesterday catching up on my styling work, which wasn't exactly rest, but it was close enough. It was a lot less stressful than giving speech, after speech, *after speech*.

My remaining roster of ten clients seemed stable for now. And to my surprise, after the dinner at The Golden Circle, I did actually get an email from Romolo's cousin about the newsletter.

He'd kept his word.

Two weeks after the election, once my obligations had ended, I'd be sent out to their mailing list.

The timing couldn't be more perfect.

I paused on the next dress. "What about this?" I pointed to a sculpted white gown. It was cinched tight at the waist before flowing into a dramatic floor-length skirt with a thigh-high slit. The neckline—an architectural masterpiece —featured a structured, asymmetrical cut. One shoulder was left bare, while the other was adorned with a folded satin detail.

"Whoa," Fabi breathed.

"Exactly."

"You always do this," she whispered. "Make me rethink everything until I'm obsessed with your choice."

"And I do it for free. Aren't you so lucky to have me as a friend?"

She elbowed me. "Hey, I'm convinced one of the reasons why you're so good at this is because I gave you free rein to edit my closet all through boarding school. That was valuable experience."

"True. You, Zo, and Nina were always game to wear the crazy looks I'd pieced together," I said with a laugh, setting my laptop down on the coffee table.

Fabi picked up her mug and sighed. "Are you sure you're

okay with this? I feel terrible that you're helping me pick out my outfit and you won't even be at the wedding."

I shrugged. "It is what it is."

Did it suck that I'd miss my best friend getting married? Yeah, it sure did. But there was a silver lining. I wouldn't have to spend the evening trying to avoid Romolo.

I was making progress on the whole forgetting him thing, I supposed. Not nearly as much as I would have liked. I still found myself daydreaming about him, wondering where he was and what he was doing. Wondering if he still thought about me. Probably not. I was sure he'd moved on. There wasn't even anything real to move on *from*. Just an unexpected, unwanted, and utterly inappropriate spark of wild attraction between two people who were *definitely* not meant to be.

I'd buried myself in work in the weeks that had followed our goodbye.

As easy as it would have been to blame Jenny for the certifiable insanity that was my schedule, it wasn't all her fault.

I could have pushed back on some of the things she wanted me to do. But I didn't. I said yes to it all with a smile, losing myself in a whirlwind of campaign events and client meetings where I bent over backward to meet everyone's expectations.

Until it had caught up to me.

Fabi sipped on her tea, still looking crestfallen about the wedding.

"Hey." I reached out and squeezed her knee. "You'll have a great time. Nina and Zo will be there, and you know they've got your back. There's no point in being upset about something we can't change."

She sighed. "I know. You're right. I just wish..."

"That my dad wasn't trying to put your future father-in-law in jail?" I asked.

She winced. "Yeah."

My phone rang. It was a client.

"I've got to take this," I said to Fabi, getting to my feet. Eliza wasn't the type of client to call just to chat. She was one of the biggest influencers in fashion right now, with a brand that had skyrocketed in the past few years. If she was calling, something was up.

"Hey, Mia. You're not going to believe what just happened."

I leaned against the kitchen island, which was only a few steps away from the sofa in my tiny East Village apartment. "Is everything okay with the dress?"

This year, I was styling Eliza for one of the most important fashion events in the city—the Stark Patrons Ball. This year, the theme was "*Notte A Venezia.*" It was such a big deal that we'd finalized her highly intricate Venetian gown months in advance. It was currently tucked away in a breathable garment bag in her closet—where, per my strict instructions, she'd also placed a humidifier to keep the air just right. No moisture, no disasters.

"If the dress wasn't okay, the first thing you would have heard when you picked up would have been my hysterical crying. It's totally fine. Don't worry."

"Thank God," I said with a relieved laugh. "So what's up?"

"My plus-one can't make it to the ball anymore, and I was wondering... Would you like to come with me?"

I blinked at one of the bedazzled canvases hanging on my wall. "You're kidding."

"I'm completely serious. I'd love for you to be there."

"What happened to your cousin? You were going to take him, right?"

"He has to stay in LA for some work thing. An audition, I think." She sighed. "He's really trying to make it as an actor. So what do you say?"

I nibbled on my fingernail. "Are you sure? There isn't anyone else you want to invite instead?"

"I can't think of anyone who'll appreciate the atmosphere more than you. It'll be a smorgasbord of fashion. Plus, you worked so hard on that stunning gown. I want to do something special to thank you."

This was...unexpected, to say the least. Eliza and I had a great professional relationship, but it had never quite crossed into friendship. There were people in the city who'd kill for an invite to this event, and she was extending it to me?

"Can I think about it?"

"What's there to think about?"

"I have to check my schedule," I said. "You know it's been crazy with everything going on."

"I'm sure your dad's people will understand. It's really a no-brainer."

Was it just me, or was she being a little pushy?

"I really appreciate the invitation. Let me get back to you."

She cleared her throat. "Right, of course. But don't think for too long. It's soon!"

Very soon. I'd have to scramble to find something to wear. I wouldn't need to go overboard, but I couldn't show up in a little black dress either. There was no bigger faux pas at these things than not taking the theme seriously.

"Who was it?" Fabi asked, tearing her attention from her laptop as I sat back down beside her.

I told her the gist of the conversation. "It seems crazy to say no, but is it really a good use of my time? Jenny's eager to put me back to work, and here I am asking for another night off?"

"You deserve a night of fun after the year you've had," Fabi urged. "You've definitely earned it. Just say yes."

One night of fun. Could I give myself that?

Maybe this was exactly what I needed to finally forget about Romolo.

I took out my phone and sent Eliza a text.

Her response was immediate.

Wonderful!!! I can't wait.

An hour later, I hurried to the studio. With less than a week until the ball, I needed to figure out what I was going to wear fast. There was a velvet dress I had tucked away that I might be able to use. It had a fitted bodice with long sleeves, a square neckline, and a lush, voluminous skirt. Alone, it was much too plain, but I could alter it and add some embellishments. Since my days off were numbered, there was no time to waste.

Leaves crunched under my boots as I made my way toward SoHo. I liked New York in the fall, though summer was my favorite season. This last summer, however, felt like it had come and gone without me truly experiencing any of it.

I hoped next year would be better, though I wasn't as confident as I wanted to be.

The campaign buzzed with energy, and while we were all trying to stay levelheaded, everything pointed toward my dad's victory. I was happy for him, but...I was also anxious.

If my dad won, he was preparing for an all-out war against the Ferraros. He was already working with the DA to build a bulletproof case. I didn't know the details, but the thought of Romolo's name potentially appearing in the case made my stomach twist.

In addition, Jenny had started hinting at what my obligations might look like once he was elected.

Obligations I wasn't supposed to have.

When she'd spoken to me about it, Romolo's words had played at the back of my head. *Tell me...who takes care of you?"*

His delivery had been unnecessarily rude, but...it had made me think.

Was there ever going to be a time when my parents wholeheartedly supported my career? Or would it always feel like a negotiation—me trying to carve out time to follow my ambitions, while they told me my time was better spent somewhere else?

I wasn't opposed to still attending an event here and there with my dad after he became mayor, but if it looked like it was snowballing into something more, I'd have to put my foot down. No matter how uncomfortable the thought of doing that made me feel.

Wrapping my arms around myself, I turned onto Broderick Lane. I was still a few blocks away from the studio when something made me stop in my tracks.

I stared at the storefront to my left.

It was Kassandra's studio. Or at least, it had been.

It was empty. A For Lease sign dangled from the door, swaying in the late afternoon breeze.

What? Kassandra had been in that space for at least ten years, and now she was just...gone. The last time I'd walked by here was maybe a week ago. It hadn't been empty then.

I stepped closer, peering through the glass, half expecting to see some kind of note or a sign announcing to a new location. But there was nothing. Just the empty space inside, stripped bare.

Strange.

When I reached my studio, I barely had my coat off before I was flipping open my laptop. There had to be something online. A post, an announcement—something.

But I didn't even have to search.

The answer was sitting in my inbox.

A message from a former client—one who'd left me for Kassandra—asking if I'd consider taking her back.

Apparently, Kassandra had sent out a notice to her client list just this morning to say she was shutting down her business and moving to Vermont.

I pressed my fingers to my lips. *Wow.* That business was her baby.

What happened?

CHAPTER 26

Mia

"Eliza! Over here! Look this way!" photographers called out, vying for my client's attention.

I fixed a wrinkle in her skirt. "Go ahead."

"You're not coming with me?" she asked, a flicker of surprise crossing her face. She looked stunning in her custom-made brocade gown, a masterpiece that had taken me and a local designer weeks to create.

"I'm going to head straight inside." For Eliza, this was a big red-carpet moment, but for me, it was a chance to spend one night under the veil of anonymity.

A mask—velvet with a pearl trim that matched the details on my gown—covered the top half of my face.

It. Was. Glorious.

I had no plans to take it off at any point tonight. The people here had no clue who I was, and I'd made Eliza promise not to out me.

I moved behind the backdrop and walked down a narrow path that was there for anyone who wanted to go directly to the museum entrance. The venue, a beautifully restored historic building from the 1940s, had originally been a family estate for one of the city's wealthiest dynasties, the Starks. Now, it was an intimate art museum with collections that rotated a few times a year.

My black velvet gown rustled around me as I stepped inside the covered courtyard where the welcome cocktails were taking place. I picked up a flute of rosé with a maraschino cherry at the bottom and found a quiet spot near the edge of the courtyard.

From here, I had a clear view of the space. Guests were slowly trickling in dressed in a kaleidoscope of flowing fabrics, intricate embroidery, and elaborate masks.

I loved it.

A grin tugged on my lips. I was so glad I'd listened to Fabi and Eliza and agreed to come. I planned to spend the evening melting into the background and feasting my eyes on the spectacle around me.

No reporters. No interviews. No speeches.

My smile faltered when I caught my reflection in one of the mirrors hanging on the wall. My hand was resting just above my chest, my fingers mindlessly tracing back and forth over the diamonds resting against my skin.

Romolo's diamonds.

It was the necklace I'd sworn I'd never wear. And I'd meant it. It had stayed tucked away in that drawer right up until tonight.

The stylist in me hadn't been able to ignore how perfectly it complemented the pearl-trimmed neckline of my dress. Just before I'd left, I'd tried it on, and, against my better judgment, I'd given in.

It was an impulsive decision. One I was already regretting. Now, every time I looked in the mirror, I'd think of him.

Brilliant, Mia. Tonight was supposed to help you get him out of your head.

I sighed. Guess I'd just have to avoid checking my reflection for the rest of the evening.

Candles flickered in the centerpieces, tuxedoed servers balanced tiny espresso cups on trays, and a five-piece band played a waltz from a small stage in the corner of the ballroom.

Eliza was already on the dance floor with a partner, along with a few other couples. I was still finishing dessert. When we first sat down for dinner, she'd introduced me to the people at our table as her stylist, Mia. Apart from a magazine editor who seemed vaguely curious, no one appeared to recognize me.

Exactly how I wanted it.

"Coffee, miss?"

"I'm alright, thank you," I said to the server at the same time that my gaze caught on a familiar silhouette on the other side of the ballroom.

Is that...?

I blinked, and he was gone, lost behind the sea of masks and Venetian gowns moving across the dance floor.

No, it couldn't be Romolo. I was most likely imagining things again. The grueling schedule of the last few weeks had done a number on me. I could have sworn I'd seen Romolo walk by the studio on more than one occasion, but by the time I'd made my way over to the window to get a closer look, there was no one there.

"You don't have a drink," Erik, the celebrity hairstylist from LA who was seated next to me, said. "Would you like to grab one at the bar?"

I forced myself to give him my full attention and smiled. "That sounds great." Was it a good idea to drink when I was already mildly questioning my grasp on reality? Probably not, but screw it. At least I could distract myself with Erik's company for a little while.

Erik got me a glass of red wine and a gin and tonic for himself. We moved to one of the high-top tables scattered on the edges of the dance floor where he began telling me about some of the projects he'd worked on this year. Despite trying so hard to stay focused, my attention was split. I tried to follow what he was saying. I really did. But my gaze kept being pulled back to the faces around the room.

The dark-haired man I'd seen was wearing a mask. It hid most of his face. Yes, he had a strong jaw, but Romolo wasn't the only man who had one of those. He also wasn't the only tall man with broad shoulders and—

"Mia."

My eyes snapped to Erik. Shoot, did he ask me something? I was about to fess up that I missed it, when he smiled and said, "Would you like to dance?"

"Sure." We'd finished our drinks, though I was so distracted I couldn't even remember drinking mine.

Maybe a dance would stop my mind from conjuring ghosts.

Erik's hand was warm in mine as he led me onto the dance floor. He looked dapper in his damask jacket. A deep-red cravat was tied in an elaborate knot around his neck, resting over his high-collared shirt.

We stopped amidst the twirling couples, and Erik's hands settled on my waist. He smiled at me. "So will you ever show me what's under that mask?"

I blinked, caught off guard by the flirtatious note in his tone. Until now, he'd seemed friendly, but I hadn't picked up *that* kind of a vibe from him.

Then again, had I really been paying attention?

There was a spark in his gaze. Maybe the gin and tonic had emboldened him.

I forced a polite smile. "I'm not sure. The mystery of it is kind of fun, don't you think?"

The way his smile faltered told me he'd expected a different response. He'd taken his own mask off a while ago.

I forced myself to study his features.

Handsome, yes, but...I felt nothing.

No acceleration in my pulse. No spark inside my belly. Nothing compared to the feverish heat I felt around Romolo.

It was depressing.

"Well, then," Erik said lightly, "I'll just have to see you unmasked some other time. Could I get your number?"

"Not if you value your ability to breathe without a respirator."

A shiver tumbled down my spine at that familiar deep voice. There was no mistaking it.

Erik froze, confusion and then unease clear on his face. He stared at the man whose presence I could feel against my back. "Excuse me?"

"You heard me," Romolo replied, his tone sharp. He stepped forward, appearing like a dark sentinel in my periphery. I refused to look at him, refused to acknowledge him even as every inch of my skin prickled with awareness.

"Ignore him," I muttered.

Erik's brow furrowed. "Do you know this guy?"

"Unfortunately, yes," I said, my eyes locked on Erik's cravat.

"You wound me." Romolo's voice dropped, like whatever he was about to say next was meant only for my ears. "And here I'd hoped you'd be happy to see me."

My head snapped toward him. "Did you real—"

My. Dear. Lord.

Like me, he was in black velvet. He wore a sexy, tailored Tom Ford that would have made him look like the perfect gentleman if it wasn't for that arrogant smirk, the snake tattoo peering over the collar of his shirt, and the rude words coming out of his mouth. The look was understated, but he wore it so damn well that it didn't matter.

Warmth pooled low in my belly. Those sparks I was just missing were back in full force.

My body was clearly happy to see him, but my mind knew better than that.

"You shouldn't set your hopes on things with a zero probability of happening," I said, meeting his gaze.

His lips twitched beneath his mask, and I saw his gray eyes twinkling with dark amusement.

The fact that I'd recognized him in a split second from across the room was *so* irritating. It was like my senses had somehow gotten attuned to him without my consent.

"My friend doesn't seem interested in talking to you," Erik said with a defiant tilt to his chin.

"She's not your fucking friend. You just met her."

"Do I need to call security?"

"Do that, and I'll break each one of your fingers before I break your neck."

Erik's hands fell away from my waist.

For God's sake. "Excuse his twisted sense of humor, Erik. He doesn't get out much."

"She's the only one who knows how to handle me." Romolo's tone was infuriatingly smug. "Now, if you'll excuse us, your presence is no longer required. Leave."

Erik glanced at me, clearly unsure what he should do.

I gave him a terse nod. I didn't want to cause a scene and draw attention to myself. "It's okay."

Erik stepped away, and Romolo wasted no time. He wrapped an arm around my waist and pulled me close. Warm fingers brushed against the bare skin of my upper back, lightly nudging the clasp of my necklace.

"Fifty carats look good on you," he murmured.

My eyes widened. Fifty carats? Fifty?!

He was certifiable.

"Take. It. Off," I said through clenched teeth. "I don't want it."

"And yet here you are wearing it."

I reached for the clasp, but he caught my wrists and held them between us.

"Shhh. Calm down," he said and then leaned forward and kissed the tops of my knuckles, his eyes never leaving mine.

My pulse skittered, and I stared at him in shock.

We were in public. There were hundreds of people around us. Someone would see us and—

The masks.

That's right. We were hidden in plain sight.

And yet he'd recognized me. Just like I'd recognized him.

"How did you know I'd be here?" My voice shook.

He released my wrists and settled his large, warm hands on my waist. My palms flattened against his chest.

"I made sure you'd be here."

"Excuse me?"

"Eliza and I are connected through a mutual friend. I asked her to let her date stay home and invite you instead. I needed to find a way to talk to you in person, and you wouldn't have agreed to that if I'd asked."

My eyes widened. He'd set this up. I'd *known* something was off when Eliza had been so pushy when she called. She'd probably been instructed to get me to agree to come or else.

"Did you threaten my client if she didn't go along with your scheme?" I demanded, appalled at the thought.

"I didn't need to," he said. "Most smart people in this city know it's good to have a Ferraro owe them a favor."

Yes, based on what my father had told me, that much

was true. Just a few days ago, I'd overheard him venting about all the people the Ferraros had in their pocket.

I stared at him, confused by those kisses, confused by the effort he'd made to arrange for us to meet. "Romolo, all this to talk? What's there to talk about?"

"Plenty." His gaze narrowed. "Why don't we start with what the fuck happened to you up on that stage last week?"

I frowned. "You heard about it?" The team had made an effort to bury any articles that mentioned my stumbling, and it hadn't become a big story.

"I saw it, Mia. On TV. You almost fell."

He'd watched the rallies? I tucked that piece of information away for a later review. "I got a bit lightheaded. That's it."

"That's it?" His hold on me tightened. "It's a bad look. You don't want rumors about Morales exploiting his daughter at the expense of her health making the news."

He was making it into a far bigger deal than it was. And why? Was he worried about me? "What do you care? I'd assume any negative press about my dad would be celebrated by your family."

His jaw ticked. "How do you feel now?"

Frustration bubbled up inside of me at the way he'd avoided my question. "Romolo, enough. Don't tell me you went to all this trouble to ask me about my health."

His gaze darkened. The masks we wore were the only reason we could have this conversation, but right now, I wanted to rip his off so that I could see his face. He'd always been hard to read. Now, it was practically impossible.

"What do you really want?" I asked.

A beat passed.

"You."

My heart leaped and then plummeted a second later.

More games. I was so tired of playing them with him.

I stopped mid-dance and pushed against his chest. "Let go of me."

His hold on me only tightened. "Listen to me," he murmured, bringing his lips close to my ear. "Please."

"Just when I'd managed to forget about you, you waltz right back into my life," I spat out. It was a lie. I wondered if he could tell.

He waited for me to still before he resumed spinning me around the room. "Lucky you," he said. "You don't want to know the things I've done to try to forget you for even a minute these past few weeks. None of them worked. You haven't left my mind for longer than a breath."

My pulse trembled.

"I can't fucking sleep. Every time I close my eyes, I see you so vividly that I can practically taste you." Romolo leaned in, brushing his lips against my temple. "I don't know what the fuck you've done to me, Berry, but I need to get you out of my system. And I think you need to get me out of yours too."

I should've kneed him in the groin—the way I did the first day we met—and fled the scene.

But I couldn't. Because despite being so damn frustrated with him, with the situation, I could relate to the feeling.

"Berry?" I asked, buying myself more time to think.

He lifted his hand and dragged his thumb over my bottom lip, pulling it down as he did it. "That's what these look like. That's what you taste like." Behind his mask, his gaze flared. "Everywhere."

The memory of him tasting me off his fingers made my breath catch. "What exactly are you proposing?"

"Simple. You. Me. A sturdy bed with a headboard, and a box of condoms. Remember how you said I hadn't earned you moaning my name? Let me fucking earn it."

Oh. *Oh.*

I teetered somewhere between insulted and turned on. He wasn't here to woo me. He was being upfront about what he wanted.

His eyes were focused on me like I was prey.

And damn it all to hell, I *was* turned on. Even though I knew it was all so, so risky and wrong.

"It's eleven. If we leave now, you'll be screaming it by midnight," he said roughly. He spread his palm open over my waist, moving his thumb up my ribcage and brushing it against the side of my breast.

My nipples tightened immediately. It was getting hard to breathe. "How do I know you're not a bad lay?"

That earned me a chuckle. "Think of what I did to you with just my fingers. Now imagine those replaced with my tongue and a nine-inch—"

"Okay, I got it." My face felt like it was about to melt off. My pussy freaking *clenched*. Was my headboard sturdy *enough*? "To be clear, you're proposing we do this tonight?"

"For a start." His voice was so low and tense. "We can continue until we decide we've had enough of each other."

"Just tonight." The masks gave us cover. I could bring him upstairs without the concierge seeing his face. But beyond that, it was too risky. "Otherwise, I'll have problems."

"I can deal with your problems. Dealt with Kassandra, didn't I?"

WHAT?

I stumbled over my feet.

No. It couldn't be. "That was you?"

His hands twitched on my waist. "I didn't like how she talked to you that day. I should have done it earlier, but better late than never."

My mouth was agape.

A mobster had run one of my competitors out of town. At least, I hoped that was *all* he'd done.

Was she still even alive?!

Heat flashed over my body. The floor tilted. The room seemed to spin even though we weren't moving anymore.

"Mia?"

My eyelids lowered. I knew what was coming, but I couldn't stop it.

"Don't let me fall," I whispered as everything around me faded to black.

CHAPTER 27

Rom

"Mia. Mia, can you hear me?"

She was completely limp. Her forehead pressed against my chest as I held her upright, her arms hanging slack at her sides.

Panic thundered in my ears, drowning out the music.

I shook her lightly. "Mia."

She didn't respond.

"Fuck." I had to get her out of here. To a doctor. To someone who could help her and tell me what the fuck had just happened.

My hands tightened on her waist, ready to haul her over my shoulder so I could carry her through the crowd fireman style, but then she stirred.

"Hey. You okay?"

She tipped her head back, looking at me with unfocused eyes through her mask. Her skin was paler than usual, her forehead glistening with a thin layer of sweat. She blinked at me, confused.

"Say something," I pleaded. My heart felt like it was on the brink of stopping. What was this? Not exhaustion. She was fine seconds ago when she was negotiating with me. Then, in the blink of an eye, she was unconscious.

This wasn't normal. Was she sick?

"Get me out of here." Her voice was weak. She clasped my shoulder with one hand. "I need air."

"I've got you."

I led her through the crowd, my arm wrapped securely around her waist. The people around us scattered the moment they saw the murderous look on my face. We moved quickly, weaving through the galleries filled with milling guests until we reached the exit and stepped out into the cool evening air.

Mia ripped off her mask and sucked in a deep breath. She was still tucked against me, and I wasn't planning on letting go of her anytime soon.

She'd said not to let her fall. Like she'd known what was coming. Whatever this was, it hadn't been a surprise to her the way it'd been to me.

We sat down on the front steps of the museum. Her color was slowly returning. I rubbed my palm against her hip. "Better?"

"Yeah." She pressed the heel of her palm against her forehead and sighed. "It always happens at the worst time."

It. What the fuck was *it*, exactly? I wanted to interrogate her and demand a full review of her medical history, but since I was the guy who'd just told her he wanted to fuck her out of his system a few minutes ago, it didn't feel like I'd earned the right.

I didn't *just* want to fuck her. But it was the one thing I thought she might actually give me.

And she'd been ready to.

Until "it" happened.

Funny how the only fucking thing I wanted now was for her to be okay.

"Is 'it' curable?" I asked, watching her closely.

"No."

My stomach plummeted. I refused to believe that. She just needed a better doctor. I doubted Morales had gone out of his way to get his daughter the best care she could get, given how busy he was showing his fucking face on every TV network in the city. Obviously, she wasn't a priority.

Mia twisted under my arm, her gaze meeting mine. "Kassandra. Is she... Please tell me she's okay."

"She's in Vermont. Opening a new studio." I needed to get someone to hack into Mia's medical records so that I could have the full picture. We had people on our team who could do it—Jimmy. Clive. If needed, I'd even ask fucking Messero for some help.

She exhaled in relief. "Next time—although I pray there is no next time—lead with that, would you? The words 'dealt with Kassandra' coming from someone like you could mean a variety of things."

"Yeah. Fine," I said, distracted. I couldn't give a fuck about Kassandra, but of course, Mia, who'd just fucking *collapsed*, was worried more about others than herself.

She rolled her head, sighed, and straightened out her back. "Okay. Let's go."

We did need to go. To a doctor who could examine her and run every test there was to run.

I made a signal to the guy behind the valet stand. He nodded and broke into a light jog to get my car. It wasn't far from the entrance. I'd handed him a bill when I arrived to park it up front.

"I'll text you my address."

I gave her a sharp look. Her address? "What for?"

A blush colored her cheeks. "We're going to my place, right? Like we...discussed."

My face twitched. Was she crazy? She still wanted to fuck tonight?

Yeah. No. Not until I knew what was happening to her and had a detailed plan for how to fix it.

"Wanna tell me what's wrong with you first?"

She dropped her hands in her lap and stared out into the street. "I don't see why I should."

Un-fucking-believable. "How about because I want to be sure you don't have another episode like that while I'm inside you?"

The blush deepened. "That's not how it works."

My Aston Martin appeared in front of us. I helped her to her feet, deposited her into the passenger seat, and went around to the driver's side.

I untied my mask and tossed it into the center console while the car's engine purred to life. Doc lived in Midtown, not far from here. I didn't make a habit of showing up at his place—he usually came to us—but it would be faster that way.

My foot pressed on the gas.

"I live in East Village," she said.

"I know where you live."

"Uh, okay. We'll come back to how you know that after you tell me why you're taking us the wrong way."

"I'm taking you to a doctor." And I was going to be in the same room where I could hear everything being said. Whatever this was, there was bound to be some clinical trial somewhere that would get her all back to good.

"Romolo, I don't need to see a doctor. I told you, I'm fine."

"And I've decided to ignore you, since you're obviously not. People don't just pass out like that while in the middle of a dance," I ground out, frustrated by her nonchalance.

She rubbed her temples. "I can't risk being seen with you at a hospital."

"I'm not taking you to a hospital. I'm taking you to my family's doctor. He's on our payroll, and he won't say a word to anyone."

"That's unnecessary. You need to calm down."

"I *am* calm." The fuck I was. I was angry at her for being so cagey and at the world for making her sick in the first place.

"It's called vasovagal syncope."

Panic gripped my chest. That sounded bad. Terrible, really. Did it have something to do with seizures? Was it a brain condition? Fuck.

She huffed. "God, you look like I just told you I'm dying."

"Are you?"

"*No.* It's a condition where the vagus nerve overreacts to certain triggers. It makes your heart rate and blood pressure drop suddenly, causing you to faint."

"And?"

"And nothing. I just try to manage it. It's not a big deal."

That was objectively untrue. "What if you were behind the wheel?"

"I rarely drive. I don't even own a car."

"And if you're alone somewhere? With no one there to catch you?"

She hesitated. "Yeah...that could be dangerous. But it's never happened when I'm alone. It usually happens when I get some surprising news." She shot me a look. "Like when someone tells me they ran my rival out of town."

My shoulders squared. *I* caused this?

"Why did you do that, Romolo?"

I stopped at a red light and closed my eyes for a second. Jesus fucking Christ. She'd just cost me a decade of my life —first from worrying that this was some incurable disease that would put her in an early grave, and now from realizing that I was the one who'd triggered the episode.

"Because I fucking felt like it, all right?" I snapped. I couldn't tell her it was because taking care of her problems gave me some sick sense of satisfaction. Because I'd derived pleasure from putting someone who'd hurt her in their place. These urges, these *feelings*, were all so fucking new to me, and I was still figuring out how to deal with them all.

At the next intersection, I took a right turn in the direction of her apartment.

"I'm sorry," I bit out. "For making you pass out."

Her stare warmed my cheek. "It's okay. You didn't know." A beat passed. "You can make it up to me."

My gaze sliced her way. "I'm not convinced you're well enough to handle what I want to do to you."

"I can handle it," she said coyly.

I scanned her for any sign she wasn't fine.

Her color had fully returned. She was biting lightly on her bottom lip as she stared ahead, like she had something on her mind.

I'd bet my entire fucking fortune that something was me and her destroying her bed.

My cock thickened. If she was game, who was I to deny her? And based on where we'd left our negotiation, all she was giving me was this one night.

Of course, I planned to use the night to convince her to give me another.

Then another.

Then another.

I'd take whatever scraps she gave me until the inevitable wave of destruction that always followed me got too close to the shore.

And when it did, I'd walk away. For good.

CHAPTER 28

Mia

Romolo parked the car in a miraculously open space a block away from my building and cut the engine.

I glanced at my phone. "Well, you wasted a bunch of time driving the wrong way. It's a quarter to midnight. Probably not enough time—"

"Get out of the car, Mia," he said, his voice low and calm as he pulled his mask back on.

My skin buzzed with anticipation as I opened the door. The sports car was so low that I had to wait for Romolo to round the hood and help me to my feet. The goosebumps on my skin had nothing to do with the cold, but when he saw them, his jaw clenched, and he took out a coat from the trunk and tossed it over my shoulders.

Then he wrapped his hand around mine and didn't let go as we power walked to the entrance of my building.

I was making questionable choices. I knew that. Romolo was Gino Ferraro's son. A man with a crooked moral compass who'd sent my business rival out of state because he "felt like it." I had no doubt it was far from the worst thing he'd ever done.

But all those things didn't change the cold, hard fact that I was drawn to him. And I was tired of resisting it.

We had a spark. An attraction that we'd tried to put out with distance, but that hadn't worked.

It was time to try something else.

The concierge at the front desk of my building made some comment about our outfits, but all I could muster in response was a breathless giggle. Romolo didn't even look at him. He just dragged me to the elevators and punched at the button with impatient force.

Ding.

We stepped inside. Romolo pressed the button for my floor—somehow he knew that too—and the doors slid shut.

The next thing I knew, he was on me. I gasped as my back hit the elevator wall, his hands gripping my hips, his mouth crashing against mine like he was starved for it.

The kiss was urgent. Greedy. His hips rolled into me, and I whimpered at the feel of his thick, hard length pressing into my stomach.

"Fucking finally," he muttered, teeth grazing my bottom lip before sucking it into his mouth. "I've been burning for you, Berry. Feels like a fucking disease."

His words made my blood thrum. "Charming," I managed to say as his fingers dipped inside the neck of my dress. "You really know how to make a girl feel special."

He pinched my nipple and placed a kiss along my jaw. "You are special." His hot breath brushed against my ear. "Your cunt might be the only cure."

I moaned at the filth coming out of his mouth. I'd never been with a guy who talked like that, and I'd never expected how it would turn me on.

His lips moved to my neck, and his teeth scraped against sensitive skin. "Can't fucking wait to be inside you."

I was so ready. I wanted this man to do dirty, filthy things to me. Things I'd sometimes imagined, but had always been too shy, too scared, to mention to any of the boyfriends that I'd had.

With Romolo?

I wasn't scared. The raw, carnal part of me I'd hidden away was ravenous for him. We only had tonight. There was no time to ease into it. No reason to hold anything back.

I wanted to be used. Spanked. Fucked so hard that every time I took a step for the next few days, I'd feel a twinge that reminded me of him.

It was depraved. It was unhinged.

And it had me soaking wet.

He carried me from the elevator to my door and made out with my neck while I fumbled for my key inside my purse.

"Faster," he growled, voice thick with need.

"As if you're not the reason I'm struggling," I panted, finally closing my fingers around the keychain.

His hand cupped my breast.

I dropped the keys.

He made a low, frustrated noise, set me on my feet, and snatched the keys up himself.

The lock clicked open.

We stumbled inside.

I hung his coat on a hook while he ripped his mask off and threw it aside.

"Bedroom," he said, obviously uninterested in familiarizing himself with where I lived. I didn't blame him. I was so turned on that I felt like I was about to combust.

"Here." I moved toward the bedroom door, feeling him close at my back.

The moment he saw the bed, he tossed me onto it. I barely had time to flick on the bedside lamp before he crawled on top of me and busied himself with the bodice of my dress, looking for a way to get it off.

"Buttons. On the back."

He flipped me over like I was a doll and swore. "Mia, there's a hundred of them."

I giggled into the duvet. "Sorry."

"I'll rip it open."

"Don't you dare. I love this dress."

He made a frustrated noise and turned me back over, his dark eyes burning into mine. "No fucking time." He shoved my skirt up to my waist, dragged me to the edge of the bed, and dropped to his knees.

His lips found my inner thigh, brushing over the sensitive skin. I erupted in shivers as he moved higher, closer to where I really wanted him, his tongue darting out to taste my flesh.

My clit pulsed in anticipation. It had been a very long time. I'd been too busy to even get myself off these days.

His nose bumped against the gusset of my panties. I heard him inhale, which made me blush, but the needy groan that followed was profoundly flattering.

One of his hands tightened around my thigh. "Did you go swimming earlier?"

My face heated. "Shut up."

His finger hooked around the wettest part of my underwear. "These are ruined, Berry. I think I'll keep them, though."

I gasped when his finger made the slightest contact with my clit. I was already so sensitive and engorged. My pussy was practically begging to be touched.

He tugged on the fabric, dragging the soaked panties down my legs and carefully pulling them over my heels. We were in such a rush I was still wearing my Jimmy Choos.

His gaze met mine. "Five minutes left."

"Doubt you can do it," I challenged.

He smirked. "Brace yourself, sweetheart."

And then he slung my thighs over his shoulders, grabbed two fistfuls of my ass, and brought me right up to his mouth.

The first lick sent a shock through my system. I moaned, my eyes wide as I stared at the ceiling and wondered how his mouth could be so *hot*.

He did it again, spreading me open and licking all the way from my ass to my clit, until every nerve ending I had stood at rapt attention. When he started drawing tight circles around the bud, a wave of spasms ran through my body.

I clutched the duvet, holding on for dear life as everything inside me began to tighten like a coil. The view of his dark head between my thighs only got me hotter, but I couldn't look away.

I liked seeing him there. *So much.*

His fingers teased my opening before sliding in. I was so wet, there was barely any friction. My pussy clenched, and a rush of warmth spread through me. God, this was intense. I wasn't sure I was going to survive the part at the end.

He kept lapping at me as he curled his fingers just so and—

"Ahh!" I dug the backs of my heels into him and arched off the bed. I was right there, right on the edge. "Oh God. Ohhh Jesus."

"Wrong name." His breath was hot against my aching pussy. "Be a good girl and play by the rules."

I tugged on his hair—I *needed* that mouth on me again— and he obliged, circling his tongue over my clit and working me into a frenzy.

And then he sucked. Hard.

My body tensed, the pressure in my core almost too much until—

The coil snapped.

Pleasure slammed into me.

And because I *was* a good girl who followed rules, it was his name I moaned as I shattered.

CHAPTER 29

Rom

Mia was still twitching as I slid her thighs off my shoulders and sat back on my heels to admire my handiwork.

Fuck, that was the prettiest pussy I'd ever seen.

It glistened with her wetness, dripping down her ass and pooling on the duvet.

She moved to close her legs, but my hands tightened on her thighs, keeping her spread open. "Let me look at it," I growled.

Her muscles relaxed. I loved that she was indulging my new obsession.

My eyes traced over those pink, puffy folds. I imagined feeding my cock between them and shuddered. I was so fucking hard that I was pulsating.

With effort, I tore my gaze away. If I wanted to last more than a single thrust, I needed to cool down.

She was still catching her breath, so I decided it was time to get her heels off. I was pretty sure I had marks from them on my back—not that I minded. Making her fall apart had been glorious. Somewhere in the top five experiences of my life. She tasted just like I remembered, like a ripe fucking raspberry—sweet with a little tang.

I grabbed her foot and propped it on top of my thigh. There was a thin strap around her ankle, held together with the world's tiniest clasp—what the fuck was up with women and microscopic closures on everything? I undid it and pulled the shoe off. Her toes were painted.

Pink.

I slid my thumb over them.

Then I did the same with her other foot.

"Thanks," she said weakly.

The next item on my list of things I needed to remove from her body was that dress. Yeah, she looked stunning in it when we were on the dance floor, but now it was just a nuisance.

I sank onto the bed beside her, gave her a bruising kiss, and then flipped her face down onto the mattress.

"Fuck me," I grumbled as my fingers closed around the first button. "They're tiny and the same color as the fabric. How the fuck did you get this on in the first place?"

One popped open.

"Patience," she said.

Then two.

"Not my fucking virtue."

Three.

"Thank you for not ripping into it like a caveman."

Four.

"Don't thank me yet. I'm still considering it."

She laughed.

Slowly, the two sides of the dress parted, revealing swaths of smooth, golden-brown skin.

I wasn't even close to being done, but I couldn't fucking resist. I leaned down and pressed my lips to her spine, kissing vertebra by vertebra as they appeared. Goosebumps spread over her skin.

It dawned on me I never did shit like this. I wasn't gentle when I fucked. But with her, I couldn't help it.

I wanted to savor this.

After another few buttons, the dress had finally loosened enough for me to slide it off her shoulders. My gaze raked over the expanse of her bare back, and I traced my fingers along her ribcage as I slowly peeled the gown down, exposing more and more of her. She shivered under my touch, her breath catching when my hands reached the swell of her ass.

She let me grope her for a bit before she rolled onto her back with the dress pooled around her hips. Her eyes were heavy-lidded, her lips swollen from our kisses.

She wasn't nearly as shy as I'd expected and lifted her hips and pushed the last of the dress down.

Bare.

Finally, completely bare.

I licked my lips and let my eyes slide down her body. Over her full breasts—sensational—to the dip of her waist —sexy as hell—to the flare of her hips—made for me to grab.

Perfect. She was the most perfect thing I'd ever seen.

I placed my hands on her thighs. My lungs rose and fell as I watched the contrast of my skin against hers.

Slowly, I slid my fingers upward over her hipbones, over her ribcage, to the swell of her tits.

God, they were magnificent. Soft, full, perky. I thumbed her nipples, watching them harden to points while she squirmed.

My mouth watered. I was overwhelmed. I didn't know where to fucking start. I wanted to lick, suck, and grab at everything, all at once. Her body was turning me into a glutton.

While I was struggling with indecision, she wrapped her

hands around my wrists and tipped her head sideways, like she wanted me to lie down.

I did, not feeling like myself.

She climbed on top of me and settled on top of the tent in my slacks with a pressure that made me groan. Her dark hair tumbled down to frame her face.

This view was even better, gravity pulling her tits down into perfect globes. I filled my hands with them and sighed. She was a fucking dream.

"You're beautiful," I murmured.

Her fingers brushed my jaw, tracing along the stubble, her touch featherlight.

"You're overdressed," she whispered.

Slowly, she undid the buttons of my shirt, pushing the fabric open once she reached the last one. Her lips traveled over my torso, pressing light kisses against my abdomen, my nipples, my collarbones. Her nails scraped over my abs, making me twitch against her.

My palm smoothed down her back, all the way down to her ass. I wanted to be inside her, but I was also enjoying her teasing. The way she seemed to be as fascinated with my body as I was with hers.

It might be the only thing she'll ever like about you.

The thought was followed by a pang inside my chest that I ignored.

She sat up and stared at me, her gaze traveling over my torso as if wanting to map all the details out. And then her hands drifted to my belt. "May I?"

"Yeah."

She undid my belt. Pulled down my zipper. Glanced at me shyly. "Maybe I want to hear it too."

"Hear what?"

She wrapped her hand around my cock and pulled it out. "You moaning my name." She slid down my legs until her face was level with it. "Otherwise, I might wonder what that sounds like, and the whole point of tonight is to get it out of our system, right?" She touched her lips to the swollen head.

I groaned, so fucking turned on, and so fucking pissed that for her, this was all about one night. Was my ego really so big to think a single orgasm could make her putty in my hands? It was irrational.

But there was nothing rational about how I felt about her.

"Right."

Her tongue darted out, licking around the crown. "We should do everything we've fantasized about."

My brow furrowed. How long was her list? Because we sure as fuck weren't going to get through mine in one night. Not when every time I looked at her, I found another thing to obsess over.

Fuck, I was in so deep.

"Just fucking suck on it, Mia," I growled, wishing the never-ending monologue inside my head would just shut up.

"Patience really is not your virtue," she mused right before she dipped her head and took my cock all the way to the back of her throat.

CHAPTER 30

Mia

He was so big that I could barely fit half of him in my mouth, but every time I heard him say my name, I tried harder.

He moaned it. Grunted it. Cursed it.

And when his balls tightened in my hand and his cum flooded my throat, that "Mia" sounded like a plea.

He had his fingers in my hair while his hips made shallow thrusts as he rode his high. Eventually, his groans turned into harsh breaths, and God, there was nothing quite like it.

I slurped him all the way down, licking over the head until not a drop of his cum was left.

When I finally sat up, the sight below couldn't be more satisfying. He looked destroyed.

"And we haven't even fucked yet," he mused, more to himself than to me.

I fell beside him on the bed. "Need a break?"

He tugged me against him and pressed his nose against my hair. "Yeah. With you sitting on my face."

I laughed. "I need a break too. I'm going to get some water. Want some?"

He squeezed my ass. "I'll get it."

"You don't know where anything is."

"I'll figure it out," he said, sliding off the bed. The view of his tatted back as he walked out of the room ensured my eyes didn't stray from him for a moment.

I slid under the duvet. My heart raced inside my chest, and my body buzzed.

I was satisfied. Yet not.

I was enjoying this so much that I wasn't sure how I'd feel tomorrow morning when Romolo left and everything went back to normal.

Me, living my life, doing everything I could for the campaign.

Him, living his life, doing...whatever it was that he did with his days.

What *did* he do with his days?

He came back in with two glasses of water and handed one to me.

"What kind of work do you actually do for your family?" I asked, my gaze sliding down his chest and settling on his abs. He worked hard on that body.

"Why?" he asked with an arched brow.

My eyes moved back to his face. "Just curious."

"I run a nightclub," he said. "But I work on some other things too."

"What kind of things?"

"All kinds."

"All kinds" sounded ominous. A part of me was curious, but another part much preferred not to find out. If I thought too hard about what I was doing and who I was doing it with...

I gulped down my water. It was just one night. I wasn't risking the campaign. No one knew he was here, and no one would find out. I'd even keep it a secret from friends, because honestly, I didn't know how I'd explain it to them.

But I didn't have to think about all that right now.

"It's called Black Silk," he said, placing his empty glass on the nightstand. "I'd invite you to visit, but it's probably not a good idea for you to be seen there." Some darkness slipped into his expression, and he looked away.

What was on his mind? I wondered if he felt conflicted about being here, about giving in to this attraction. After all, I *was* still the enemy. Even if I didn't really think of him as one.

His family is the reason your uncle is dead, a voice in my head reminded me.

An uncle I never knew. An uncle I never loved. But I loved my dad, and even if the fight he was fighting wasn't my own, I was still loyal to him.

It's just one night.

"That's okay. I'm not much of a nightlife person anyway," I said softly.

His Adam's apple bobbed. The air in the room felt charged with something that neither of us dared to address.

My attraction to him burned like a flame in the pit of my belly, but that wasn't the only reason I hadn't been able to forget about him all these weeks.

For me, it was deeper than that.

I had no clue what it was like for him.

"So is it working?" I asked, putting my glass beside his. "Are we getting each other out of our systems?"

He dragged his palm over his jaw and looked at me thoughtfully. "Not sure yet." His voice was gruff.

I bit my lip. "Better get back to it then. The night won't last forever."

His nostrils flared, and something about the way his shoulders dropped a little made my chest clench. But before

I could make sense of his body language, he sank onto the bed.

A frisson zinged up my spine as he peeled the duvet off me, revealing me inch by inch. The caress of his gaze sent heat spreading through my core. He looked at my body with such fascination—now and earlier—and I wished I was brave enough to ask why. I wasn't the first woman he'd slept with—far from it.

I remembered Harper. That selfie of him and another girl on his phone.

Those memories made me want to sink my nails into him like they were claws and demand to know what he was thinking. I gave my head a shake as if to dispel the ridiculous urge.

I had no right to feel possessiveness. Jealousy. He wasn't mine. All we had was this one night.

He brushed his lips over my nipple. "Fuck. Left the condoms in the car. I'll go grab them."

"I have some," I said cheerfully to mask the tightness in my throat.

"Do you?" He lifted his narrowed gaze to my face, and I could tell this news pissed him off.

He didn't like being reminded I'd been with other people? Well, he could join the damn club. At least he'd never had to listen to a man proclaim his love to me.

"Yeah, I do." I slid out from under him. "One second."

I crossed the room toward the en suite bathroom and opened the cabinet behind the mirror.

There was a box. Closed.

Should I open it to make it seem like some had been used? No, that was too petty.

When I returned, he was sitting against the headboard, waiting. I tossed the box at him. He caught it with distaste and turned it over to read the back.

"Wow." I propped my shoulder against the doorframe and crossed my arms over my chest. "Never thought *you'd* need to read the instructions."

He shot me a glare. "I'm checking to make sure they're not expired."

"They're not that old," I said, keeping my voice casual.

His jaw ticked.

"Get over here." The words came out rough.

The moment I reached the bed, he yanked me onto his lap.

I yelped. "Rom!"

His lips brushed mine, teasing before he bit down just hard enough to sting. When he pulled back, his brows were still furrowed in displeasure. "Who bought these?"

"Me." My palms flattened against his chest, and I could feel his steady heartbeat.

"Can't imagine you walking into a convenience store and asking for ribbed for her pleasure—"

"The Internet is this magical place where you can buy just about anything and get it delivered to your door. You should give it a try sometime."

"Ha. Ha. Good one," he said in a deadpan.

My fingertips trailed over the hard angle of his jaw. "Anything else you want to ask me?"

His palms flexed on my waist. "When was the last time you fucked someone, Mia?"

Heat rose to my cheeks. Damn it. He'd called my bluff. I knew I didn't owe him an answer, but I gave it anyway, "Two years ago."

His palm slid up my stomach, carving a path between my breasts before wrapping gently around my neck. He exerted just enough pressure to send a jolt of electricity through me. "*Who.*"

"I'm not telling you." I had a feeling they might end up

in Vermont if I did. "When was the last time *you* slept with someone?"

His thumb traced slow strokes against the side of my throat. "Two months."

Jealousy wriggled into knots inside my stomach. I shouldn't have asked.

But then, I did the math. "So...around the time of the engagement party?"

"The week before." Darkness and something else danced at the edges of his stare.

"And no one since?"

He didn't answer. He just let go of my throat, cracked open the box of condoms, and fished one out.

"Hmm." A slow smile tugged on my lips. "Wonder why."

He rolled it on. "Beats me."

I laughed, and happiness fizzed like champagne inside my chest.

"Something funny?" A warning seeped through his voice.

"Yea—ah!"

His palm landed against my ass in a sharp, stinging smack that sent heat rushing through me.

"That's for all that fucking sass." His grip tightened on my hips. "Now, get on your hands and knees, Berry. I'm tired of not being inside you."

What did it say about me that I scrambled to obey?

The sting from his slap faded beneath the soothing warmth of his palm as he rubbed over the spot. Then he hauled me closer, positioning me just where he wanted. The head of his cock pressed against my entrance.

My core clenched, as if inviting him in.

His fingers wound into my hair, coiling it tightly around his fist, and he pulled until my back arched.

Then, in one slow, controlled motion, he pushed inside me.

I moaned. It was a tight fit.

"This still funny?" he taunted as he pulled out before thrusting back in.

"A bit."

He tugged me harder against him and picked up speed. His hips smacked into mine, his balls slapping against my clit while the diamonds still around my neck bounced with every thrust.

"How about now?"

"Romolo," I moaned, sweat slicking my back.

"You said everything we've fantasized about, right? I wonder how funny you'll find it when I'm deep inside of here."

I barely had time to register before his thumb pressed against the other hole.

I whimpered against the shallow intrusion. "Who says I'll let you?"

"Did you let *him*?" he growled, his pace turning rougher, harder. "The one you went Internet shopping for?"

Oh, he was *really* jealous.

A breathless laugh lodged in my throat, and I bit down on the inside of my cheek to keep it at bay.

"No." I panted as he fucked me like he wanted to punish me, like he wanted to erase my memories of anyone who'd come before him. "Never."

His cock thickened inside me. "Atta girl." He reached around me, his fingers finding my clit. He slid them over it in tight, merciless circles, like that was my reward.

It was so good that I sobbed into the duvet. Somehow, he knew how to work my body better than I did, which was why I opened my mouth and said, "I'd let you."

"Ah *fuck*." Whatever restraint he still had snapped. He

went at me like a wild animal. I clutched at the sheets, whimpering as he got me closer and closer to the edge. My pussy spasmed around him, willing him to go harder, deeper.

I pushed myself upright until my back met his chest, and wrapped my fingers around the headboard. His palm slid around my throat again, applying the perfect amount of pressure as he drove into me from behind.

I turned my head, and his mouth crashed down on mine in a searing, hungry kiss. The combination of his tongue tangling with mine and his fingers moving in tighter and tighter circles finally threw me over the edge.

My body clenched around him, pleasure exploding in waves, and his rhythm turned frantic, his fingers digging into my hip. One more stroke, and he groaned with his own release, his body curving over mine. "*Fuuuck.* You were made for me, Berry."

Butterflies exploded inside my belly. I was spent. Breathless. Dazed.

Even if this night was a reckless mistake, it was the best damn mistake I'd ever made.

CHAPTER 31

Mia

When I cracked open my eyelids, the first thing that greeted me was smooth, tattooed skin. My cheek was pressed against Romolo's chest, rising and falling in sync with his slow, steady breaths.

I blinked against the sunlight flooding the bedroom.

It was morning.

Crap.

It was *morning*. We were only supposed to take a nap.

It was over. Our one night was up. And what had it gotten us?

A pit yawned open in my stomach as I sat up and looked down at Romolo's sleeping form. The hard edges of his face had softened, the usual tension smoothed out. His dark lashes fanned across his cheeks, and his brows were unknit for once. He looked younger. Softer. Almost...gentle.

The diamond necklace he'd given me rested on the bedside table. I slid my fingertips over the stones and exhaled.

There was no future here. None. The fact that I had to keep reminding myself of that was ridiculous. But my skin itched with the need to keep him for just a little longer.

I lay back down, tucking my body against his warmth, pressing my lips to the side of his throat, and pretended to sleep.

A few seconds ticked by. Then, he stirred. Yawned. Brushed his lips over my temple in a touch so tender it cracked something inside me.

Romolo was a contradiction—rough and ruthless one second, tender the next. And that mix? It threatened to undo me.

"Good morning." His voice was thick with sleep, and the greeting was followed by his palm lazily cupping my ass.

"Shh." I burrowed closer against him, inhaling his scent, fighting against the tightness inside my throat.

The thought of him getting dressed and walking out the door cleaved me in half. My emotions bubbled just below the surface, threatening to pour out.

It's just sex. You've had casual sex before.

Yeah. Right.

The only problem was that nothing about *this* actually felt casual. Not when he said things like I was made for him.

I sat up, overwhelmed by the mess inside my head, and stared out the window.

His palm pressed against my bare back. "Mia—"

Click.

My spine straightened. That... That sounded like a door unlocking.

A sharp, cold pulse went through me.

I shot out of bed, snatched my robe from the chair, and yanked it on.

"Stay here," I whispered.

Romolo swung his legs off the bed, already reaching for his boxer briefs. "Who is it?"

"I don't know. I'm going to check."

His frown deepened as he pulled them on. "I'll go."

"No." I grabbed his wrist and squeezed. "Are you crazy? No one can see you."

"If it's an intruder—"

"I'll scream, and you can come running, okay?"

His jaw tightened. He didn't like it, but I pressed my index finger to my lips and slid out the door.

Jenny.

She stood by the kitchen island, a stack of folders in one hand, typing something on her phone with the other.

Shoot. I'd given her a key to my place for emergencies, but she'd never used it before. "Jenny? Can I help you?"

She jerked, seeming surprised to see me. "You're awake."

"What are you doing here?"

She gave me a strange look. "Dropping off the letters you need to sign for the animal rescue charity. You said you'd be sleeping in late after your party, and that I could just come right in. Is everything okay?"

God, she was right. The memories hit me all at once. How had I managed to forget she was supposed to stop by this morning? "I'm sorry," I stammered. "It was a late night."

Jenny cocked her hip and leaned against the counter, sliding her phone back inside her purse. "Have fun?"

"Yeah. Yeah, it was..." I scrambled for words. "Beautiful event. Everyone's gowns were stunning. And the art... The art was amazing. Rembrandt, I think."

Jenny smirked. "You look exhausted. Had a few drinks? Nothing I should know about, I hope?"

"No, no. Nothing at all."

Her gaze swept over me, searching for clues of misbehavior. I kept my face neutral, refusing to give anything away, but a prickle of annoyance appeared in the back of my mind.

Jenny often treated me like I was a misbehaving teenager, even though nothing was further from the truth.

Until last night.

A beat passed before she seemed satisfied. She turned toward the door. "Great. I should get ba—" Her body froze mid-step.

I followed her gaze, and my stomach dropped.

Hanging on one of the hallway hooks was Romolo's coat, just where I put it when we stumbled in yesterday.

Jenny glanced over her shoulder, one brow raised. "Is someone else here?"

Panic wrapped around my lungs and squeezed.

Stay cool.

A slew of excuses threatened to spill past my tongue, but I managed to keep my mouth shut long enough to decide I didn't owe Jenny an explanation. "Don't worry about it."

A slow, knowing smile spread across her lips. "What's his name?"

I crossed my arms over my chest. "I'm allowed to have a private life, aren't I?"

She narrowed her eyes at my attempt at setting a boundary, like *I* was the one out of line. "Could've texted me, you know. I would've left the letters with the doorman."

Thank God Romolo had worn his mask last night. Even if she asked the doorman about my guest, he wouldn't be able to tell her anything identifying.

"I honestly forgot you were coming by, but thanks for dropping everything off. I'll make sure to get it done today."

Jenny's eyes flicked to my neck.

Shit.

"Maybe cover up that hickey for the event tonight," she added, a cool note slipping into her tone.

My hand flew to my throat, and heat rushed up my face. "I will."

Jenny smirked. "I'll let you get back to it then." A wink. "Have fun."

I forced a shaky smile. "Bye."

The moment she left, I locked the deadbolt and slid the chain across. Why hadn't I done that last night? My back connected with the door, and my heart pounded against my ribcage. That was way too close.

Romolo appeared on the threshold of my bedroom. He was mostly dressed, his long fingers working a cufflink through a buttonhole. "One of your father's assistants?"

"Yeah. I completely forgot she was stopping by." It was easy to forget all kinds of things when I was all wrapped up in him.

Like the fact that actions had consequences.

Unease clogged my lungs and bled into the air with my next exhale. I wanted to crack a window open, but more than that, I wanted to kiss him one more time.

I couldn't.

One cufflink done, he moved on to the next. His gaze skimmed over me but didn't linger, like there was nothing left for him to see.

Swallowing past the ball in my throat, I brushed my palm over the kitchen island. "I guess this is goodbye, then."

He tugged on his sleeve, his movements as slow and deliberate as the next words that came out of his mouth.

"I'm not done with you yet, Berry."

CHAPTER 32

Rom

My plans never seemed to work quite right when it came to Mia.

The morning after was supposed to be the grand finale. I'd fuck her slow, drag it out until she was writhing, bring her right to the edge, and then refuse to let her come until she agreed to see me again.

It was crude, but I was ninety-nine percent sure it would have worked, because there was no denying how her body responded to me.

We were fucking electric. Even now, my cock was half hard just from looking at her—her robe loose around her shoulders, her lips pink and swollen, her skin glowing in the soft morning light.

Instead of putting my plan in action, the fucking assistant had showed up. *Jenny.*

She'd spooked Mia. I could see it in her eyes. The walls were going back up. She was preparing to push me out the door like last night was something that needed to be erased.

Bitterness stabbed through my chest, the pain turning sharper when Mia said, "We agreed on one night."

I scoffed. "You fell asleep halfway through."

Her eyes narrowed. "So did you."

"I woke up in the middle of the night but decided to let you sleep." She'd looked exhausted. I'd lain there in the dark and watched her breathe. The image of her stumbling on that stage had come to me, and I'd decided to wait until the morning to have her again. She needed rest.

Her bottom lip disappeared beneath her teeth. "Really?"

Her skepticism pissed me off. It's like she thought I was beneath that kind of a gesture.

I reached for my phone and tossed it to her. "Since you know my passcode, why don't you check my messages? I texted Cos at three a.m."

She got into the phone and then frowned as she swiped her thumb over the screen. "Why did you tell him you spent the night at the club?"

I arched a brow. "Would you prefer I told him I spent the night inside you?"

Red crept up her cheeks. She shoved the phone back at me, her jaw set. "We can't."

I took a step forward. She took one back. Again. Again. Until her spine pressed against the door and her hard nipples—fuck me—pressed against my dress shirt.

"Don't tell me you don't want this."

Her head tipped back. Her gaze flicked to my mouth. "It's not about what I want."

"Why not?" My voice dropped lower. "For once, Mia, why can't it be *all* about what you want?"

She swallowed hard. "Because that's se—"

"Selfish?" I cut in. "Last night, you were selfish. How did that feel?" I slipped my fingers between the folds of her robe, slid them down, and pressed into her slick heat. She gasped, her hips tilting into my touch. "Didn't it feel so fucking good?"

She squeezed her eyes shut like she was trying to block me out.

"Look at—"

"No." She shoved at my shoulder to break free and stalked across the room until the kitchen island was between us. Her eyes blazed with frustration, mirroring my own. "What are you even asking for? Specifically."

"More time." My voice was rough. "More time to be with you."

"To be with me? You mean to *fuck me*, right?"

My jaw tightened. "Yes."

Her lashes lowered, like that wasn't what she'd wanted to hear. But I was probably just projecting. "How do you possibly see this playing out? If anyone finds out—"

"No one will find out. Leave it to me. I'll find ways for us to meet without anyone knowing."

"Why should I trust you?" she demanded, her palms flat against the counter. "I still don't even know what you wanted from me in the first place. Why did you come to my studio? How do I know this isn't just the continuation of some kind of a plan?"

Her voice was laced with something deeper than suspicion—hurt.

I exhaled.

She had me there.

How the fuck could I ask her to trust me when I hadn't been honest about a single goddamn thing?

Trust was a two-way street, wasn't it? And if I wanted her to give me something, I had to give her something first.

A small crumb of truth. Just enough to make her give me a chance.

No matter how small, it's a betrayal to the family.

I gritted my teeth. Morales wanted to end us, and here I was considering whether to tell his daughter our suspicions about him, all so she would see me...for what? A few more days? Weeks, if I was lucky?

Worth it. So fucking worth it.

Despair at my predicament dripped through my veins like slow-acting poison. Women like her were the reason men like me got themselves killed. What would she do if she realized the power she had over me?

I clenched my fists against the roar inside my head.

Fuck it. At the end of the day, what real damage could I cause by telling her the truth? I was convinced she didn't know anything about Morales anyway.

"My mother suspects your father has a secret backer, someone with a vendetta against us who's pushing him to go after us aggressively."

Her eyes widened. "What? That's nonsense."

"Is it?" I studied her face. "No one fucking buys that he's doing this just because of his brother."

She let out an exasperated breath. "We already talked about this. He just wants justice."

I smiled. "He spent most of his life running a company, and now, at fifty-five, he suddenly decides to run for mayor and make this his life's mission?" I took a step closer. "Has your uncle's death really tormented him his whole life?"

She frowned. "I don't know, Rom. How am I supposed to know that? It's not like he tells me all of his inner thoughts."

"If he did have a secret backer, you wouldn't know it. Your dad wouldn't tell you the truth. He knows *you* wouldn't stand for something like this."

She gave her head a hard shake. "He would never. He's a good man."

I scoffed. "A good man who lets his daughter run herself into the ground? Who lets your business fail because of his own selfish demands? Who makes it your job to take care of your stepmother?"

Her expression darkened. "Do not come after my father, Romolo. This isn't helping your case."

I raised my hands. "Fine. Fuck it. But that's the truth. That's why I came to you. And when I realized you didn't know anything, I backed off."

Silence stretched between us.

She looked down at the counter. "That's the only reason you backed off?"

My defenses surged. How much more could I tell her before I seriously fucked myself? If she suspected how deep this went for me, she'd cut it off. She'd try to save me from the pain that awaited us at the end.

But I didn't want to be saved. Who said I deserved it?

"You kept my secret," I said gruffly. "That meant a lot to me."

Her gaze lifted to my face, and her expression softened.

The thoughtful way she studied me made me feel like I was being drawn into quicksand. The longer I stayed here, the deeper I sank. And the worst part? I wasn't even trying to claw my way out.

"Okay, Rom," she said finally. God, I fucking loved hearing her say my name. "I'll see you again. But we have to be careful."

I nodded, my relief edged with bitterness about how uneven this whole thing was. "Give me your phone."

She unlocked it and placed it into my open palm. "What are you doing?"

"Syncing our calendars so I can see when you're free." I walked over to my coat and pulled out a second phone. "Take this. It's a burner. We'll use it to communicate."

Mia stared at it, then back at me. "You came prepared with a burner? I thought you said this was just one night."

I shrugged. "I always carry one. Just in case."

She hesitated and then took the phone. She seemed to buy it.

Good. The lie was a hell of a lot more believable than admitting I'd come here with a plan—an entire fucking plan —to make sure she'd keep seeing me.

I couldn't tell her the truth. That I felt something for her. That I didn't know what the hell to do with these feelings. That at the end of the day, I knew there was no real future for us.

I didn't believe in fairy tales.

Let alone one that could happen to me.

But maybe, just maybe, I could have her for a little while.

Just for a little while.

CHAPTER 33

Mia

What I agreed to do with Romolo was reckless. Plain and simple. The second I'd said yes, a weight had settled on my shoulders, and it hadn't lifted in the two days since he'd walked out my door.

I wasn't a risk-taker. Years ago, when I set up an online investment account, I'd taken a survey that had labeled my risk tolerance as low. That had always felt like an accurate description of me. Low risk. Low drama. Low chance of doing anything that might implode my life.

And yet here I was risking everything.

I couldn't let myself dwell on what would happen if we were caught—because whenever I did, panic coiled tightly around my throat.

My dad would be gutted. The campaign would have a PR nightmare on their hands. My friends would question my sanity. And with good reason, because despite everything I was gambling, I still couldn't bring myself to regret it.

I'd relished our night together. And I wanted more.

More rough kisses. More mind-shattering sex. More *him*. *More. More. More.*

It was an incessant chant inside my head, and I was well aware that this wasn't mere curiosity anymore. It wasn't even me chasing a dark thrill after a lifetime of denying myself anything of the sort.

This was about how he made me feel. A little braver. A little bolder. A little more selfish.

I never thought I'd like being selfish. It went against everything I believed. But maybe I only liked it when I was being selfish with him.

We had a narrow window of time to enjoy each other before reality caught up with us.

After my dad won—and at this point, his victory was all but assured—everything would end. Romolo wouldn't want anything to do with me once my father and the DA launched their investigation into his family. And I wouldn't be able to stand by and watch his world get torn apart by someone I loved.

The buzz of a phone inside my purse chased off the hollowness that accompanied that thought.

It was the burner.

> Be ready outside your building at 6:30 p.m. I'm picking you up.

Giddiness fizzed and popped inside my chest as I hurried back home. I'd decided to walk back from my last meeting instead of taking a cab. It was just before six, which meant by the time I got there, I'd have just enough time to shower and change into something I hoped Romolo would appreciate for a bit before he tore it off me.

Just as I reached my block, my purse vibrated again—my normal phone this time.

"Hey, Mia, can you talk?" Eliza sounded frazzled.

"Yeah, what's up?"

"I'm freaking out. We're supposed to have a shoot for my new collection tomorrow, and the stylist just disappeared on us."

I frowned. "Disappeared?"

"She's not answering her calls, not replying to emails—nothing. Either something happened, or she took our deposit and ghosted. But we have to get these photos done, Mia. If we can't shoot tomorrow, I'll have to reschedule everything—photographer, models, hair, makeup. And that could take weeks."

I could practically hear her pacing. She'd told me about this collection at the ball—it was the biggest launch for her sunglasses brand yet.

"I'm desperate," she admitted. "I know you don't usually style for brands, but I trust your eye. Would you do it? I know you'd kill it."

I bit my lip. I'd have to cancel on Romolo if I agreed to help her. "How many looks?"

"At least ten. I'll send over the styling deck. We have most of the wardrobe, but the stylist was still pulling some pieces."

"Okay, let me take a look." I sat on my building steps, opened my laptop, and connected to my hotspot.

The deck loaded—a seventies-inspired aesthetic. Big frames, flared silhouettes, earth tones, bold textures. The base pieces were solid: silky blouses, structured blazers, vintage denim, and a few crocheted details. But the statement pieces were missing—the items that would tie the whole vision together and really sell the collection.

I tapped my nails against my laptop, thinking. "What happened to the stylist's pulls?"

"No clue. She was supposed to confirm today, but now she's just gone."

I'd need to source fast. Most of my usual showrooms in SoHo would be closing soon—if they weren't closed already.

"You need at least one killer fur-trimmed coat, a slinky halter dress, and some platform boots. Do you have any of that?" I asked.

"We've got platforms, but no coat. No dress either."

I rubbed my temple, feeling torn. I didn't want to cancel on Romolo, but I couldn't leave Eliza stranded. She was one of my oldest clients, and she needed me right now. Not to mention I still felt weird about how Romolo had strong-armed her into inviting me to the ball.

Guess I still had leaps to go when it came to being selfish.

"All right. I can't promise anything, but I'll try my best."

"You're a lifesaver. Can you be at the shoot tomorrow?"

I pulled up my calendar. My morning was free until about two p.m., when I then had a prep meeting with my dad's team. I was expected to attend an evening event where I had to say a few words. It was tight, but if I started early and talked to Jenny about coming late to the prep meeting, I could maybe pull it off.

"We'd have to start first thing in the morning if you want me there for most of it. Like six."

"Done. But will you have time to gather everything?"

"It'll be tight," I admitted. "I'll pull what I can from my closet, hit up contacts, and if I have to, I'll buy a few pieces. Can you drop off what you already have at my studio in a few hours?"

"You got it. You're an angel. Thank you, Mia."

"See you in a bit." I hung up and fired off texts to my showroom and PR contacts, then I grabbed the burner and sent a text to Romolo. My fingers drummed against my thigh as I waited for a reply.

A few minutes passed. Romolo didn't respond, and neither did most of the other people I'd messaged. The ones who did answer came back with the same answer—"Sorry, nothing in stock."

Damn it.

I tucked a strand behind my ear, mind racing. There had to be something. Somewhere.

Then it hit me.

Two weeks ago, I'd walked past a boutique on Madison Avenue—Late Republic. Their window display had a full seventies-inspired capsule collection. Velvet suits, slinky halters, faux-fur coats.

I grabbed my bag and slid my laptop inside. If they still had inventory, I might just have a shot at pulling this off.

I started down the stairs just as a familiar Mercedes pulled up to the curb. Guilt crept up my back. Guess Romolo hadn't seen my text.

His gaze lasered in on me as I slid inside the passenger seat. The car smelled like him, and it made me want to burrow my face against his chest before I broke the bad news, but there was no time for that.

"I'm sorry. I can't—"

He reached over, pushed his fingers into my hair, and slanted his lush mouth against mine. I let out a small moan at the taste of him. Heat licked at my skin, coaxing me to deepen the kiss. He felt so good, and I wanted to melt into him, but there was an incessant buzzing in the back of my mind, reminding me that I had no time to waste.

He let out a frustrated groan when I tore myself away. "Rom, I have a work emergency. I sent you a text."

"Yeah, I saw. Decided to come anyway." His jaw hardened. "Getting cold feet, Berry?"

If only he knew how badly I wanted to climb all over him right now. "No. It really is an emergency."

His brows furrowed. "What happened?"

I brought him up to speed on the situation with Eliza.

When I was done, a sardonic smirk tugged on his lips. "You and your fucking savior complex."

That stung, but I hid it. "I have to run to Late Republic." My hand was already on the door handle when his palm appeared on my thigh.

"I'll drive you," he said roughly.

I glanced at him, taken aback. "You don't have to. I can take the train."

The car doors locked with a muffled click. "I said, I'll drive you. Where is it?"

"On Madison Avenue," I said after a beat.

He shifted into drive and pulled onto the road.

My teeth sank into my bottom lip. "Rom, I'm probably going to be up all night working on this. If you're hoping we can still—"

"Jesus, Mia." He shot me an annoyed glare. "Just let me fucking help you."

I bristled at his tone. "I didn't realize sleeping with you came with additional perks."

"It doesn't. But you're the first woman I've fucked who has a tendency to pass out when she's anxious or stressed. You cracking your head open while getting off the 6 train would put a fucking damper on things, don't you think?"

He was being crude, but I sensed that I'd hurt him by insinuating he was only helping me to get into my panties later. I breathed in deeply and allowed the sting of it to melt away.

"Thank you," I said, and I meant it.

His hands tightened around the wheel. "Sure."

"Do you mind if I work while we drive?" I asked.

He gave me a look, like *what do you think?* "Mia, do what you need to do. You don't need to ask for my permission."

There was no other word to describe the sparkling warmth that slid into my veins but fondness.

I was fond of Romolo Ferraro.

If I lingered on that thought, I'd never get anything done, so I tucked it away and got my laptop out of my bag.

CHAPTER 34

Mia

Traffic was brutal. Romolo did his best to navigate through it while I studied the styling deck, but it was still a few minutes past seven by the time we pulled up to Late Republic.

I jumped out of the car, nerves jittering beneath my skin, and jogged to the door.

It was locked.

Inside, there were no customers. Only staff tidying up.

I knocked lightly against the door. A security guard glanced my way and just shook his head.

Damn it. I kicked myself for not calling ahead. What was I going to do now? Nothing else was open, and most of my contacts hadn't answered my texts.

I could see if Fabi, Nina, or Zo had anything, but I was looking for something so specific that it was unlikely they would.

On the other hand, the perfect coat sat right there, just behind the glass.

Romolo appeared at my side. "They're closed?"

I nodded, needles pricking the back of my throat. "Yeah. I think I'm officially screwed."

He took a step forward and began to bang on the glass.

"Rom, I already tried," I said, alarmed at how hard his fist hit the damn thing.

So was the security guard inside. His head snapped toward us, brows knitting together, his frown deepening into something hostile. He stomped toward the door, already shaking his head like we were a couple of hooligans trying to break in.

The door cracked open just enough for him to scowl at us. "Store's closed."

Romolo didn't acknowledge that. Instead, he asked, "How much do they pay you per hour?"

The guard blinked. "Excuse me?"

"Your hourly rate." Romolo's voice was smooth, unhurried. I wished I knew where he was going with this. "What do they pay you?"

The man dragged his tongue over his bottom teeth. "Thirty bucks an hour."

Romolo reached into his pocket, pulled out his wallet, and produced a staggering number of hundred-dollar bills. He counted them out efficiently, stopping when he reached a grand, and held out the cash.

"That should cover an hour of overtime."

My mouth popped open. Was he trying to bribe him? I'd never bribed anyone in my life. Never even thought to try.

The security guard's annoyance gave way to apprehension. He let out an uncomfortable laugh. "Look, man, that's generous, but we've got a store policy. I can't let you in."

My stomach sank. I hadn't even realized I was hoping that trick would work, but I guess I was desperate enough that I was okay with bending a few rules.

I took a step back, ready to leave, but Romolo didn't budge.

He put the money back into his wallet and slid the wallet into his slacks. I watched as his hand brushed over the side of his jacket just enough to tug it back slightly.

The guard's eyes flickered downward and widened. His face lost all color. "Ah, shit."

What had just happened?

Then I remembered when I'd had a similar reaction back in my studio.

My pulse skittered against my neck.

Romolo was flashing his gun.

"They don't pay you enough to handle that," Romolo said in a low voice that made the hairs on the back of my neck stand straight. He sounded so damn scary. If I were the guard, I would have peed my pants.

The man swallowed hard, throat bobbing. I could see him putting it together—the gun, the money, the way Rom carried himself. It only took a second for him to decide this wasn't a fight worth picking.

"Shit. Yeah, of course. You got it, man."

He stepped back and pulled the door open, dipping his head slightly as he gestured us inside. His voice was suddenly respectful. "Please, sir. Come on in."

Romolo's palm settled on the small of my back, guiding me forward. The touch was warm, firm, possessive, and it made something far hotter than fear bleed into my veins.

The security guard locked the door behind us before rushing toward the two sales associates and whispering in a hushed, frantic tone. Probably something along the lines of *act normal and don't piss him off unless you want to die.*

There was a lot I wanted to say to him, but I settled on, "You're nuts."

"Comes with the territory."

"What territory?"

He leaned down, pressing his lips to my ear. "The territory you waded into when you slept with a gangster."

My eyes widened, and my thighs... God, they *clenched*. That was the first time he'd ever referred to himself as that in front of me, and it *should not* have made me feel so hot.

"What if they call the cops?" I whispered, squeezing my legs together to relieve the sudden ache.

"I'll handle it," he murmured. "Now go get what you need."

I hesitated, glancing at the sales associates. They stood frozen behind the counter, their nerves written all over their faces.

Romolo jerked his head in their direction. "One of you. Come here and help my girl."

The statement of ownership in that sentence sent a shiver through me.

All of this felt surreal. I should have been horrified by what he'd just done. This man had bribed and threatened his way into a closed store for me.

Instead, I felt like I was floating off the ground.

He was taking care of me.

I didn't have time to process *that* and what it meant, so I turned to the sales associate and explained to her the kinds of pieces I was looking for. She gave me a nod and said she'd be right back.

The faint sound of Romolo's voice drifted through the store, smooth and low as he spoke to the security guard. I couldn't hear what he was saying, but the security guard was visibly sweating. Maybe Romolo had simply told him his last name. I had to remember that most people feared that name, just the way I used to fear it.

But not anymore. I wasn't afraid of the mobster who casually flashed his gun at people, showed up to appointments with bruised knuckles, and threatened to snap a man's neck just for talking to me.

Our eyes met briefly across the room. The smirk he wore seemed to convey he was perfectly in control of the situation. He gave me a wink.

It brought a smile to my lips and heated my cheeks.

The assistant brought out a dozen or so pieces and laid them out in front of me. The coat I'd seen in the storefront window was a given. A bold red dress caught my eye. It would look perfect layered with a turtleneck Eliza already had. The wide-cut pants in a psychedelic print screamed seventies, as did the scarf with a similar print.

After some back and forth on sizing, I had what I needed. It hadn't even been an hour.

I headed to the register to pay. The attendants, who now seemed a bit more relaxed, even gave me a few shaky smiles as they folded the clothes and placed them into glossy red paper bags.

As I pulled out my wallet, one of the women shook her head. "He said he'll pay for everything in cash."

Awkwardly, I slid the wallet back into my purse. I guessed Romolo didn't want any record of us being here, which made sense in case the staff tried to report this. But there were cameras hanging up above—

An arm wrapped around my waist. A warm, solid chest pressed against my back. "The security guard will erase the footage. They won't say a word about this."

My heart pitter-pattered against my ribcage. "Thank you."

"You're welcome." Romolo's lips drifted over my temple before he let go of me and moved to the counter to pay.

I stared at his back, attraction simmering inside my veins. I wondered how I'd gotten here. No matter how hard I tried to summon some disapproval for what he'd done in the past hour, I wasn't getting anywhere with it.

Instead, I was grateful and...*turned on.*

I swallowed. Good girls didn't sleep with gangsters.

But maybe I was tired of being good.

CHAPTER 35

Rom

I leaned back in the chair and watched Mia scribble on the pages scattered all across her desk.

We were at her studio and she was in her element. Her expression was taut with focus, the soft glow of the desk lamp casting shadows over the delicate curves of her face. Even exhausted, she was fucking beautiful.

She glanced up, catching me staring. "You know, you don't have to stay. You're probably *so* bored."

Bored? I was entranced. Seeing her like this stirred something in me. I was an intruder on her process, but I didn't give a fuck. She could try to get me out of here all she wanted. I wasn't leaving. This area was safe during the day, but all kinds of fucked-up shit happened in New York during the late hours of the night. I'd know.

"I'm not going anywhere. You need someone to keep an eye on you."

A smile tugged on her lips. "How noble."

Noble? I was only indulging my obsession.

I dragged my thumb over my bottom lip, my body heavy against the armrest as I took her in. I was soaking up every moment while I could, knowing that soon enough, I wouldn't have this.

I had power, strength, and money that could buy almost anything.

But it was useless when it came to solving the only problem I cared about. Keeping her.

There was softness in her gaze when she looked at me now, which made me think she was once again looking for the good inside my myriad of bad. If we woke up one day in a different country with no pasts and no history, maybe this *thing* between us could stand a real chance.

But that was a dream. Detached from reality.

My problem remained, and it had no solution at all.

The air in my lungs thinned.

I pushed off the chair, needing something to do, needing space from the thoughts clawing at my head. "I'm going to get us something to eat."

She kept writing. "I'm not hungry. I'd kill for a coffee, though."

"You haven't had dinner. You'll need the energy if you're pulling an all-nighter."

"You're very bossy. You know that?" Her gaze flicked up, playful.

I rounded the desk and slid my fingers into her hair, gripping just enough to tip her head back.

Her lips parted. Her brown eyes went wide. Her elegant throat arched, bared for me like an offering.

My fist tightened in her hair. "Don't pretend you don't like it when I boss you around, Berry."

Her tongue darted out to swipe across her lip, and I bent down and kissed her.

Heat dripped into my veins. Blood rushed to my cock. Her scent wrapped around me, slipping into my tight lungs.

She smelled the way she always did—like my undoing.

Ten minutes later, the damp brick pressed into my back as I stood outside the sushi joint and waited for my order. A cool mist had settled over the city, but my thoughts were an angry blaze.

In some ways, the short time we'd had together was for the best. She'd see the parts of me I wanted her to see, but she'd never get close enough to touch the rot inside me.

She was too fucking good for me.

If she knew the things I'd done, she'd run and never look back.

I ran my fingers through my hair, exhaling hard.

The clock was ticking. We were less than a month out from the election, and according to Mother, the world was ending. Morales was still winning. The Colombians still hadn't signed the deal. And it was only a matter of time before she started asking me again about Mia.

It was that last one that made a chill creep into my bones. How far was I willing to go to protect her?

The door swung open, the chatter of the restaurant spilling onto the street. "Sir? Your order is ready."

I grabbed the bag and the coffee, tipped the waiter, and made my way back.

When I walked into the studio, Mia was pacing, her phone pressed to her ear. "Jenny, this is important to me. No, I won't be able to dial in. I have to be present for the shoot. I'm just asking for a little flexibility."

I put the food down.

Mia stopped pacing and exhaled. "I'm not going to the prep meeting. Send me the files, and I'll review them. I understand you're not happy. I have to go. I still have a ton of work to do. Bye."

She hung up and tossed her phone onto the desk. "*Jesus.*"

"If you give me her address, she can be dealt with."

A coarse laugh escaped her as she tilted her head and met my gaze. "Don't tempt me."

I wasn't joking. The way these people treated her like someone with no life of her own pissed me the fuck off.

Her eyes shifted to the paper bags on the desk. "Sushi?" Her lips curved. "That's my favorite. How did you know?"

"Just a guess." I wasn't about to tell her I'd stalked her Instagram until I could recite what was in every picture she'd ever posted.

"Sit," she said. And instead of taking the chair across from me, she slid onto my lap.

My hand gripped her waist while she took the containers out from the bags, her long hair brushing against my chest. I swiped it off to the side of her neck and pressed a kiss to her throat.

She popped a piece of sushi into her mouth before turning slightly and offering one to me. I accepted and chewed it carefully, but she caught the grimace that slipped through.

"Oh," she said, eyes widening. "You don't like it?"

My fingers slipped under the hem of her shirt, tracing the dip of her waist. "I'm more of a steak-and-potatoes kind of guy."

She rummaged through the bag until she pulled out the beef teriyaki I'd also ordered. "Why didn't you say anything?"

Because I'd fucking eat anything she offered me just for the sheer pleasure of being fed by her. "It's not that bad."

She picked up a piece of the beef with her chopsticks. "Here."

I accepted the piece before pulling her closer to me. Having her in my lap shifted my appetite to other things. She shivered as the hard ridge of my erection pressed against her ass. "Or maybe there's something else you'd like instead," she murmured, lowering her voice.

I dragged my nose over her shoulder, inhaling her scent. "You need to eat first."

"Don't tell me what I need," she whispered, rolling her hips against me. "I know what I need."

She put the food down and stood up.

I tilted my head, a pleasant buzz settling beneath my skin as I watched her hike her skirt up her thighs. "Mia—"

My words strangled in my throat as she reached underneath and slid off her panties, the lace disappearing between her fingers. She leaned in and slipped them into the pocket of my jacket, her lips brushing my ear as she whispered, "What I need is you inside me."

Fuck. Me.

The spike of arousal was so violent it gave me tunnel vision. It was amazing how a few words from her were enough to shake my control. "Turn around and bend over your fucking desk," I rasped.

A hitched breath. A spark in her eyes. She shoved the containers aside, and napkins fluttered to the floor as she did as she was told.

Her obedience made me ache.

I dragged my palms down the backs of her thighs, gripping her flesh, feeling the way she shuddered at my touch. Slowly, I lifted her skirt, bunching it around her waist.

A glance down at her bare cunt had me bracing my palm against the edge of the desk and fumbling with my belt.

She reached between her thighs, fingers circling her clit.

I loved that she wasn't shy when it came to sex. At one point, I'd fantasized about her being demure and cautious, but by now I'd realized I preferred her just the way she was. Blushing but eager. *Oh so fucking eager.*

"Who said you could do that?" My voice came out rough

as I tugged my belt from my slacks. "I'm the one who makes you come." I grabbed her wrists and pulled them behind her back, pressing her against the desk.

She rubbed her bare ass against the tent in my slacks and tried to wiggle free. "You're taking too long."

"If you don't behave, I'll make you."

A muffled moan. "Then make me."

I exhaled.

Black leather against delicate wrists. The clank of the buckle. A twitch in her fingers as I pulled the belt taut.

She squirmed and made soft, muffled protests, but she was so goddamn wet that a glistening trail ran down her thigh.

My thumb stroked lazily over the curve of her ass, drifting closer and closer to her center. I ran it over her puckered hole and then dipped it lightly into her pussy.

"You've made a mess of yourself," I muttered, dragging my thumb through her slick folds. She gasped, her muscles tightening, her back arching into my touch. "Is this all for me, Berry?"

She made a whimper. "Please..."

I coiled the belt around my fist and rolled down my zipper, the sound of it pouring through the air. "Remember that you asked for this." I fisted my cock and ran the thick head along her entrance.

A beat. Then, "Use me, Rom."

My vision darkened. I sank into her with a groan, and *fucking Christ*, she was so tight and warm, somehow even better than before. Raw pleasure ripped through me as I pressed my pelvis flush against her ass.

I smoothed my palm down her back. "You have no idea how good you feel, Berry. No fucking clue."

Then I realized—no barrier. Nothing between us.

I hadn't wrapped up.

My entire body went rigid.

I hadn't done this since— No. I wasn't going to think about that right now.

This was *nothing* like that time.

This was intimate. Mind-melting. *Perfect.*

My head fell between my shoulders. My body shook with the effort it took me to stay still. "Mia, I—"

"I'm on the pill," she whispered. "Don't stop."

Two words.

And I lost it.

I snapped my hips forward, burying myself deep. She sobbed out my name, her head bouncing with every thrust.

"Rom. Oh God—"

I bent down, curling my body over her, wanting to be closer to her still. My teeth slid over the shell of her ear. "You can take it, baby. Fuck, you take it so well."

I fucked her like that—hard, fast, relentless—until my balls tightened, until I was right on the edge. But I didn't want to come like this.

I wanted to see her face when I filled her.

It took me a second to pull out. Three seconds to remove the belt. Five to flip her, lift her into my arms, and slam her against the wall.

But the handful of seconds it took me to sink back inside of her stretched into a fucking eternity as we held each other's gazes, the truth crackling between us.

This wasn't just sex.

She knew it. I knew it.

But neither of us said a goddamn word.

Her legs were locked around my waist as I pumped in and out and groaned at how good she felt. My fingers found her clit, stroking and teasing as I watched her fall apart in my arms.

She clenched around me, her body trembling, her nails digging into my shoulders.

"You gonna come for me, Berry?" My lips trailed over the veins in her throat as I tasted her skin, nipped at her jaw, bit at her lips.

She gasped, thighs squeezing tightly around me, her orgasm ripping through her.

That was all it took.

My body tensed, and a low growl slipped through my clenched teeth as I spilled inside of her. My hands gripped her hips, keeping her where she belonged.

With me.

I moaned against her neck and moved in and out of her, fruitlessly trying to chase away the storm inside my head.

We were both lying to each other.

And neither of us had any fucking clue how to stop.

CHAPTER 36

Mia

"Over a million views in one week is remarkable," Corine, my dad's social media manager, said, grinning as the waiter dropped off her pasta. "And listen to these comments. 'Go Mr. Morales. Finally, someone making sense.' 'Okay, but that outfit? He ate.'" She looked up at me. "Nice work, Mia."

I smiled as I cut into my salmon. "Just doing my part."

"I'm confused. Ate what?" Lionel asked, brow furrowed. At seventy, he was one of the campaign's oldest advisors.

"It means he looked good," I explained. "It's Gen Z speak."

He shook his head, still looking lost.

I dabbed my napkin against my mouth to hide my smile and caught Jenny's glare from across the table.

She was still pissed at me for skipping the prep meeting last week to do Eliza's shoot. The way she was acting, you'd think I committed a capital offense.

I was getting tired of her attitude. I'd only missed a handful of commitments all year, and I was doing my best. Showing a little grace wouldn't kill her.

At least the shoot had gone well. And Romolo...

Romolo had stayed with me all night. He'd even dropped

me off at the location in the morning, despite me insisting—repeatedly—that he didn't have to.

After the third time I'd said it, he'd shot me a look, his grip tightening on the wheel. "I'll do what I fucking want to do, Berry."

That had shut me up.

The rest of the drive had been tense. Not because we'd fought, but because we'd both known what had happened in the last eighteen hours.

The unspoken rules had been broken.

He wasn't treating this like just sex. And the part of me that still believed in self-preservation wished he would. Because the alternative was a ten-letter word.

Heartbreak.

Since then, I'd seen him three more times.

At a thin-walled brownstone he owned, where he'd kept me quiet with his palm over my mouth.

At a hotel in Brooklyn, where steam had curled around our bodies, and we'd left handprints on the shower stall glass.

At a cabin upstate, where we'd made lo—I mean, fucked—under a canopy of stars.

And every time, the lines had blurred a little more. The breathless excitement, the sensation of falling...it all lasted for precious seconds at a time before the dread swooped in.

November 8 was just around the corner.

"We're excited to see how the new ads perform," Corine continued, drawing me back to the conversation. "They're hard-hitting. Great storytelling. We're hoping to win over the last holdouts in the suburbs."

"Let's monitor the comments closely," Dad said. "I want to see early—" His voice cut off as his gaze snapped to something behind me.

The table went silent.

"Is that who I think it is?" Corine whispered.

I glanced over my shoulder, and my stomach filled with shards of glass.

Romolo and his family had just walked into the restaurant.

Our table wouldn't have been more tense if someone had announced a bomb threat.

"Should we leave?" Mike, one of my father's aides, asked.

"No." My dad stared at the group on the other side of the restaurant as he wiped his napkin over his mouth. "That would make it look like we're intimidated."

I barely heard him. My senses had locked onto Romolo, who was oblivious to my presence. He stood near the entrance in his dark-green wool coat and a scarf wrapped around his neck.

Behind him, Cosimo looked tired. According to Fabi, he'd finally agreed to meet her, then rescheduled because he was constantly traveling. Alessio—the third Ferraro brother—stood beside Cosimo, tattooed and unreadable.

Ahead, at the reception desk, were their parents.

I'd seen photos, but seeing them in person was different.

Romolo's mother—statuesque, with sleek silver hair and crimson-painted lips—had a smile that was meant to put people at ease, but the regal way she carried herself radiated quiet authority. It was her—not her husband—who'd dreamed up the ridiculous theory about my dad's funding. I could tell just by looking at her that she didn't sit on the sidelines. She was an active player in their game.

Her husband's presence wasn't loud, but it was impossible to ignore. Gino Ferraro was in his late fifties, and like his wife, he had a head full of silver. The fact that neither of them did anything to try to hide their age felt like a deliberate statement.

They were the top dogs. They had *no one* to impress.

This was a high-end restaurant, the kind where business deals were whispered over polished silverware. The Ferraros' entrance turned heads at nearly every table. As they followed a server toward their seats, whispers rippled across the room.

I swallowed hard.

My father was fighting for power. The Ferraros already had it. They were feared. Respected. Revered. And they wouldn't go down without a fight.

Nerves crawled over my skin. *Don't look this way.*

But as if she'd heard my thoughts, a familiar pair of gray eyes found me.

Not Romolo's.

His mother's.

A flicker of recognition crossed her face before her gaze slid to my father. She touched Gino's arm, her lips moving in a whisper only he could hear.

He followed her line of sight, his steps slowing. His sons noticed, and their heads turned in unison.

That's when Romolo saw me.

His expression turned to stone.

Gino Ferraro adjusted his suit jacket and began to make his way toward us. Only Romolo followed.

Oh God.

I sank deeper into my seat, gripping my napkin with trembling fingers.

My father had never spoken directly to Gino Ferraro. He'd dismissed the man's attempts to meet with disdain.

Now, he couldn't avoid them—not unless he wanted to bolt from the restaurant like a coward.

"Carlos Morales," Gino said smoothly, his voice easily carrying through the hushed dining room. "It's about time we finally met, don't you think?"

My father didn't rise to meet him—an unspoken slight.

Instead, he leaned back in his chair and tossed his napkin onto the table with casual defiance.

"I was hoping it would be in a courtroom with your hands shackled behind your back."

A burning heat spread over the back of my neck as I stared at the tablecloth. That seemed unnecessarily aggressive. Was Dad trying to provoke him?

Gino's chuckle was dismissive. "You have quite the imagination. As far as I know, they don't put shackles on innocent men. Especially when those men make the kinds of generous contributions that I've made to the city you claim to love so much."

"Generous contributions?" Dad cocked a brow. "You mean the filth you flood our streets with? The families you destroy? We'd be better off without your generosity."

Gino's stance shifted, his expression darkening. "Your conspiracy theories about my family are getting creative, but that's all they are—theories."

I risked a glance at Romolo. His jaw was tight, his hands shoved deep into his pockets. He was looking at everyone but me.

The same couldn't be said for Vita Ferraro. She stood with her sons where Gino and Romolo had left them, her sharp gaze trained on my face.

My stomach tightened with unease. What was she searching for?

I forced my expression into a blank mask. I wouldn't give her anything to analyze, to pick apart.

Meanwhile, Gino and my father continued their verbal sparring.

"You have no shame," Dad said. "Your arrogance will be your downfall, Ferraro."

Shut up, I willed my father. *Stop before you make this worse.*

Instead, he leaned forward, his expression turning harsher. "And if you think your sons will be spared in the investigations I'll launch with the DA the second I'm elected, you're wrong. Every last one of you will pay."

The last of Gino's smirk vanished. The threat to his sons had struck a nerve.

"It's too bad your wife isn't here, Morales. I would have loved to meet her. But it seems your family is plagued by tragedy—first your brother, then your wife's unfortunate condition." His gaze slid my way. "Let's hope the unlucky streak doesn't extend to your daughter."

My lungs stilled at the barely veiled threat. Some people around the table audibly gasped. My father didn't move. But if looks could kill, Gino Ferraro would be dead.

"We should let them get back to their lunch," a rough voice cut in.

Everyone was staring at my dad or Gino.

But Romolo was staring at me.

The restraint spelled across his features set off a warning flare inside my belly.

I shook my head. Just slightly. A silent plea not to come to my defense.

How did I know that's what he wanted to do? It was a gut feeling, but I trusted it.

His gaze softened.

"Goodbye, Ferraro," my father ground out. "Enjoy your last few weeks of peace. After I'm mayor, you'll only ever relive the feeling on your deathbed."

Gino didn't respond, just turned and strode away, his steps measured, unbothered.

Romolo lingered for a moment longer, then he followed, leaving a silence so heavy it felt like the whole room was holding its breath.

CHAPTER 37

Mia

My father hadn't said a word since the Ferraros had walked off to their table. The rest of our group had made a few weak attempts at small talk before giving up and focusing on their plates.

No one wanted to seem like they were eager to rush out of here, lest the Ferraros think they'd managed to scare us, but honestly, I couldn't wait to leave. The people at our table shot me worried looks from time to time, likely remembering Gino's parting words. Their attention made me more uncomfortable than the threat itself.

When the waiter came by to ask if we wanted dessert, Dad shook his head and asked for the bill.

Thank the lord.

"I need the bathroom before we go," I said.

"We'll wait outside," Jenny replied, already rising from her seat.

The corridor was quiet, save for the soft hum of the dining room's chatter. I headed down the hall toward the restrooms. I was halfway there when the men's room door swung open, and Romolo stepped out.

My lips parted on a breath.

There he was. Alone. Both of us were. But with my father and his team and Rom's family just a few feet away we couldn't speak, we couldn't linger. Still, an invisible thread pulled us toward one another.

Each step felt heavy, my legs like concrete. His haunted eyes locked onto mine, and time seemed to slow.

I wanted to tell him I was okay. That he didn't need to worry about me. That I didn't hold him responsible for his father's actions, just like I hoped he didn't hold me responsible for mine.

But all I could do was stay mute.

As we passed, our hands brushed. A jolt of electricity raced over my skin. I wanted more so badly that I turned my fingers just enough to let them slip into his for a brief reckless second. Then I pulled away and disappeared into the ladies' room.

When I came out, Jenny stood at the end of the hall, a strange expression on her face. "I got your jacket from the coat check."

"Thanks." I took it from her hands. "Ready to go?"

"Yes," she said, her tone clipped.

We stepped outside. My father and the rest of his team had already left for a meeting across town. Jenny and I didn't need to attend, so we'd take a cab back to the campaign headquarters.

She flagged one, and we climbed in.

"Well, that could have gone worse, I suppose," I said, forcing a lightness I didn't feel into my tone. "Any plans for Halloween?"

Jenny stared out the window and didn't answer.

Frustration bubbled up inside of me. "Really? You're giving me the silent treatment now? Jenny, this is getting ridiculous. It was one prep meeting. You have to let it go."

Her head snapped toward me, her eyes sharp. "I know you're sleeping with him, Mia."

My jaw snapped shut. Her words might as well have been a slap.

How?

Did she see Romolo and me as we passed in the hallway? No. She hadn't been behind me. I was sure of it.

My grip tightened around my purse. "What are you talking about?"

"Don't play dumb. I saw Romolo's jacket in the coat check. It's the exact same jacket that was hanging in your apartment when I dropped off the cards that one time."

Crap!

My mind raced. I needed a reasonable explanation. Or maybe I just need to deny, deny, deny.

I feigned annoyance. "Do you think he's the only man in this city who owns that jacket?"

Her eyes rolled, like she wasn't even remotely buying my shit. "Please. He spent that whole unfortunate encounter avoiding looking at you. And when he finally did?" She scoffed. "Jesus, Mia. He looked at you like you were *his*. I'm surprised no one else noticed."

The shrill wail of an ambulance siren cut through the air. Anxiety tightened around my throat. If Jenny told my dad, my whole life would implode. Especially after how badly that lunch had just gone—my dad wouldn't even try to understand. He was on a goddamn warpath.

The only way I could salvage this was if I stayed calm and chose my words carefully.

Jenny clasped her hands in her lap, her knuckles white. "I'm waiting for your explanation."

"We met at a party. It hasn't been long," I hedged.

"Is it serious?" She was in damage-control mode, trying

to assess the threat. Depending on her assessment, she'd decide whether to loop in Dad or not.

I needed to defuse her.

"It's nothing. A mistake." The lie burned across my tongue.

She huffed. "Bullshit. I know you, Mia. You wouldn't risk all this over a casual fling. So be honest with me. How bad is it? Do you love him?"

Love. The word dripped from her lips like an accusation.

A lump thickened my throat. The backs of my eyes prickled. I turned away before she could see my face crack.

Do you love him?

It was a question I hadn't dared to ask myself.

I didn't know the answer. Or maybe I did, but I wasn't ready to confront it.

Even now, my body ached for his presence. To press my face against his chest, feel his arms tighten around me, hear that low, familiar murmur against my ear. He was one of the most dangerous men in this city, but somehow, he had become my safest place.

The hardened exterior that masked something deeper. The sharp edges softened by moments of tenderness. The darkness I wanted to believe I'd shed some light into.

He wasn't an easy person to understand. Or to love.

But I'd fallen anyway.

The street beyond the window blurred.

"Who do you love more, Mia?" Jenny's voice sliced through the air. She didn't try to soften the blow. "Him or your father?"

I swiped a tear sliding down my cheek with the back of my hand. "That's not fair."

"Lots of things in life aren't fair," she retorted sharply. "Romolo Ferraro is an expert in unfairness. Just look at what he and his family do. Last week, there was an explosion at a warehouse in Brooklyn. Three dead. Rumor is, it was his family sending a warning to some gang trying to move in on their turf."

"That's a rumor." My voice shook.

"They're fucking criminals," she spat. "You know this, Mia. How can you turn a blind eye to it? I thought you were better than this."

Impotent fury scraped through my chest. She was right. He *was* a criminal. And the Mia from a few months ago would have folded under the weight of that truth.

But I wasn't the same woman anymore. I'd changed. And I couldn't reduce Romolo to just that single label.

My teeth clenched. "You don't know him."

"And neither do you," Jenny shot back, her anger rolling off her in waves. "If you think he has even a single redeeming quality, you're deluding yourself. If you don't end it, I'll have no choice but to tell your father. There's too much at stake."

"This has nothing to do with the election." If Jenny just kept her mouth shut, no one would find out.

And yeah, I had to end it. Eventually. But I wanted to do it on my own terms.

She leaned closer, her voice dropping to an icy calm. "We both know that's not true. I'll have you put on house arrest if I have to. You *cannot* see him again."

"You have no right to control me like that!" I snapped.

"I might not have the right, but I have the power. If your father knew what you've been up to these past few weeks, he'd give me carte blanche to do whatever I think is necessary to keep you in line. It would be for your own good. When you wake up from this madness—and that's exactly what this is—you'll realize just how close you were to making the biggest mistake of your life."

I felt like I was suffocating. "I've done *everything* you've asked of me this entire year."

"And it will all be for nothing if you screw up these last few weeks."

The car slowed to a stop outside the campaign offices.

Jenny's gaze assessed me coldly, as if she were seeing me for the first time. "You have three days to end it. After that, I'll do whatever it takes to protect this campaign."

Then, with a shake of her head, she opened the door and stepped out—leaving me behind. Shattered.

CHAPTER 38

Rom

The second crystal tumbler smashed against the window, and shards rained down onto the hardwood floor. "That son of a bitch!"

Dad didn't lose his temper easily, but the disaster at the restaurant had pushed him over the edge. The drive back to the penthouse had been the tensest fucking car ride of my life.

"I'll call the staff to clean this up," Mother said, eyeing the broken glass.

"Not now," Dad barked. "You can handle a little mess, Vita."

Jesus. He was snapping at her. That's how you knew it was bad.

I walked over to the bar and splashed some whiskey into the last surviving tumbler. I needed a fucking drink. Rage still simmered beneath my skin at the veiled threat against Mia. But more than anything, I was furious with myself. I hadn't been able to stop it. Hadn't been able to defend her.

The only comfort was knowing I'd never let my father touch a hair on her head. I didn't care what it took. If I had to play her personal bodyguard, so be it.

He. Would. Not. Hurt. Her.

"How did we let it come to this?" Dad seethed. "How is he still leading in the polls? We've spent months digging, and what do we have? Nothing."

Mother's sharp gaze snapped to me. "The daughter, Romolo. You were supposed to have something we could use weeks ago."

My jaw clenched. "I'm working on it."

"No. We're done waiting," Mother snapped. "If she doesn't have anything useful, then we use her. We're out of time. Where are the photos?"

The photos. The compromising ones of me and Mia that I told her I'd get.

They didn't exist. Never fucking would.

"Pictures are easy to Photoshop," I said dismissively. "It's a weak plan."

"Then get a video. Quickly. Humiliate her in it. Even if it doesn't sway the election, it'll sting. Morales won't be able to bring her out for the rest of the campaign."

Bile rose in my throat. She was out of her fucking mind. Was she actually asking me to film a sex tape—one designed to degrade Mia—and release it?

"You've done worse," she said coldly, as if sensing my hesitation. "Don't act like you're above it."

A charged silence filled the room. Alessio watched me with furrowed brows. Cosimo's expression was harder to read, but his eyes flickered with something that might be concern.

They didn't know what she was referring to.

Thank fuck for that.

It was true. I had done worse.

But that was before I met Mia. When the family was all I had. Now I had something more, even if it was just fucking fleeting. I wasn't going to repeat my past mistakes with Mia, no matter what it cost me.

"Romolo."

My gaze snapped back to Mother's. "Yes?"

Arms crossed, she tilted her head. "Is there a problem?"

I took a slow sip of my drink. "No. I just think we don't have time for petty distractions."

"It's an order. End of discussion."

"Fine," I gritted out. "Give me a few days." When I came back empty-handed, I'd be ready with an explanation. Something along the lines of Mia refusing to see me this close to the election. For all I knew, after that fucking lunch, that might already be the truth.

That encounter had been a brutal reminder of why our days together were numbered. And it made me want to break something.

Dad leaned back in his chair. "We have to prepare for Morales's win. He's too confident. There's a chance he has something on us."

"You're letting him get into your head." Mother's voice was tight. "He doesn't have anything. We have to stay calm, be smart, and keep a tight rein on our operations and our people."

My father picked up a heavy paperweight, his fingers flexing around it. "If this deal with Alvarez falls through, it'll shake the confidence of our partners, not to mention the family."

"I just got some news," Cosimo said, eyeing his phone. "We got access to the flight logs for Alvarez's private plane. It looks like he came to the States last week. Landed at a small private airport at the Finger Lakes. We weren't able to track them past that, but we'll be ready if he returns. Know anyone in that area?"

My grip tightened around the glass.

The Finger Lakes?

Mia had mentioned Morales had a meeting there over Labor Day weekend.

Dad's gaze flicked to the city skyline. "No one comes to mind, but it's a good lead. Any further movement—anything else you find out about that visit—I want to know immediately."

The whiskey burned as it went down my throat. A coincidence?

My gut said no.

But if Mia's father was involved with the same people trying to sabotage our deal with the Colombians...it would mean a level of corruption even my mother hadn't anticipated from him.

I could ask Mia. Try to get more information.

If she was still willing to speak to me at all.

CHAPTER 39

Rom

The hotel was a small, understated brick building nestled on a quiet street in the Upper West Side. There were only ten rooms, and I had booked the presidential suite for Mia and me. She was running late, and I needed something to take the edge off, so I went down to the bar.

It was nearly empty, occupied only by a few neighborhood regulars drinking wine in worn leather chairs. They minded their business. I minded mine.

Loosening my collar, I took another sip of whiskey, trying to temper the tangle of emotions clawing at my chest.

Mia had taken her time replying to my text yesterday. Long enough for me to sweat. Long enough for me to get a bitter taste of what was waiting on the other side of this.

My life without her in it.

I'd always known it would come to this. That we had an expiration date. But now that it was staring me in the face, I still couldn't bring myself to accept it.

Impossible ideas swirled through my head.

Ideas like walking away from the only life I'd ever known. Ideas like taking her with me, whether she liked it or not.

But deep down, I knew I couldn't do it. I was a selfish bastard, but I couldn't ruin her life just to keep her in mine. That knowledge was driven by something stronger than my selfishness, something I refused to put a name on.

I'd always thought this kind of obsessive attraction burned fast and bright before fizzling out, but with Mia, it had followed a different path.

It had led me straight to my doom.

The revolving door spun, and there she was.

The hard set of her mouth told me something was wrong. A sliver of worry curled inside my stomach, adding to the stress, anxiety, and fucking dread that had been festering ever since yesterday afternoon. She crossed the empty lobby and headed straight for me.

I stood as she approached, bracing myself, wondering if she was only here to say goodbye.

"Mia—"

She pressed herself against my chest and wrapped her arms around my waist.

Inside me, something shook.

I exhaled, locking my arms around her as I pressed a kiss to the crown of her head.

"Baby, what's wrong?"

The bartender started to approach, likely to take her drink order, but I shot him a glare that sent him scurrying back to the other end of the bar.

Mia tilted her head up. Judging by the red around her eyes, she'd been crying.

It fucking killed me.

"Jenny knows."

Son of a bitch. My grip on her tightened. "How?"

"She recognized your coat from when you were at my place. Confronted me after we left the restaurant."

Fuck. My coat? I should have known better than to wear the same one I had with me the night of the ball.

"She told me I have to stop seeing you...or she'll tell my dad."

My whole fucking body tightened with the knowledge of what was coming next. It was like watching a car crash happening in real time. There was no way to stop it. She was going to tell me we were done.

She stared at me, her eyes shimmering. "Rom, I—"

"It was always meant to be temporary," I cut in.

Coward.

If I said it first, I could pretend it wasn't ripping me open.

A notch appeared between her brows. "That's not where I was going. I've been thinking and..." Defiance and a hint of desperation crossed her face as she flattened her palms over my lapels. "Tell me the truth, Rom."

"What truth?"

"How do you really feel about me?"

I bit on the inside of my cheek. This was even worse. She was calling my bluff.

How do I feel about her?

I'd spent years trying *not* to feel, only for her to barge into my life and crack the floodgates open. I felt too fucking much when it came to her. And if she knew what she meant to me, she'd have power over me.

It made me feel fucking vulnerable. I hated it.

And yet the answer was right there, clawing at my throat, desperate to be freed.

"Mia..." I drifted off, indecision shredding through my lungs.

She let out a breath. "If we're honest with each other, maybe we can figure this out." Her forehead pressed to my chest, and her voice was quieter now. "I *want* to figure this out."

I cupped the back of her head with my palm and stared at the ceiling.

Would she still want to figure it out if she knew about the skeletons I hid in my closet? There were so many things she didn't know about me. So many things that would eventually make her pull back.

Going further down this path would only make it hurt worse—for both of us—when it happened.

She took a step back. "I'll give you a moment to think on it. I'm going to use the bathroom. Get me a drink." A soft smile. "Something you think I'd like." She squeezed my hand and disappeared around the corner.

I waved the bartender over and ordered her a berry-infused gin and tonic, my mind racing a mile a minute.

What I wanted with her was a fantasy strung together by wishful thinking and delusions. But Mia saw the world differently than me—full of goodness. Full of possibility. Full of fucking hope.

It was so tempting to see it her way, to let myself get carried away with it.

My fingertips traced the edge of a coaster.

The truth.

The truth was that I fucking loved her.

A light touch skimmed my back.

"I ordered you a gin and tonic," I said.

"Not my favorite, but I'll take it."

My spine went rigid. That voice didn't belong to Mia.

I turned and came face-to-face with Harper.

Son of a bitch.

"Romolo," she said with a tight smile. "What an unpleasant surprise."

What were the chances we'd run into each other here? Then it hit me. We met here once when I was sleeping with her.

I was so agitated last night that I'd forgotten this very inconvenient fact when I picked the meeting spot.

"Harper," I acknowledged, my nape prickling. If she saw Mia, she might recognize her from TV.

That couldn't happen.

"This is a nice place. Quiet." Bitterness dripped from her words. "I come back here from time to time."

"Maybe you should come back tomorrow instead." My voice dropped to the kind of tone that usually made people scurry.

But it didn't faze Harper. She ignored the suggestion, her gaze flicking to the cocktail the bartender had just set on the counter.

"Who are you waiting for?"

I stood up. If she wouldn't leave, then I would. Mia couldn't walk in on this. "I've got somewhere else to be."

Her hand shot out, and her fingers clamped around my wrist. "I took your awful advice and left him. Turns out the prenup was airtight. I walked away with nothing."

My jaw clenched. "Not my fucking problem."

She set her purse on the counter and leaned in. "You ruined my fucking life."

I scanned her over, paying attention to the details. Gaunt frame. Dull hair. Dark bags under her eyes. She looked sharper and harder than the last time I saw her back in Messero's bedroom.

I hadn't felt a thing then, not even pity. I used to be good at numbing my emotions. But now, a twinge of regret appeared at the back of my head. "I didn't do anything you didn't want me to."

"You saw an unhappy woman and took advantage."

I picked up my drink and took a long pull, but it didn't help. Acid slid down my throat. I didn't believe in signs or messages from the fucking universe.

But this?

This felt like one.

This is who you are. This is what you do. You really think telling Mia you love her will be enough for her to stick by your side when she finds out?

Harper's teeth glinted in the low light. "If you hadn't sunk your claws in me, I might have stayed with him. Instead, you fucked me up, and by the time I came to my senses, it was too late." She sighed heavily, like someone mourning a tragedy. "I wish I'd never met you."

A pit opened in my stomach.

Not the first time I'd heard those words.

In my head, their voices synchronized, echoing over each other, growing louder.

Then a third voice joined.

Mia's.

I didn't ever want to hear her say it. Didn't think I could survive it.

Me loving her wasn't going to be enough. Us trying to find a way to be together would only implode her life and her relationship with her family.

For what?

I wasn't fucking worth it. Eventually, she'd figure that out.

Harper's fingers brushed my chest. "You're poisonous, Rom. I hope one day it kills you from the inside out."

She wouldn't have to wait long. Venom burned through my veins as I came to terms with what I had to do.

I shoved Harper's hands off me and walked out of the bar.

Mia might have led me to my doom.

But I wasn't going to take her down with me.

CHAPTER 40

Mia

Romolo was waiting for me outside the bathroom. "Finally. Let's go."

He grabbed my hand in a grip that was too firm and dragged me to the elevator.

My brows pinched together as I struggled to keep up with his long strides. "What's going on?"

"Nothing." The tendons in his neck were taut from the way he was clenching his jaw.

This wasn't nothing.

"Did something happen? Rom—ouch, you're hurting me!"

He dropped my hand like it burned him and curled his fingers into a fist at his side. A flash of something—regret?—crossed his face, but it was gone in an instant.

"We need to talk," he said stiffly. "But not here. I got us a room."

The way he touched me, the coldness in his eyes...it was like he'd become a stranger in the span of a few minutes.

Confusion knotted in my stomach. Umm, what the hell had happened in the five minutes I was gone?

The elevator ride up was silent. The air felt thick,

heavy with a tension that I didn't fully understand. Romolo didn't move, didn't blink. It seemed like he didn't breathe. He just stared at the doors like he was willing them to open faster.

My wrist still felt the sting of his grip. I rubbed it absent-mindedly. Out of the corner of his eye, he saw the motion and flinched. His face twisted.

"I'm sorry," he muttered, the words rough, like they'd been scraped from his throat.

"It's fine. Are you okay?" I couldn't make any sense of this weird shift in his mood.

No answer. When we got to our floor, he stalked down the short hall, obviously expecting me to follow.

The room was nice—tasteful, understated decor in muted shades of gray and blue. But I barely registered the details before the door slammed shut and Romolo's gaze locked with mine.

It was so intense, so dark, it stole the air out of my lungs.

"It's over."

My stomach plummeted to somewhere in the vicinity of my shoes.

"We both know there's nowhere for this to go from here."

I stared at him, stunned. This wasn't how this was supposed to go.

In the bathroom, I'd given myself a pep talk, psyching myself up to be honest with him. To tell him the truth about how I'd fallen for him.

Because if we were ready to admit it—to say it out loud —there had to be a way to make it work. I didn't have a plan. Just a desperate desire to try, and a bone-deep faith that together, we could figure it out.

I thought Romolo would want to try too. By now, I trusted my intuition when it came to him.

Something must've happened in the last few minutes that had set him off.

But I wasn't going to give up on us that easily.

"I asked you a question before I went to the bathroom." My voice sounded far steadier than I felt. "Answer it."

He strode toward the minibar. "What do you want me to say?" His hands shook slightly as he unscrewed a tiny bottle of whiskey and sloshed the amber liquid into a glass. "That I wish we had more time?" He tossed the shot back, his throat working as he swallowed. "We both knew this was never going to work long-term."

A hollow ache bloomed inside my chest. "Rom, just answer the question."

How do you feel about me?

His gaze flicked over me. He shrugged. "You were a good fuck."

The world blurred at the edges, tears stinging my eyes. His words cut deep. I wanted to scream, to demand an explanation for why he was being such an asshole.

Breathe. Just breathe.

He didn't mean it. I knew he didn't. He was angry. Lashing out. Scared.

Scared of *what*?

The desire to understand him steadied me, even as my eyes burned.

"Bullshit." I took a step forward, hands clenched at my sides. "What happened out there?"

He gripped the edge of the minibar. "Nothing happened. Let it go, Mia."

"Why should I? Why should I let you lie to me?"

"All we had was sexual chemistry. It would have fizzled out sooner or later. Go home and tell Jenny we're done." He swiped a hand across his mouth, like he was trying to erase the taste of those ugly words.

Rom was a good liar, but even he couldn't reduce us to two people who'd only slept with each other.

"Something triggered you out there. I wish you would just tell me what it was instead of pushing me away." I took a breath, steeling myself. "Rom, I care about you. I..." The word I was looking for got stuck inside my throat.

Why was this so hard? Why was I so scared?

I wanted him to say it first. I'd spent my life telling my dad and my stepmom that I loved them only to get nothing in return more often than not. There was a fear embedded deep inside me that no one would ever say it to me and mean it.

And right now, when he was like this?

I couldn't do it.

Romolo exhaled, staring down into his empty glass. "Let's play it out. Pretend I say the words you want to hear from me." He pushed off the bar and stalked toward me until he had me backed against a wall. His arms caged me in, his palms flat against the wall on either side of my head. "Then what?" he demanded.

I tipped my head back to meet his gaze, my pulse a wild throb in my throat. "We could keep it a secret until the election, and then..." I drifted off, unsure. I didn't have all the answers, damn it. "And then, we'll find a way to tell my family."

"You'd lose them."

"Not necess—"

"*Mia*," he cut me off. "You'd. Lose. Them. Maybe not forever. But for a while. And no matter what I think about your dad, it's obvious you love him. That would be the price you'd have to pay to be with me."

He stared at me, as if trying to make sure his words were sinking in.

They were.

And maybe he was right.

But I wasn't going to lose faith. Just because something seemed impossible, didn't mean it wasn't worth fighting for.

"And what would you get in exchange?" he continued, his eyes burning into mine. "I'm fucking defective, Mia. I've got this thing in me that makes me bad for people. It always happens. *Always*. I ruin their lives. I fuck things up."

My mind raced. What was he talking about? "I don't understand."

He touched his forehead to mine, a heavy sigh spilling past his lips. "I'm bad for you, baby. So fucking bad."

My instinct was to soothe him. I brushed my fingers over his cheek before settling them on his chest. His heart was pounding beneath my palm. He stared at me, his gaze like a dark abyss, filled with self-loathing.

Whatever Romolo thought about himself was obviously distorted. I knew it wasn't the whole truth. He wasn't the villain he painted himself as, at least not with me.

My thumb brushed over his cheekbone. "Rom, you can't predict the future, or what will—"

He swiped my hand away and took two steps back, dragging his fingers through his hair in clear frustration. "I saw Harper."

"What?" I asked, disoriented. "When?"

"Just now. Downstairs. She told me how everything fell apart for her after our fling. The end of which you witnessed at Messero's party."

A prickle of realization appeared at the back of my mind. So that's what'd happened while I was gone.

His throat worked. "I don't want to make your life fall apart too. You might not even see it coming, but one day, you'll wake up in the midst of ruins and ashes. You'll look around and realize, bone-deep, that you'd made a mistake choosing me. Then, you'll want to leave." He paused. "And here's the thing, Mia." His tone darkened. "Once you're mine, I won't *let* you. If we cross this line, there'll be nothing that can save you from me."

A shiver ran down my spine. I shut my eyes and took a steadying breath. "What makes you think all these awful things about yourself? You haven't been bad for *me*. You've made me stronger and more courageous. You've made me feel accepted and safe. Two months ago, I would have walked out of here the second you said we were over. And now, here I am, fighting for this. For us."

He flinched, like I'd physically hurt him.

The silence in the room was loud.

A few beats passed before his shoulders sagged. It was as if all the tension, all the fight, had abruptly drained out of him, leaving him exhausted and empty.

"You want to know who I really am?" His voice was hoarse, no more than a rasp. "Fine. Here's what I do for my family, Mia. I trade in secrets, favors, and threats. I manipulate people. Find their weaknesses. Dig into their lives until I find dirt. If I can't find any?" A smile touched his lips, but there was no humor in it. It was a bleak, bitter thing. "I create it. And then I use it to make them serve the interests of the family, whatever those happen to be at the time."

My heart raced. In politics, they had people like this too. Power brokers, fixers, men who operated in the shadows.

Yes, I could see it. I could see Romolo being that.

The photo of me he'd taken. The one I'd deleted from his phone that night in the Hamptons.

My chest tightened, a vise squeezing my lungs. That had been him trying to create dirt on me, to gain leverage over my father. But in the end... he hadn't used it. He'd let me erase it.

I pushed off the wall and took a step toward him. "You

could have ruined me ten times over by now. But you haven't. Don't you see? You're different with me. I trust you."

"Stop." He held up a hand. "Stop trying to find good in me where there isn't any."

"I don't need to try. I've already found it. You're not the monster that you think you are."

"You don't fucking know me," he snarled, a trapped-animal desperation in his eyes. "That's the problem. If you did, you'd know I'm capable of anything."

I tilted my chin up. "What else do I need to know?"

"Jesus, Mia." He stared at me for a long moment, the muscles in his jaw working. Then, suddenly, he turned and sank down onto the edge of the bed.

Silence again, thick and heavy. I watched him wage some internal war with himself, his fingers curling into fists, his knuckles turning white.

Finally, he spoke, his voice so low I had to strain to hear it. "The summer I turned eighteen, a few months before I was supposed to be made, my mother came up with a plan..."

CHAPTER 41

Rom

The summer I turned eighteen, a few months before I was supposed to be made, my mother came up with a plan for how to compromise the new police chief.

She called me into her study the morning of a party she was hosting at the penthouse.

It was early, and I'd barely woken up, but the penthouse was already buzzing with activity. Decorators and caterers were coming in and out every five minutes, their voices carrying through the hallways. I locked my bedroom door before I went to talk to her. I didn't want someone snooping through my shit.

Cos and Alessio had both moved out, and I was counting down the days until I could do the same. It wasn't that living with my parents was horrible—I barely saw either of them—but moving out meant something. A rite of passage. That, along with getting made, would mean I was officially a man.

Mom stood by the window, looking out at Central Park, a serene smile curving her lips.

When she turned to face me, the smile slowly melted away.

"Caterina told Aunt Paolina you kissed one of her friends at the barbecue last week."

Heat blasted across my cheeks. Fucking Cat. The next time she called me for a ride home from one of her Brooklyn raves, I'd tell her to hitchhike.

"Am I in trouble?" I asked, feeling like a total tool. Why the fuck would I be in trouble for kissing a girl? I was eighteen. By the time Cosimo was my age, he'd already lost his virginity. And Les—he didn't talk about that kind of thing, but I had a hunch he'd done it with one of the cleaning girls before he moved out.

I could have done it by now too, if I'd wanted to. But I hadn't.

Because deep down, I had this stupid idea that I'd wait. That I'd save it for someone who actually mattered.

Of course, I'd rather take a kick to the balls than ever admit that to anyone. It made me sound like a pussy.

Mom shook her head, her tone eerily calm. "You're not in trouble. But tonight, I need you to kiss someone else."

I frowned. "What?"

She moved to her desk, opened a drawer, and pulled out a photograph. She slid it across the polished wood toward me.

I hesitated before picking it up, unease sliding down my back. The woman in the picture was old enough to be one of Mom's friends, maybe even older. Her heavily made-up face did nothing to soften the deep lines across her forehead, and her too-bright smile reminded me of the overeager chaperones at school dances.

"You want me to kiss her?" I asked, incredulous.

Mom nodded. "Yes."

"I don't understand."

"She's the police chief's wife," Mom explained, crossing her arms. "Alana taught at a high school until a few years ago, then she was quietly let go. Rumor has it she was involved with a student." A pause. "Of course, there's no evidence of that. Or if there was, it's been buried."

I stared at her, waiting for the punch line that never came. She was serious.

"If she likes younger men, Romolo," Mom added, "she'll like you."

A cold, slimy feeling settled in my stomach. "You're joking."

She smiled faintly. "You're very handsome. You know that, don't you?"

Yeah, I knew that. Girls at school had always said yes when I asked them out. I never struggled for attention. But right now, I wished I could disappear. Fade into the background. Become invisible.

"She'll be at the party tonight," Mom said matter-of-factly. "Her other weakness—besides younger men—is her love of climbing the social ladder. I met her a few months ago, and we've become...fast friends."

I blinked. "Doesn't she know who you are? I wouldn't think the police chief would want his wife spending time with our family."

"I told her it's all unsubstantiated claims. That people judge based on old history, not the truth. That seemed to resonate with her—for reasons we can probably imagine."

I looked back down at the photo still clenched in my clammy hands, the edges curling under the pressure of my grip. "And what do you want me to do?"

"When she arrives, I'll introduce you," Mom said. "Talk to her. Be charming. Offer to show her the art gallery. And when you're alone in there, I want you to kiss her."

"What if she doesn't want me to?" A million tiny worms crawled under my skin.

Mom took the photo from me and slid it back into the drawer. "She will."

～

The party started at seven, and by eight, the penthouse was packed with guests. Overlapping voices, laughter, and the clinking of glasses filtered through the air.

Dad wasn't around—he had been called away to Italy on business—and my brothers were nowhere to be found either. I hovered near the bar nursing a beer, too nervous to mingle with anyone. My eyes scanned the room, watching for the woman Mom had shown me earlier.

At around 8:15, she arrived.

"This is my youngest son, Romolo," Mom said, gently guiding me toward her.

The woman looked a little younger than she had in the photo, though still like someone's mom—a friend's mom. Her gaze swept over me, from my head to my shoes, before settling on my face. Her eyes shone with something I couldn't quite read, and her lips curved into a smile.

"Romolo," she said, her voice soft. "That's a beautiful name. So nice to meet you."

She slid her hand into mine, and her fingers were cool against my palm. If she noticed how clammy it was, she didn't mention it. Instead, she seemed fascinated by my face, staring at me so intently it was like she was committing me to memory.

Self-consciously, I wiped my free hand over my freshly shaved jaw. I was still unable to grow a decent beard, so I always made sure to get rid of the wispy patches that cropped up every few days.

"Is this your summer between high school and college?" Alana asked.

"Yeah, I just graduated last month," I said, "but I'm not going to college."

"Excuse me," Mom interrupted with a polite smile. "I have to greet a few other guests."

"Of course." Alana barely acknowledged Mom's departure. Her gaze never left mine. "How come?"

I shrugged, shifting my weight. "I think I'll just help my dad with some of his businesses. He owns a lot of companies, and he likes having family he can trust running them."

She laughed. "Well, you must be a very smart young man if he trusts you to jump right in. Graduated with good grades?"

I gave a modest nod. "I did all right."

"I used to be a teacher, you know," she said, turning her wineglass in her hands. "I taught math and accounting to twelfth graders."

"You don't teach anymore?"

Her smile didn't waver, but something in her eyes cooled. "No, I don't."

"Do you miss it?"

"Sometimes. But I have two kids—thirteen and fifteen. They keep me busy. Soccer practice, tutors, all of that. It's always a struggle to find time for myself." She glanced around the room. "Meeting your mother has been wonderful. She's so kind. She's introduced me to new people and given me a reason to get out of the house. You're very lucky to have her."

The beer bottle was warm in my hand. "Lucky, yeah."

That was one way to put it.

Mom wasn't warm, not in the way most people thought of mothers. Her love was sharp-edged, conditional. But she took care of me and my brothers. She had high standards for us. So high they sometimes felt impossible to reach.

Maybe tonight I could show her that I was capable. That I could be the son she needed me to be.

"Would you like to see the art gallery?" I asked.

Alana smiled. "That sounds lovely."

I left the beer on a table and led her through the crowd. The gallery wasn't much—just a room at the back of the penthouse with paintings packed onto its walls. A few narrow windows let in slivers of natural light, but the space was mostly shadowed, designed to showcase my parents' collection.

"They're big fans of Japanese art," I explained, walking toward a large canvas of a snowy winter day set against the backdrop of Mount Fuji.

"This is beautiful," Alana said, her gaze shifting between the paintings and me. She seemed more interested in studying my face than the art on the walls. "And what about you? Do you like it?"

Caught off guard, I ran a hand through my hair. "I think it's cool, but...it's not really what I'd put up in my own place, you know?"

She grinned, seemingly charmed, like I'd said something far cleverer than I had. "Are you planning on moving out soon?"

"Yeah," I said. "Just starting to look at apartments. My brothers have already moved out, so I'm the last one left."

She nodded, stepping closer until we stood shoulder to shoulder in front of the painting. "And did you have a girlfriend at school, Romolo?"

Her voice had changed, turning lower, softer. I noticed the faint flush creeping up her neck, the way her arm brushed against mine—lightly enough that she could pretend it wasn't deliberate.

Adrenaline flushed through my veins, making me feel a little sick.

"I didn't," I said slowly, turning my head to meet her gaze. And then, because I knew what she wanted to hear, I added, "I prefer older women."

Her lips parted slightly. Her pupils dilated.

The moment hung heavily between us, and I knew what I had to do.

Revulsion clawed at my chest, but I shoved it down.

I leaned in and pressed my lips to hers.

It was brief—two, maybe three seconds. I didn't use tongue, but she let out a soft gasp. When I pulled back, her eyes were heavy-lidded, her expression slack.

I couldn't tell if she was pleased or just surprised.

A beat passed. The silence stretched until I couldn't bear it anymore. What if Mom had been wrong?

Panic flared.

"I'm sorry," I stammered, the words tumbling out of me. "I shouldn't have done that."

I turned to leave, already trying to figure out how I'd explain this to Mom, but before I could take a step, fingers curled around my wrist.

"Romolo."

Her voice was thick.

I glanced over my shoulder.

She licked her lips. "You don't have to apologize."

And then she closed the distance between us and kissed me again.

I didn't sleep that night. The party stretched into the early hours, music and conversation bleeding through the walls long after I'd locked myself in my room. When the penthouse finally fell silent, it was past three a.m.

I lay on my back, staring at the ceiling, trying to make sense of the sick feeling in my gut.

The door creaked open.

I sat up, muscles tensing, but it was just my mom. She stepped inside with something in her hands.

"Romolo?"

"Yeah?" I flipped on the bedside lamp, and its soft glow illuminated her face. She didn't look angry or pleased—just neutral.

Without a word, she handed me the papers she was holding.

Photos. Of me and Alana in the gallery. Kissing. Every angle captured in stark detail.

I looked back at her, my stomach twisting. "Is this... okay?"

A small smile tugged at her lips. "You did well."

She turned toward the door but paused at the threshold, glancing over her shoulder. "You'll see her again next week. She'll be coming for tea every Wednesday from now on."

And then she was gone, leaving me alone with the evidence of what I'd done.

Every Wednesday for the rest of the summer, Alana was there at noon.

My mother always ensured we had time alone, excusing herself for at least half an hour each visit. Her reasons grew increasingly flimsy—an urgent phone call, a sudden need to check something in the kitchen, an errand that couldn't wait. Alana never seemed to question it. Or if she did, she didn't care.

The dining room where Alana and I met had multiple hidden cameras. At first, she dressed modestly, but as the weeks passed, her outfits became more revealing—plunging necklines, tighter fits, shorter hems. We'd kiss. Sometimes she'd take my hand and place it on her breasts. Other times, she'd touch me over my clothes until my body couldn't help but react. But she never took it further.

My mother never said it outright, but I knew my job. I had to make Alana believe I wanted this. So I played along, even though my stomach turned every time she touched me.

One afternoon, the housekeeper walked in at the wrong moment. Alana's hand was resting on my groin.

The look on her face—the way all the color drained from it—stayed with me longer than any of Alana's touches. Made me feel something close to shame.

That evening, I overheard my mother speaking to the housekeeper in the kitchen, her voice firm and unyielding.

The housekeeper never stepped into the dining room on Wednesdays again.

My sleep started to get all fucked up. Nightmares. Sheets drenched with cold sweat. The nights before Alana's visits, I rarely managed more than a few hours' sleep.

I didn't know how much longer this was supposed to last. No one had given me an end date.

By the end of August, I was still trapped in this nauseating routine when my mother announced she was hosting a big end-of-summer party at the house in the Hamptons.

"I want you to go up a day early," she said, typing something on her phone, her attention elsewhere. "The caterers arrive in the morning, and I need you to supervise. You'll get there Friday night. I'll come up early Saturday afternoon, and the party will be that evening."

"Okay," I said, hesitating before adding, "Mom, did you look at the apartments I sent you?"

She finally glanced up, irritation flickering across her face. My living situation was another thing outside my control. I was still in my parents' penthouse, dependent on their finances until I got made and could earn my own money. The apartment hunt had been her idea, but every time I brought it up, she brushed me off.

"I'll look after the party, Rom," she said dismissively, turning back to her phone.

I scratched the back of my head, my frustration mounting. "And this...thing with Alana? How much longer do you think it'll last?"

Her eyes snapped to mine. For a moment, I braced for a reprimand, but then she smiled—a slow, thin thing that didn't reach her eyes.

"Make sure you please her this weekend," she said coolly. "After that, I think we'll call it a day. I've got almost enough on her as it is."

The air in the room felt suffocating, but I nodded. The end was near.

The soft drizzle outside tapped against the windows as I lounged on the sofa while *The Dark Knight* played on TV. The glow from the screen flickered across the dim room. A half-eaten bowl of popcorn sat beside me, untouched for the past half hour.

I wished Cosimo or Alessio had come with me to the Hamptons tonight, but they had other plans. They were always busy with something. Meanwhile, I felt stuck in a purgatory I couldn't wait to escape.

I didn't plan to stay up late. My sleep was still fucked up, and I didn't want to be a groggy mess for tomorrow's event.

The movie credits began to roll when a knock at the door startled me.

I frowned, pushing off the couch. No one else was supposed to be here tonight.

When I peered through the peephole, I froze.

Alana stood on the other side, her hair damp from the rain, dark spots blooming across her blouse.

I opened the door. She gave me a breathless smile, though she seemed nervous. "Your mom told me you'd be here."

A cold prickle crawled down my spine.

She did?

Fuck.

I had assumed my mother would want me to kiss Alana again during the party, but now, realization sank in.

That wasn't the plan.

This—tonight, while we were alone—was the plan.

"Won't you invite me in?"

I raked a hand through my hair. "Yeah. Sorry. Come in." I stepped aside, catching the faint scent of alcohol as she brushed past me. Glancing out, I saw her car parked in the driveway, rainwater glistening on its hood. She'd driven here after drinking.

I shut the door and followed her into the living room. "Is everything okay?"

She whirled around too fast, her arms flailing slightly before falling to her sides.

"Yeah," she said, but it came out brittle. "I just had a fight with my husband. It's a long story, but I couldn't stay there anymore."

"You have a place in the Hamptons?" I asked.

"A friend's house. The kids and I have been here for the last two weeks. My husband works in the city during the week and only comes down for the weekends, but—" She waved a hand, dismissing the thought. "I don't want to talk about him anymore."

She sank onto the sofa, her gaze landing on the frozen credits on the TV. I hesitated before sitting beside her, and the cushion dipped under my weight.

"Do you want to watch something?" I asked. How was I supposed to act around her when she was in this kind of a mood?

She shook her head, her eyes distant. I could tell her thoughts were elsewhere, likely consumed by the fight she didn't want to discuss.

"No, Romolo, I don't want to watch anything." Her hand appeared on my thigh. "Being with you makes me feel young again, like I'm just a girl with her whole life ahead of her. You make life...less heavy."

She slid her fingers upward, and my muscles stiffened. Should I stop her? Let it play out?

Then, before I could decide, she began unbuttoning her blouse.

Frantic. Clumsy. Her fingers ripped through the buttons, and the fabric fell open to reveal the lace underneath.

She climbed onto my lap. "I don't want to talk anymore tonight," she whispered, her lips grazing my ear. "I just want to feel something good."

The faint tang of alcohol clung to her breath, mixing with her perfume. It was sweet but stale, like fruit that had gone bad.

My pulse quickened, not with desire, but with unease. She fumbled with the zipper on my jeans as she lifted her breasts to my face.

I forced myself to respond, dragging my tongue over the lace of her bra. It was mechanical, detached. Her gasps told me she liked it, though my stomach churned with every second that passed. She dug her hands deeper into my jeans, her nails grazing my skin as she wrapped her fingers around my dick.

"I want this," she murmured.

My eyes shot open, panic flooding my chest. This was more than she'd ever wanted from me before.

And I... I didn't want this. I didn't want *her*. Kissing her had been bad enough, but now...she wanted me to go all the way.

Which meant she'd be my first.

In my desperation, I confessed, "I've never done this before."

She froze. For a moment, I thought—hoped—it might make her rethink what she was doing. But when I met her eyes, there was no hesitation there. Only a glint of excitement.

A slow, knowing smile spread across her face. Leaning in, she pressed her lips just under my ear and whispered, "I'll make it good for you."

A strange pressure built behind my eyes, like my head was being squeezed in a vise. It felt like I was coming untethered from my body, drifting above the scene instead of living it. Her hands were everywhere, touching me, squeezing me.

And then, inexplicably, I was hard.

I didn't know how it happened, didn't want it, but there she was—climbing onto me, lifting her skirt. Nothing underneath. There was a flash of bare skin before she sank onto me. The warmth of her engulfed me, and though it felt oddly comforting, it also felt wrong. So wrong. My mind screamed at me to stop it, but my body didn't listen. I just sat there, useless, frozen, while she moved against me.

She gripped my shoulders, her nails pressing into me. "Look at me, Romolo," she said, her voice distorted, like I was underwater, and she was speaking from above.

I blinked at her, my focus slipping in and out. Her face blurred, and the pressure around my head tightened.

Suddenly, she stopped. Her entire body stilled as her gaze darted past me and confusion skated across her face. "What is that?" She pointed at something behind me.

"What?" My voice came out rough. I tried to turn, but her weight pinned me in place. "I can't see."

Without warning, she scrambled off me, hurriedly buttoning her blouse. The hunger that had fueled her minutes ago was gone, replaced by something close to panic. "What *is* that?"

I zipped up my jeans, still sluggish, and followed her stare. A vase of fresh flowers sat on a nearby console table.

I hadn't noticed the vase when I first came into the house, but now I wondered how I could have missed it. Fresh flowers in a house that wasn't supposed to be cleaned until tomorrow?

I squinted. Wait. Did it just—

There.

Alana pushed past me and moved toward the vase. With shaking hands, she yanked out a rose where the blinking light was hidden. She plucked the tiny, thumb-sized camera from the petals and stared at it, her face a storm of emotions —shock, betrayal, fury.

My stomach plummeted. Mom had ordered someone to install a camera. Likely, there were many others hidden throughout the house. But this one was defective. It had flashed. A rookie mistake.

Fuck.

She hurled the camera to the ground and stomped on it. Once. Twice. Three times. The crunch of plastic and glass filled the room, but she didn't stop.

"Alana, that's enough!"

She whirled to face me, eyes wild. "Tell me what's going on, Romolo. Now!"

I think she already knew.

Her palm flew to her mouth, muffling a strangled gasp. The puzzle pieces fell into place, each realization sharpening her expression into one of horror. "That camera. There've been others, haven't there?"

I nodded, my throat dry.

"This was planned," she whispered.

I couldn't answer.

Alana crumpled to her knees, her body shaking as she clawed at her cheeks. "No. No, no, no. Romolo, please. You can't do this to me."

"If your husband plays by our rules," I forced out, "the pictures and videos will never see the light of day."

She shook her head, her tears flinging into the air. "You don't understand! After the last time— He told me he wouldn't protect me again. If he finds out, I'll lose everything."

Mom believed the police chief wouldn't want these pictures to surface, that he'd cave to our demands to protect himself. But looking at Alana trembling and broken on the floor, I wasn't so sure anymore.

"If they come out, it won't just be your reputation that's damaged," I said, my voice low. "It'll hurt his too."

She wasn't listening. Her sobs grew louder as they spilled out of her. "This will ruin everything! Romolo, please, I'm begging you. You can't do this to me."

"It's not up to me." The edge of frustration in my tone masked the guilt twisting in my gut. "This wasn't my plan."

She lifted her tear-streaked face, her eyes pleading. "There has to be something I can do. Please, anything. I'll do anything."

"It's not me you need to talk to. It's my mom."

The way she wept cut deep into my conscience. But I was doing this for the family. Mom and Dad said we all have to make sacrifices for the family. It's how my brothers and I were raised.

"Look," I said, rubbing the back of my neck. "You'll be

able to talk to her tomorrow. Let me take you home. You've been drinking. You shouldn't be driving like this."

I tried to help her to her feet, but while she'd welcomed my touch earlier, now she tore her hand out of my grip like she'd been burned. I grabbed my keys and a jacket before opening the door. She stumbled out into the rain, which was heavier now, and slid into the passenger seat of my car.

The squeaking of the windshield wipers and her weeping bled into the air. Her head was bowed, her hands trembling in her lap.

Guilt still churned inside me. I knew my family's world was ruthless, full of difficult choices and cold calculations. But seeing the fallout up close like this? It was different.

Was it supposed to feel this awful?

Or was I just soft?

I tightened my grip on the wheel. Next week, I was expected to prove myself. To put a bullet in a traitor's skull and solidify my place in the family. That act would set me on the path to being Cosimo's underboss when he took over as don.

I wasn't a kid anymore. I had to be willing to do whatever it took.

"Romolo," she whispered, her voice raw. "My kids need me. Their names are Grant and Tessa. If this comes out, my husband will make sure I never see them again. He has the power to do that, you know. He's got all the judges wrapped around his little finger."

My knuckles turned white against the wheel.

"You have to talk to my mother," I forced out. "There's nothing I can do to help you right now."

Her head shook violently, her movements erratic and aggressive. She was falling apart right before my eyes.

I pressed harder on the gas. Anything to make this drive end faster.

Her fingers suddenly dug into my thigh, sharp as claws. "I made a mistake," she choked out. "A horrible mistake. Haven't you made mistakes before?"

I swallowed hard, eyes fixed on the slick road glowing under the headlights, and stayed silent. Nothing I said would help.

"Maybe you haven't," she continued. "Maybe you haven't because you're so young. When you're young, the mistakes you make... They don't matter. You don't know any better." Her voice cracked. "But, Romolo, I'm not eighteen. I'm forty-eight. I won't get a second chance if my life falls apart."

She pressed her nails harder into my leg, her other hand grabbing at my arm now.

"Romolo, do you understand? I won't have a second chance!"

"Alana, let go of me." I was trying to keep my eyes on the road, but she was distracting me. Hurting me.

She tightened her grip. "Don't you understand, you stupid boy? God, I wish I'd never met you!"

"Let go!"

Her screams grew louder, and in the chaos, I lost control of the car. The wheel jerked sideways as the tires skidded against the slick pavement.

We were on a bridge. A narrow one crossing one of the lakes.

The rain blurred everything.

The railing shattered.

For a split second, we were weightless.

Then, with a deafening crash, the car plunged into the lake.

Cold water surged in through the cracks around the windows, filling the cabin. Darkness swallowed everything. No headlights. No streetlamps. Just ink-black water, rising fast.

Alana was still screaming, a piercing sound that echoed in the confined space.

"You have to get out!" I yelled as I fumbled with my seat belt.

"Grant, Tess, I'm so sorry," she sobbed. "I'm sorry."

Fuck. She was in shock. She wasn't even trying to free herself.

I unbuckled my belt and reached over to help her. "Alana, listen to me. You need to go through the window."

She looked at me, her eyes wide and terrified, and nodded.

The force of the water rushing in nearly choked me as I rolled down the window on my side. I threw myself through the opening. We were sinking fast.

My foot got caught in the seat belt. For a moment, blind panic took hold. I thought it would drag me down, that I'd drown right there tied to the car. But after a few frantic yanks, I broke free.

The darkness outside the car swallowed me, disorienting me.

My lungs burned as I kicked upward—what I hoped was upward.

Finally, I broke through the surface and gasped for air. I swam to the bank, every muscle in my body screaming, but when I pulled myself onto the shore, a new kind of panic sank its teeth into my chest.

I didn't hear Alana.

She hadn't come up.

Did she even try to get out of the car?

"Shit!" I shouted into the night, my voice hoarse. I couldn't leave her.

I turned and swam back to where the car had gone under. I dived under the dark, frigid water, but it was as black as ink below the surface. I couldn't see the car. I went under again. And again.

Each time, I came up empty.

Minutes stretched into what felt like hours. My limbs grew heavy, my lungs burned. It wasn't until my body gave out—until I physically couldn't keep going—that I realized...

She was gone.

I dragged myself out of the water with my last bit of strength and collapsed on the bank. My body was shaking, my wet clothes clinging to my skin.

I patted my jacket and felt the solid shape of my phone inside the inner zip pocket. It was waterproof and had done its job. The phone still worked.

Staring at the screen through blurry eyes, I called my mom.

"Come get me."

"Where are you?"

I gave her my location and hung up.

It took her nearly three hours to arrive. When she did, she was flanked by some of my father's men. By then, the rain had stopped, but the chill hadn't left me.

She sat beside me and handed me a blanket. I wrapped it around myself, my teeth chattering.

She looked out over the still, dark water. Silent.

"Is she dead?" I choked out.

"I'm sure she is," she said, sounding utterly calm.

My throat tightened, and then the tears came, hot and uncontrollable. "Mom, how did this get so fucked up?"

She lifted her hand and rested it lightly on my shoulder, but there was no warmth in the gesture. My body turned toward her, aching for something—comfort, solace, anything—but instead of pulling me in, she cleared her throat and stood.

A gaping hole tore open inside me. I couldn't hold back the sob that ripped through my chest. "Tell me everything will be okay," I pleaded.

"It's a shame. We almost had him."

"Him?"

"Her husband. He would have done whatever we wanted once he saw the pictures and video." She made a thoughtful sound. "He still might to ensure her memory isn't tainted by her misdeeds."

For a moment the pain was too much for me to even breathe. It was everywhere—my lungs, my limbs, even my teeth. *Everything* hurt.

"Mom," I gasped, "I need—"

"Next time, try to stick the landing, Rom. You ruined the perfect plan."

I couldn't listen to this. I ruined her plan? I ruined a *fucking person*.

Entrapped her.

Killed her.

I pressed my hands to my ears and rocked forward, but her voice still sliced through.

"On second thought, maybe this was for the best."

I pressed harder.

She crouched in front of me and yanked one of my hands down. "You left New York a boy," she said, fingers digging into my chin. "Now you're a man. Now you understand what it takes to stay on top. To run an empire that destroys its enemies. You don't flinch. You don't break. And you. *Can't. Be. Weak.*"

Her face was no more than a smudged blur in the dark. "I was concerned whether you'd be able to kill that traitor next week. Worried if you might embarrass me." She let go of me and straightened out. "Now I know you'll get it done."

I curled into myself, forehead pressed to my knees. My

jeans were still damp. The fabric smelled musty, earthy, slightly rotten. I breathed through the scent, trying to ground myself, trying to pull myself back from the spinning void that had cracked open inside my skull.

I was breaking. Every emotion clashed at once—hurt, guilt, disbelief—until I couldn't tell where one ended and another began.

My eyes squeezed tighter. Tighter. Just when I feared my mind would burst, all of the pressure suddenly released.

Something let go.

Numbness rushed in like a merciful tide. It dulled everything—my thoughts, my memories, even the shape of Alana's face in my mind.

A breath escaped.

I felt nothing.

It was easier feeling nothing.

My mother cleared her throat. "Wipe your tears and let's go. The men will handle the clean-up. We have a party tomorrow."

CHAPTER 42

Mia

I've never wished death onto someone before, so this was a new experience. The rush in my veins. The prickle of heat creeping over my nape. The twisting, sick feeling inside my gut.

Vita Ferraro was a monster. And she deserved to *die*.

Put me and that vile woman in a room, hand me a gun, and I'd pull the trigger without any remorse.

I sat on the floor, my back pressed against the wall, my fingers frozen into claws against the carpet. Rom's words played over and over in my mind, each horrifying detail searing into my brain. Nausea churned in my stomach.

This couldn't be real. It was too awful, too cruel. The thought of a teenage Romolo being exploited and traumatized by the two people who should have protected him—his mother and a teacher—made me want to scream.

Rom had spoken in a voice so hollow it made my bones ache.

I'd tried to move closer to him while he was talking, but he stopped me with a flick of his hand. His empty gaze hadn't lifted from the floor. He'd barely moved from his spot on the edge of the bed, his broad shoulders curled inward as if he were trying to disappear inside himself.

Now that he was finished, silence reigned.

The sun had long since vanished, leaving only the glow of the bedside lamp to paint his face in deep shadows. Shadows that seemed to extend far beyond the room, sinking into the spaces inside him where he had locked all of this away.

"I'm so sorry," I breathed past the lump in my throat. Sorry didn't begin to cover it.

It all made sense now with sickening clarity. The car accident, the panic attack...

He still loathed himself for the role he played in that entire situation, despite being the one betrayed and abused.

I understood now why he thought he didn't deserve anyone's care and love. His own mother hadn't given it to him.

God, that thought made me see red.

I got to my feet and took a tentative step toward him. The need to comfort him, to hold him, to tell him everything *was* going to be okay gnawed at me.

He must have sensed my approach, because his head snapped up, and his eyes found mine. He looked startled. Like he'd woken from a trance.

I barely had time to process it before he shot to his feet and staggered toward the bathroom.

The door slammed shut.

A second later, I heard him throwing up.

I pressed my palm over my mouth, muffling a sob.

Vita. Deserved. To. Die.

And so did Alana, but fate had already taken care of that woman.

Even after all these years, what those two had done still haunted him. Still tormented him from the inside out.

If there was some way to take that pain away, I would have done it in a second.

Swiping at my damp cheeks, I paced the room, my body thrumming with restless, helpless rage and the need to make him understand that none of this changed anything between us.

I wasn't going anywhere.

The retching stopped.

The faucet turned on, then off.

A long moment passed before the door finally opened.

Rom stepped out, his gray eyes locking on mine.

I lifted my shoulders in a small shrug. "I'm still here."

He frowned, like he couldn't quite make sense of it. Like he'd expected me to be gone.

Without a word, he brushed past me and went to the window, resting his palm against the frame as he stared out.

I moved to stand beside him. "You're not a monster, Rom. You weren't before you told me that horrifying story, and you aren't now."

His teeth grazed his bottom lip, like he was thinking about it, considering my point.

I stepped closer. Wrapped my arms around his stony form. Pressed my face into his shoulder.

"I'm sorry," I whispered. "About what happened to you. You were eighteen. Just a kid."

"I knew what I was doing," was his gruff response. He was stiff. Unmoving.

"You wanted your mom's approval." I pulled back enough to look at him. "Your mother set it all up. She didn't give you a choice. She ordered you to do it. She was the adult in the situation, and she failed you. And let's not even talk about how wrong Alana was…"

A shudder ran through him.

Anger coiled beneath my skin. "I hope I'm never in the

same room as your mother again, because I won't be able to hold myself back. How dare she? How *dare* she do that to you? Oh, I could kill her."

His face twisted, a deep crease forming between his brows like once again, he couldn't understand what I was saying.

"No." He shrugged off my embrace and took a step back. "That's not how it was. She's not blameless, but I was the one who did those things. It was my choice to follow her orders."

"It didn't seem like much of a choice. She was your guardian. You lived in her house. You were dependent on her."

"Even after I was no longer dependent on her, I *still* followed her orders. For many years." A shadow passed over his face. "I've hurt people. Killed people. And I did it without remorse. I don't want you to delude yourself into thinking I'm a good person. I'm not."

"You didn't follow her orders when it came to me."

That made him pause. Think.

"People can change," I said softly. "You don't want to hurt me? Then, don't. It's that simple. And forgive yourself for what happened to Alana. You were a victim in that situation."

His entire body went rigid. A bitter, disbelieving laugh tore from his throat. "Victim?" The word was a harsh whisper. "You think I was the fucking victim?"

Stupid. Stupid!

I swallowed hard. That was the wrong word. The absolute wrong word to use with someone like him. Someone used to being powerful and in control. "I just meant—"

"I know exactly what you meant." He sneered. "You really are fucking naïve."

My stomach clenched. "Rom—"

"I've never been a victim." He yanked on his jacket, fists tight. "And if you think I have been, you're even more wrong about me than I thought."

I felt like an idiot. Why did I say that? He wasn't ready to hear it. Maybe he never would be. "Rom, I'm sorry."

He gave his head a hard shake. "I survived. I did what I had to do. I made my choices." His eyes burned into mine. "I don't need your pity. In fact, I don't need anything from you."

Romolo turned and without looking back, walked out of the room.

The door slammed behind him, leaving only the remnants of his anger and indignation lingering in the air.

I sank onto the windowsill, a sob wrenching from my throat.

What had I done? Why did I say that?

Romolo had handed me a piece of his soul, and I'd mishandled it. I'd tried to wrap it in words he didn't want, didn't need. Tried to fix something that wasn't mine to fix.

I just wanted to help him see it wasn't his fault. That his mother and Alana had broken him long before he ever broke anyone else.

But I said too much. Or maybe not the right thing at all.

The shadows seemed to press in, heavy and close. I buried my face in my hands and cried.

We were like two magnets reversed—drawn to each other with a force neither of us understood, only to be repelled every time we got too close.

And still, we kept trying.

Like some part of us believed we could overcome the laws of physics. Make the impossible, possible.

Or maybe just me. At what point did optimism cross into delusion? Whatever that point was, I had a feeling I was close.

I wiped the backs of my hands under my eyes and stumbled to the bathroom.

I needed to clean myself up and go home, where I planned to drown myself in a bottle of wine.

But as the faucet ran, something caught my eye.

Lying on the counter, out of place, was an old tube of my lip gloss.

CHAPTER 43

Rom

My fist slammed into the bag, and a sting of pain shot up my forearm. I didn't catch a goddamn wink of sleep after I left Mia last night, and I'd been in the home gym for two hours.

There was too much pent-up energy in me, too much tension, and it had to go somewhere.

Mia knew everything now. Everything. I'd cut myself open and let her sift through my insides.

I couldn't fucking believe I'd told her. It was reckless.

That story? It was supposed to die with me. But I told it anyway, thinking out of desperation maybe it would make her realize she was better off without me.

I was ready for that. For her disgust. For her to walk away.

But I'd braced for the wrong thing.

She still wanted me. And I had no fucking clue how to handle her compassion.

It shook something loose inside me. Rattled the foundations of my world. Made me feel *weak*, and that was so much worse.

The past belonged in the past. There was a reason I never revisited it. There was no point. You couldn't change it.

And trying to reframe it—to assign new meanings and put different labels on things—made me question my role in it all.

Was I the victim? Or the one who let it happen?

Nah. I wasn't a goddamn victim.

"Fuck!" Another strike sent a sharper pain through my arm. I stepped back from the bag, my chest heaving as I tried to catch my breath.

My phone rang from the bench. The screen lit up with Cosimo's name.

I answered on speaker. "Yeah?"

"We got the Colombian contract," he said. "Alvarez negotiated an extra ten percent out of us, but whatever. Nothing major in the grand scheme."

I flexed my hands, wincing at the dull ache. "Congrats. How'd you pull it off?"

"Flew down there yesterday. Three-hour meeting. Explained to Alvarez how with Messero and us joining ranks, it'll take the authorities a long time to stop us from moving product—that is, if they even have a case. Meanwhile, the other options they've been considering won't stand a chance. I made it clear we'd put every resource into taking them down. Called their so-called safer bet a goddamn fantasy."

"You didn't think to use that angle earlier?"

"I did. But I didn't know who the other buyer was until now. Once I had a name, I could paint a better picture. Show them exactly how fucked they'd be if they went with them."

"You got a name?" I hadn't brought up the Finger Lakes connection to Mia. With everything going on, it wasn't exactly top of mind.

"Yeah. The Santoros."

The name lit something faint in the back of my brain. "Sounds familiar..."

"They were big in New York decades ago," Cos said. "Lost a war to the Riccis about thirty years back. Got run out of the city."

I dragged a hand through my hair. "What the hell do they want with us? We weren't even part of that war."

"No fucking clue. This whole thing's sketchy. They've been dormant for decades, but it looks like they've rebuilt and are making a move. They think they've got the connections to make it work, but they're wrong. I told Alvarez their story's bullshit."

"You think the Santoros have tricked him somehow? Why even consider them?"

"Fuck if I know. Alvarez doesn't overshare, but he listened to me. After a whole hour talking to his team behind closed doors, he came out saying they're going with us."

"You already told Dad?"

"He's pleased. Mom too."

Just the mention of our mother put me back on edge.

I was done listening to her. Done doing her bidding.

I should have stopped a long time ago. But it wasn't until I revisited that summer—and saw Mia's reaction—that it finally landed.

If I didn't want to follow Mother's orders anymore, I didn't fucking have to. What was she going to do to me? Berate me? Glower at me? Ban me from the fucking family for defying her?

Let her try. If it came down to it, my brothers would have my back.

When I was a kid, she seemed all-powerful. Towering. Infallible.

But I wasn't a kid anymore, and whatever power she still had over me... I was the only one giving it to her.

"I think Dad knows something about the Santoros," Cos

said, pulling me back. "But he's keeping his mouth shut. Wouldn't tell me anything."

I frowned. "The fuck?"

"I'm going to try to get more out of him tonight. They want to celebrate. Mom's already got the staff calling family, setting everything up. Party's at seven. You're expected to be there."

"I'll be there."

The Santoro family. It was a power play—a way for them to claw their way back into the city. But something didn't add up.

Should I call Mia and ask her about who her father met at the Finger Lakes?

If the Santoros were also backing Morales, this was even more convoluted.

She probably didn't want to hear from me, but if her father was tangled up with people like this, I needed to make sure she was protected. That she wouldn't get caught in the fallout.

I swiped my palm down my face.

Or maybe I was just looking for an excuse to hear her voice again.

The penthouse was already packed with family by the time I showed up.

After months of feeling like the axe was about to drop, we finally had something to celebrate.

Everyone was in a good mood. Everyone except me.

Unease ate at me as I stood by the unlit fireplace, watching my cousin Joe shove bruschetta into his mouth. Mia calling me a victim had made me irate. At the time, I'd felt nothing but rage. But after two hours of beating the hell out of that punching bag, regret had started to creep in.

Every time I slipped my hand into my pocket, my fingers instinctively searched for the lip gloss I'd stupidly left behind by the hotel sink.

That had been before I came out of the bathroom, when I'd been sure she'd be gone.

Only, she wasn't.

The whole time I was with her, I'd agonized over how to keep her.

And she'd offered me a chance to figure it out.

If I hadn't lost my shit, things could've gone very differently.

She had hope.

All I had was fear.

Coward.

"Jesus," Cosimo muttered, appearing at my side. "You look like someone pissed in your drink."

My response was a dismissive grunt.

"This got something to do with the Morales girl?"

I eyed him. "Why would it?"

"You looked like you wanted to fucking murder Mom when she asked you to tape her."

My grip tightened around the glass in my hand. "I'm not seeing her anymore."

"No?"

"But no one's going to fucking touch her unless they want a gun shoved down their throat."

Cosimo adjusted his watch, chuckling. "Interesting."

"Is it?"

"You went from seeing her, to not seeing her but acting like her guard dog. Care to explain?"

"Not really." Truth was, I could've used some advice. But

opening that door meant unpacking a lot of shit I wasn't ready for.

His voice dropped lower. "What Mom asked you to do crossed a line. What did she mean when she said you've done worse?"

Annoyance crackled over my nape at his prying, but when I caught his gaze, something in his eyes diffused it. A hint of concern.

I remembered our conversation at The Golden Circle dinner. More accurately, the conversation he'd tried to have, one I'd intentionally dodged.

Even after telling Mia, the idea of sharing the worst night of my life and everything that led up to it with another person made me sick.

Shame, guilt, and something even colder churned inside my stomach.

You. Can't. Be. Weak.

Since that night, I'd built walls around every part of me that could be broken, that could hurt.

Walls that protected me and kept everyone out.

But Mia broke through. And as fucking vulnerable as her seeing me made me feel, it gave me faith, for the first time, that things could change.

That maybe, I didn't have to be bad for her.

Tell him.

My eyes scanned around the room. I wanted to, but there were too many people around. "It's not the right time to get into it. Let's talk later."

He studied me for a bit longer, then nodded. "Sounds good." He sipped his drink. "Had a chance to talk to Dad yet?"

I shook my head. "Not yet."

"Fuck," he muttered with a laugh. "Look what Aunt Lisa brought."

Our aunt had just stepped into the living room, cradling a bonsai tree like it was a newborn.

I chuckled. "Dad's going to be thrilled. One more for his collection."

Cosimo swiped a palm over his mouth. "That thing looks heavy as hell."

"Let's go help before she drops it." We weaved through the crowd, making our way over.

"Zia, are you trying to butter up Dad?" I teased as I lifted the tree from her arms.

"Oh, you're a blessing, Rom," she panted, pulling out a handkerchief to dab her forehead. Her face was flushed from exertion. "I wanted to get him something to mark the occasion. I wasn't sure I'd make it up here with that thing."

"Where's your husband?" Cos asked.

"He's under the weather," she said. "Told him to sleep it off instead of spreading his flu to everyone."

I nodded at the tree. "We'll take this to Dad's office for you."

She gave me a quick smile, but her attention seemed elsewhere. Her eyes flicked between me and the party behind me. "Thanks. I've got to grab a tray of ziti from the car. I'll be right back." She hurried out toward the foyer, glancing back once before disappearing down the hall.

The tree was heavier than it looked. Cosimo held the office door open for me as I hauled it in and set it on an empty spot on the windowsill between the other bonsais already there. We were about to leave when Dad walked in, Alessio behind him.

Dad's gaze went straight to the tree. "What's this?"

"A gift from Zia Lisa," I replied, stepping aside to give him room.

A faint smile tugged at his mouth. He approached the tree, inspected it briefly, then turned to us. "Sit down," he said, gesturing to the sofas. "I need to have a word with you boys."

Cosimo and I exchanged a look. This had to be about the Santoros.

Finally, we were going to get some answers.

"Anyone need a drink?" I asked. When no one replied, I walked to the small bar in the corner and grabbed a glass. The tumblers Dad broke a few days ago had been replaced.

Les and Cos sat down, but Dad stayed by the window, his hands resting on the sill as he stared at his precious trees.

A foot tapped against the floor. Cosimo probably. I got the sense he was annoyed by this secrecy when he was the one who'd closed the Colombian deal.

I leaned back against the wall, drink in hand, not in the mood to sit.

Seconds ticked by.

Dad was sure as hell taking his time.

"As you all know by now, it was the Santoros trying to sabotage the Colombian deal," he finally said. "There's something I need to tell you about that family."

I took a sip and—

BOOM.

The world cracked open. The air turned solid, slamming into me like a crushing wave. My ears screamed—no, roared—until everything cut out, leaving behind a ringing so sharp it felt like blades slicing through my skull.

Heat clawed at my skin. I was on the floor. My palms pressed into something jagged—glass? I couldn't tell. Everything around me was engulfed in smoke.

Move. You need to move.

A dark form appeared next to me.

"Rom, you okay?"

It was Cos. He kneeled beside me, his gun already

drawn, his face covered in blood. Behind him, our uncles and cousins were swarming into the room, shouting in confusion.

"Fine," I choked out, coughing. "What happened?"

"A bomb. Can you stand up? Alessio's out cold."

I grabbed his arm and forced myself to my feet. The ringing in my ears had softened enough for me to hear the chaos coming from outside the room.

Cosimo tugged me forward until my feet bumped against something soft.

It was Alessio, unconscious, lying behind the sofa with blood soaking his clothes. Fuck. Was he even alive?

"Can you pull him out of here? I need to check on Dad."

I grabbed Alessio under the arms. One of my cousins appeared beside me and grabbed his feet.

"You ready?" he shouted. "On three!"

We lifted Les and carried him into the living room, where the women were crouched on the ground, their hands covering their heads.

My mother rushed to me. "What happened?"

"I don't know. Something exploded." I pressed my fingers to Alessio's neck.

He was still breathing.

"Someone call Doc!" I shouted as I searched for injuries. There was glass embedded in his shoulder, and there was a burn on his arm, but nothing life-threatening. He must have hit his head hard, though.

"He's on his way!" someone shouted back.

"Did anything go off here?" I asked, lifting my gaze to my mother. But she was already gone.

I wiped my forearm across my eyes and blinked, trying to clear the fog in my brain. Everything felt sluggish, like I was operating at low capacity, but the damage in the living room didn't seem too bad beneath the smoke billowing in from Dad's office.

The bomb had gone off only in there. Who the hell could've planted it?

Planted.

The bonsai tree?

No. *Fuck.*

Was that the bomb? Dad had been standing right next to it.

"Keep an eye on him," I barked at my cousin as I got to my feet.

I was halfway to the office when I heard my mother's scream.

CHAPTER 44

Mia

Balloons bobbed against the fluorescent lights of the campaign office. A handmade Happy Birthday sign hung on one of the walls. On the table in front of me sat a paper plate with a slice of untouched confetti cake.

We were here for someone's birthday. Whose? I had no idea. An email had told me to show up, so here I was. The Uber ride from my apartment had been a blur. My body had arrived where it was supposed to be. But my mind?

My mind was elsewhere.

When I got home last night, I poured myself a generous glass of red wine and sat on the sofa in the dark silence of my apartment, turning everything over.

At first, my thoughts were doused with doubt and insecurity.

Had I fooled myself into believing Romolo felt something real for me?

No. I knew deep in my heart I hadn't.

If I'd learned anything about Rom in the last few weeks, it was that he didn't show you how he felt with his words.

He did it with his actions.

The way he lost it when he thought I was seriously ill.

The warmth in his gaze when he'd cup my cheek and say things like, "You'll be the death of me, Berry." The fact that he took my lip gloss and apparently carried it around for nearly two months.

Even when he'd pushed me away, he worried about ruining my life... He was trying to protect me from what he saw as the biggest danger of all—himself.

The clues had been there. All I'd done was piece them together.

He cared for me. And God, I wanted to scream at him for making me hurt, as much as I wanted to comfort him for everything he'd been through. If only he'd let me help him chase his demons away. If only he'd been willing to try.

A part of me wished I'd been brave enough to tell him how I felt, but another part was relieved that I hadn't.

I couldn't say it to him and not hear it back. It would destroy me.

My gaze found my father, standing by the watercooler, talking to one of the staffers.

It killed me when I'd say those two words to him at the end of our weekly phone call when I was at boarding school, and he'd just say goodbye. Every time, it left me guessing where I stood with him and my stepmom.

When I was younger, I looked a lot like my mom. For a while, I'd wondered if that was why Aris never warmed up to me, or why Dad pulled away the way he did. But my face changed as I got older, and by the time I was fourteen, I didn't resemble her as much anymore.

So then I started to worry if it was something deeper. Something within me.

Maybe I was just... not good enough.

A braver person would have asked. But I'd always been too afraid of the answer. So I tried to please everyone, and fix everything that might be wrong in hopes that one day, everything would be right.

My shoulders curved inward. It was all so exhausting.

I hadn't been living my life the way *I* wanted to. I'd allowed others to set my priorities. Steer my choices. Shape me into what they needed.

You've been betraying yourself over and over again.

I was even doing it right now.

Across the room, Jenny was talking to some of the staffers. Their laughter grated against my nerves.

I wanted to be home, curled under a blanket, music playing in my ears to drown out my thoughts. Or even just to be with my friends. I knew they would lend a sympathetic ear even after they found out about the secret I'd been hiding from them.

I didn't want to be here.

Yet I was.

I drew in a long, slow breath.

Maybe it was time I actually listened to myself.

My hand closed around my purse.

I'm leaving.

A weird sensation tugged on me, like someone was watching.

I scanned the room. It was my dad. He was still mid-conversation by the watercooler, but his eyes were on me.

Had he picked up on the fact that I was about to leave? The usual pang of guilt hit me, but I chose to ignore it.

I shot him a tight smile. He returned it, but it was somehow off.

Was he annoyed with me? For once, I couldn't bring myself to care. There were more pressing things on my mind, including what I was going to tell Jenny tomorrow. According to the deadline she'd given me, I still had another day.

The way things stood, Romolo and I were over.

But I hadn't given up yet. Maybe it was best to call him and see if we could meet one more time now that we'd both had a day to cool down.

I reached into my purse, pulling out my phone to request a car, maybe text Fabi for advice. God knew I needed it.

"Hey, guys, turn up the news!" someone shouted.

My hand was still in my purse when I looked up and froze.

A skyscraper filled the screen, smoke pouring from a blown-out window near the top.

My stomach dropped. I pressed my fingers to my lips, breath catching in my throat. If you're a New Yorker, that kind of image isn't just unsettling. It rips something open inside you.

"What happened?" someone yelled.

"Just listen!"

The voice of the news anchor came on. "It seems the explosion occurred on the seventy-seventh floor of 214 W 57th Street, which is a luxury condominium. Reports indicate a loud blast, though the cause remains unknown. Paramedics and police are on the scene. John, do we know whose penthouse this might be?" The anchor addressed the reporter who appeared in the frame beside him.

"It's unconfirmed," the man replied, the bottom of the skyscraper visible behind him. "But records show there's one unit per floor in this building. If the explosion was in fact on the seventy-seventh floor, it might belong to Gino Ferraro, a prominent businessman in the city."

My shock morphed into something colder. The words sank into my skin, filling my veins with ice.

No. Don't panic.

It was unconfirmed. Even if it was Gino's penthouse, that didn't mean Romolo was involved.

He was fine. He *had* to be fine.

I needed to call him. Right now.

The room around me blurred as I stumbled into the hall. My trembling fingers rummaged through my bag, looking for the burner. I pulled up Romolo's contact and dialed.

It rang. And rang.

No answer.

I tried again, praying that each beep would be the last one and I'd hear his voice. I'd laugh at how scared I'd been. Tell him my heart almost stopped, but it was fine now, everything was fine.

Beep. Beep. Beep. *The person you are calling is—*

I hung up and tried again, the swell of panic rising up my throat.

Stay calm. He's probably just busy.

Beep. Beep. Beep. *The person you are calling is not available. Please leave a message after the tone.*

"Rom, I just saw the news." My voice shook. "Please call me back. Or send a text if you're busy. I need to know you're okay. Please."

My thumb tapped against the screen. I covered my face with my hands as anxious waves rolled through my body. If he was in that penthouse when the explosion happened—

No. Don't.

I could go there. See if the first responders had more information. It was better than standing and doing nothing.

I turned and froze.

Dad and Jenny were just outside the room I'd run out of. They were watching me. Listening.

Jenny looked nervous. Dad's expression was grim.

My pulse drummed against my ears. How long had they been there? What had they heard?

Dad took a step toward me. "I didn't want to believe it, Mia." His voice was low. Hard. "But it looks like I was wrong."

I shook my head. My heartbeat was deafening. "Dad, I don't have time for this."

"Jenny told me everything." Red was creeping up his neck, spreading over his face. "Romolo Ferraro? Really, Mia?"

He knew.

But none of that mattered.

Not right now.

"I have to go. I need to—"

He stepped in front of me, Jenny flanking him. "You're not going anywhere," he said.

There was no point in trying to fight back the panic. I couldn't. My flight instinct kicked in, and I surged past them, clutching my phone and my purse to my chest.

The exit wasn't far. Just around the corner. I'd be out on the street in a few seconds, and then I'd get into a cab and deal with all this later. After I found Romolo. After I was sure he was okay.

I turned and skidded to a halt. Two security guards stood by the exit.

There was nothing relaxed about their body language, but I moved toward them anyway. They weren't going to stop me—

They stepped forward, blocking my path.

"What are you doing?" I demanded. "Let me pass."

They didn't budge.

I whirled around, my desperation rising. "Dad, please. Not now. I have to make sure he's okay."

His gaze darkened until it was pure coal. "I said, you're not. Going. Anywhere."

There was no reasoning with him. I turned back to the guards. "Get out of my way."

Instead of acknowledging me, they glanced over my shoulder toward my father, as if waiting for him to issue a command.

A beat.

Then one of them moved and grabbed me by the arm.

"What are you doing?" I thrashed against his hold. "Let go of me!"

A kick to his shin made his grip loosen, and I ripped my arm away and took a step back.

My thoughts raced like wild horses. Why were the guards here instead of outside where they normally stood?

It was like they had been waiting for me.

The realization hit me all at once.

This was an ambush.

My dad had anticipated this. He'd waited to see how I'd react to the news to confirm what Jenny had told him. But in order for that to be true, he would have had to know about the explosion in advance.

The ground beneath me seemed to tilt. I felt like I was about to throw up. It was hot. So hot.

No. Not now.

My knees gave out, and I fell. And this time, there was no one there to catch me.

CHAPTER 45

Rom

"Do you have any suspicions about who's behind this?" the detective asked.

I glared at her through narrowed eyes. "No. For the third fucking time."

The dissatisfaction wafting off her was almost as strong as her cloying perfume. "Neither did your brother. He also had no clue why there were no remnants of the bomb at the scene."

"Yeah. Isn't that your job to find out?" The plastic chair creaked beneath me. "We both know this is a waste of time."

Blood was still caked to my face. They'd sent Alessio to the hospital and dragged Cosimo and me in here for questioning.

As if we'd ever say a damn word.

She chewed loudly on a piece of gum. "I'm going to let you go. For now. But, Mr. Ferraro, I hope I don't have to warn you against trying to take things into your own hands."

"I've got no clue what the fuck you're talking about."

"It might seem like a great idea to you right now, but trust me, it won't in the morning."

"For fuck's sake, Detective. I don't need your advice. I need to help my family make arrangements."

She sniffed. "Sorry about your father."

Dead. My dad was dead.

Didn't seem real. We used to joke he'd outlive all of us.

I wouldn't have believed it if I hadn't seen the body—or what was left of it—myself.

The detective clicked her pen once. "All right. We're done here. For now."

A cop escorted me down the hall and to the lobby. Cosimo stood outside, barking orders into his phone next to a running car that had one of our guys in the driver's seat.

As soon as he saw me, he gestured for me to get in before doing so himself.

"How's Alessio?" I asked, grabbing a bottle of water from inside the door.

"He'll live," Cosimo said. "A concussion and a fractured arm. Could have been a lot worse. Besides Dad, he was the closest to the bomb."

"Have our guys found anything?"

"They're analyzing the bomb fragments right now," Cos said.

We got as much of the debris out of the penthouse as we could before the cops showed up. We didn't need them sticking their noses in our business. No one in the family would talk. Everyone knew better than that. While the detective tried to put together a theory based on the scant evidence we'd left for them, we'd track down who'd done this.

And we'd make them pay.

Whoever had ordered the hit were dead fucking men.

I swiped my palm over my mouth. "It was the fucking bonsai. Have you talked to Zia Lisa?"

"She never returned to the party, and she's not picking up her phone. We're going to her house right now."

"Fuck, seriously?" In the aftermath of the explosion, things had been chaotic. We'd only had minutes to get the key evidence out of the penthouse before the cops and the paramedics had shown up. Some of the family had scattered —leaving the building before it became a crime scene— which was exactly what we'd wanted them to do.

There was no way Aunt Lisa had known what she was bringing into the house. But if she hadn't come back with her pasta dish...

Jesus. Was she involved?

"The Santoros have motive," Cosimo said, still typing something on his phone. "Revenge for us getting the deal. They found out last night. They might have been planning a surprise for us for a while in case it happened."

I finished the water and crushed the bottle between my palms. "Who the fuck are these people? Dad was going to tell us right before. Mother must know. They've never had any secrets between them."

Cosimo's jaw tightened. "She knows. She's still being questioned at the precinct. I've arranged for someone to wait for her there, and he'll call me when she's with him. We'll talk to her then."

Out of habit, I reached into my pocket for my phone, but it wasn't there. I remembered losing it in the chaos...

Fuck. I needed to call Mia.

I didn't call her before the party. I'd put it off since I was still trying to figure out exactly what I wanted to say.

But after the explosion, once the shock had worn off, everything had become clear. Brushing fingers with death had a way of cutting through the noise.

She'd stayed. Despite everything, she'd stayed.

And that could only mean one thing.

Romolo, I...

Christ, I walked out on the only woman I ever loved. And if my gut was right, she loved me too.

Not the kind of love I was used to—one that came with checks and balances and interest payments—but the real fucking deal.

I wasn't going to let it slip through my fingers. I would fix everything I ruined with her, and then I'd spend the rest of my life doing everything I could to never ruin it again.

Mia Morales was going to be *mine.*

"Need to use your phone," I said to Cosimo. As soon as we figured out what the fuck was going on with Aunt Lisa, I'd go to Mia. But first, I had to call her. If she saw the news and heard my family's name mentioned, she'd worry, and I didn't want her to worry about me.

He tossed me his device. Mia's numbers—both the one for the phone I'd given her and her regular one—were stored in my memory. I'd made a point of memorizing them just in case, the same way I had my brothers' numbers.

It went straight to voicemail.

Without my phone, I couldn't check her calendar. Maybe she was doing an interview or at some event. I'd try again later.

"For some reason, I always thought Dad would be shot," Cos said, his voice rough. "And that he'd manage to kill whoever got him."

"I think that's how we all hope to go. No one wants to be killed by a faceless killer."

"Or by a fucking plant."

I dragged my thumb over my lip. "It means you're don now." The capos had to swear loyalty to him, but it was a formality. We'd handle it after we dealt with more pressing matters, like figuring out who the fuck had killed our dad.

Cosimo took the phone from me and slid it inside his

jacket, his expression unreadable. If he was hurting inside, he wasn't showing it. He was already behaving the way the head of the family was expected to behave in a situation like this.

We'd crossed the bridge and were now in Hoboken, just minutes from where Aunt Lisa and Uncle Mario lived. When we pulled up to their two-story home, their cars were missing from the driveway, and all the lights were off.

"I assume you called Uncle Mario too?"

"Yeah. No answer."

We got out of the car, and the cold night air bit at my skin. I glanced through the windows, watching for any movement inside while Cosimo rang the doorbell. The house was eerily still. No one was moving inside.

"You see any neighbors around?" Cos asked.

I scanned the street. "You're good."

Cosimo's shoulder slammed into the wood with a heavy thud, and the door buckled under the force. We stepped inside and flicked on the lights.

"Son of a bitch." The words escaped me in a harsh breath.

Most of their stuff was gone.

The silence in the house was deafening, broken only by the soft creak of floorboards beneath our feet. Every room we checked confirmed the same thing—Aunt Lisa and Uncle Mario had cleared out. They'd left the furniture, but they'd taken their personal belongings.

"They didn't just leave," Cosimo muttered, running a hand through his hair. "They fled."

My fists clenched at my sides. "She knew. She fucking knew what she was bringing into the penthouse." The fact that this had come from someone within the family cut deeper than I'd expected. "Do you think Mario was involved, or just Lisa?"

Cosimo shrugged, his expression grim. "Does it matter? They're both gone now."

"We need to find them."

"We'll find them. But right now, we need to regroup. There's too much we don't know. Were they carrying out someone else's orders, or acting on their own? We need to talk to Mom to find out if anything had happened between Dad and them recently. Let's go," he said, jerking his head toward the door.

I followed him out. The car was still running, our driver waiting for instructions. As we slid into the back seat, Cosimo was already on his phone, giving orders to start a search for Lisa and Mario.

I stared out the window as we drove away from the empty house. My mind drifted to Mia. She must have heard the news by now.

When Cos was done, I took his phone again and dialed her number.

Both of her phones went straight to voicemail.

My gut tightened. What was going on? It was possible she'd tossed the burner in the garbage after yesterday, but what about her other one? I couldn't remember her ever having her phone off for so long.

I tipped my head back and blew out a rough breath. I needed to wash this blood and grime off my skin and calm the fuck down. She was probably just busy.

But even as I told myself all that, I couldn't shake off the feeling that something was wrong.

CHAPTER 46

Mia

I woke with a gasp, my body jerking upright. The sunlight streaming through the window was so bright it seared my eyes. I threw up a hand, squinting as my vision swam.

My head was heavy. Sluggish. And it hurt.

I reached back instinctively, fingertips grazing something foreign.

A bandage.

This wasn't my apartment. I blinked hard at the ceiling overhead, trying to make sense of it—crown molding, a familiar crack in the paint near the corner vent...

The Upper East Side apartment.

My childhood bedroom.

The memories came rushing in, faster than I could process them.

Someone holding me back, their fingers tight around my wrist.

My dad's strange stare. The smoke billowing out of a skyscraper window.

Romolo.

"No!"

I tore the covers off and flew to the door, ignoring the

pain that was erupting inside my skull. I didn't care. I had to get to him. I had to make sure he was okay.

The handle wouldn't give. It was locked.

Panic surged. I hammered my fists against the door. "Let me out! *Let me out!*"

Footsteps echoed on the other side. A low male voice murmured to someone. Then—*click*—the lock released.

The door swung open.

I stumbled back as a man I didn't recognize appeared in the doorway. There was a stethoscope slung around his neck.

"Good morning, Mia. How are you feeling?"

"Get out of my way," I whispered harshly, eyeing the gap between him and the frame. It was too narrow for me to pass through. I'd have to shove him out of the way.

He didn't move. "I'm a doctor and I'm here to check on you. How's your head?"

Tears blurred my vision.

No. Get yourself together. Focus.

I forced myself to look him straight in the eye. "I want to leave."

He gave me a sad, almost pitying smile that made my skin crawl. "I'm afraid that's not possible."

He stepped inside, and that's when I saw them. Two men in security uniforms posted just behind in the hallway.

It was the same guys who'd blocked my way out of the campaign office. And now they were here to do...what?

Keep me from leaving?

The doctor noticed me looking and gently pushed the door shut. "Please, sit. I need to examine you." His voice was almost drowned out by the roar of blood rushing in my ears.

I was being held captive.

By my father. Who else? He must've ordered this.

My hands skimmed over my hips. I was still in the same

dress I'd worn yesterday. Had I been out all night? That didn't make sense.

"Vasovagal syncope only knocks me out for a few seconds," I said, turning to the doctor. "Why was I out for so long?"

He cleared his throat and looked away as if my question made him uncomfortable. "You hit your head when you fell. The bandage is there for the cut."

"The hit to my head knocked me out for over twelve hours?" I didn't believe him. "If it was that bad, I would have been taken to a hospital."

A flush rose in his cheeks. "Due to your agitated state before the episode, we decided it was best to administer a sedative. I gave you something mild to help you rest."

Oh...my God. He'd *drugged* me. With my Dad's consent.

I burned with fury. The sun was still too bright, too aggravating. I strode across the room to close the curtains and jerked them across the rod so hard the fabric tore at the top.

The rip grated right over the pulsing ache in my skull.

I stared at the flap of fabric. "Is that what you're here to do again?"

"No, Mia. You don't seem agitated to me anymore. Let's keep it that way, okay?"

Slowly, I turned. A ballet dancer twirling in her enclosure. I felt stiff enough for the image to fit.

The doctor patted the bed, his leather satchel at his feet. "Please. We need to check for a concussion or any complications."

Where was my phone? I scanned the room, just in case, but as expected, it wasn't anywhere in sight. They'd probably taken it.

The doctor watched me closely. He was middle-aged,

gray peppering his hair. A thick mustache sat under his broad nose.

What on earth would compel *him* to be involved in this? Money? A favor called in?

His body was rigid, like he wasn't completely at ease.

That was something. He was likely my best chance at getting out.

Tempering the rising urge to throw the Hippocratic oath in his face, I moved to the bed. The mattress made a soft whine as I took a seat. "Is my dad here?"

"I don't believe so." He placed the stethoscope gently on my chest.

"Who let you in?"

"Your stepmother."

The blood inside my veins froze over.

Not just my dad. They were both in on it.

It had all been pointless. The nights I'd spent taking care of Aris. The year I'd given to help Dad win the election. The dreams I'd let slip away. The ways I'd abandoned myself.

None of it had mattered. *I* didn't matter. Not to them.

"The explosion in Manhattan," I rasped. "Do you know if anyone died?"

The doctor hesitated. "I heard there was one casualty."

The room tilted. I wanted to throw up.

"Who?" The word barely made it past my throat.

"I don't know. Please turn so I can check the laceration on your head."

I shouldn't have let Rom walk out of that hotel room. I should have run after him and just *fucking told him* I loved him.

Now I might never get the chance.

A strangled moan, low and raw, tore from somewhere deep inside of me.

When I first met Rom, I thought we were opposites. He

was rough where I was gentle. Abrasive where I was soft. Disillusioned where I was optimistic.

But we were the same. Both of us were starved for the love we'd never received.

The only difference was I'd kept searching for it.

He'd stopped.

"Please," I begged. "Just tell me who it was."

"I don't know," he said emphatically as he pulled at the bandage. "Are you experiencing any visual disturbances?"

"Let me use your phone. I can check online."

"Mia, you need to answer my questions."

"No," I spat. "I'm not experiencing any fucking visual disturbances."

His jaw tensed, but he said nothing.

I rolled my lips between my teeth and tried again—softer this time. "I won't call anyone. Just a quick check. Please."

"The guards took my phone before I came in. The cut looks fine to me. We're almost finished."

The memory of Jenny's words wormed its way into my head. *I'll have you put on house arrest if I have to.*

Well, here I was.

She hadn't even given me the three days she'd promised.

Looking back, it was obvious. She never intended to. Three days would have been enough for me to derail things. Of course, she didn't want to risk it. Not with a promotion riding on my dad's win.

"I just need to check your pupils," the doctor said.

"This is illegal." My voice shook as the light from his flashlight flooded my eyes. "They can't keep me locked in here against my will. When you leave, call the police."

"All done. I don't see anything to be concerned about."

"You know this isn't okay," I whispered. "Help me."

The doctor put his flashlight back into his bag, avoiding

my gaze. "I'm sorry, but I can't." He zipped up the bag. "Miss Morales, I want you to rest for a few days. If anything feels worse, let the guys outside know. I'll come back to check on you."

Despair clawed its way through me.

He moved toward the door and knocked twice. "We're done."

The lock clicked. The door opened.

I didn't know when I'd get another chance. I lunged.

My shoulder slammed into the doctor's, knocking him off balance. I shoved past, ignoring the startled shout from the guard.

The front door was just ahead.

I could do it.

I could make it.

Arms appeared around me, hauling me off the ground.

"Let go!" I screamed, thrashing against the guard.

"Miss Morales!" the doctor called. "Please calm down. Agitation could make you feel worse."

He could shove his fake concern straight up his ass.

"I said let go!" I kicked, fought, desperate to break free.

"MIA."

A familiar voice cut through the chaos, making me grow still. I snapped my head toward the sound.

My stepmother stood at the end of the hallway. Her cane rested in one hand, and her hair hung loose around her shoulders.

"You can't do this," I snarled.

She began her slow journey toward me. The doctor slipped out of the apartment, leaving me alone with her and the guards, one of whom still had his arms locked around my shoulders.

I twisted in his hold. "Tell him to get off me. I'm leaving."

She stopped in front of me, her lips pressed into a thin, unforgiving line. "How could you do this to your father?"

"Do what, exactly?" My voice trembled. "How have I harmed him? What exactly did I do that justifies you holding me here?"

She scoffed, her eyes narrowing. "You're lucky no one found out. You know very well what would happen if your relationship leaked to the media. You and Gino Ferraro's son…" Her lip curled. "He and his family will rot in prison—or at least the ones still alive."

My heart slammed against my ribs. "Who died in the explosion?"

She knew, I was sure of it. But her expression didn't give anything away.

"Aris. Tell me. *Please.*"

She shifted her weight, her heavy silver earrings jingling. "Helping your father with the campaign was a privilege. And yet you were always so ungrateful. Always complaining about how busy you were."

"A privilege?" I shot back, my voice raw. "It was an obligation forced onto me."

She took a step closer. "I would've done anything to take your place."

"And I wish you had! I never wanted it!"

"So you tried to sabotage your father's dream in some kind of childish tantrum? Now he knows I was right about you, Mia."

I stared at her. "What?"

"I told him from the beginning—you were bad luck. I felt it the moment I met you. I never liked you, never wanted you around. Even as a kid, the sweet and innocent exterior you put on was all fake, wasn't it? When Carlos sent you away, it was bliss. But then you had to come back."

A tear carved a path down my cheek. There it was, all

out in the open. I didn't have to wonder anymore. Her words confirmed all the fears I'd carried deep inside my heart.

She didn't love me.

She never had.

I wasn't her daughter in any way that mattered.

To her, I was an inconvenient burden, nothing more.

"Dad asked me to come back," I whispered. "He *asked* me to come back and take care of you. What kind of a bad intent could you have possibly seen in that?"

"You liked parading yourself around here, reminding me of everything I couldn't give him," she spat. "You've caused me so much pain."

A bitter taste flooded my mouth. How was it possible for her thinking to be so twisted?

"I tried to tell Carlos I didn't want you here, but he wouldn't listen. He'll listen now. Now that he sees you for what you really are."

Dark thoughts pressed in. Her words tore through old wounds, digging into places I'd never managed to heal.

She loathed me this whole time. What kind of person looks at an eleven-year-old girl and decides she's bad luck? Who spends years trying to push her only remaining parent away?

My stomach twisted.

This was whose approval I'd spent years chasing?

The thought felt laughable now.

She could hate me. The whole damn world could hate me.

I didn't care anymore.

I just needed Romolo to be alive.

CHAPTER 47

Rom

The capos were packed into Cosimo's living room, waiting for him to issue orders. Everyone was itching for a fight, but we weren't going out to hunt the people who did this tonight. We weren't ready for that. Not yet.

The bomb fragments told a story. This was a sophisticated device—well beyond what our aunt or uncle could've cobbled together, let alone acquired. Whoever built it knew exactly what they were doing.

The current theory? Someone handed Aunt Lisa the bonsai to deliver, but she had to know it was a bomb, otherwise she wouldn't have fled.

We suspected it was the Santoros—who else?—but we were still looking for proof, and more importantly, information on the family.

They were ghosts. No one had heard from them in decades.

Messero was helping. He'd called earlier to give his condolences and reaffirm his commitment to the joining of our families. That was a good thing. After a hit like this, we were vulnerable.

I was doing what I could on my end—calling contacts

and chasing down leads—but my head wasn't fully in it. I couldn't stop thinking about what was going on with Mia.

It had been nearly twenty-four hours since the explosion, and still nothing from her.

I stepped out onto Cos's back patio and crossed the lawn to the picnic table beneath the old oak tree. The air was still, but the quiet didn't soothe me.

I took out my phone and dialed Mia again.

No answer.

Fuck. There was no way she would've let her phone die and stay off for an entire day.

Something had happened. I could feel it.

And I was done waiting around.

I pulled up Nina's number and hit dial.

She answered right away. "Rom? Your mom's still here."

"I'm not calling about her." That was another problem I wasn't going to deal with right now.

After leaving the precinct late last night, our mother had gone straight to her sister's place—Nina's mom's house. Cos called her to get information about the Santoros, taking it for granted that she'd tell us everything she knew.

It was always dangerous to take anything for granted as far as Mother was concerned.

She wouldn't say a fucking word.

Claimed she was grieving and would talk when she was ready.

We were all grieving. But we still had shit to do. In our world, grief was a constant—you learned to function with it humming in the background. She knew that better than anyone.

Keeping secrets now, after Dad had just died? Fucking absurd.

We were giving her twenty-four hours to pull herself

together. After that, she'd have no choice but to tell us what she knew.

I scratched my thumb over the scruff on my jaw. It was getting long. "Have you heard from Mia?"

There was a pause. Then a suspicious, "Why?"

She didn't know about me and Mia. And maybe Mia would be pissed I outed us, but her safety was my priority. And really, I was done hiding how I felt about her. All the fears that had felt so heavy back in that hotel room now seemed irrelevant.

I needed her safe. I needed her with me.

And if I had to beg her to forgive me for the stupid shit I'd said, I'd get on my fucking knees and beg.

"Mia and I have been seeing each other. We had a fight two days ago, and I haven't heard from her since. I'm getting worried."

Nina groaned. "Of course you decide to tell me this today, when I'd be an asshole if I jumped down your throat. Look, if you had a fight, she probably just doesn't want to talk to you."

"Our fight wouldn't make her keep her phone off for an entire day. Including the burner I gave her. Has she called you?"

"No." A hint of concern slipped into Nina's tone. "That's weird. She never goes dark like that."

"I'm going to look for her. Any chance she's somewhere besides her apartment or the studio?"

"It's Saturday," Nina said, thinking. "She usually visits her dad and stepmom in the morning. Maybe she's still there? I can send you the address."

"I have it."

"Rom, wait—if she didn't tell us about you, she definitely didn't tell her family. You can't just show up there."

"I don't care. I need to know she's okay."

She let out a surprised breath. "You actually sound worried."

"I *am* worried." I clenched my fist. "She means a lot to me."

A pause. "Excuse me?"

"I'm losing my goddamn mind over here, Nina. I'm not messing around. If you know where she is, you need to tell me."

"Jesus. Okay. I mean, I don't understand any of this, because why the hell did Mia not say *anything* to us, but I can hear that you're serious. I swear I haven't heard from her. I'll call Fabi and Zo and check if they have."

"Keep me posted," I said and hung up.

The concierge at Mia's building wasn't cooperative—until I stepped around the desk and pressed a gun to his throat.

That changed his mind.

According to him, she hadn't come home last night.

Back on the road, I strangled the steering wheel as I sped toward her studio.

It was past eight p.m., and most of the shops in SoHo were closed. I turned onto Broderick Lane.

The blinds were pulled shut over the windows, but the light in her studio was on.

I didn't bother looking for parking. I just drove onto the curb, left the car running, and jumped out. She didn't have employees or anyone else who used that space. It had to be her.

Had she decided to drown herself in her work to get our last meeting off her mind?

I hoped that was all this was, even as guilt stabbed through me. I had a lot to apologize for.

But when I tugged the door open, Mia wasn't there.

Instead, a woman in a yellow blazer with curly hair and a pen lodged behind her ear worked on a laptop at Mia's desk.

A memory stirred. I'd seen her before. She'd been at that lunch with Morales when my family walked in on their group.

Our eyes connected. Her face blanched.

"What the fuck are you doing here?" I growled.

Her chair screeched as she pushed back, eyes wide. "Don't come any closer."

That voice. It was the same voice I'd overheard at Mia's place when one of her father's staffers showed up to drop off documents.

I smiled at her coldly. "Jenny."

Her eyes were the size of saucers.

Scared?

Good.

She'd tell me everything I needed to know.

"Where is she?" I growled.

Her throat bobbed. "I don't know."

I stalked toward her and fisted both hands in the lapels of her blazer, yanking her hard against the wall. "Start fucking talking. Why are you here?"

She clawed at my arms. "Just to answer some emails!"

I glanced over my shoulder at the laptop. I recognized the background. It was Mia's. "Why are you answering *her* emails?"

"I can't tell you. He'll fire me."

"What do you care about more? Your job or your life?"

Her lips trembled.

My fists tightened, bunching the fabric. "I don't like hurting women, Jenny. But if you don't tell me where Mia is, I will throw you through that fucking window and run you over with my car. It's a shitty way to go. Don't fucking tempt me." I jerked my head at the laptop. "What are you writing in those emails?"

"That Mia will be out of office until after the election," she choked out.

"And why would that be?"

When her eyes flickered with hesitation, I lifted her several inches off the floor. Her shoes scraped against the wall. "Talk. *Now*."

"Please put me down!" she wailed, her nails dragging across my hands.

"Answer me," I roared. "Where is she?"

"She's at home with her parents!"

"Why is her phone turned off?"

"They took it from her. She's not allowed to leave until after the election. Please, I can't breathe!"

I dropped her. She collapsed to the floor, gasping for air.

"Why the fuck would Morales do that?"

"Be-because he knows about you and her. He doesn't want her to see you again."

Rage pulsed through me. Every fucking gut feeling I had about Morales was confirmed. He didn't give a fuck about his daughter. The only thing he cared about was himself.

I had to get Mia away from him.

He was keeping her locked up like a prisoner, but not for long.

Because I was getting her out.

CHAPTER 48

Rom

Adrenaline still pumped through my veins by the time I returned to Cosimo's. I'd gotten more out of Jenny before I left—two guards were stationed with Mia. Taking them out wouldn't be hard, but if Morales had backup, there could be trouble. I didn't want to risk firing a gun with Mia nearby, which meant I needed my own manpower.

I wasn't taking any chances. All that mattered now was getting her out—fast and clean. If something had happened to her, if she'd been hurt in any way, Morales was a fucking dead man.

I found Cos pacing in his office. He was visibly agitated, and he wasn't alone. Mother sat on the sofa, dressed head to toe in black, and Alessio stood nearby, his fresh cast slung over his chest.

"Romolo," Cosimo snapped, "you missed quite a show. Mom arrived here just as I got a call from our lawyer. Turns out, there's a page missing from Dad's will." He stopped in front of her. "She was about to explain how that happened."

The words I'd planned to say—*I don't have time for this*—froze on my tongue.

What?

This morning, just before sunrise, Cosimo and I had gone out to the backyard to get some air. We'd sat at the picnic table under the tree and ate cold leftover pizza one of the capos had ordered. When he'd brought up that summer again and asked what happened, I'd finally told him.

It should've been the most uncomfortable conversation of my life—and in some ways, it was. But it was also cathartic.

I'd talked. Cos had listened. When I'd finished, he cleared his throat and said he wished I'd come to him back then.

I'd told him there was no changing the past. But from now on, I wasn't following Mother's orders.

He'd nodded. *"Good,"* he'd said. *"Because I'm the don now and the only person you answer to is me."*

Mother's gaze flicked to me and then back to him. The lamplight made her silver hair glimmer in a disconcerting way. "I don't know what happened."

Cosimo crossed his arms. "Don't know? The safe where the will was kept has only three keys—one with Father, one with the lawyer, and one with you. There's a record of you accessing the safe yesterday. You didn't even bother hiding your tracks."

Mother didn't flinch under Cosimo's glare. "I was there to get jewelry for the funeral. I didn't touch the will."

Cosimo scoffed. "The missing page specifies who gets control of the family. What are you playing at?"

"I'm not playing at anything. But without that page, succession has to be a discussion."

I let out a sharp breath. The fucking audacity of this woman. This was a new low. Did she really think this blatant attempt at a power grab would work?

"That's insane," Alessio said. "Everyone knows Dad

intended Cosimo to be the don. The capos are ready to follow him."

"Maybe your father changed his mind," Mother said, smoothing her palms over her mourning dress. "He was disappointed with Cosimo's immaturity regarding his upcoming marriage. A person ready to lead this family wouldn't behave like that."

"That's bullshit, and you know it." I stepped closer to Cos, who looked like he was barely restraining himself from snapping her neck. "Dad never expressed any doubts about who should succeed him."

"Maybe not to you," Mother countered. "But he did privately to me. And I agree with him. Cosimo still has growing up to do."

I shook my head. It was all bullshit. Dad may have given her an unusual amount of power, but he'd groomed Cosimo to take over as don from basically the day he was born. "None of us have time for this pointless discussion. We all know Cosimo is the don. Did you really think Alessio or I would take your side?" I turned to Cos. "I've got a lead on Mia. I have to—"

"Mia?" Mother interjected.

"Yes, Mother. Mia." Cos and Alessio already knew the abridged version of our story—I told them before I ran out to search for Mia earlier.

Mother was about to get an even shorter summary. "She's mine. Off-limits. Forever."

Her gaze narrowed. There was a time when that look from her would have made me feel two feet tall, but incredibly, now it barely registered.

"Ah," she said. "That explains your utter incompetence when it came to her. I didn't expect Morales's daughter would be smart enough to outmaneuver you. But maybe you're not as smart as I believed."

"Thanks for the opinion no one asked for," I said. "You can think whatever you want about me, but if you so much as touch a hair on Mia's head, I'll rip you apart with my bare hands and feed you to the fucking dogs."

Her face paled. She wasn't used to anyone standing up to her, and it showed. Satisfaction unfurled inside me at how quickly things were changing. Funny how sometimes change seems impossible, but really, all it takes is a single leap of faith.

"We're a family, Romolo," she said. "Or did you forget? With your father gone, all we have is each other."

"Spare me," I snarled. "It was never about our family. Not for you. Family doesn't fucking do the things you've done to us."

"I *raised* you," she bit out.

"No. You *used* me. I was your tool. But I'm done being useful to you. My loyalty's with Cosimo. The fucking leader of this family. And if you're trying to undermine him, then you're not family anymore."

Deep lines marred her forehead. The fact that she was losing was finally hitting her. "Cosimo doesn't have what it takes. I do. I've led alongside your father for almost thirty years." Mother's eyes flicked between us before she dropped her final card. "Here's the hard truth. None of you have any idea what you're up against. You've tried to figure out why the Santoro family is targeting us, and you've found nothing. That history's been erased. I'm the only one who knows the full story."

Cosimo walked around his desk and sat down. "We'll figure it out."

"You won't." Her voice rang out. "The Santoro family killed Gino, and this is only the beginning. I know them. I know I can lead us past this threat. But without me, you've already lost."

I exchanged a glance with my brothers. We were all thinking the same thing.

"We'll take our chances, Mother," Cosimo said, cold as ice. "Get out. I don't want to see you again."

Mother stared at him, fury twisting her face. "You're making a big mistake." She grabbed her purse from the coffee table and stormed out, slamming the door behind her.

"Fucking finally," I muttered. I had to get out of here. "Morales is keeping Mia locked up in his apartment. I'm taking a few guys and getting her out."

Cosimo nodded. "Take who you need."

It didn't take long to gather the men. We got into three cars and hit the road.

Within an hour, Mia would be with me. And if Morales thought he could stand in my way, he was about to learn just how far I'd go to protect what's mine.

CHAPTER 49

Mia

The sharp click of a door closing yanked me from a restless, sweat-soaked nap. In my dreams, skyscrapers burned and their flaming husks sent dark smoke billowing across the horizon.

I untangled my legs from the skirt of my dress and sat up slowly, eyes landing on a tray of food by the door.

I didn't want it. The tight knot in my stomach had nothing to do with hunger. Just stress and a desperate, gnawing need for answers.

All I wanted to know was if Romolo was still alive. If that one casualty the doctor mentioned was him.

Being kept in the dark like this was cruel. But maybe that was the point—to hurt me as much as possible. To make me pay for daring to defy them. Or maybe just for existing.

But I wouldn't lose hope. It was the one thing that kept me from spiraling into despair.

Swallowing past the ball in my throat, I walked to the window. Outside, the Met's grand facade was bathed in dramatic light. A few people were sitting on the steps, their phones glowing in their hands.

I'd never been more desperate to trade places with anyone. They had what I longed for—freedom and the ability to reach out to the world beyond. My palms pressed against the cool glass, my breath fogging up the surface.

Just then, a wispy tendril of a memory appeared at the edge of my awareness.

The news of the explosion hadn't triggered my loss of consciousness.

Neither had my father finding out about Romolo and me.

Something else had done it. Something so outlandish that it seemed utterly impossible.

Just before I'd passed out, I'd wondered if my dad had anticipated the explosion.

My spine straightened.

How else would he have known to post guards at the campaign office? Why else would he and Jenny have followed me when I fled the party?

It was like they were waiting—waiting to see how I'd react. To see if I'd be upset. If I'd panic.

If I'd immediately try to contact the man I loved.

I began to pace.

Romolo's words echoed in my mind. *"My mother suspects your father has a secret backer, someone with a vendetta against us who's pushing him to go after us aggressively."*

At the time, I'd dismissed it. But now? Now, I wasn't so sure.

What if my dad *was* working with someone who hated the Ferraros?

Hated them enough to plant a bomb?

My stomach dipped.

I'd met most of the people who'd donated large sums to the campaign—or at least, I thought I had. But my father could have taken money from someone in secret. It's not like I had access to his financial records. I wouldn't know.

My dad isn't capable of that.

That's what I would have thought if I wasn't currently being held prisoner in his own home.

No, I was done being naïve. Done jumping blindly to his defense.

If the Ferraros were right about my dad, I wanted to know. I deserved the truth about who I'd been helping all this time. What was I complicit in?

I bit on my nail. Would he lie straight to my face if I asked him directly?

Yeah. Possibly.

But it was worth a try.

My gaze swept the room. It was a small, sparse space—one bed, an armchair, and a desk. I opened the drawers, rifling through remnants of my childhood: colored pencils, erasers, old notebooks. The bottom drawer was a chaotic mess of cords, toys, and forgotten objects. I sifted through it, untangling wires and brushing off dust. And then I found it —a voice recorder.

I remembered using it years ago during long walks in Central Park, recording ideas for outfits or creative projects.

It didn't turn on, so I swapped out the batteries. The red light blinked to life.

A breath escaped my lungs. This would work.

I didn't know if Dad would tell me his secrets. But if he did, I'd be ready.

It was past nine p.m. when I heard the sound of footsteps—sharp, rhythmic clicks of dress shoes echoing on the hardwood floor. They grew louder, closer then they stopped outside my door.

"How is she?" I heard my father's voice.

"We served her dinner at seven," one of the guards replied.

My heart began to race. I had a plan now. It hinged on my ability to lie convincingly, but I had no choice. This was my best shot at getting the truth.

There was a long pause. Was he going to come in or leave me here like some discarded piece of luggage?

"I'd like to speak with her."

I darted back to the bed, turned on the recorder, and wedged it between the mattress and the wall just as the lock clicked and the door creaked open.

My father stepped inside, briefcase in hand, his mouth set in a flat line. He looked older than he ever had before, and for a brief second, something like pity scraped at my chest, but just as quickly, it vanished.

My stepmother had tried to pit him against me. As far as I could tell, his resistance only stretched to the times when I could still be useful to him.

Maybe he loved me in his own sad way, but it wasn't enough. I was done begging for his scraps.

He set the briefcase on the floor and eyed the untouched dinner on the floor. "You didn't eat."

I shrugged. "Didn't feel like it."

He nodded like he understood. "The doctor told me you're fine. We were worried for a second. There was a lot of blood."

I rolled my lips at the flicker of concern in his eyes. If I wanted him to confide in me, I had to pretend like I was starting to come around to seeing his side. So I stayed silent, waiting to see what he'd say next.

"I'm sorry we had to do this, *cariño*." He sat down on the

edge of the bed, some distance away from me. His cologne, usually a comforting scent, now turned my stomach. "But you're not in the right state of mind. That man clearly managed to trick you. You were always too trusting, Mia."

Yeah, and you know that well, don't you? You used it to your advantage.

My gaze fell to my lap. "I know. I'm sorry." *Lie.* I hoped I was selling it. "I've been thinking over the last few hours since I'd talked to Aris." I picked at a nail. "I... She said some things that upset me. But now...I can see that she was right. I made a huge mistake, Dad. I don't know how it happened."

"How did you meet?"

Is Romolo alive?

I had to bite on my tongue to stay silent, to breathe through the urge to ask the one question consuming me.

"At a party. It was an accident."

He scoffed. "It's just as likely it was all planned from the beginning."

"Maybe you're right." I lifted my gaze to his. "But I never told him anything about you. I swear, I didn't."

Some of the lines in his forehead softened. "Good. That's good." He sighed. "Romolo wanted to use you to hurt me. And he succeeded. Even if you told him nothing, he still managed to fool someone very important to me."

Important? I guessed you could say I was important— the way an expensive painting is important, there to impress and be shown off at the right moments.

"Knowing he compromised you hurt me." Dad's voice hardened. "But what awaits him once I'm in power will be a thousand times worse."

My eyes fell shut.

The wave of relief that swept through me rattled at my heart.

It took everything I had—*everything*—not to let my expression show it.

He was alive. Somewhere out there. Heart still beating.

"It will be easier now, with Gino Ferraro dead."

My eyes shot open. *Gino.* Rom had lost his dad. "He was the single casualty?" I asked, lifting my gaze.

Dad nodded. There was a smirk on his face. "My first campaign promise came true before I'm even elected. But I'm not done. We'll focus on his sons next."

Focus. What did that mean? At this point, I wasn't sure if he wanted to launch an investigation or if he just wanted to take them out, guilty verdict or not.

Ask him. Do it now.

"Dad, how did you know the explosion was going to happen?"

A flicker of shock passed over his expression.

I thought of the recorder and hoped I hadn't accidentally blocked the mic when I shoved it behind the bed.

"You were waiting to see my reaction to the news," I continued when he stayed silent. "The guards were ready to stop me from leaving. How did you know?"

He looked down at his hands.

I licked my lips. "You know who's behind the explosion, don't you?"

Silence.

"Dad, I've worked tirelessly for you this past year. I want you to win. Even if I've made mistakes, I still want you to win." My nails dug into the palms of my hands. "Romolo told me his parents suspected you have a connection to some of their enemies."

His head snapped up, and his eyes hardened.

"Is that true?" I asked.

The words hung there, thick with tension.

I waited.

Waited.

Waited.

He swallowed, then he reached over and tucked a strand of hair behind my ear. "It's just a temporary arrangement."

My heart pounded in my chest. It was working. "With who?"

"Rena Santoro. A friend from college."

Santoro. I racked my brain. Then it hit me like a bolt of lightning. Two years ago, when Dad sold the family grocery chain business...

"Weren't they one of the investors who bought the business?"

He cleared his throat. "Yes. The business was bankrupt."

What? I didn't know that. "You said you sold it because you wanted to do something new."

"Also true. But we were in trouble, Mia. The market had turned against us. We lost money for years. Rena Santoro approached me two years ago with an offer that she'd find investors to buy the business at a premium price, and in exchange, I'd run for mayor on a...certain platform. It was a good deal. If I hadn't taken it, my father's business—one he built from the ground up—would have died."

I was reeling. So this—his entire campaign—wasn't about service. It was about salvaging a mess he'd made with the business that had been handed to him.

"A certain platform?" I forced out. "To hunt down the Ferraros?"

"It's a platform I wholeheartedly agree with. The Ferraros killed your uncle. In the decades since, they amassed excessive power in this city. They are due for a reckoning."

"But these people... the Santoros..." I swallowed hard. "Dad, if they're behind that bomb, they're criminals too."

My dad's mouth flattened. "I can't control the Ferraros,

but I can control the Santoros. They helped fund the campaign, but once I'm in office, they'll fall in line with my agenda."

My breath caught. *Fall in line?* The people who planted a bomb in a residential penthouse? I stared at him, stunned. "You made a deal with exactly the kind of people you condemn the Ferraros for being."

He gave me a dismissive glance. "I don't expect you to understand."

Hot shame and rage battled in my chest. This was the man I had defended. The man I'd tried so hard to see as good. My father, who I'd believed was guided by principle and integrity. But I'd been clinging to a lie. Shielding myself from truths I didn't want to see.

Not anymore.

I rose to my feet. "You're right. I don't understand it even a little. That explosion could have killed a lot of people."

"But it didn't." His voice was cold. "It only killed one don, and he deserved it. He was an awful, awful man."

"You're no better," I whispered.

The door burst open behind me.

I spun, heart hammering. When I saw who it was, tears seared my eyes and my chest hitched on a ragged breath.

Romolo.

He stood in the doorway in a leather jacket, chest heaving, fists clenched, eyes wild.

Our gazes collided.

"Mia," he rasped.

A sob tore from my chest, and I ran to him, a burst of frantic energy propelling me straight into his arms.

He'd come for me.

He'd found me.

This nightmare was over.

With him, I was finally safe.

CHAPTER 50

Rom

Mia's small body trembled in my arms.

She mumbled something that might have been *you found me*, and my cold, black heart broke at the thought of her locked in here, wondering if anyone was coming to get her out.

She'd never have to wonder again. She was fucking mine.

Leaning down, I brushed my lips against her ear. "I'll always find you, Berry."

My hands roamed over her back and arms, checking for any injuries. When I felt the bandage on the back of her head, my body stilled.

She must have felt the tension coiling inside me because she rubbed her cheek against my chest and whispered, "Just a cut. I'm okay."

A cut. How?

My eyes snapped to the man responsible—her father. He stood frozen by the bed, his expression dark with rage.

"Who let you in?" he bit out.

I smirked coldly. "I have ten men with me. We let ourselves in."

Mia pulled away and darted toward the bed. She grabbed something from behind the mattress before returning to my side.

Her father's eyes never strayed from me. Maybe he knew better than to look away from someone who could end him within seconds.

Tempting. So fucking tempting.

"What kind of father does something like this to his own daughter?" I asked.

A flush crept up his neck, painting his face crimson. "I'm not going to stand here and be lectured by you."

"I'm ready," Mia said.

Morales's jaw ticked. "I'm going to get you arrested for this, Ferraro."

"No, you're not." Mia's voice was low but firm. "Do you really want me to tell the police, never mind the press, about how you sedated me and kept me locked up here against my will?"

Did she just say "sedated"?

I saw fucking red.

My fist collided with Morales's nose before my brain could even fully process what I was doing. The need to make him pay was too strong to resist.

Morales fell onto the bed, clutching his face as blood dripped down his chin.

A hand appeared on my back, curling into my shirt. "Rom, don't. I'm okay."

Nah. I was only getting started.

I took a step and my shirt pulled around me.

"*Rom.* I want to go."

I froze. She sounded tired. Spent.

Fuck. Of course she was. And I was here to get her someplace safe, not indulge my violent urge to make anyone who harmed her pay.

Morales could wait. He'd get what he deserved eventually.

"You're going to look back on this and realize it was the biggest mistake of your life, Morales," I ground out at the pathetic man staring up at me.

Mia's hand slipped into mine.

His eyes darted toward Mia. "You can't trust him, Mia. He's manipulating you. You'll regret this."

"The only thing I'm regretting is all the time I wasted helping you," she said.

Pride surged through me. *That's my fucking girl.*

"He's a criminal," Morales spat. "He'll spend the rest of his life behind bars. Is that the kind of life you want?"

"I'll choose him over you any day."

God, I wanted to kiss her. To seal her words with a promise. But I needed to get her out of here first.

"Morales, if you ever try to hurt Mia again—if you even think about pulling a stunt like this—you'll have a war on your hands. I will hunt you down and rip you apart limb by limb. So think carefully about your next move." I tugged her closer. "Come on."

We moved down the hall, flanked by my men. The two guards we'd taken down when we came in were now unconscious on the floor, wrists bound, duct tape over their mouths.

One of my guys was locked in a stare-down with a woman—Mia's stepmother. She leaned heavily on her cane.

"If you walk out that door," she called out, voice shaking, "you will never be welcome back, Mia."

These fucking people. My protectiveness surged. I wanted to wipe those words from Mia's memory so that they couldn't hurt her.

But when I looked at her, all I saw was quiet resignation. No tears. No anguish. Just an unshakable calm.

"You made it abundantly clear that I've never been welcome," Mia said, her voice even. "I thought about what you said to me earlier. Thought about it long and hard. You've always wanted kids. I could have been that daughter you wanted. I'm sorry that you didn't have it in you to love me. That hurt you more than it will ever hurt me."

The room went silent. The kind of silence where you could hear the faintest shift of breath.

Her stepmother's grip tightened on the cane.

"Let's go," Mia said. "There's nothing left for me here."

We walked out. My men took the stairs while we got into the elevator. As soon as the doors slid shut, she sagged against me, her facade cracking.

I cupped the back of her neck, careful not to touch the bandage on her head. "I'm sorry it took me this long to get to you."

Her body shook with silent sobs.

It fucking gutted me.

Why the hell did I wait? Twenty-four hours hadn't felt like much at the time, but now I regretted every second I wasted hoping she'd call. I should've known better.

"Fuck, baby. I'm so, so sorry. I screwed up. But I'm going to make it up to you, I promise. I—"

She lifted her face from my chest and looked at me with her puffy, red eyes. "They wouldn't tell me who died in the explosion until just before you showed up. The whole day, I thought you might be—" Her voice broke as she clung to me tighter. "All I could think about was if it was you."

My chest clenched. They'd purposefully kept her in the dark. Purposefully made her worry.

Monsters. They were fucking monsters to do this to the sweetest goddamn girl in the entire world.

I cupped her cheeks, tilting her mouth toward me. "Berry, I'm hard to kill."

A tearful laugh slipped from her lips. "Please stay that way."

"I plan on it."

And then I bent down and kissed her.

~

As soon as I got Mia into my car, something inside me unknotted. *Mission accomplished.* My body buzzed with relief as I hit the gas.

Outside, the city smeared past us in black and neon streaks. For a few seconds, we were silent, just basking in each other's company. Her intoxicating lily-of-the-valley scent filled my lungs and squeezed like a fist around my heart.

I had her. And I wasn't ever letting her go.

"Mia." My voice was rough. "The last time we talked, I said a lot of stupid shit." Stupid didn't even begin to cover it. "I pushed you away because I didn't think I was good enough for you. I ran because you called me something I couldn't stomach. Something that made me feel weak. I acted like a fucking coward. But I've realized some things since then."

She listened to me silently, her profile lit by the light coming from the dash.

"Maybe I was a victim back then," I said quietly. "But I don't have to keep being a victim of my past. Fuck the past. It doesn't get to define me." My palms tightened on the wheel. "Before, I only knew how to destroy. But now? I'll learn how to build. If you'll let me, I'll build a life with you. One where you will feel safe, loved, and so fucking cherished that you will never doubt that you belong by my side. Not for a single second."

She let out a small, shaky breath. "Rom..."

"I want to be the man you deserve and I know I fucking can be. If you give me another chance, I'll spend the rest of my life proving it to you."

My heart thumped against my rib cage.

I waited for her to say something. Anything.

Finally, she sniffed. "I can do another chance."

Relief flooded through me. *Thank fuck.*

Three simple words—the ones I should have said back at the hotel—burned in my chest, demanding to be set free.

I needed to look at her while I said them.

My foot pressed on the brakes. We were in the middle of a block. Cars cruised by. A couple headlights flashed. I didn't care.

"Rom?" she asked, startled. "Why are we—?"

I unbuckled and turned toward her, every part of me trained on her face. She blinked at me, wide-eyed.

"I'm answering your question. The one you asked that night."

A car honked behind us. Another. Didn't matter.

I took her hands in mine and ran my thumbs across her knuckles. "I love you." The words scorched their way out of me. "I love you like I've never loved anything in my goddamn life. It's terrifying. It's relentless. You've gotten under my skin and into my soul, and you didn't even try. Somewhere along the way, I stopped being mine and became yours."

Her lips wavered and tears clung to her lashes.

"I wasn't living before I met you, Mia. I was just existing. Trying to drown the parts of me I couldn't face. But you— you came in with all your light, and suddenly there was nowhere left to hide. You cracked me open. Made me *feel* again."

She bit on her lip, emotions flickering across her face.

"I'd tried to run from those feelings. But I'm not running anymore. I fucking love you."

She reached out and pressed a trembling hand against my cheek. "You're not a coward," she said softly. "You're the very opposite. All you needed was a bit of time." Her thumb brushed over my jaw. "I'm so proud of you, Rom."

Inside me, everything melted.

A smile tugged on her mouth. "And I love you too. So damn much." The next moment, her lips were pressing against mine.

I cradled her jaw and pulled her closer, my tongue sliding into her mouth, hungry to taste her, feel her, memorize her all over again. I kissed her like a man finally touching heaven after crawling through the pits of hell.

When we finally broke apart, she rested her forehead against mine, her breath shaky and warm. "I missed you," she whispered. "When I thought you might be gone…" Her voice cracked. "I regretted not telling you I loved you earlier. I'd wanted to, you know. But I was scared too. Scared I'd misread you. Scared you'd break my heart."

I brushed my cheek against hers. "You didn't misread me, Berry. You saw me more clearly than anyone ever has. It was never about getting you out of my system. I just wanted to have an excuse, any goddamn excuse, to be close to you. No matter how I tried, I couldn't stay away."

She kissed me again. "You don't have to try anymore. Just be with me, Rom."

"HEY!" someone behind us yelled. "MOVE IT OR WE'RE CALLING THE COPS!"

Mia choked out a laugh, wiping her eyes. "Maybe we can continue this somewhere we won't get arrested?"

I grinned and eased the car back into motion. "Fair. I'm not eager to end up in that precinct again."

"They brought you in for questioning?"

"Right after the explosion," I said. "Fucking mess. But I'm fine now. I've got you."

She fell quiet, and then, softly, "I'm sorry about your dad."

The grief hovered, just beyond reach. I hadn't let myself feel it yet. Not fully. Not with so much chaos happening around me.

"I feel a hell of a lot better now that I have you with me. I'm taking you to my place. We'll grab your things from your apartment tomorrow. I want you somewhere safe, while my brothers and I handle the fallout."

"What are you planning to do?"

"Retaliation isn't optional. If we don't do anything, we'll look weak. But there are a lot of unanswered questions."

"Do you know who planted the bomb?"

"My aunt, but she's long gone. We think the people behind her are the Santoros—this old mob family that's suddenly resurfaced." I paused, unsure if I should tell her more. I didn't want to give her any more stress, but at the same time, she deserved the truth. "We're almost certain they've been funding your dad, Mia. We don't have proof yet, but there's been too many signs that point that way."

Mia was silent. She hesitated for a moment before slowly opening her palm to reveal a voice recorder. "I think I have something that can help you."

I shot her a quick glance. "What's on that?"

She held the recorder up. "Let me just play it for you."

CHAPTER 51

Mia

"You've got to be fucking kidding me." The harsh words rolled off Rom's lips as he drove into the parking garage of his condominium.

I had just finished playing the recording. The one in which my father admitted to working with the same family that had killed Romolo's dad.

"You were right," I said softly. "And I was just too naive to even consider it."

His hand moved to my thigh. "He hid it from you well," he said, slowing the car to a final stop. "Even I started to doubt our suspicions after I'd spent months chasing dead ends and finding no proof."

"Here it is now." Dad had no idea I'd recorded his confession. He probably didn't think I was capable of outsmarting him.

Romolo shut off the engine and the car went quiet. "What do you want to do with this?"

I turned the recorder in my palm. For such a small thing, it was surprisingly heavy. As was the decision I had to make.

"If the last twenty-four hours have taught me anything,

it's that blood doesn't make a family," I said. "It's our actions, our words, and the choices we make. You had no idea what would happen when you came for me, Rom, but you did it anyway." I rolled my lips and raised my gaze to his face.

His brow was furrowed.

"I want you to have this," I said. "These people already tried to kill you once. I can't just sit back and wait for them to try again. If my father gets elected, they'll have too much power. It has to stop."

His eyes dropped to the recorder in my hand. He didn't take it yet. He was still giving me an out.

"Are you sure?"

"I want to keep you safe. If this helps, then it's worth it."

"This is enough to end your dad's campaign and earn him jail time. Are you really ok with that?"

"It's yours, Rom."

His fingers brushed mine as he took the recorder. His expression softened, though I could still see the war playing out behind his eyes. He didn't want me to regret it later.

I wouldn't. Not for this. Everything was different now. My priorities had changed.

Doing what felt right to me wasn't selfish—I saw that now. It just meant honoring my own truth. Listening to my gut.

And right now, my gut screamed at me to do everything I could to keep Romolo safe.

"Thank you," he said, slipping the device inside his jacket.

"You probably want to take that to your brother."

Romolo reached over and pushed a strand behind my ear. "He can wait."

A smile pulled on my lips. "Time to show me your lair?"

Warmth sparkled in his gaze. "You ready?"

I nodded. *So ready.* I was curious to see where he lived. All this time, I couldn't come here because we couldn't be seen together.

Now we could do whatever the hell we wanted. God, it was sweet.

The elevator ride was fast, and my heart thumped inside my chest as the screen counted up to the penthouse floor.

Finally, we stepped into his abode. The scent of cedar and clean leather hit my nose as he led me through the foyer.

The space was sleek and masculine—dark floors, warm lighting, rugs that softened each footstep—but it was also lived in. Plants were tucked in corners. Books and records sat out on surfaces.

It smelled like him. It felt like him.

And I already loved it.

He led me through the living room, past a movie playing on the TV, to the window that stretched from floor to ceiling. Manhattan sprawled beneath us, glittering and infinite.

A moment later, his arms wrapped around me from behind, his lips brushing my neck.

My eyes fluttered shut. "Rom?"

"Yeah, Berry?"

"Has it hit you yet?" I whispered. "We don't have to hide anymore."

He pressed a kiss just behind my ear. "You mean I get to show you off? Walk into a room with you on my arm?"

I giggled, leaning into him. "Yeah."

"I'm torn," he murmured. "Between proudly displaying you to the world and keeping you all to myself."

I turned in his arms, placing my hands on his chest. "Option two. At least for a little while." My teeth sunk into my bottom lip and Rom's gaze dropped to my mouth.

"How's your head?" he asked, tightening his hold on me.

"It's just a cut." I slipped my palm between us and stopped when I reached the bulge in his slacks. "Not nearly enough to prevent me from getting what I want."

A low groan slipped past his throat and he scooped me up like I weighed nothing. "Have I ever mentioned how much I love it when you're not shy about it?"

"Not in words. But it's loud and clear now."

He carried me toward the hallway, but halfway there, he paused, turned, and headed toward the coffee table. With me still in his arms, he crouched to grab the remote, and turned off the TV.

I arched a brow. "Saving electricity?"

He chuckled and placed a kiss on the tip of my nose. "No distractions."

Dark bedroom. Cool sheets. His warmth melting into mine.

Strong hands slid beneath my shirt. A thousand butterflies stirred in my belly.

The world saw this man as rough, brutal, cold. A man built to break things.

But I knew better.

I'd seen the tenderness. The patience. The way he held me like I was something sacred.

And maybe, just maybe, I was. To him.

My fingers curled into his shirt. "You asked me once who took care of me. I didn't have an answer back then. I do now."

The gray in his eyes softened and he leaned down, pulling gently on my bottom lip. "Always, Berry."

I smiled against his mouth, something fierce and beautiful blooming in my chest.

With him, I didn't have to shrink myself. I didn't have to play small or quiet down the parts of me that wanted more.

With him, I was safe to be exactly who I was.

And for the first time in my life, love didn't feel like a sacrifice.

It felt like freedom.

CHAPTER 52

Rom

"The shocking revelation has put Carlos Morales's entire campaign at risk," said the news anchor on the TV. "The audio recording was apparently made by his own daughter, Mia Morales. We've not been able to reach Mia for comment. It's unclear what prompted her to expose this evidence of wrongdoing by her father, but it's safe to say New York City constituents are grateful she bravely revealed the truth. The FBI and NYPD have launched investigations and will be auditing Morales's campaign finances."

The camera cut to a second anchor. "With the election only a few days away, it's hard to imagine how Morales can recover from this blow. He campaigned on his tough stance against organized crime, which makes this revelation—that he accepted funds from an organized crime family—particularly hypocritical."

I sank back in my chair and dragged my thumb across my bottom lip. *It worked.*

The day after Mia gave me the recording, I played it for Cosimo. Within the hour, we'd emailed a copy to every major news outlet we could think of. We knew they'd fall over themselves to be the first to report on it. This was a juicy story that would get them views.

Now, three days later, we were having a watch party in one of the meeting rooms at Black Silk. This was the third station saying more or less the same thing.

The main takeaway? Morales was fucked.

Mia sat at the far end of the table, her hands folded in front of her. I studied her expression, looking for any sign of discomfort and found none.

Cos muted the TV and leaned forward, his gaze sliding over the capos seated around the table.

"With Morales neutralized, our full focus shifts to the Santoros," he said. "Prepare for long nights ahead. Anyone has a problem with that, come talk to me."

Silence.

"All right, show's over," I barked. "Everyone out. I've got work to do."

The capos filed out. At the far end of the table, Mia rose to her feet.

"We owe you a debt," Cos said to Mia as the door closed behind the last capo. "From this point forward, you're under the family's protection."

Mia's expression didn't shift. "I think Rom's got that covered," she said.

Damn right, I did.

"But how about you promise not to hurt my best friend?"

Cos frowned. The wedding with Fabiana had been moved up to next month. No more delays. The alliance with the Messeros mattered now more than ever.

He was doing what a good don did—putting the family first. I just hoped, for his sake, that his good intentions held after the vows were exchanged.

If not, he'd upset the woman I loved. And that wouldn't fucking fly.

"I won't," he said, jaw tight.

Mia held his gaze for a beat, weighing him. Then she nodded.

"All right. Nice little heart-to-heart," I said. I was eager to be alone with Mia. We haven't spent more than an hour apart since I got her away from Morales, but I still couldn't get enough. "Goodbye, Cos."

My brother shot me a glare but headed for the door.

Mia moved to follow.

"Not you, Mia," I called out.

She glanced at me. "I thought you had to work—" She registered the hungry expression on my face. "Oh."

I caught the sound of Cos's knowing chuckle. "Should I close the door?"

"Obviously," I barked.

The second he was gone, I crooked my finger at Mia. "Come here, Berry. Why the hell did you sit all the way over there?"

She blushed as she walked toward me. "I wasn't sure if I even belonged here today."

I grabbed her hand and pulled her onto my lap. "You don't belong *there*, but you do right here." I nuzzled my nose against her neck and stole a kiss. "Give me an hour and I'll be done." We had dinner plans at a hot new spot in town she'd been wanting to try. "Did you bring your laptop?"

Mia nodded. She'd agreed to work from my place this week, but she was itching to get back to her studio next week. I'd said yes, because I was powerless to deny her anything—though I'd made one thing crystal clear: she wasn't going anywhere without her four bodyguards.

"Actually," she said, playing with the collar of my shirt, "I wanted to stop by my apartment before dinner."

My hand tightened on her hip. "Why?"

She sighed. "This dress is the only thing I have at your

place. I can't keep taking client Zoom calls in your T-shirts, Rom. I've been telling everyone I'm going through a grunge phase. That excuse is going to wear thin fast."

"I like you in my T-shirts." I bit lightly on her shoulder.

"I know," she said with a laugh. "But I think you like me even more out of them."

"Fair."

"Either option isn't exactly professional attire. I need to grab some things."

"I'll buy you a new wardrobe." I should have thought of that by now, but I really *did* like her in my shirts.

She gasped, scandalized. "Rom, my closet is carefully curated. I've spent years hunting down some of those rare vintage pieces. And you know, it's quite a bad practice to buy all your clothes in one go. It's much better to add to your collection slowly, with intention. So that every piece makes sense and fits with your style."

I grinned. God, she was adorable. "Forgive me for that offensive suggestion. What was I thinking?"

She swatted at me. "I need to go home."

"Then we'll go together and pack everything up."

"I was only going to grab a little."

"Nah. Take it all."

Her eyes searched mine. "Are you asking me to move in?"

"I've gotten used to waking up with you beside me. I can't go back to not." My hand slipped under the skirt of her dress, fingertips tracing along her inner thigh.

A smile tugged on her pretty little mouth. "So needy."

"Is that a yes?"

"I'll think about it."

"Berry," I groaned, lifting her from my lap and settling her on the edge of the desk. I anchored my palms on either side of her hips and hovered close. "Don't torture me. What do you want? You want me begging on my knees?"

She bit on her lip, eyes dancing, and shrugged. "Maybe."

I sighed. "Fine. For you, I'll get on my knees and beg."

And then I sank to the floor, slid off her panties, and devoured her. Her moans filled the room. I could live a thousand lives and never get enough of this.

Afterward, her fingers tangled in my hair as she caught her breath. I rested my head against her bare thigh, enjoying her warmth, her scent.

"I love you," she whispered.

Warmth spread through my chest. Every time she said those words, it made me want to howl.

I stood, kissed her deeply, and murmured against her mouth, "So... is that a yes?"

She wrapped her arms around my neck and smiled up at me. "It's a hell yes."

God, I fucking loved this woman.

Mia was my peace in the chaos. My compass. My fucking redemption.

And every single part of me belonged to her.

EPILOGUE

Mia

The wedding venue was a gorgeous farm in upstate New York. The Ferraros and the Messeros had descended onto its snowy grounds in the first week of December, arriving in a motorcade of bulletproof black SUVs, lush burgundy rose wreaths pinned to the trunks.

Those same roses filled every corner of the reception hall, the farmhouse bridal suite, and lined the aisle of the chapel where the ceremony would take place. They were beautiful—burgundy was Fabi's favorite color.

But in a certain light, that color reminded me of blood.

I snipped through the thread I was using to hem Elena's dress and let the fabric fall to the floor. "How's that?"

Fabi's sister slid her heels back on and walked up to the mirror. "Perfect now. Thanks, Mia."

Elena had returned to New York two nights ago and was planning to leave tomorrow evening. It seemed to me that every time she looked at Fabi, she couldn't help but wonder how long she had left before she was also ordered to return. Elena didn't want to leave Switzerland, and something told me she wouldn't be nearly as amenable as Fabi when the time came.

"Anyone else?" I asked, glancing around at the brides-maids. Fabi had asked me to style the girls after I'd been officially invited to the wedding, and I jumped on it despite only having a few weeks to find the dresses. It meant a lot to be a part of her big day.

"Stop fussing over us," Zo said. "Sit down and have a drink."

Everyone had a glass of champagne in hand, each of them trying a little too hard to keep the mood light. The air was tinged with tension, and it was starting to show.

It hurt, watching Fabi power through it. She deserved joy. Pure, unfiltered joy. Not this tightly wound version of a celebration.

She drifted toward the window, her wedding gown shimmering in the afternoon light. She looked like a princess in that dress, and I didn't know how Cosimo could look at her and not feel *something*.

"It's snowing," she said quietly.

I moved to stand beside her. "It's beautiful, isn't it?"

She smiled, but it didn't reach her eyes. "I'm going to get some air."

"I'll come with you," Nina offered, already rising.

Fabi shook her head. "I just want a few minutes alone." She reached for the fur shawl she'd wear during the ceremony—the chapel didn't have heating, so we were all bundling up—and slipped out of the room.

The second the door clicked shut, we all looked at one another.

"Is it just me," Zo asked, "or does she seem... off?"

"She is off," Elena said, her jaw tightening. "But she's not letting anyone in."

"Something changed," Nina murmured. "Since Gino Ferraro's funeral. She's quieter. Sadder."

"I noticed it too," I said, remembering that day vividly.

I'd gone to the funeral with Romolo, and Fabi had stood beside Cosimo for most of the day. I saw them talk and, naively, thought it was a good sign.

But ever since, something in her had shifted. Whenever I asked about it, Fabi brushed me off.

I gave it a few more minutes before pushing to my feet. "I'm going to check on her."

The farmhouse had an old-world charm that made you feel like stepping back in time—exposed stone walls, deep windowsills, and lanterns made of wrought iron and glass.

I followed the hallway past antique portraits and vintage rugs, toward the wide balcony where Fabi's silhouette appeared beyond the glass doors.

When I saw she wasn't alone, I halted.

Cosimo stood beside her.

There was at least a foot between them but it looked like they were talking. Didn't anyone tell him it was bad luck to see the bride before the wedding?

I stood there for a moment, trying to decide if I should go back, when I felt a soft touch on my lower back. "Hey, you," came Romolo's voice.

I turned. "Hey."

Gray eyes. Ink-black hair. A smile that was reserved just for me. The sight of him melted something in me. He had a way of making everything feel solid. Steady. Safe. His presence was a grounding force I'd desperately needed over the last month.

A month ago, he pulled me out of that apartment and into the wreckage of a life I didn't recognize. Everything had fallen apart.

But with him by my side, rebuilding hadn't been as hard as I'd thought.

One month.

It had been one month of living with him. Sharing his

space. Learning his routines. Marveling at how seamlessly we fit into each other's lives.

My business had exploded—in the best way. The Golden Circle referrals were still pouring into my inbox, weeks after I'd been sent out to the list. I'd onboarded ten new clients over the last week—the kind of clients I never would have thought I'd be capable of having.

And my father... Well. He was now under a federal investigation for fraud and collusion. After his spectacular plummet in the polls, the election had gone to the incumbent, Mayor Wilson.

Every time a story about Dad came on the news, Romolo would silently appear beside me, offering comfort and support.

I kept reminding him I was okay. I was done playing savior for those who didn't deserve it. My father had made his own choices. His own bed. And now he could lie in it.

Romolo studied me now, his gaze warm and steady. "What are you doing out here, Berry?"

I nodded toward the balcony. "I came to check on Fabi. She's out there with him."

His brows lifted slightly. "Cos?"

"Yeah."

We both stared through the glass for a moment, watching them. Two people caught in something complicated.

"What do you think the odds are they'll come back in and tell us to cancel the wedding?" I asked, half-joking.

Romolo shook his head. "Zero. Cosimo's not backing out. Not now."

"I hope they're not signing themselves up for a lifetime of misery." I wasn't so concerned anymore about Cosimo being the kind of guy who would physically hurt Fabi, but that wasn't the only way you could hurt someone. And Fabi had a gentle heart.

"She'll be fine," Rom said, his lips brushing against my ear. "Give it a few months and she might have him eating out of the palm of her hand. Happened to me, didn't it?"

I laughed. "Is that how you'd describe it?"

"More or less." He laced his fingers through mine. "Come on. Let's give them some privacy. I want to show you something."

His hand was warm and steady in mine as he led me down the hall and up a narrow staircase tucked just behind the main corridor.

Behind a small door was the attic. I expected a tiny room with creaky floorboards and dusty boxes, but it turned out I was completely wrong.

The attic had been converted into a small sewing workshop. Sunlight streamed in through a round window, spilling across vintage mannequins, bolts of fabric, and a wooden worktable covered in spools of thread. A dress form stood in the center, half-draped in a gown made of creamy, thick linen.

My mouth parted in awe. "Rom... this is incredible."

Romolo's arm curved around my waist. "The owner said it used to belong to his grandmother. Now his daughter uses it to design period pieces. I thought you'd enjoy seeing it."

I turned slowly, soaking it all in. "This place is magic. Being here is giving me some interesting styling inspo."

"Me too," he said, his voice low. "You'd look brilliant in white."

My cheeks heated. "Rom."

"Too fast?"

"We've only lived together for a month."

"When you know you know," he simply said, making my stomach flutter. "And trust me, Berry. I fucking know."

His hands slid to my waist as he brought our bodies together. I rose onto my toes to kiss him, and he met me halfway, his lips slanting over mine with a hunger that sent a shiver down my spine.

He pressed me gently against the wall with his solid, strong body, our mouths never parting. One of his hands slid beneath my dress, fingers grazing my thigh with teasing slowness.

I melted into his touch. Into his scent. Into the way he made me feel like I was the only thing in the world that mattered.

His hard length pressed insistently against my belly.

"I want you," he rasped.

"The ceremony's about to start," I said, barely able to get the words out as his lips dragged along my neck.

"We've got time," he muttered, fingers slipping beneath my panties, finding me already wet. "And I'm going to love the way you'll blush, standing there in front of everyone."

I shivered as he teased my entrance. "Why would I blush?"

His voice dropped to a rough whisper. "Because every time you move, you'll feel my cum dripping down your thighs."

His fingers curled inside me, coaxing a soft cry from my lips. I clenched around him, dizzy with need. Suddenly, every reckless thing he was saying sounded like the best idea I'd ever heard.

I reached between us, undid his trousers, and curved my palm around his cock.

His forehead dropped to mine as I pumped him slowly. "Fuck. That's it."

We worked each other into a frenzy until we were both right on the edge. And then he was lifting me with a firm grip on my ass, while I scrambled to tug my dress out of the way.

He sank into me with a hiss and a shiver. "Jesus, Mia."

My legs tightened around him and his hips began to move, dragging pleasure through me with every thrust. I clung to his shoulders, held together only by his grip and the rhythm of our bodies.

"Good?" he breathed, voice tight.

"So good," I gasped, thighs trembling.

His hand cupped the back of my head to keep me steady as he drove into me harder, deeper.

"Fuck, baby," he grunted, his mouth hovering over mine. "I'm close."

"Me too," I whimpered, heat coiling low in my belly, my nails digging into his back.

One more thrust. Then another.

And then we shattered—together.

I buried my face in his neck, muffling my moan, while his arms held me through it, his body pulsing inside mine.

For a few long seconds, we just stood there. Breathless, tangled, sated.

Eventually, his lips brushed over my temple. "I'm so fucking in love with you."

My heart swelled. I tilted my head up to meet his gaze, smiling as I cupped his cheek. "I love you too, Rom." I bit my lip. "And on second thought... I think I like fast."

Q&A WITH AUTHOR
GABRIELLE SANDS

Q: Who asked for this Q&A?
A: Literally no one. Which is why I'm here, writing both the questions and answers myself like a lunatic.

Q: …Okay.
A: Look, I just want to chat to my readers a bit. Is that a crime?

Q: Don't you have a newsletter for this kind of thing?
A: I *do*! You can subscribe at: *www.gabriellesands.com/ subscribe/*. I try to keep it interesting, relevant, and free of boring life updates like "I reorganized my desk today." But I get it—not everyone wants another email in their inbox, even if it contains juicy sneak peeks into my books and an occasional guest spot from my characters.

Q: So you're just… talking to yourself at this point?
A: Yes, welcome to the glamorous life of an author. Anyway, let's move on to actual book questions before I start monologuing about plot holes I cried over at 2 a.m.

Q: If you had to pick: Team "Lock Vita Ferraro in a Dungeon" or Team "Push Her Off a Cliff"?
A: Honestly? Either works. If you've read my previous books, you might've had *feelings* about Vita. She was always shown through the eyes of characters who didn't really know her—and as Romolo explains, his mother is a world-class actress (sans Oscar). She puts on an act with just about everyone but her husband and sons. Exploring who she really is was enlightening. I won't spoil what awaits her, but she will definitely play a prominent role in this series.

Q: Who the heck are the Santoros?
A: Ah yes. The mysterious Santoros. You'll get a better look in the next book... and an even closer look after that.

Q: That flashback chapter was *a lot*. Was it hard to write?
A: Probably one of the hardest things I've ever written. One of my editors even suggested cutting it, thinking it was too much of a risk. But I kept it in because I wanted you to feel —viscerally—what Romolo had gone through and to understand the pain that shaped him.

Q: How did you come up with Mia's character?
A: Once I understood Romolo, I started thinking: What kind of woman would both challenge him *and* offer him the kind of love he doesn't think he deserves? Enter Mia. Writing her made me want to reach through the page and hug her. Haven't we all, at some point, tried to earn love by pleasing others? Watching her try to win the approval of people who were supposed to love her—it broke my heart.

Q: What do you hope readers take away from their relationship?
A: There's a line in Chapter 46 where Mia says, "But we were

the same. Both of us were starved for the love we'd never received. The only difference was I'd kept searching for it. He'd stopped." That line, to me, captures both of their journeys. By the end of the book, Mia isn't searching anymore. She has love—real, unconditional love. And Rom? He's no longer holding back. He's discovered that love is worth fighting for and that he's capable of becoming a man who can give it.

Q: Why wasn't there more Alessio in this book? Don't you know he's a fan favorite?
A: Oh, I know. I'm well aware Alessio captured a lot of hearts with his appearance in *When He Takes*. But this was book one of a new series, and I had a *lot* of ground to cover. So much world building. Introducing all the new characters. Setting the stage for the Ferraro family drama, which will stretch over the four books. And of course, giving Romolo and Mia space to work through all their issues while getting it on in multiple locations. It's a lot. But trust me, Alessio's time is coming. Will he still be into coffee by then? No promises. He's a man of intense (but short-lived) obsessions.

Q: I loved this book. How can I spread the word?
A: You're my favorite. Please leave a review on Amazon, Goodreads, or BookBub—they really help! You can also shout about it on Instagram, TikTok, Threads, Pinterest, Facebook—whatever your platform of choice is. Tag me (@authorgabriellesands) so I can come flail in the comments.

Q: So Fabi and Cosimo are next?
A: Yes! I swear, by the time I'm done with him, Cosimo will be eating the crumbs that Fabi drops. It's gonna be delicious.

Q: Anything else you'd like to say?
A: Thank you for reading Be With Me! I love and appreciate my readers so much. I wouldn't be here without you!

ALSO BY GABRIELLE SANDS

THE FALLEN

When She Unravels: Valentina & Damiano

When She Tempts: Martina & Giorgio

When She Falls: Gemma & Ras

When She Loves: Cleo & Rafaele

FALLEN GOD DUET

When He Desires: Blake & Nero

When He Takes: Blake & Nero

All of Gabrielle's books are set in the same dark world filled with romance, suspense, and mafia intrigue.